Petr Zhgulyov

CITY OF GOBLINS

Don't wait for miracles. Make them happen!

IN THE SYSTEM BOOK 1

Magic Dome Books
in collaboration with 1C-Publishing

City of Goblins
In the System, Book 1
Copyright © Petr Zhgulyov 2020
Cover Art © Vladimir Manyukhin 2020
English Translation Copyright © Sofia Gutkin 2020
Published by Magic Dome Books in collaboration with 1C-
Publishing, 2020
All Rights Reserved
ISBN: 978-80-7619-220-1

TABLE OF CONTENTS:

PROLOGUE

EVERYTHING ONCE CREATED will someday die. Our world is no exception. The heat death of the universe. For most, this fact is too far into the future and too doubtful to worry over. Having accepted one's death, it is much easier to accept the destruction of all and sundry. There were god-like beings, however, who could survive until this moment and who had no desire to obediently await the inevitable. It seemed that one of them had found a solution. If the problem was that energy gradually disperses in space, would it not be better to gather it all himself? A desire of madness, even for a deity.

The Devourer began a war, consuming star system after star system, waging battles against his own kind and taking their power... Slowly, too slowly. The universe is enormous and most of its inhabitants had no desire to be consumed, and so it came about that everyone took up arms against him.

There came a moment when the Devourer realized that he was bound to lose, but he did not admit defeat. Instead, he destroyed himself and created the System. The Great Game, which drew in countless worlds and continued to constantly spread.

A Game in which his enemies continued what he had started.

A System that would allow the universe to come to its end, and then, using the energy absorbed over billions of years, create the world anew.

Attention! The System has granted you the status of one of the seven First Gods of Order. Please select your incarnation from the regional list.

Europe. France. A young woman, casting a regretful glance at Aphrodite, picks the one slightly higher on the list.

Attention! The Greek Pantheon has been generated. Hera has come into this world!

Eastern Asia. PRC. An elderly Chinese man makes his choice.

Attention! The Asian Pantheon has been generated. Guan Yu has come into this world!

Africa. Nigeria. A youth barely out of childhood...

Attention! The African Pantheon has been generated. Great Set has come into this world!

North America. USA. An office clerk grimaces, picking uncertainly among the local gods. Maybe he's heard of this one before?

Attention! The North American Pantheon has been generated. Quetzalcoatl has come into this world!

South America. Brazil. A tourist lounging on the bed...

Attention! The South American Pantheon has been generated. Inti has come into this world!

Southern Asia. India. A monk in one of the numerous temples in this land.

Attention! The Indian Pantheon has been generated. Shiva has come into this world!

Europe again, northern this time. Denmark. A minor official...

Attention! The Scandinavian Pantheon has been generated! Odin has come into this world!

CHAPTER 1

ACTIVATION

THERE ARE PLENTY of good things in life, and one of them, undoubtedly, is sleep. There is a reason that people say you should 'sleep on it'. If you're sad, afraid or lonely, go to sleep and it will all pass. At least, until you wake up again. This method had always worked for me before, cutting off my problems better than alcohol or drugs. Besides, I never had much interest in the latter, and it's not like I had money to splurge after being recently fired. Hmm...

This dream was different from the thousands I'd had before, not least because I clearly remembered everything that came before and knew that I'd definitely gone to bed. I knew this a bit too clearly for a dream. A standard menu appeared before my eyes,

Start Spiel?

Ja/No (Die)

[0] — I have read and agree with the Terms of the Contract.

Why the mix of languages? Bad localization? Man, my mother did say that nothing good would come of these games... Ten or fifteen years ago. Who would have thought that it wouldn't happen immediately, but many years later?

This thought didn't stop me from agreeing to the terms of the contract without reading the text, by moving the cursor left and choosing the first option. Yes.

✼ ✼ ✼

In the very same minute, thousands of people around the world saw a similar menu, although it varied slightly for each person. Different languages, slightly different phrases and fonts...

Start Game?

Yes/No?

A man who was president of a large company didn't like to rush important decisions and his intuition told him that this decision was important. And urgent. However, experience told him never to agree to the terms without checking everything first. It took him only a minute to skim through the Agreement but when he finally, prodded by a vague anxiety, reached for the left button, he found that it had already disappeared. The remaining option glowed and shifted into the center, transforming from the brief 'No' into the frightening 'Death'. What?

Trial failed. The Player's position has been taken.

This message was the last thing that he, and three other candidates, saw before they turned into clusters of energy and information. The creation of a player was an energy-intensive process and the System preferred to save its internal resources, concurrently adding new information about this world to its database. Only one person passed in a pool of 5-6 candidates – the one who first accepted the offered terms. Perhaps it was unfair, but the mechanism couldn't care less if it didn't get in the way of reaching the Goal.

The man died in his sleep, from severe exhaustion, the doctors later said. Around five thousand such deaths took place that night. A drop in the ocean of humanity, and so nobody noticed the loss. A drop from which the first one thousand players were born.

Attention! You have passed the preliminary

trial!

The System (75%) is active. Connecting to the **Server (50%)**... Status obtained: **Player!**

Creating **database** for the new world... **Scanning** character. Checking **parameters**. Please wait.

I floated in emptiness with no awareness of my body and no idea about what was happening. About a minute later, when I was getting seriously worried about being stuck here forever, a table popped up.

Ivan V. Susanin

General ID: unknown.
Local ID: Z-8.
True Name: Ivan V. Susanin.
Age: 24 years (8954 days).
Race: human (97%).
Gender: male.
Level: 1 (0/20 System Points).
Available: 0 System Points (SP).
Parameters*:
Strength: 6/10.
Agility: 7/10.
Intelligence: 7/10.
Vitality: 6/10.
Stamina: 6/10.
Perception: 7/10.
Luck: 2/10.

Race Parameter:
Intuition: 9/10.

*For the human race, 10 is the maximum possible natural value. First Barrier.

System Skills:
Player (F)
— Intuitive interface (F, 1/1).
— Help (F, 1/1).
— System Language (F, 1/1).

Achievements and Titles:
Eighth (personal, unique) — sometimes ill-luck is so great, that great fortune passes close by. Special skills are hidden.

It was like in a game. The slowly growing panic retreated slightly. I glanced over the text and fastened my gaze on the last line. I wasn't given time to study what was written, however, as a new message appeared.

Attention! Do you wish to change your tag? Yes/No?

(60, 59, 58...)

A timer? I confirmed my 'wish' immediately and mentally erased my surname and middle initial. This didn't seem sufficient so I erased my first name, too. Right, now my tag... Eighth? A chill ran down my spine. No, better not use my achievement as a name. Or is it a title? OK, whatever...

(52, 51, 50...)

Despite my decision, the timer remained and continued its countdown, so I had to hurry. Just Ivan? No. Even ignoring the fact that half the villains in Hollywood movies were called that, it was my real name. Should I pick a foreign one? That felt fake. Something flashy like Superman or Night Shadow? I'm not a twelve-year-old boy.

It will be... it will be... Vasya. Well, why not? In that case, let it be Vasily. **Confirm**

System Name: Vasily

Truly an 'intuitive interface'. The controls were straightforward, reminding of a standard OS.

The System accepted my decision without even trying to add a couple of numbers to my tag. Which wasn't that surprising, considering the number assigned to me. If I was indeed the eight, it was unlikely that the others have already taken the most popular nicknames. Of course, if there was even a restriction on originality. My real name didn't disappear, it simply dropped one line down and was labelled 'True'. What was the point of that?

Attention! Do you wish to hide your True Name?
Yes/No?

Of course. The System thought for a moment and the word 'hidden' appeared in brackets next to my name. I felt instantly calmer and finally returned to studying the table. Well, was there a help menu?

There was. As soon as I focused on one of the parameters, a brief description appeared.

Strength (6/10) — *corresponds to physical fitness.*

Helpful... They might as well have written "strength corresponds to strength". Although, if this was a dream, I had nobody to blame but myself for the puny description. But the more things unfolded, the less I was sure of my initial conclusion. The question wasn't even if it was a lot or a little, but rather how much it corresponded to reality?

If one assumes that only a few people in the whole of humanity had a 10, then world athletes could only get 8 or 9. Perhaps a couple of years ago, I would have scored a solid 7, but I'd become less active since I'd returned from the army and started working. I didn't have the time, nor, to be honest, the desire for regular training. Still, you wouldn't call me a weakling...

Agility (7/10) — *corresponds to overall mobility.*

An equally useless description, but the number was acceptable. I hadn't gained any extra weight, after all, and remained quite, um, mobile. Plus, I'd done a lot of stretching in my childhood.

Intelligence (7/10) — *corresponds to memory, processing speed and brain development.*

Seven. Almost too much. I'd finished university but couldn't boast of any high marks, and I'd done plenty of stupid things during my life. Nevertheless, according to the System, I was a long way from a genius.

Vitality (6/10) — *corresponds to wound healing, immunity and life expectancy.*

Well, a 6 for *vitality* looked rather poor. If I took 120 years as the maximum, 1 point was equal to roughly 12 years. Hence, the System predicted my death at around seventy years of age...

Bloody hell, why was I taking these numbers seriously? Although... why wouldn't I? It was a strange situation but right now, all I could do was keep calm and wait for events to unfold. Why not take the situation seriously in that case? If this was reality, I would be at an advantage, and if it wasn't, I wouldn't lose anything by it.

Stamina (6/10) — *reduces the accumulation of fatigue, determines the time required for proper rest and sleep.*

There was nothing surprising there, it was the obvious consequence of my past year of sedentary work.

Perception (7/10) — *responsible for the senses and attention to detail.*

A 7 was quite good, I'd never complained about my powers of observation. Perhaps it was due to my little hobby? It's well known that as people get older, they become more and more absorbed by their own thoughts and pay less attention to their surroundings. Once I'd noticed this tendency in myself, I consciously forced myself to note minor details. If you keep your eyes open, you'll always spot something interesting. And it will be harder for a person to spring something on you.

Luck *(2/10) — corresponds to probability.*

I only had a 2 here... Hmm... All my life, I preferred not to believe in luck, considering it a kind of compilation of events that couldn't be predicted. All our problems are the results of our actions, and blaming them on the powers that be or something similar is not a good habit.

Nevertheless, I was hard put not to admit that I was suspiciously unlucky at times. For example, I would randomly pick the most difficult question in an oral exam, and then pick the same question when I was retaking the exam. Such things didn't always happen, but they happened often enough. Still, I'd never slipped on a banana peel and had somehow survived almost a quarter of a century. And two was more than zero.

Intuition — *allows decisions to be made based on ambiguous facts. Maximum for the human race — 10.*

Unlike the previous parameter, this one was close to maximum. Which was surprising, considering the example with the exam questions. Perhaps I had drawn out the unlucky piece of paper again not by chance, but because it had seemed vaguely familiar? After being handled by students, the papers lost their anonymity. One acquired a slight crease, another had a barely noticeable spot. Perhaps it wasn't even bad luck? After all, even if it had been a difficult question, I didn't give into the temptation of not studying it, and eventually passed the exam. Hmm...

I didn't know what to make of that, I had to keep going. But where? Surely, I wasn't going to remain here forever, in this emptiness? The System unfroze and reminded me again of its existence.

Attention! Select a primary skill (74%).

— *Minor magical ability (F, 1/5).*
— *Sword fighting (F, 1/5).*
— *Dagger fighting (F, 1/5).*
— *Axe fighting (F, 1/5).*
— *Mace fighting (F, 1/5).*
— *Spear fighting (F, 1/5).*

...

— *Hand-to-hand combat (F, 1/5).*

I skimmed through the list. There were plenty of options, covering almost all bladed weapons. It was hard to miss the fact that all the skills were combat ones. There were no offers of teaching me to grow flowers or play chess with great skill. It didn't take a genius to figure out that the game would focus on fighting. Not the cheeriest conclusion to make.

The events seemed less and less like a dream and more like virtual reality, in the way science fiction authors liked to describe it. Sadly, scientists had never managed to invent those 'full-immersion capsules'. Like any potential psychopath, I couldn't accept the possibility of my own madness, just like other, even crazier theories. Let's not get carried away. Let's assume that I really will have to fight, and I need to pick the most useful skill right now. Of course, I would have preferred a firearm, but there were no range weapons in the list. There was magic, however...

Minor magical ability
Rank: *F.*
Level: *1/5.*
Type: *Characteristic.*
Description:

— *Uncovers the Wisdom parameter (86%) +1 point.*

— *Instills the basics of magical ability, however, you will need to go a long way before you can gain some benefit from it.*

The first thing I noticed that it was a *characteristic* and not a *skill*. Basically, it was a way to gain a ninth parameter. As the *help* showed, the numbers in brackets that kept popping up were the 'match value of the term'. It seemed that *Wisdom* was responsible for magical abilities, while the term itself was taken from a game and reflected the matter quite closely. For those 86%.

What idiot would say no to magic? But something stopped me from acting rashly. Was it really the best option? Could it be a trick? For example, there was no guarantee that there would be combat spells available. Or if there were, that they would be strong enough. Everyone had at least a vague idea of how to use a sword, but what about magic? Not even magic but something similar to this term? It's quite an ill-defined notion in Earth's culture. I started at the table, deep in thought, looking for a hint.

Attention (Intuition)! Existing combat skills are insufficient. The characteristic is not recommended as the first choice.

Aha! Looked like it was a bad idea. The hint actually gave me more than it seemed at first glance. If magic wasn't recommended as the first choice, did it mean that there would be opportunities to obtain it later? I hoped so. I couldn't see any classes here, so I shouldn't hurry and follow clichés. Let's go over it all again...

Why is it here at all, if it's not recommended? As a trick? Or is it simply an option for those who are already masters of combat? Or professional soldiers at the least? Whatever, what's next on the list?

Sword fighting

> **Rank:** *F.*
> **Level:** *1/5.*
> **Type**: *skill.*
> **Description:**
> — *Teaches one how to use a sword.*
> — *Slightly adjusts the body for the chosen weapon type.*

I scanned the list of other skills. They were surprisingly repetitive, with the only difference being the kind of weapon I'd learn to use. I had the same problem here as with magic. I had to hope that I would be given a weapon later on, otherwise I'd have to choose hand-to-hand combat. Since magic was not recommended...

Attention (Intuition)! The characteristic is not recommended as the first choice.

Or not. These types of hints appeared with a delay, almost reluctantly. But nothing of the sort appeared when I looked at the weapon skills. Therefore, it made sense to assume that I'd be given a weapon. Let's stick with that. Otherwise, I could end up being too clever for my own good.

Attention! If you do not make a selection in 5 minutes, the skill will be chosen randomly.

(300... 299... 298...)

Yet another timer forcing me to hurry. Grr... What was the point? Well, five minutes was quite enough to review my options again. Especially since the timer seemed to apply to choosing a skill and not as an overall limit.

The choice of optimal weapon usually depended on the balance stipulated by game developers, which could be completely different from real life. Since I had no other options, I decided to base my decisions on reality. As much as I could, really, considering that my knowledge of medieval weapons was mostly theoretical. It was based on books, films, and games, of course...

Alright, let's start again. The sword is the 'king of weapons' and seems like the obvious choice. I'm sure that most players, who don't pick magic, will pick a sword. Whether this is the right decision will largely depend on opponents. For example, what am I going to do with a sword if I have to fight against wild animals? Such as a bear? Plus, a sword is quite a broad term. It can be two-handed, one-handed or even a mix of the two, a bastard sword. It could have a variety of sizes, weights and shapes of the blade and cross guard. And this variety is not just for fun, each option is designed for a particular situation and a particular opponent. Still, it wasn't a bad option.

Magic. Let's go over it again. I would have to be guided by common sense and guesses rather than facts. I didn't need to mention how 'strong' it was in real life, but it was endlessly popular in gaming. Mages are usually powerful in later stages of the game, but have difficulty leveling up and are weaker than fighters at the beginning. And there was no guarantee that I would be given combat spells. Should I ignore the warning? No, if I was sure that I'd have access to magic only at the start, I'd have done so, but... For some reason, this time I was certain that I would get another chance.

Daggers? Not a serious weapon. They're too short and are only good against an unarmed opponent. It's more of an accessory weapon. To finish off a wounded enemy, to slice some bread...

I discarded the idea.

Axe... Not only a weapon but also a useful tool. However, it's almost impossible to block attacks with an axe and it requires a shield to go with it, or better yet, a full suit of armor.

Mace... Worse than an axe in many ways, although it has its pluses. It's unlikely to get stuck in an opponent's corpse. And there'd be less blood. In the Middle Ages, warrior monks had used blunt weapons specifically to circumvent the religious ban on spilling blood. Not that I had taken such vows, so I might as well look for something else.

I glanced down the list and stopped at the next item.

Spear fighting
    Rank: *F.*
    Level: *1/5.*
    Type: *skill.*
    Characteristics:
    — Teaches one how to use a spear.
    — Slightly adjusts the body for the chosen weapon type.

Not the most obvious option but probably the most universal. I had no idea whom I'd have to fight against, while a spear was suitable against both animals and humans. The main advantage, and simultaneously, the disadvantage, was the weapon's length. It limited its use indoors and at close range, but enabled one to keep an opponent some distance away and, in most cases, to land the first blow. In a bout between a swordsman and a spear fighter, with no armor and roughly equal skill, I would probably place my bets on the latter.

In addition, if I wasn't issued a spear after all, I'd be able to make a primitive one myself. If the location allowed me to find a stick, of course.

(23...22...21...)

Time was slipping away and I couldn't put my decision off any longer.

Attention! Do you wish to study the skill 'Spear fighting'?
Yes/No?

Reconfiguring.

As soon as I made my choice, the world seemed to explode and unfamiliar knowledge poured into my brain. The foundations... Types of spears, stances, how to correctly hold, thrust and slash, how to care for the weapon. Having obtained the basics, I followed my intuition and focused my attention on one of the memories, in which a young warrior skillfully used an infantry spear. It was two-meters long, with a wide blade that allowed him to stab and slash. It wasn't created for fighting in formation, it was a loner's weapon. As soon as I concentrated on the image, the flow of memories changed, focusing on this type of spear in particular. It was as if I had gone through many months or even years of training in those short moments.

The 'teachers' passed by in quick succession, but their opponents remained only blurred silhouettes. Shadows. The picture gradually dulled and began to fade, indicating that the course was coming to an end. I felt disappointment, as if there was something missing. Something important for my... survival? I needed... I needed more. If I would be forced to kill, I needed more than bare theory.

Attention! Checking access rights of (Eighth)... Approved. Censorship (51%) has been removed!

What bloody censorship? The picture grew brighter again and shimmered as scenes of battle appeared. The opponents became flesh and blood, and new knowledge flooded into me, albeit of a different kind. How it feels when a weapon plunges into flesh, pleas for mercy and the splash of blood on the face. The shock of the first kill, replaced by the indifference of a hardened professional. And corpses, corpses, corpses. Mainly human, but there were other creatures whose names I didn't know. *One who wants to live needs to be able to kill.* It was not my thought but it felt so *right*.

"Damn." I came to, lying on the floor and struggling to catch my breath. I had a body again. I tried to remember the last battle scenes, but the faces of those killed were blurry as if decades had passed, and evoked no strong emotions. My cramped muscles were gradually relaxing. The very same muscles that I needed for spear fighting, and many of which I hadn't used since birth. The stone floor wasn't especially cold but I knew that such sensations could be misleading and made myself get up. It seemed that I had been lying here for quite some time.

I was right. No matter what this was, it felt nothing like a dream. Such dreams didn't exist – everything was too realistic, my thoughts were too clear, everything was just... too much! I wasn't wearing any clothes, which I could consider as indirect evidence that I had landed here straight from my warm bed, since I normally slept naked. My own body looked utterly familiar, including the moles, scars and even dental fillings. I pinched myself, already knowing the result. It hurt.

"Looks like I'm here in the flesh," I muttered just to hear my own voice. "The question is, where is 'here'?"

A chill ran down my spine, intermingled with anticipatory fear. It looked like this would be *interesting*, at the least. Not the cleverest and in many ways, artificial thought, but right now, it kept the panic at bay. If life had taught me anything, it was to keep myself under control in critical situations.

I was in a strange room of around ten by ten meters, with a slightly glowing ceiling and a single set of doors. Or perhaps they should have been called 'gates', for doors seemed too trivial a name for them, stone-bound and decorated with an ornament, even if they were a bit small. I hoped it was a real exit and not some sort of fresco.

The temperature was rather comfortable and I had enough air, although I couldn't see any source of ventilation. There was nothing in my memories to tell me how I'd gotten here. The last thing I remembered was coming home and crashing into bed. I could have had a memory blackout, but it seemed unlikely...

"Fine," I licked my dry lips. If I couldn't get out of here, I didn't know what would kill me first: a lack of air, thirst or fear.

I was forced to console myself with the thought that if someone had cast me into this room, it was unlikely so I could die in here needlessly. I had to keep going, especially as the route was clear. And no, I didn't mean the gates. A semitransparent bag hung in the air nearby. So, this was virtual reality, after all? My whole life experience contradicted the facts, so I couldn't quite puzzle it out. It was pointless to keep guessing, but if this wasn't a hint, then I knew nothing about games. As soon as I touched the strap, the bag became solid and dropped over my shoulder. It didn't feel too heavy but it certainly wasn't empty.

Bottomless bag

Class: *F.*
Status: *System artifact.*
Description:
— *Bag for a beginner. Part of a basic kit issued to all players.*
Properties:
— *Allows system items to be carried between locations (83%). Items not belonging to the System will disappear on transfer.*
— *Conceals the size.*
— *Reduces the weight of stored items tenfold.*
— *Slightly slows down spoilage of stored items.*
— *Scalability (1/7). Can be improved by combining with other identical items.*

The *help* worked in the 'real world' too, and the descriptions were quite helpful this time. I tipped the bag upside down and spilt its contents onto the floor. Bingo! A pile of clothing, underwear, boots, a flask of water. I screwed the cap back on. Judging by the smell, all these goodies hadn't appeared out of thin air but had been lying in storage for many years.

Remembering the System's love of timers, I

tried to get dressed as quickly as possible. As I did, I tried to examine the items I'd been given, but the clothing was very simple with a paramilitary style. Pants, shirt, a jacket with pockets for... armor plates? It reminded me of a bulletproof vest. The clothing was free size and was easily adjusted to fit me using archaic belts and ropes. The boots were a little big but fitted fine with foot wrappings. I hopped on the spot, noting that the outfit was surprisingly comfortable.

Although the flask was silver, the water inside wasn't of great quality, stale but still drinkable. I hoped so, at least. I rinsed out my month, put it back in the bag and finally noticed a small steel plate with an image of a spear on it.

Execute initial activation of the Weapon Card? Yes/No?

Yes. Images of different types of spears appeared in my head, as if inviting me to choose. Long and short, throwing spears and cavalry spears, they zoomed through my mind in endless succession. I focused, trying to imagine the right type, since I doubted that I would be given a choice every time. A beam of light finally shot out of the card, which formed into a spear.

"Damn it," I muttered, grabbing the shaft. "Life didn't prepare me for this."

The spear was around two meters in length, and made from a type of hardwood. The wide, leaf-shaped tip could be used to slash and stab. Yari? Bear spear? I had trouble with the classification but it was the exact type of spear that I had focused on during my skill training. It was exactly what I wanted to get. Apart from a machine gun, of course.

System Spear

Rank: *F.*
Material: *gun steel, unknown wood.*
Length: *2 m.*
Weight: *3 kg.*
Description:
— *System Weapon. Enables the owner to absorb 40% of the spiritual and life force of the victim.*

So, what could I tell from all this? Firstly, there were no damage indicators typical of games. Secondly, the weapon was of high quality, but I doubted that I was its first owner. There were slight scuffs on the shaft, dark spots and fine scratches on the blade... The spear had clearly been used long and hard.

I looked at the card again. It had changed after activation and was now showing the exact spear I held in my hands and not some abstract one. The card itself now looked faded. I immediately wondered if I could return the weapon. The answer was simple. As soon as I touched the spear to the card and made a wish, it instantly turned into a beam of light and disappeared inside, while the card regained its colors. Here and now, alongside everything else, this seemed quite normal. Also, I tried to guess the size of the 'armor plate' pockets in my jacket and found to my surprise that they matched the dimensions of the card.

I recalled the weapon and made a couple of practice moves. The spear felt perfect in my hand, as if I had spent a long time mastering the craft. Or was it just a skill for now? I tried a spin but it wasn't too impressive – my new-found mastery didn't extend to such tricks. There weren't many moves but they were extremely practical. The level of a soldier from the Middle Ages rather than a Shaolin monk. Save one's strength, don't leave oneself open and, whenever possible, land the first blow. Not necessarily a mortal one, for even a superficial wound sharply reduced an enemy's fighting ability. Pure pragmatism...

I suddenly felt a mild alarm but didn't understand the reason at once. There wasn't a clear warning this time, but somewhere at the edge of my consciousness, an invisible timer was counting down the last few minutes given for preparation.

(2:34... 2:33... 2:31)

I wasn't going to check what a delay would

entail. I returned the weapon to the card, slid it into a pocket on my chest, slung the bag over my shoulder and headed to the one and only 'door'. If this was a dream, I would believe it once I woke up. If this was virtual reality, then, considering the lack of such technology on my home planet, I would probably wake up in the tender tentacles of some aliens. Well, if this was something else... At some point, the situation would become clear. There was no point in torturing myself with doubts, I needed more facts.

As soon as I pressed my palm to the gates, a new message appeared:

Attention! Destination selection is impossible! First trial! Select difficulty level:*

Minimum (F)/Easy (E)/Normal (D)/Above normal (C)/High (B)/Very high (A)/Maximum (S)

*The higher the level, the higher the reward.

Right, and the higher the likelihood of defeat. I'd have to be an idiot to choose the maximum difficulty without having any idea of what was going on. Especially since the default level was F. But would that be too cowardly?

I paused and then moved the cursor one step to the right. Strangely, this calmed me down. I dropped my head to one shoulder, moved the cursor a bit further and felt a stab of fear. Even further? I felt even worse. OK, let's stop at easy level.

Attention! Decision has been recorded!

Task No. 1
   Type: Defense.
   Information:
   The Celestial City of Sar once belonged to a race of... searching for counterpart... **goblins (83%).** Their... searching for counterpart... **gods (57%)** were defeated and vanquished. However, for as long as not all altars are captured and the city still stands, the battle continues and hope remains!
   Number of players: *1000.*
   Global objective:
   Difficulty level: A.
   — Reach and defend the central altar. Repel the assault on the city.
   Reward:
   — Varies.
   Allies:
   — City Defenders.
   — Allied Players.
   Presumed enemies:
   — System Creatures.
   — Chaos Creatures.
   Local objective:
   Chosen difficulty level: E.
   — Survive for a minimum of 24 hours.

— Obtain Level 2.

Reward:

— First mission bonus: earned System Points are doubled.

— The Player's rank increases.

— Shard coordinates.

— Soul Stone.

— Temporary access to the **Server.**

Penalty for failure:

— Unknown.

All I needed to do was reach Level 2? It didn't sound that difficult. Maybe.

The door opened but all I saw beyond was a strange mist. I cautiously stuck out my card, and once I had made sure that nothing happened to it, took a step forward. Time was running out, and what other choice did I have, anyway?

CHAPTER 2

ALL YOU NEED IS TO KILL

FELL FROM A DECENT HEIGHT and rolled along the ground, my body painfully striking several rocks. I kept silent despite the pain and immediately got back on my feet and pulled the spear out of the card. Although I couldn't see any danger nearby, I didn't bother putting away the weapon.

The world around me looked... strange. Heavy clouds obscured the sky and hinted that it was going to rain soon. I had expected to land in the midst of battle after such a briefing, but if there had been a battle here, it was long over. The houses, their style reminiscent of the European Middle Ages mixed with Ancient Rome, were not quite in ruins but had fallen into disrepair, and had been abandoned by their inhabitants quite a few years ago. Not centuries, though, since even the wooden structures were still standing, to say nothing of the stone ones. Could it be that the intelligence obtained by the System was several decades out of date? As if it was reading my mind, the System reacted,

Attention! Correcting task!

Task No. 1

> **Type:** *Looting.*
> **Information:**
> *The Celestial City of Sar once belonged to a race of* **goblins (83%).** *Their* **gods (57%)** *were defeated and vanquished. Although their enemies withdrew, a* **necromantic curse (65%)** *hangs over the capital. The city's central districts are controlled by the* **undead (93%),** *while the outskirts are being looted by the surviving defenders and their descendants. Formerly allies, the living and the dead now fight each other for access to the* **altar.**
> **Global objective:**
> *Difficulty level: A.*
> *— Capture the altars(?) of the fallen gods and dedicate them to a new owner.*
> **Reward:**
> *Varies depending on the choice.*
> **Allies:**
> *— Players (1000/ 1000).*
> **Assumed enemies:**
> *— System Creatures.*

— The Undead.

— Goblinoids.

Local objective:

Chosen difficulty level: E.

— Obtain Level 2.

— Survive for 24 hours.

Reward:

— First mission bonus: earned System Points are doubled.

— The Player's rank increases.

— Soul Stone.

— Temporary access to the Server (50%).

— Shard coordinates.

Penalty for failure:

Unknown... Correcting...

— Player status reduced to Hero status (84%).

— Inability of system return to the home location until the global objective is achieved.

I read the last point and frowned. Change in status to Hero level? Following the game's logic, this didn't sound promising. Inability to return to the 'home location'? Did it mean Earth? On one hand, this didn't sound good at all, but on the other hand, it suggested that if I achieved the local objective, I would be able to return home. It was better than the uncertainty before the information had corrected itself.

I automatically licked a scratch on my arm and pulled a face. All the stats, tasks and parameters indicated a game, but the taste of blood, dirt and saliva were real. I kneeled, examining the grass growing between the pavement slabs, pulled out a stalk and turned it around in my hands. A bird chirped overhead. Taste, touch, hearing, smell and sight were all too realistic for me to believe that it could be a mirage. Although my body felt unusually light, as if a weight had dropped from my shoulders. I performed a little jump. Was it higher than normal? Either I had suddenly gained a lot of strength or the gravity here was slightly lower. Not a huge difference but certainly noticeable. How would it affect my reflexes?

Deciding where to go wasn't much of an issue. If you have neither map nor compass, all you can do is wander blindly. First, it would be good to find some cover.

I strode towards the closest building that looked like it hopefully wouldn't collapse in the near future. It was immediately clear that I hadn't been the first. The house had been completely cleared out. Even the furniture had been chopped up for firewood, although the fireplace hadn't been lit in a long time. I remembered the second briefing. It was hard to imagine that the looting had been done by the undead. It seemed more logical to assume that I had landed somewhere near the outskirts and had every chance of meeting some goblins. Or something similar, since the match value was only 83%. They could look quite different to the 'traditional image'. It was something to keep in mind.

As I had rightly worried, even a small difference in gravity had a substantial effect on the accuracy of my movements. Familiar actions required a different amount of force and my body needed time to adjust. I found a suitable area and spent about ten minutes performing careful spins with the spear to get used to the changes, trying not to make too much noise and not forgetting to glance around from time to time. It wasn't enough, I really needed weeks of training but I didn't have enough time. I had to keep moving since I was only given a day for everything.

Since I had nothing better to do, I started collecting samples as I walked, throwing bunches of unfamiliar grasses into my bag. I threw them in with the roots intact since they didn't take up much space. If this was a different world, even the weeds had enormous research value. Although, judging by the description of the bag, I'd have difficulty bringing them home. But perhaps I could level it up to Level 2?

I could see no enemies nearby, nor allies. Which was odd, considering the declared numbers. How were they doing, anyway?

Remaining players: 453/1000.

"Son of a..."

The counter blinked and the number changed to **451/1000.** These losses reminded me to be cautious and I gave up on my weed collection. My allies were being massacred. Less than 30 minutes had passed and more than half of them were already dead. And it didn't look like this game had a respawn point. What would happen if I died here? I had no intention of finding out. Until I saw a respawn with my own eyes, I would behave as if I had been given only one life.

Sometime later, I discovered that the number of allies had more or less stabilized and felt a little calmer. I could only guess the reasons for such massive losses, but then I remembered the task correction. It was possible that some of the players, who had chosen the lowest difficulty level, had been dropped closer to 'past allies' who were now the undead. While those who had selected the higher difficulty levels had been sent to the front, where the goblins now wandered. There was a reason why they had been removed from the list of allies, right? A mistake. If I still believed that this was a game, it would have been easier to accept. Something gave me the chills again. Damn.

Carefully checking that the beams were still sturdy, I climbed up to the roof of a nearby building. I couldn't make out very much from the third floor but the city took up a huge area, sprawling below me in all directions.

Not far away, I spotted a lazy drift of smoke, an obvious sign of human presence. Or, in our case, goblins. I decided to head over there. Task, weapon, enemies. It wasn't hard to figure out how to gain experience points here. Time was passing and there was a chance that I wouldn't meet anybody if I kept wandering aimlessly. I didn't know if I would have the strength to fight a goblin, but I definitely had no desire to tackle the undead. Even if knew where to find them...

I laid aside the fact that I was planning to kill sentient beings. If goblins were even slightly like humans, they were bound to give me a cause for aggression. It was unlikely that I would come across women and children in a city filled with the undead, so I would probably find wandering warriors. The big question was which of us would die... The answer lay ahead of me.

I always suspected that modern people have problems with the sense of self-preservation. As soon as something explodes or bursts into flame, they run towards the source as if they're immortal. It looked like I was no exception.

A desperate, pain-filled scream came from beyond the houses and was sharply cut off. Clearly, someone had just died and this was a powerful argument for heading in the other direction. Nevertheless, I did the opposite, carefully moving towards the potential danger.

What can I say... I was right. There were three goblins, and despite some differences with the 'classical image', they generally looked as I had expected. Black skin, around five feet tall, with unusual facial features and pointed ears that stopped me from confusing them with any human race. They didn't look like complete savages in the way that goblins are usually portrayed. Their clothing appeared quite decent, albeit slightly old-fashioned. Pants, kaftans and even some kind of armor. They were also quite well-armed, with simple but obviously metal weapons: a bear spear, an ax and a club.

By the time I arrived, my 'fellow sapiens' were almost done stripping a player's corpse. His equipment kit looked like mine, while this slightly overweight imbecile had picked a sword as his weapon. Why imbecile? Because he had been killed with the very same weapon, his neck half-severed. One of the goblins was admiring the trophy and in his hands, the relatively short weapon looked like a bastard sword. I narrowed my eyes, activating the *help*.

Goblin. Level 2

The same signs appeared above the heads of his companions, glowing blood red to clearly signal their enemy status. I felt a sense of dark satisfaction observing this scene. The question of whether killing goblins was ethical had smoothly transformed into a question of whether I would have enough strength for it.

"Ha-a!"

Even while pillaging, the natives remained on guard, and my appearance was immediately spotted. I considered my prospects, put on a fake smile and headed towards them, casually holding my spear. How strong were they? How fast? Did I have any chance of winning? I judged my chances of running away as even lower since the modern world hadn't equipped me for endurance running and the goblins seemed smallish but hardy. Despite my expectations, they didn't rush to greet me with happy squeals, their faces instead showing something akin to fear. It appeared that they had met humans before and were wary of them, to say the least.

"No. Player mumble-mumble. Mumble-mumble strong!" growled the leader, leaning on the sword and beating himself on the chest. Although I couldn't understand most of the speech, a few words were quite clear. It seemed that the goblin knew several System words but it clearly wasn't enough for a proper conversation. There were other possibilities, of course... One of which my predecessor had tried, judging by the drawings in the dirt.

I didn't get a chance to inspect the scratches. One of the goblins, seeing the direction of my gaze, bashfully erased the evidence of past negotiations with his foot. The second creature hurriedly hid the severed head behind his back. What a picture — the player had tried diplomacy but was unsuccessful. They broke his legs, took his sword, made him kneel and then tried to chop his head off with the same sword, finishing the job using the axe. I didn't bother listening to them but switched to a run.

"Ra-a-a!"

The goblins backed away, their leader swung the sword but needn't have bothered, obviously lacking the sword-fighting skills. I slowed down and let the blade pass before me, then swung the spear and sliced through the goblin's throat. For a moment, I felt something pass through the spear shaft and into my body...

Attention! You have gained 4 SP! (4/20).

I twitched from the strange energy wave that swept through my body. Hmm, four System Points at once, not bad. A light appeared around the fallen goblin and a card floated away from his body and hung in the air. What the?

The brief distraction almost cost me my life. I barely managed to deflect the second goblin's spear, which he simply threw at me. Considering the lack of armor and close distance, this could have been the end. The third goblin leapt forward but his abilities didn't even reach Level 1 of the system skills. Easily parrying the swing of his club, I stabbed the spear into his chest without any pity. He had practically impaled himself on it. The goblin's eyes bulged, he clutched at the shaft as blood ran from his mouth, jerked several times and then died.

Attention! You have gained 2 SP! (6/20).

It was only half of what I had gotten last time, so it seemed that the number of System Points directly correlated with the enemy level. Hell, this isn't the time...

The spear head had gone in too deep, so I discarded it and picked up the trophy one. Luckily, my opponent took this chance to escape rather than attack. I took a run up and flung the spear with all my might after him. It whistled through the air and pierced him in the back. There was no message this time, so after collecting my own weapon, I cautiously approached the fallen enemy. Was he pretending? No, the goblin was dead and unlike the leader, he wasn't wearing any chain mail so the spear had gone right through him. An impressive pool of blood had already gathered under the body. The corpses looked quite realistic in this 'game' and I could have probably used them to study goblin anatomy if I so wished. Hmm, coming back to collecting samples, should I stick one of them in my bag? A goblin weighed about 40 kilograms and even if my bag reduced the weight tenfold, it would still be four extra kilos. Moreover, even though the corpse was still glowing, there was no guarantee that I could take it with me. Fine, I'd leave that for the future.

The triple murder and the bodies lying on the ground triggered no special emotions in me, as if I had done this dozens of times before. No feelings of disgust or a need to empty my stomach. Even the smell of blood seemed vaguely familiar... for all that today had been the first time I had killed an intelligent being, even if it wasn't human. I doubted this was due to my natural equanimity, more likely a consequence of the learnt skill. Although the absence of guilt was likely unrelated to that. I really did think that the goblins deserved to die. I am sure that given the chance, they would have happily finished me off.

Speaking of which, I hadn't gotten any points for the last kill. I even jabbed my spear into the body a couple of times but to no avail. I concluded that I had to kill using the System weapons, otherwise it didn't count. A total of 6 SP for the skirmish, while I needed 20 to reach the next level. So, to complete the task, I needed to kill another seven first-level goblins. A victim number that not even many maniacs could boast of...

Nevertheless, these thoughts didn't stop me from looting. I first approached the semi-transparent card that still hung in the air against all laws of nature. Looks like the game has loot? As soon as I grabbed it, the card solidified and turned into a blank steel plate. Interesting.

Clean skill card
  Rank: *F.*

Description:
— *Allows one of the **Player's** skills to be recorded by paying for it in full.*
Saturation:
0/ 10 SP

Why do I need it if I can purchase any skill directly from the System? Or... Mentally, as if I had done this hundreds of times before, I called up the menu and found the relevant section.

Attention! Connection with the Server is lost! Skill base is unavailable!

Great, just great. I remembered the thousands of skills that I hadn't even looked through properly, believing that there would be time in the future. If leveling up was random here, this severely limited my choice of strategy. Plus, it was going to be harder to obtain magic. There was some good news – I didn't need the connection to look through skills I'd already acquired. I could even improve them. The second level of *spear fighting* cost 20 SP. Alright, now wasn't the best time for digging around in the interface.

There was no other System loot but there were the dead player's items.

System Sword
Rank: *F.*
Material: *steel.*

Length: 75 cm.
Weight: 1.3 kg.
Description:
— *System Weapon. Enables the owner to absorb 40% of the spiritual and life force of the victim.*

I swung the blade a few times but felt no enthusiasm. Without the appropriate skill, the sword was more dangerous to me than to my opponent. It took some time to find the card, which I eventually found on the main goblin. I inserted the sword back inside it and stuck it into one of my many pockets.

Remembering about the *bottomless bag*, I took the second one, reread the description and, without thinking too much about it, tried to put the new bag inside the old one. The bags resisted. It was like trying to connect two magnets, but I eventually succeeded.

Do you wish to combine items?
Yes/No?

As soon as I picked 'yes', the bag made a hungry chomping sound and swallowed its twin. That's it?

Bottomless bag (2/7)

That's it. The bag's appearance didn't change at all and its characteristics remained at the same level. To complete the transformation, I had to feed the cannibal bag another five of its fellows. Where would I get them? A rhetorical question. I doubted this was going to be the last time that I would meet some goblins. Plus, sooner or later, I was going to come across other players.

Having finished my pillaging, I placed the other player's equipment in my bag, as well as the few goblin items that were worth keeping. The axe, a couple of silver ornaments, a small pot, a handful of coins, several bags of grain, salt, a knife... I thought about it and also took their water flasks. Although not much time had passed, mine was already half empty, and I had no idea where to find water. The state of the local microflora, bacteria and other such things also remained an interesting and unanswered question. One that I wasn't going to worry about right now, since I could do nothing about it. Easier to discard these unhelpful thoughts than to try and find evidence of a strange alien disease in myself. Interestingly, the player kits, although similar, also had minor differences. Another small detail to add to my collection of facts.

I threw the extra weapons into some underbrush. I didn't touch the bodies since I had no way of hiding the evidence of the slaughter. I simply covered the fallen human with the goblin's cloak, which wasn't long enough and left his head and feet sticking out from underneath.

The easy victory did not go to my head as I

was aware of how closely I had skirted death. If everything had gone a bit differently, if there had been more goblins, it would have been my body lying on the ground. My next step was clear — find other players. Of whom 402 still remained, including me. The drop in our numbers had slowed down but hadn't stopped. I needed allies. Only an idiot would try to fight alone when there was an opportunity to join with others like him. The humans were bound to start gathering in bands, and if I didn't find companions now, I was likely to have problems with more than goblins in the future. I was certain that sooner or later, someone would have the bright idea of checking how many points were awarded for killing a human. Not now, but closer to the System deadline. It was a big city and it took time to find goblins... Humans too, but I doubted that the System had dispersed us too far. Or perhaps my view of things was overly gloomy?

CHAPTER 3

THE FAILED ALLIANCE

HE NEXT MEETING occurred about twenty minutes later and I'd heard the stamping of feet and the heavy breathing in advance, and so had enough time to hide behind the nearest fence.

Human. Level 1.

This was the only information provided by the System. Unlike the crimson of the goblins, the stranger's status glowed a pale green. The man looked to be around thirty, wearing the regular player clothing already smeared with mud and blood, an axe in his hand, and an unhinged look in his eyes. He checked behind him several times, as if fearing pursuit, and kept turning his head from side to side, probably in search of cover. The rickety fence I was crouching behind no longer seemed like a safe hiding place.

The fugitive saw me and croaked something, but I was already disappearing inside the nearest house. The man sped up, apparently hoping to join me, but in that moment, a rider appeared from around the corner. Riding a horse and not some local beast. I heard the twang of a bowstring, the player screamed and tumbled to the ground, letting go of his weapon and clutching his pierced leg, right in front of my hiding place. His eyes, full of genuine pain, met mine. I put a finger to my lips, nodded slightly, and stepped to the side. The man seemed to get the message. In any case, he didn't beg for help, thus giving away my position, but grit his teeth, picked up his weapon and backed away to the opposite side of the street.

Goblin. Level 8.

The enemy approached and the System cheerfully revealed his level. His status glowed a much brighter red than that of those first goblins. As for his strength... I hadn't noticed any difference between Level 1 and 2, and the goblins were comparable to human adolescents in their strength. The archer, however, looked noticeably different. He was taller, more muscular and even his movements seemed more dangerous. I wasn't sure I could handle him in a fair fight.

The only positive was that the rider was alone, which seemed slightly odd. He clearly wasn't poor, with his opulent clothing, chain mail, a silver-encrusted helmet, and a rich set of weapons at the saddle... Was his retinue lagging behind him?

The goblin watched coldly as his victim tried to flatten himself against the wall of the house, the axe held out in front of him. Brave but naive. The bow twanged again and another arrow pierced his victim's shoulder. The movement took only a couple of seconds; the goblin was a master of his craft. It seemed that the archer wanted something from the human, since he hadn't killed him at once.

Returning his bow to its saddle pouch, the goblin dismounted and drew out a dagger. He took a step toward his helpless victim, who was clutching his injured shoulder.

"How many *players* have come? How many are still alive? What is your task this time?"

This goblin spoke the system language quite fluently. Not that it provided any opportunities for negotiation — he was too dangerous for that. Nevertheless, by leaving his bow behind, the goblin had made a mistake I hoped would prove fatal to him. A short dagger against my spear, and even the seven levels between us wouldn't help him.

"Don't kill me, I'll tell you everything. There's only a thousand of us," the player revealed this 'military secret' without hesitation, grimacing from the pain. "We must last one day and get to Level 2."

"Newbies, then? Father will be pleased," the goblin smiled coldly. "You named only the minor goal. I don't believe your gods sent you here for something so small. What else do you have to do?"

"We... we must capture the altars in the center of the city."

"Scavengers." the goblin muttered, raising his dagger. "Well, you have been honest with me. Put down the axe and your death will be quick."

"Wait, I have something else to tell you."

I carefully exited the house, trying to make as little noise as possible, but the rider still managed to react and, without turning to look at me, leapt several meters away. In one jump! My spear pierced nothing but air.

"Watch out, he's very fast!" the man stated the obvious. "I was beginning to think you were going to leave me to die. Thank you, thank you!"

"How could I?" I smiled without not taking my eyes off the goblin, and shifted to stand between him and the horse. How could I not interfere? Although the player's confession might have been an attempt to distract the enemy, I'd bet nine out of ten that he would have revealed my position if I had tried to remain hidden. If only the goblin had killed him right away...

The rider paused, grimacing nastily and watching the wavering point of my spear like a snake. This time, he said nothing. I kept silent too, my gaze locked on him. My nerves were stretched taut and I sensed that if I let my attention wander for even a second, the enemy would take advantage of this opportunity. I wanted to blink so badly. The tension grew with each passing second, drawing closer and closer to the point when the mind would succumb to instinct, making me step toward the danger. The spear no longer seemed like such a clear advantage. Considering the goblin's speed, all I could hope for was a counter strike. If he dodged, I wouldn't be able to gain enough distance to try again.

A belated thought came that he might have weapon cards with him. The goblin glanced at his saddle, where hung an impressive mace. Damn... I realized that I had allowed myself to get distracted and let the enemy out of my sight for a moment. Without thinking, on instinct alone, I jabbed my spear down and to the left. The spear struck armor, slid across the metal, and then, with almost no resistance, sank into flesh. The wound wasn't deep and the goblin reacted immediately, jumping back and holding the cut closed with his other hand.

Still, this was the end, for the spear had pierced his shoulder and had struck an artery, judging by the amount of blood. The goblin only had a few seconds left. I took no chances and put more distance between us, knowing that a mortally wounded enemy was doubly dangerous.

The goblin's eyes flashed with rage and

desperation, and he charged. Not at me, but at the wounded man. I leapt after him and plunged my spear into his back as he stood over the injured player. The chain mall screeched yet managed to deflect the blow, and the goblin struck again with the dagger. I pressed harder, pushing the tip deeper into the flesh.

Attention! You have gained 16 SP! (22/20)

Attention! You have reached Level 2! (2/40)

Additional: You have 2 parameter points available.

Task has been updated!

I pushed my now-dead enemy aside and bent over my ally, trying to assess his injuries. Unfortunately, I couldn't see much because of the clothes, but the slowly spreading blood stain on his chest didn't bode well.

"Are you alive?" I asked rhetorically.

The man wheezed in response. The jacket had provided no protection from the dagger, and the goblin had struck twice. He hadn't even drawn out the dagger the second time, and it still stuck out from the man's side. Not to mention the arrows...

"Do you know what's going on? Where are we?"

"I don't know... I don't want to die."

Words spoken by almost every person whose time had already run out. I could console myself with the fact that this was a game and he would respawn. Hope, like the belief in heaven and hell. The player uttered a sob and tried in vain to clutch at me with a blood-spattered hand. Maybe if I could get him to a hospital and straight into surgery, he could still be saved, but there was clearly no ambulance or field hospital in this place. The player seemed to know that.

"It hurts... Pull it out."

If I let the dagger be, he would last a little longer, but I looked at the blood trickling from his mouth and nodded. The man was doomed.

"Just a second."

As soon as I touched the dagger, a wave of energy surged through it.

Attention! You have gained 10 SP! (12/40)

I didn't have time to enjoy the unexpected bonus.

Attention! For murdering an ally, you are marked with the Bloody Spot!

Bloody Spot

*Only the strong can break the rules! For the duration of one day, any **Player** can kill you* *without incurring any punishment. The possibility of resurrection on the altar is blocked.*

Blasted buggy System! It didn't seem to care that I was only trying to help. The message hit me like a bucket of cold water. The altar, possible resurrection... this information was important but paled against the main fact. Ten SP! To get that much experience, I would have had to kill five goblins of the same level! This information was dangerous, a temptation of how easy it would be to level up.

A translucent card formed over the dead player's body. However, it was much more vivid this time. I could get loot from players, too?

Mask of the Faceless Killer (49%)*

Material: *unknown leather.*
Class: *E.*
Type: *System artifact, scalable.*
Description:
The rules are the same for everyone, but the weak will die anyway. So why shouldn't they serve as a stepping stone for your ascension?
Properties:
— Hides the face and all system information about the player.
— Changes the name to match the mask.
— Temporarily severs the link with the altars, preventing resurrection.

Available to the first 10 players in the new world who have killed an ally.

A mask that can hide a killer's identity. What is this, if not a clear offer to start exterminating one's allies? Given the promised doubling of points at the end of the mission, it was more than tempting. It was unlikely that the System would be this generous in the future. Of course, it didn't mean that I would rush to kill everyone I met, without understanding what was happening. It was... A possibility to consider. Even if I returned home at the end of this mission, I could no longer believe that it would all be over.

I removed the mask from the storage card. It looked like someone had been skinned. True, someone green and scaly, so there was no need to worry that the donor was human or goblin. A slight feeling of revulsion didn't stop me from placing the artifact against my face, and the mask instantly stretched and enveloped it. I didn't have a mirror but I found a puddle and admired the twisted reflection. It was horrible. A monster looked back at me from the water, with the words *Faceless Killer* in deep red letters above my head. With such a description, the name *Cain* would have been more appropriate, surely.

Attention! Sync level increased!

The name wavered and changed to the new

version. Cain. This only made the situation seem even crazier. I could influence such things?

I turned back to the corpses. The Level 8 goblin had also dropped a card.

Archery

Rank: *F.*
Type: *skill.*
Level: *1/5.*
Description:
— *An archery skill taken from one of the goblin tribes.*
Saturation:
0/10 SP

I checked my statistics. Well, I had completed half of the task and my level had increased automatically, using up twenty SP at once. I still had twelve points remaining, about a third of what I needed to reach the Level 3.

Would you like to learn the skill Archery? (10 SP)
Yes/No

After briefly thinking it over, I agreed **(2/40)**. The process was markedly different this time. The *Spear fighting* skill I had obtained directly from the System was like an endless labyrinth, where I could choose between thousands of paths. This time, there was little general information and almost no choice. It felt like an extract of the dead goblin's memories and skills. I suppose bows are more similar than spears, and if you can shoot from one type, you can use any other. If you have the right physical abilities, of course.

Now came the time for the weapons that the goblin had left strapped to his saddle. The horse recoiled at my approach, looking doubtfully from me to its dead owner. Apparently, having come to some conclusion, it decided to flee. Alas, I couldn't let this happen.

I took a step forward and hurled my spear, which flew about five meters and pierced the horse's side. The horse trotted another ten meters before it collapsed, fortunately onto its other side and without damaging my weapon. I didn't dare to pull the spear out at once, mindful of the hooves. I circled around the poor beast, carefully put my arms around its head and cut its throat with the goblin's dagger. Another System weapon, as it turned out. The dagger obviously absorbed something, but I didn't get any system points and the energy flowed through me without leaving a drop.

Interesting... Does the System discourage the murder of defenseless creatures? After carefully examining the dagger, I understood why the goblin had been so eager to use it to finish off his victim that he had even dismounted from his horse.

System Dagger

Rank: *E.*
Material: *steel.*
Weight: *0.4 kg.*
Type: *System weapon, normal.*
Description:
— System Weapon. Enables the owner to absorb 50% of the spiritual and life force of the victim.

This weapon had a higher rank than my spear, and therefore allowed me to gain more experience. The goblin had been killed by his own greed, together with arrogance and carelessness.

The same greed threatened to be my undoing since I doubted that the goblin had been travelling alone. I had to leave immediately, but I couldn't do so before I collected the extensive loot. The deceased player, whose name I would never know, had a full set of system items, including the bag. The goblin had four such bags, which allowed the artifact to complete its evolution.

Marauder's Bag

Class: *E.*
Type: *System artifact.*
Description:
— Conceals the size. Reduces the weight of stored items twentyfold.

— *Allows you to transport System objects between locations.*

— *Allows objects not related to the System to be transported to the **home location (83%)**.*

— *Slows down spoilage of stored items.*

— *Allows you to transport bags of a lower rank without them being consumed.*

— *Scalable (1/7). It is possible to increase the rank by combining identical items.*

Although the artifact's total volume was less than all the absorbed bags, the ability to transport items to a 'home location' more than made up for it. If I wasn't mistaken, it meant Earth... Apparently, I could take some trophies home from this world. Perhaps if I improved the bag again, I'd be able to bring something useful here. The goblin world certainly lacked a machine gun...

My joy was dampened by the contents of one of the bags, which clearly explained how the goblin had acquired so many artifacts. Three human heads rolled out: a middle-aged man, an old man, and a woman. Three cards, most likely belonging to the deceased, contained different types of bladed weapons: a Cossack saber, a sword, and a dagger. I glanced at the counter.

Remaining players: 392/1000.

Yet less than a quarter of the allotted time had passed. The dead goblin alone had caused four deaths! The statistics were depressing.

However, I had no time for regrets. I moved on to the most important trophy — the bow, for which I had high hopes. Although it was a System item, just like the clothing, and wasn't even a class F artifact, it could be placed inside the last card in the goblin's possession.

Archer's Kit

> **Rank:** *E.*
> **Type:** *set.*
> **Description:**
> *Allows typical items from a set to be placed inside, by marking them with the System label.*
> *Time until conversion into a System object —*
> *20 days.*
> **Contains:**
> *— Goblin Bow.*
> *— Archery Outfit.*
> *— Renewable Quiver. System artefact, rank E.*

I suspected that this card had once contained the complete artifact set, but only the quiver now remained. At least, there was no separate card for it, and after a brief inspection, I concluded that everything else had been locally made and transformed into a System item by the power of the card. There was an archer's ring, glove and spare bowstring.

Renewable Quiver

Material: wood, leather.
Class: E.
Type: System artifact.
Description:
— Transforms arrows placed inside into System weapons. 1 arrow/day.
— Capacity: 12/20 arrows.

Although the bow was designed for a goblin, I struggled to pull the string taut. I feigned a couple of shots, drawing the string back and then returning it to the resting position. There weren't many System arrows, but I found two normal quivers in the bags with thirty arrows in each. There were armor-piercing arrows, hunting arrows, and finally, blunt arrows with a lead ball on the end. Each one was slightly different, with marks that allowed the owner to pull out a specific type of arrow.

I fired a dozen arrows, testing my newfound skill. My accuracy left much to be desired. The arrows were obviously not factory-made and each one flew a little differently, but I could definitely hit a post from thirty meters away... And that's after shooting a bow for the first time in my life! Unfortunately, I only managed to pull out half the arrows, while the others lost their tip or broke completely.

I threw everything of any interest into my

bag, including the goblin corpse, since the bag's characteristics allowed me to do so, and jogged away. I was looking forward to increasing my parameters by using the points obtained at this level. Something that was impossible in the real world.

VASILY

General ID: unknown.
Local ID: Z-8.
True Name: Ivan V. Susanin (hidden).
Age: 24 years.
Race: human (97%).
Gender: male.
Level: 2 (2/40 System Points).
Available: 2 SP.

Parameters:
Strength: 6/10.
Agility: 7/10.
Intelligence: 7/10.
Vitality: 6/10.
Stamina: 6/10.
Perception: 7/10.
Luck: 2/10.

Race Parameter:
Intuition: 9/10.

System Skills:
Player (F)
— Intuitive interface (F, 1/1).
— Help (F, 1/1).
— System Language (F, 1/1).
— Archery (F, 1/5).
— Spear fighting (F, 1/5).

Achievements and Titles:
Eight (personal, unique) — sometimes ill-luck is so great that great fortune passes close by. Features unknown.

Cards and Items:
Rank F: spear, sword, axe, saber, cutlass, foil, empty skill card, Bottomless Bag (2/7).
Rank E: dagger, Archer's Kit, Marauder's Bag (1/7), Mask of Cain.

I closed the menu. So, what was I missing? An obvious option was to gain more *Intelligence*, but I always liked round numbers, so I decided to add one to my *Intuition* first. There was a tickling sensation inside my skull that lasted a couple of minutes. Goosebumps appeared all over my body... And the statistics number changed.

Attention! Your understanding of the System interface has improved.
Congratulations! Your Intuition parameter has reached the limit for your race. You have

received the Identification skill (99%).

Identification

> **Rank:** *E.*
> **Level:** *1/5.*
> **Internal number:** *A5437593475.*
> **Description:**
> *— Allows you to determine the features of System objects. The amount of obtained information varies and depends on specific conditions.*
> *— Visual or physical contact required to activate.*
> *— A magic skill that requires the* **Wisdom** *parameter to be unlocked for activation.*

I placed the spear in front of me and immediately tried to test my new skill, although I could read and knew that it wouldn't work.

Attention! The skill cannot be used. Insufficient magical energy.

Something stirred deep inside me, leaving behind a strange feeling of emptiness. A sense that something strange was missing... which was to be expected, really. At this point, the skill was useless to me. Although I still had one point left, the desired parameter wasn't on the list, which meant that I couldn't yet raise my *Wisdom* level. Annoying. I wondered how much the information provided by the *Identification* skill differed from what was contained in the *Help*.

Nevertheless, the increased *Intuition* produced other effects. Such as the fact that all skills now had an 'internal number'. What was the point of that? Well, if I was to assume that the System adapted to the user and the names of the skills differed from person to person, then it would be the only way to find the right one. Which meant that only people with maximum human *Intuition* could see the numbers... Hmm. This was just the tip of the iceberg. Although the System did not provide a complete list, I kept noticing small but useful changes to the interface.

I tried to add another point to my *Intuition* but found that it was impossible. A tiny lock had appeared beside the parameter. Thinking logically, if there was a lock, there had to be a way to open it. Otherwise, at the current parameter number and values, one needed just twelve levels to pump everything to the maximum.

Attention (Intuition)! To break the first limit, you need 50 SP!

Another bonus from my increased *Intuition*? Not bad, not bad.

After a brief thought, I put the second point into *Strength* and winced in advance. What can I say? My suspicions were correct and it was *really* painful. I clung to the ground, stifling a scream and counting the seconds. My muscles were growing rapidly, as if I had completed months, if not years, of regular training in minutes. After two hundred and fifty-six interminably long seconds, it was over. Not only did my muscle bulk increase, I also seemed to grow a little taller. Fortunately, the clothes were loosely fitting and secured with numerous straps. It seemed the creators had anticipated such changes, so I quickly adjusted everything to fit my new shape. Very practical.

Why did I choose *Strength*? Well, aside from the fact that increasing it was much more obvious than increasing my *Intuition*, and provided me with new information, my reasoning was simple. I was stronger than any of the goblins from the beginning, despite not being in the best physical shape, while the natives clearly did not lead a sedentary lifestyle. In other words, their limit was probably well below ten, and even a single point invested in *Strength* would give me a significant advantage in battle.

Yes, I was going to keep fighting. One would think that having obtained the required level and assessed the danger, I would lie low. There was no point in taking a risk by biting off more than I could chew, right? Well, I didn't think so. Perhaps the people following this approach would live a little longer but they were unlikely to succeed. I wanted to be strong enough not to fear for my life.

Right now, I could only guess at what was going on, but instinct told me that it would be easier to gain an advantage early in the game. I was going to take that chance.

CHAPTER 4

BLOOD

A NOISE COMING FROM the street drew my attention. I had chosen a more secure shelter this time so I could rest, sort out my loot, and make further plans. It was the second floor of a four-story building that had been plundered many times and was unlikely to attract the attention of any looters. Despite several holes in the floor, the beams looked solid enough to support an adult's weight, and the building's entrances were overgrown with bushes.

I peeked through a small gap next to me. Two poorly dressed goblins were moving along the street, clearly looking for something. Or someone. According to the System description, even before the arrival of the players, these ruins were dangerous enough that a couple wouldn't wander through here alone. I was probably looking at scouts from a larger band.

Their behavior suggested the same. The pair stopped in front of my shelter and began to inspect the grass and bushes where I had forced my way through. Of course, I had tried to hide my tracks as best as I could, but apparently not well enough, since they had noticed something. Well, so much the worse for them.

Taking advantage of the fact that the goblins were busy studying my tracks, I stood up at the window, pulled back the string and loosed the first arrow. It whistled and half-buried itself in the collarbone of the crouching scout. He instantly dropped dead, yet there were no experience points reported.

The second goblin leaped to his feet, grabbing his club with a cry, but froze once he looked up. A moment later, he dropped the weapon as if it had burned him. I shouldn't have hesitated. The goblin saw what awaited him and his face crumpled, tears beginning to flow down his cheeks.

"Do you understand me?" I shouted, not too loudly. It should be easy to negotiate with a creature so afraid of death. The goblin sobbed something, but I couldn't understand the words. Sorry.

The second arrow cut off his cry, along with his life. I shuddered, realizing that I had been staring at the corpses for ten seconds, as if looking for an excuse. A pointless exercise in which I had achieved considerable success. Even if these two hadn't been looking for me... Whether this was a game, a dream or reality, I was still too weak to allow myself to be merciful.

"Is this ...war?" I wondered aloud. It was easier to decide now, once and for all, rather than hesitate every time and look for an excuse to kill a 'defenseless goblin'. So often, in war, there's no right or wrong, only sides to a conflict and the dead. In these circumstances, even the dead didn't always seem to be neutral.

These thoughts didn't make me feel much better. I picked up my bag and considered jumping through the window, but then headed for the stairs. A risk had to be worth it. If I twisted an ankle while trying to save a minute, I could end up losing my life.

I materialized my spear as I drew closer, carefully examining the bodies. Although there had been no system messages, I was certain they were dead. Only a corpse could lie this still with an arrow protruding from its chest.

As soon as I touched the shaft, the familiar energy flowed through me.

Attention! You have gained 2 SP! (4/40).

Hell, one could get hooked on this. I touched the second arrow and received a few more experience points (**6/40**). It seemed that ranged weapons, despite their obvious advantages, had a significant drawback. Experience points weren't awarded directly but could be obtained by anyone who touched the shaft. It wasn't great but still better than if the energy had just dissipated.

Only one card dropped from the second goblin, and it was quite symbolic.

Goblin Language

Rank: *F.*
Level: *1/1.*
Internal number: *G58648643254.*
Description:
One of the many goblin languages across an infinite number of worlds. Nevertheless, most of them are similar. Enables you to speak and write.
Saturation:
0/10 SP

I made myself a mental promise to learn this skill in the future. My immediate goal was to find and question the other players, but obtaining information from goblins looked more promising. And I'd better start with questioning those who were weaker...

The pair had nothing else on them, no system items or even any normal weapons. Just primitive garbage. Blood sprayed in my face. Damn! It wasn't that I was fixated on loot, it just helped to distract me from what was happening.

The arrows had gone in deep and I had to cut them out of the bodies to avoid leaving the tips inside. It didn't take long but was thoroughly unpleasant, and I'd gotten filthy.

I washed the blood off with water from the flask, albeit not completely. I was faced with the question of where to go next, but now I had some options. There was a map among the rider's possessions. It was quite crude, with a lot of unfamiliar notes, but it gave me a general idea of my surroundings. The city I had found myself in was huge, consisting of seven rings separated from each other by walls. It sounded crazy, why would anyone need so many walls? According to the map, someone had taken the trouble to build six inner walls in addition to the outer one.

"Right, a location for a crazy game..."

The boundary of the fifth circle contained something that looked suspiciously like a fortress. Several sections of the wall were marked with signs and probably signified passageways. There were a lot of notes, but I could only guess at the meaning of most of them. Even my current location was unknown. None of the goblins had a compass, and even if I'd found one, there was no guarantee that the map was oriented according to the cardinal directions. Plus, who knew if this planet had magnetic poles. There were fewer and fewer notes closer to the center of the city, while the greatest number was between the sixth and seventh walls, as well as beyond the city.

I thought that I was probably somewhere in the outer rings, perhaps the sixth or even the fifth circle. It made sense that there would be many more goblins in the seventh ring, while the center was occupied by the undead. There were relatively few goblins here, but they could afford to walk around in small groups. The houses had been pillaged, but not always completely. I was most likely in the sixth circle, but I couldn't be sure.

"The sixth circle of Sar." I muttered aloud. It sounded like a synonym for hell, where we had been sent for our sins. A perfect time to become a believer?

I spent a couple of hours making my way carefully in the direction I had chosen, without encountering either humans or goblins, and finally came upon a fortified wall. If I were to keep guessing, it was the fifth one. It was highlighted on the map, and if I understood correctly, it separated the goblin territory from the undead. There were four passageways marked on it, all close to one other. The road deeper into the city was covered by a square, which suggested a fortress. In other words, if I followed the road that ran along the wall, sooner or later, I would come to openings that were most likely guarded. I didn't know how many goblins there were, but I didn't want to take any chances. The only sensible way of getting to the other side was to go right over the wall. But was it necessary?

I studied the obstacle and decided that I didn't yet think so. The wall was built of stone, rather uneven and only ten meters high, but unscalable without climbing equipment. Perhaps in the future, once I had leveled up a dozen times, I would risk climbing with nothing, relying only on the strength of my hands, but now was not the time. Plus, what was I going to do there? Better to try and hold out until the end of the mission within this circle.

A pity that there were so few players for such a huge city. I had only seen twenty or so people thus far, most of whom were already dead, and the others made me reluctant to initiate contact. Not with my 'player killer' status. Still, I had to talk to someone.

Katana. Many people these days think it's perfection itself, but as for me, I thought it was best suited for home decoration. On a stand, in a lacquered scabbard, a katana had no equals. In movies, samurai easily hacked through enemy heads, armor, and in special cases, even armored metal plates, but reality was very different. In ancient times, katanas were forged from poor quality steel and were inferior even to European swords, let alone Arab ones. The special fighting style was based on parrying due to the fact that the expensive blades often broke when trying to block a blow because of the poor-quality steel. In addition, the katana does not chop as much as it cuts, which isn't bad against unarmored opponents but is a fatal flaw against even the simplest chain mail. Take, for example, the story of the forty-seven samurai, which began when their unlucky master attacked his unarmed opponent in the shogun's palace with a wakizashi — a sword paired with a katana — and failed to not only cut him down, but even properly wound him. Not because he didn't want to or didn't try hard enough or because the victim was very quick, but because the Japanese had terrible swords back then. As a result, the offender was sentenced to death and committed seppuku, while his forty-seven samurai, who at once became rōnin, finished off the hapless victim a year later as revenge. Which was in accordance with the Bushido code but against the law. It all ended rather predictably. The result was a heroic story about human stupidity and the quality of Japanese swords, which cost the lives of several dozen warriors. In summary, it was a weapon that a smart person was unlikely to choose, given an alternative.

Why the story? Because there were three of them, and two were armed with katanas. Strapping lads, if you can say that about Asians, who aren't known for being particularly tall —

about half a head shorter than me. I didn't know if they were Japanese, Chinese, Mongol or Korean since I wasn't good at telling them apart. Anyway, who said they were all from the same country? Perhaps it was an example of international friendship?

"Hey, wait! We need to talk. Don't run!"

I wasn't planning to, it was too late for that. I dropped my head slightly and put on the mask so they couldn't see my face. We had a difficult but necessary conversation ahead of us. The players stopped abruptly, their weapons at the ready. Despite my skeptical attitude towards the katana, I wasn't going to underestimate these "samurai". I had no way of knowing if the System weapons were as bad as their Earth prototype. One could find quite good replicas made in the 20th century.

"Don't worry, it's just a mask," I said, showing them my empty hands. I wanted them to know I was human so that they wouldn't try anything stupid. Which they were clearly planning to.

There really wasn't much point in putting the mask on since I already had the red status. But where was the guarantee that if it came to a fight, the System wouldn't increase my punishment?

"Why are you hiding your face... Cain?" a man in his forties came forward, leaning on a spear. He could see my nickname? "Your status is red. Did you kill a player?"

"Yes, I did." I didn't deny it and waited for him to continue. Three against one.

"There's a reason for everything. Perhaps you were defending yourself?" The ashigaru suggested sympathetically. I didn't like his tone, and I didn't like the whole situation. Why did I have to run into them?

It was too late to run. His two young companions drew their swords and flanked me on either side, but their actions lacked coordination. Were they already willing to kill humans for experience points? That was quick.

"No," I said wryly, rapidly drawing my bow out of the card and pulling several arrows from my bag. I had spent a whole hour practicing this simple move. "He was injured, and I only eased his suffering. Perhaps you will put away your weapons and we can talk?"

The arrow resting on the bowstring tempered their enthusiasm, forcing them to stop.

"A worthy act." the older man continued but was interrupted by one of the others.

"Yeah right, gaijin!" interjected the left-hand samurai. Although, judging by his speech, more likely a yakuza. Or what do they call Japanese rednecks? "Eased his suffering, my ass... How much experience did you get?"

"Do you get experience points for people?" I acted surprised. They didn't need to know the truth.

"You probably know better than we do.

Perhaps not, but the System is promising a reward of 20 SP for you," the second swordsman chuckled, taking another step forward. The spearman threw him a sidelong glance of displeasure. He didn't approve of such frankness.

"Of course, anything could have happened," the ashigaru tried again. It sounded fake.

It was clear that the negotiations had failed. The prize was too great and they had the advantage of numbers. I could see my death in their eyes. The only question left was who would earn the lucky 'ticket home'. But don't count your chickens before they hatch...

"Jokes aside. Another... another step and we'll quarrel." I let my voice tremble and stepped back, pointedly nocking the arrow again. "I s-s-suggest we put down our weapons and talk like civilized people. S-s-stop!"

"There are three of us," the ashigaru sighed, stating the unpleasantly obvious. He didn't even think of lowering his spear. "So, don't threaten us. I believe you, you didn't do anything wrong. Come on... There are too many goblins around for us humans to fight each other. There's a camp nearby, and three dozen people have already gathered there. People from China, Japan, USA, Europe, and even a Russian man! Where are you from?"

The ashigaru smiled gently and took another step forward again. Perhaps he didn't mean me any harm, but, what was more likely, thought I was a weak-willed idiot. I could practically read his mind. One more step and his spear would be able to reach me before his allies could strike. As soon as he took that step, he fell back, clawing at the arrow that had plunged deep into his chest. It's impossible to miss at such a distance.

"Go to hell!" I growled, dropping my weakling act.

The freshly baked rōnin froze for an instant and then the left one collapsed from the second arrow. The last man broke out of his stupor and charged, forcing me to drop my bow and switch to my spear. Despite my training, I barely had time to change weapons, parry the blow, and jump back, increasing the distance between us again. One-on-one.

"You killed them! Killed them!" the samurai decided to start yelling instead of attacking me. Was he hoping that someone would come to his aid? His companions could only wheeze.

"That's right." My tone was as cold as ice. "But you still have a chance. If you put down your sword and answer my questions, I will let you go. You didn't see my face, right?"

I had to make sure that this was real. No, I no longer had any doubts, but I wanted my suspicions confirmed. A few questions...

"Ha! Do you think I'm stupid?" the guy laughed hysterically. "I'll admit that you played well, but I know your weakness. You're an archer! This is the spear of the player you killed, right?

Without the appropriate skill, it's just a stick against my sword. I will avenge my brothers! Die!"

"If you're wondering, I was going to keep my word." I sighed.

Attention! You have gained 8 SP! (14/40)

Sword versus spear... My theory was confirmed, and victory came easily enough. His companions were still alive, but not for long.

Attention! You have gained 10 SP! (24/40)

Attention! You have gained 10 SP! (34/40)

I wiped clean the E rank dagger, which I had used to finish off the two wounded men, stripped the corpses in what was quickly becoming routine, dragged the bodies away from the road and hurried away from the 'scene of the crime'. I was only six points away from reaching the third level.

✿ ✿ ✿

The ashigaru hadn't lied about the camp. I lay on the roof, observing a squat stone house that had probably once been an administrative building. At least 30 people had gathered below. Different ages, different nationalities and races. Thankfully, I couldn't see any children or elderly. There were only seven women and they kept themselves apart from the rest. I counted just five people who had reached Level 2. Given how much time had already passed, I couldn't imagine how the others were going to complete the task. Many were wounded, some sat staring blankly ahead, dried tracks of tears on their grimy faces.

A few were training, but not many. It was hard to tell what weapons they had since most players didn't keep them in sight, but at least half of the remaining adults carried swords. As I had thought, the most obvious choice and therefore the choice of the majority. I wondered how many of these swordspeople had chosen *magic*. It looked like I had significantly weakened this 'army' by killing that trio.

I wasn't impressed. They had posted sentries, yes, but I'd been watching them for half an hour and they hadn't even moved. Most of these warriors were amateurs who wouldn't even be able to deal with an equal number of goblin warriors. Perhaps it was a good thing that I couldn't join them. I had no way to help them and with such baseline data, this temporary alliance was doomed to end in mutual slaughter. If the goblins didn't get them first. Or their own leader...

Player. Level 2.

The status of the tanned man glowed a

bright red, but no one seemed bothered as his charisma had won them over. The player walked slowly through the crowd, smiling and speaking words of encouragement. Like a wolf in sheep's clothing, inspecting the sacrificial flock. To reach Level 2, you had to kill a dozen goblins or 'just' three people. It was difficult to know what his ratio was and how he had killed his human victim. Or several victims.

Was I being too prejudiced? I didn't look any better myself. However, even if my suspicions were correct, the wolf was unlikely to get the chance to satiate himself on human flesh. I wasn't the only one observing the camp as I could see goblin scouts sneaking around nearby.

If I knew anything at all, the goblins would do more than just look. It wasn't really any of my business, but I decided to interfere. After all, I had no other allies and human losses had already exceeded all imaginable limits. I pulled out a shirt that had belonged to one of the dead men, cut off a strip and wrote a short message using blood and a stick. The words were composed of strange characters that didn't look like the letters of any human alphabet, but they were perfectly readable, as if I had spent my entire life writing in the System's language. If the goblins did attack, the players would have a chance to reach the second level without resorting to extreme measures like killing allies...

When I was done, I tied the rag to an arrow

and fired it into the ground. The sentry, who was a good two meters away from the arrow, reacted with commendable speed. He dived into the building on all fours, without even trying to analyze the situation. Good reaction, perhaps he would survive.

"Murderer! Goblins! Help!"

I doubted that the people he was protecting would survive. He only started shouting once he sure that he was safe. Fifteen or so players ran out in response to his shouts, while the rest hid.

"Calm down!" the wolf stopped the growing panic and immediately noticed the note tied to the shaft.

My face was obscured by the mask so I didn't even try to hide, standing up to my full height and holding the bow above my head. I stood like this for several seconds, then crouched down behind the parapet. I rolled and hurried to leave the exposed position. I was more concerned about the goblins than the players, so I spend a lot of time and effort disguising my tracks. Was it just me or had it become noticeably darker?

It had been such a long day that I had almost forgotten that it was bound to end sooner or later. Evening abruptly turned to night, and with it came absolute darkness. I was unhappy to discover that this planet had no moons and the scattering of stars gave off almost no light. You never get such pitch blackness in a modern city. Even if the sky is overcast, there are glowing windows, streetlights, neon advertisements and the headlights of cars as they sweep past. It would have been enough to orient me, but here and now, I couldn't even see my own hand raised in front of my face. Only the few dim lights overhead showed me that I hadn't gone blind.

I had never been afraid of the dark, but in a strange world, surrounded by enemies, I struggled to remain calm. I felt helpless. How much light did goblins need? Could they move around with only the stars to light their way? Did the undead need light?

Given the twenty-four hours allocated for the mission, I knew that I had to wait out the night, but I didn't know if the deadline was at dawn or when that would be. In any case, I intended to remain awake until the end. I hadn't planned to start a fire and it was too late now to change my mind. There was a set of flint and tinder somewhere among my things, but even if I could find them, there was no way I could get a fire built and started in this darkness.

Luckily, I had chosen quite a good spot, on the roof of one of the houses, to make it harder to reach me. The stairs had collapsed, the entrances were blocked by mounds of stone, and the neighboring houses were a little lower. In other words, it was almost impossible to reach my hiding place without making any noise, but there were plenty of ways for me to escape. I just had to make a couple of jumps... Accurate jumps, for which I really needed to see where I was aiming.

I lay on the roof as it released the day's heat, wrapped in several trophy cloaks, and felt the air grow colder. It grew even darker as clouds gathered, depriving the world of its last source of light. However, I found it reassuring. Even nocturnal predators needed some light to search for prey, which meant that my life was unlikely to be in danger until dawn.

Well, not counting the possible cold and pneumonia. I wrapped the cloaks tighter around myself against the drizzling rain. It was going to be an unforgettable night. I was bored so I pulled up the interface to pass the time.

I had to admit that no matter who had created this game, the interface was simple and clear, reminiscent of many familiar games of our time. There was a main page and a bunch of information tabs, half of which were unavailable. "No connection to the Server... Insufficient access rights..."

I studied the interface for several hours, adjusting it to suit myself. I hid the skill numbers, for example. I discovered that I could display the name and level for allies. I moved the life and stamina bars to where I could see them — even if the numbers didn't make the same sense as they did in games, they still gave me an idea of how bad things were... In the end, I didn't notice when I dozed off.

I slept badly and not for very long. For several hours before sunrise, I was plagued by angry howling and screeching coming from somewhere below. Somebody had found my hiding place and wanted to get to know me better. I sat listening to the noises until it grew light, clutching an axe in my hand since a spear or a bow would not be much use in the dark...

Despite my slight misgivings, morning came but did not bring me much joy. I stood at the edge of the roof, looking down at, if I had to judge by his clothing, one of the goblins I had killed the day before. The goblin was practically frothing at the mouth as he waited impatiently for me to descend. The System readily provided me with an explanation:

Wight. Level 1.

The undead? To be honest, the goblin didn't look like a decomposing corpse, but he had grown some impressive fangs and curved claws. He took a run up and leapt at the wall, trying to sink his claws into it, but failed and slid back down to the ground. Well, perhaps there was a reason why the locals had a penchant for chopping off heads. The corpse looked far more dangerous than he had when still alive. I drew my first arrow... Five minutes later, I released my twentieth. I saved the System arrows, using up the usual ones and simultaneously trying to discover the enemy's weak spots. Blunt arrows worked best since a successful shot shattered bones. The others didn't do much damage. Even now that he looked like a porcupine and no longer dangerous, the wight continued to shift around.

I sorted through the cards and chose a suitable weapon, then jumped onto the next roof. Then to the next one, a little lower, and finally onto the ground, where the wight was waiting for me. Broken in bone but not in spirit. It would have been nice to reach the next level, but despite the temptation, I didn't dare to try and finish off the revenant with a dagger. I picked up the axe that had formed in midair, and stepped forward to the now-motionless monster, cutting off his head. On my fifth attempt.

Attention! You have gained 4 SP! (38/40)

Strangely, the wight was worth twice as many points as the goblin had been when alive. And a little less than I wanted. Only two SP were needed to reach Level 3, so I had to kill someone urgently. My desire only grew stronger as I picked arrows out of the dead man's flesh and counted the broken ones. I hated this work.

I'd been right — there was a reason why the goblins had been hanging around the players yesterday. The approaching band numbered fifty or so individuals, with some of them at Level 2 or 3, and the strongest at Level 7. Hastily assembled militia, by the look of them. Not many wore armor and their weapons seemed equally inadequate but many of the goblins carried bows. Only a small portion of the group looked impressive enough to be professional warriors. Did the humans stand a chance? Difficult to know. Theoretically, yes.

The goblins seemed to share my low opinion of the humans' combat abilities. Their leader uttered an order and the archers scattered, taking up position on the roofs. Fortunately, nobody picked my position — a strange 'recognition of merit' from the professionals.

The majority of goblins disappeared inside the surrounding houses, while ten of the most pathetic and bedraggled-looking individuals headed for the camp. They dashed into the square, their shouting making the sentries retreat into the building, and then started throwing stones at the building. Then, pretending to lose interest in the fugitives, they began to rummage through the things left behind beside the well. In this moment, they looked exactly like the stupid savages portrayed in numerous book illustrations. Like easy prey.

Who was going to buy it? Despite my warnings, the players bought it. There was a belligerent shout, and people poured outside for the easy experience points. The goblins made a convincing show of fright and retreated as fast as they could, which only served to whet the humans' appetite. I could have intervened again and warned them about the ambush, but... the players needed the experience if they want to make it on time. The mission was coming to an end and this was likely to be their last chance. I wouldn't have had time to stop them anyway.

The fleeing goblins ran past the ambush site, behind the thin line of spearmen, and turned around. Stones flew again, but this time fired from slingshots rather than thrown by hand. The players, shocked by the sudden counterattack and the new enemies pouring out of the surrounding houses, panicked and stopped, instead of smashing through the thin line of spearmen. Then the archers stood up on the roofs.

"Ambush!" somebody screamed at the top of their lungs, and then everyone started yelling, making it nearly impossible to make anything out.

Right, here we go... I stood up, firing the first arrow. A goblin archer on the other side of the street grabbed at the protruding shaft and fell over the parapet. I saw three more archers from my position and each got an arrow. Not that each shot was fatal and sometimes it took more than one. The goblins still managed to loosen a couple of arrows, aiming for the legs. There were too many archers for me to change the overall outcome of the battle.

It was a sad and instructive sight. I could hardly call it a fight, more like a thrashing. Once they found themselves in the trap, few humans tried to fight, while the majority dropped their weapons and begged for mercy, or attempted to escape. The people who had brought up the rear or who hadn't joined the chase for whatever reason, now scattered with no thought for their comrades. The goblins, however, were in no hurry to kill and were happy to take people captive. Only a few of the higher-level warriors armed with System weapons, acted ruthlessly. They cared more for experience points than for slaves. As I watched, the goblin whom I assumed to be the leader reached Level 8 and then Level 9. He didn't reach Level 10 because there was no one left to kill. All the players had either died, been captured or managed to escape. Not many of the latter...

Smashing a staff in two and raising his sword over a cowering young woman, the chief looked around and, finding that the battle was over, changed his mind. Interestingly, I couldn't see the "wolf in sheep's clothing" among the dead or those taken captive. Had he escaped? I shook my head and ducked down, continuing to track what was happening.

The goblin chief said something and gave the girl a slight kick, but she only shook her head in fright. The goblin growled again, louder this time, so that even I could hear the threat in his voice. The girl lowered her gaze and began to untie her clothing with trembling hands. Was he checking out the "goods"? The goblin reached for his belt and I realized that I was being overly optimistic. Was the leader seriously going to take her right there in the open?

The chief thus sealed his fate, relieving me of any remaining doubts. It wasn't even about rescuing the damsel in distress, for the young woman was only at Level 1 and had almost no chance of escaping the goblins. The problem was the goblin himself. A leader who could bring an entire squad of warriors to hunt down players was too dangerous to leave alive. Who knew how many times I'd have to come back here? Of course, I should have killed him earlier, in the midst of the fight, but I hadn't been able to catch the right moment. There was no way that the murder would go unnoticed now, but so what? I was far enough away that I could almost certainly escape. The important thing was not to miss.

"Drop dead!"

The bowstring sang. The arrow pierced the chief just below the left shoulder blade, throwing the goblin forward onto the half-naked victim. It was an armor piercing arrow so even the chain mail didn't help him much. It was a great shot, and I had used a System arrow. The girl twisted around and grabbed the shaft, driving it deeper in, and her level rose to second at once, confirming that the goblin leader was dead.

I didn't know whether to call it luck since the goblins didn't seem to take those who had reached Level 2 prisoner. At least, I saw only first-level newbies among the survivors. The young woman clambered out from underneath the corpse with obvious difficulty, leapt to her feet, snatched the card out of the air and ran, while also managing to scoop up her jacket from the ground. She's quick...

I automatically sent an arrow into the goblin blocking her path. This was the last straw. The enemy finally spotted my position and dozens of eyes locked on me and a single roar of anger left their throats. Shit.

It was time to run, but I hesitated just long enough to see the results of my actions and let loose a few more arrows. The girl had managed to break through the encirclement but was being pursued by three goblins, so I didn't rate her chances too highly.

Some of the prisoners also tried to take advantage of the situation, but without much success. The goblins had abruptly changed their minds about taking prisoners. Even my arrows weren't much help. One person managed to jump through a window while another couple began to fight in the face of certain death... I no longer saw their fate as I hurried to make my escape. They had probably bought me 10-20 seconds of time. May they rest in peace.

CHAPTER 5

THE ESCAPE

I SOON REGRETTED improving my *Strength* rather than my *Stamina*. Or at least my *Intelligence*, because maybe then I would have had the sense not to get involved.

The goblins seemed determined to avenge their leader. I glanced behind me. There were six of them, and they were higher levels ones: two Level 3 goblins and four Level 2 ones. More had given chase initially but the weaker ones had fallen behind. Considering the shouting I heard behind me, I doubted that I could lose them completely. Not only that, but the risk of more locals joining the chase was growing by the minute. Or there could be a dead end ahead, since I had chosen the road at random. Not to mention the simple risk of twisting my ankle. The hatred I felt towards my pursuers grew as fast as my fatigue. Unlike the goblins, I couldn't count on any help.

"I hate goblins," I whispered. It was practically my motto...

I ran into a house, spun around, and shot an arrow at the pursuer who appeared in the doorway. The fastest one. The goblin attempted to swerve belatedly, but the opening was too narrow, and he only succeeded in getting the arrow through the chest instead of through the heart. Then again, I wasn't so good with the bow that I always hit the center. My vindictive joy outweighed even my regret at losing a System arrow and the well-deserved experience points. I should have grabbed the normal one, but I had already spent nearly all of them. There was no time to repeat the successful shot. The wounded goblin was pushed aside by his fellows, and all I could do was rush to the nearest window. I wasn't ready to fight five enemies at once.

My gaze darted to the right and up, where the timer was counting down the seconds. The deadline was less than an hour away, but would I survive for that long? Out of a thousand players, only one hundred and eighty-four remained.

✳ ✳ ✳

I'm... ready to... keel over. I felt like a soldier staying behind to cover the withdrawal of my comrades, ready to give my life in hopeless combat for the chance to lie down for a few of minutes... The *Stamina* bar, which I had moved to the left corner last night, mocked me by being almost half full, despite how I felt. I wanted to dump the bag, but I knew that I would seriously regret it if I survived. Even if the things inside weighed ten times less than normal, there were still plenty of them.

Only four goblins were chasing me now. One at Level 3 and three at Level 2. I had killed the fifth, and the sixth had gotten lost somewhere, which was good. Even though the pursuers looked tired and had fallen back, it would be naive to hope that they would give up before me.

"Bastards!"

I stopped and drew my bow with difficulty, but before I could fire, the goblins scurried away, immediately finding cover. My arms were shaking and I didn't have the strength to hold the bowstring taut for long. I began to slowly back away, using the seconds I had gained to rest. I didn't need to win, I just need to hold on until the timer ran out. I could only guess at what would happen next, but I would have given up long ago if not for this hope. Or, more accurately, I would have turned around and fought the goblins... But even if I managed to finish off these four, I'd have wasted time and given the others a chance to catch up. And any injury I sustained would leave me with no chance of continuing this 'marathon'.

Damn, damn, damn. What did I care about

the goblin leader? What did I care about that stupid girl? I could have been lying on a roof somewhere right now, watching the clouds and waiting for the timer to finish its countdown.

One of the goblins pulled a horn from his bag and blew a long note. Within twenty seconds, there were answering sounds coming from several directions. I felt my body freeze — not due to magic, but due to the primitive terror of a trapped animal. It seemed that I had gotten carried away with the game, and was going to die for real. There was nowhere left to run, with the wall I'd seen before rising on one side, unscalable without climbing equipment, and my enemies waiting for me on the other side. The goblins weren't faster than me but other teams had obviously joined the hunt. Unlucky.

I looked around, desperate for any opportunity, and finally spotted a tall tower nearby. I started running again.

✹ ✹ ✹

The creatures took their time, since my arrows had taught them to be careful. My chances of winning dissipated when a dozen more warriors joined them. Now, all I could do was run, and run, and run. While I still had a place to go...

"I hate goblins." It had become a mantra from which I drew my strength.

The tower wasn't that close, and I arrived

there completely out of breath. I spun around and let an arrow fly. The goblin who rushed in after me managed to cover himself with his hand. The wound wasn't fatal, but he didn't dare to continue the attack and scuttled back outside.

Come on... There were several rooms on the ground floor, but it was hard to miss the stairs. One of their nasty mugs looked through the window, demonstrating that I had been surrounded. If I had a little more strength left, I would have tried to break through, but right now, the only way was up. I hate goblins. I hate stairs. I hate...

Gasping for air, I began my ascent. The goblins burst, screeching, into the tower, and my arrow, fired almost blindly, didn't stop them. I missed. I hate goblins. Have I mentioned that before? My hatred gave me strength, and I sped up again, not letting my enemies catch up with me.

The first and sprightliest goblin sprang forward, but the step collapsed under him and he stumbled and fell with a cry. The railing here was long gone, yet I doubted that he had fallen to his death. We weren't that high off the ground, but at least he was no longer a threat. I wished I could finish him off... I hate goblins. My thoughts grew muddled. The *Stamina* bar was less than a fifth full. Which was funny, but I needed strength and air to laugh, so I didn't.

I drew my bow again and fired, knocking another goblin into the gap. That's better... Even if the shot wasn't fatal, we were up high enough for me to hope he'd broken his neck. Should I walk backwards? I'd just stumble and fall, and it would all be over. I was in no hurry to shoot again, not wanting to provoke the goblins — I was quite happy with our precarious equilibrium. A few seconds of blissful rest, then my enemies began to climb up again, shouting. They had nowhere to go on this staircase, and they refused to give up. The only thing that saved me was that the creatures were also tired, and seemed afraid...

I put away my bow and kept running. My heart was pounding so hard that I wondered if I die of a heart attack before the goblins got me. I hate goblins!!! With this thought in mind, I finally reached the roof. There was nowhere left to run. I needed a chance, something that would let me last a little longer. Just a little longer.

Attention! Improve the Spear fighting skill to Level 2? (20 SP)

Yes! (18/40) Images flashed through my mind again, wasting the seconds I'd saved with my last sprint. Faster and faster... The goblins didn't dare to burst through the doorway all at once since too many had met their end by my arrow. Faster...

"R-a-a-a-a!"

One of them was literally pushed forward, and the others followed. When the horde burst out on the roof, I smiled wryly. There was nowhere else to run. The images that flickered through my mind overlapped with reality. I swung my spear, slicing open the throat of the first enemy.

Attention! You have obtained 2 SP! (20/40)

I cast the goblin with the pierced throat off my spear. The first points I'd obtained since I'd had gotten caught in this mess, and possibly the last. I dodged a thrown cudgel, catching it a little with my left shoulder. The injury was not severe enough to stop me from holding a weapon. The enemies kept multiplying. I stabbed them with my spear, but there were too many. I retreated slowly to the edge of the roof, trying hard not to trip and let one of the bastards get too close. If I fell, they'd trample me. If I allowed them to come any closer, the spear would be useless.

"R-a-a-a-a!" I shouted now, gaining another second and making the goblins take a step back. It wouldn't work a second time.

How much time was left? I couldn't even check. I thought the timer should have gone to zero a long time ago, but the fighting continued. I no longer believed that I could survive, yet held on by sheer stubbornness. An enemy spear grazed my brow, but no blood flowed despite the pain. Oh, yeah, the mask...

An arrow flew from somewhere behind me, from the ground, miraculously not hitting me, but producing a fit of fear and anger. I couldn't fend off a bunch of goblins while dodging arrows being fired at my back. Two enemies rushed toward me at once, trying to impale me on their spears. I repulsed one but the second struck me hard in the chest, making me freeze from the unbearable pain. A second later, I realized that the pain wasn't so bad, for the blow had landed on one of the cards. Nevertheless, the interruption proved fatal — I had to take a step back to avoid the next blow. It was a single step, but now there was only air beneath my feet.

Was this the end? I relaxed in anticipation of hitting the ground, but even so, I didn't let go of the spear. I wanted to say that I hated goblins, but I lacked the energy even for that. I was simply too tired.

Congratulations! Mission complete
Would you like to leave the location?
Yes/No

The rush of adrenaline, the desperate plunge, the darkness and being unable to feel my body... It was like death, in a way. The only evidence that I had managed to click "Yes" was the game interface floating before my eyes.

Mission statistics

Global mission (A): not completed.
Personal mission (E): completed.

Players: *1000.*
Killed: *827.*
Completed: *97.*
Failed: *76.*

In other words, just one in ten had completed the task. Pretty disturbing statistics. Another 76 people had survived, but failed to complete the mission and were stuck in the goblin world. Even if they survived, I didn't envy them their fate.

Attention! The Shard coordinates have been recorded in the database.

Attention! Added bonus for the first mission (x2) is 70 SP! (90/40)

Attention! You have reached Level 3! (50/60)
Two parameter points are available!
Accessing the Server... The player's rank has increased to E!

Attention! You have obtained the Soul Stone!

Attention! You can choose an E-ranked ability. Time is limited.
Remaining: 29 minutes 59 seconds

Half an hour... Wow, the System was now warning me about how much time was allocated?

I wondered if this was due to the new rank or the ten in *Intuition?*

I forced myself to concentrate, since who knew when I would get another chance. This time, the list of abilities was much more extensive, while the allotted time was too short. Tens of thousands of options, so that I didn't even know where to start. Many of them, however, were displayed but unavailable, requiring lower-ranked skills or a certain parameter level. Only ten seconds ago, I had been regretting not reaching the fourth level, but now I was glad of it — the level increased automatically, so I had the opportunity to obtain several skills at once. I remembered eyeing one of them earlier...

Study the Fundamentals of Magic? (10 SP)
Yes/No

Attention! The *Wisdom* parameter has been unlocked (+1). You now have access to magical energy!

Wisdom added another scale, which the System named *Mana* **(67%)** and immediately offered to configure its display. By default, one unit of *Wisdom* was split into 100 *Mana* units, probably allowing you to better meter the time or skill strength in the long run, but you could change the ratio slightly. The effect would be purely visual, so I didn't change anything, just glanced at the upper corner, where a third bar, a classic blue one, had been added to the red life bar and the yellow stamina one.

Now I had to decide on the high-level skill promised by the System. For that I had to understand how severe my wounds were, while I was floating 'in the void' and couldn't feel my body. I wasn't sure when the transfer had occurred, whether it was the second before impact or the second after. Fortunately, a sleepless night spent studying the interface had not been in vain, so I knew where to find the answer. I opened the menu and found the right tab among all the others, which showed the condition of my body. The picture had changed slightly since my last visit, becoming more clear and detailed.

A full-size model of a man unfolded before me. Numerous arrows pointed to areas of damage, which were marked with a particular color. Mild injuries were green, moderate ones were yellow, and the serious ones were red. I didn't have any injuries marked red, just a couple of light yellow ones and a whole bunch of green ones. So, a large number of bruises, abrasions, and even a few shallow cuts. How deadly was this?

Prediction (intuition).
At the current health level, the probability of recovery is 77% in 2 weeks... The probability of death during this period is less than 1%.

That was if I did nothing at all, I guessed. If I treated the wounds, the probability of recovery would increase significantly. I clearly hadn't reached the ground, which significantly increased my freedom of choice.

Select an E-ranked bonus skill automatically? Yes/No

What a stupid question, of course not, I'll figure it out myself. I didn't want to choose healing as the first E-ranked skill, but I couldn't resist the temptation of examining my options. There was plenty of choice here, from general skills like *Minor Healing* and *Regeneration*, to specialized abilities like *Dampening Pain* or *Stopping Bleeding*. I even studied several options in a little more detail.

Regeneration could potentially regrow an arm, but required ten units of *Vitality* to study it. And recovery would take many months at the first level.

Resilience increased the corresponding parameter by one point for each level for twelve hours, and therefore, everything associated with it. *Immunity*, first and foremost. The cooldown was a month, however.

Minor Healing was tied to *Wisdom*, which I had little of, and healed specific wounds, but, again, at low levels and without a large store of mana, its effectiveness was low.

The *Mystical Hand* required the *Chakra*

(51%) or *Wisdom* **(86%)** parameter. Envelops the hand with energy, allowing it to penetrate through flesh and perform operations, selectively affecting the body. Has combat potential.

Chakra... I would have laughed, but the low degree of correlation indicated that this was simply the most understandable concept for me. Another parameter that I couldn't access. There were dozens, perhaps even thousands of options on the list, many of which, if transferred to the real world, like *Longevity* or *Improved Immunity*, would be priceless. Alas, in my situation, they were practically useless. The prospect of dying of old age seemed exceedingly remote. They were also difficult to use in battle since they took time and mana, and if I lost, the goblins would probably just finish me off. No, I needed something else...

A spell like a *Fireball* or an *Ice Arrow*? This option looked quite interesting but still insufficient. It would work well against a single enemy, but my bow was more practical in this case, and it didn't require mana. Plus, according to the descriptions, basic spells were inferior to firearms, which meant that they would be of little use in the real world. Unless I needed to get into places where I couldn't bring guns, but I wasn't planning on becoming a professional killer, right?

Looking at the descriptions of spells, I once again congratulated myself for not choosing magic at the start. If these abilities were being offered as E-ranked skills, you could be sure that no one would provide them 'upfront'.

A summoning category? It contained only minor familiars. Which, apart from everything else, were mortal, with no guarantee that they would be reborn. The System didn't provide any explanations in this regard. A magic scout would be handy, but I had to choose carefully. An E rank skill was worth one hundred SP, and since the level increased automatically, I wouldn't be able to save so many points for a long time to come. Only after Level 6, if these trends continued. It was too much of a long shot, considering how difficult it was to score points.

I needed something that would increase my survivability and combine well with the skills I had already obtained. *Stone Skin*? Becoming invulnerable to bladed weapons was tempting, but I could only maintain this defense for a very short time. Twenty seconds per unit of *Wisdom*? If goblins were smart enough to keep their distance for that long, and they weren't idiots, it would only delay the inevitable. Skills of disguise? Hmm... In response to my thought, several hundred options appeared, of which I chose two.

Disguise (F, 1/5) — *bestows knowledge on how to remain unnoticed. Cost* — *10 SP.*

An F-ranked skill was just a set of knowledge and experience, but it would be very useful to me, especially when combined with the next magic skill.

Invisibility (E, 1/5) — *creates a controlled cloaking field over the player and their equipment for a period of 100 seconds per unit of **Wisdom**. Cost: 100 SP (free).*

If I increased my *Wisdom* by two points, I would have five minutes of invisibility — more than enough time to escape. In addition, *Invisibility* did not need to be used continuously, so I could simply activate it at critical moments.

I confirmed my wish to study these skills and immediately winced from the information flooding into my brain. Although I couldn't feel my body, which also wasn't a pleasant feeling. The flow soon dried up, but I still had 30 points to spend.

Medicine of the Earth (F, 1/?) — *medical knowledge from a remote corner of the System.*

Attention! The database is currently incomplete, improvement is limited. The database needs to be updated for further development. Contact with the Server required!

Ignoring the warning, I confirmed my wish to learn this skill. I may not have learned about magical healing, but this skill would come in handy. My mind grew fuzzy but I could not allow myself to be weak. I almost habitually outlined the fields that I wanted to study: human anatomy, first aid, dissection, field surgery... I already knew a lot of this, but now the System was filling in significant gaps and organizing the information.

Time was running out, but I still had 20 SP left, and it seemed like I didn't have time to spend all of them. I had to set aside 10 points for learning the *Goblin language*... Why waste a card if I could obtain the skill directly? Knowing the number, it was easy to find. **Study.**

Attention! Consecutively learning a large number of skills at such a low level of Intelligence can negatively affect your well-being.

The System demonstrated an uncharacteristic but sneering concern for my health. **Accept**. Knowledge poured into me again, and included not only the spoken and written language, but also vague images portraying the life of the natives...

The last few seconds evaporated, the world flickered, and I woke up. I had a body again, reminding me of how painful it was to be alive.

Damn, damn, damn... I opened my eyes in the same hall where it had all begun. Stone ceiling and a stone floor, already stained with blood. The portal that I had walked through twenty-four hours ago and that I automatically tried to crawl away from, until I realized there was nothing to fear.

The Summoning Portal. Temporarily inactive

How long had I been lying here? Judging by the amount of blood that had pooled around me, a long time. More than the time allocated for me to choose my skills. I had a splitting headache from the knowledge I had acquired: advanced *Spear Fighting*, *Disguise*, *Medicine*, *Goblin language...* *Invisibility...* The information was jumbled and random facts kept floating up, producing a dull ache in my temples. They had warned me that I shouldn't learn so many skills at once, that I needed to let the information settle.

I muttered the filthiest curse I could muster in the Goblin language. The classical skill of provocation — an insult that can only be washed away with blood.

The adrenaline that had let me fight despite the wounds was gone, leaving me tired and aching all over. I had felt this rotten only a couple of times before in my life. It was all drowned out by the growing fear and despair. Is this the return that the System had promised? I noticed another timer:

Time remaining: 4 minutes and 12 seconds

And then what? Do I go home? Do I return to the goblins? Or will I be cast somewhere else? All this time, I had subconsciously feared that there would be no return home after the first trial, but rather a second, third, tenth... I wouldn't last long at this rate.

Nevertheless, I was alive, so it was too early to give up. I forced myself to stand. I returned in the same state as I had left the ruins, with my clothes torn, a spear in hand, and covered in scratches, dirt, and blood — both my own and someone else's. Strangely, there was plenty of blood, but no dirt, as if it had all been left behind in the goblin world. Was it because the dirt didn't belong to the System? This was convenient since I didn't have to worry about infection.

I hoped the System destroyed viruses and such, since I wouldn't want to pick up some alien bug... or bring it back to Earth.

A new wave of nausea came over me and I pushed away all these useless thoughts. There was very little time left. The room had changed since the last time I had been here, with eight new exits appearing alongside the portal. Seven portal gates clustered along the left wall, but only one gate had appeared in the wall opposite the *Summoning Portal*.

Time remaining: 3 minutes and 5 seconds.

From a mathematical point of view, it made

more sense to check those seven first. However, logic suggested that the way home was hidden behind the standalone gate. I limped toward it. Having reached my goal, I put my hand on the drawing to the right of the arch and saw the question I had been craving to see.

Do you wish to return to the home location of Earth?
Yes/No

Yes! Yes!! Yes!!! I hadn't checked where the other gates led, but there was little time left, and frankly, I didn't much care about this in my current state. I practically collapsed into the activated portal.

Attention! You have failed the hidden quest!
You refused to become a follower of one of the seven gods of the home location. You have received the status 'Seeking a patron'. Under the influence of the title Eighth, it has changed to Atheist.

Status: Atheist.
Features:
— *Worsens the gods' attitude to the player. The effect depends on the specific god and can vary widely.*

I paid little attention to the brief message. I would think about all this later.

APPENDIX

CHARACTER TABLE NO. 1

VASILY

General ID: unknown.
Local ID: Z-8.
True Name: Ivan Vladimirovich Susanin (hidden).
Age: 24 years.
Race: human (97%).
Gender: male.
Level: 3 (10/60 System Points).
Available: 10 SP.

Parameters:
Strength: 6+1=7/10.
Agility: 7/10.
Intelligence: 7/10.
Vitality: 6/10.
Stamina: 6/10.

Perception: 7/10.
Luck: 2/10.

Race Parameter:
Intuition: 9+1=10/10.

Additional Parameters:
Wisdom: 1.
Available points: 2.

System Skills:
Player (E, 1/1):
— Intuitive interface (E, 1/1).
— Help (E, 1/1).
— System language (F, 1/1).

Combat Skills:
— Archery (F, 1/5).
— Spear fighting (F, 2/5).

Secondary Skills:
— Disguise (F, 1/5).
— Medicine of the Earth (F, 1/?).
— Goblin language (F, 1/1).

Features:
Minor magical ability (F, 1/5) — provides
a unit of *Wisdom* for each level.

Rank E Skills:
— Invisibility (E, 1/5) — creates a cloaking

field around the hero.

— Identification (E, 1/5).

Achievements and Titles:

Eighth (personal, unique) — sometimes bad luck is so great that great luck passes close by. Special features unknown.

Atheist — reduces the favor of the Gods.

Cards:

F Rank: spear — 2 items, sword, axe, saber, rapier, katana — 2 items, empty skill card

E Rank:

— Archer's Kit: regenerating quiver (E), Goblin bow (-), Archer's ring (-), spare bowstring (-).

— System Dagger (E).

— Mask of Cain (E).

Other:

— Marauder's bag (E, 1/7) — 1 item.

— Bottomless bag F (E, 1/7) — 2 items.

— Flask — 9 items

— Player set — approximately 9 incomplete sets.

— Non-System items. Goblin weapons and gear, goblin corpse, plants.

CHAPTER 6

THE RETURN

I LANDED ON THE BED and rolled off it onto the carpet. The pain was overwhelming and all my wounds opened again. I got to my knees and collapsed back down again, but happily. It was my familiar one-bedroom apartment on the outskirts, where I had gone to sleep over a day ago and which I thought that I might never see again. I had come back home.

Getting up again was even harder but I dragged myself into standing, threw my bag into a corner, and staggered into the bathroom. A green monster stared back at me from the bathroom mirror. "Mother of..."

It was the mask. I'd forgotten about it. There was a thin, crusted gash above my right eye. I hadn't imagined it and someone had thrown a spear at me right at the end. If it had landed any lower, I would have lost an eye. I uttered a weary curse and removed the mask, throwing the instantly hardened artifact into the laundry basket. Blood started seeping from the gash, forcing me to squeeze my eyes shut and press a towel to it.

I turned on the tap and had a long drink, then undressed slowly, resisting the urge to cut the numerous belts with a knife. I really looked like something. Although most wounds were superficial, my appearance was disturbing. I soaked the towel in water and began to carefully wipe away the blood, wincing from the pain. My muscles were clearly outlined beneath the skin, the result of increasing *Strength.* I didn't have much fat before, but the last 24 hours had eliminated it completely.

I decided not to take a bath and washed the blood off in the shower. Then I took out my first aid kit and treated the cuts. The dirt had remained back there, in the other world, so I didn't have to stress about infection. I bandaged myself up. Some of the wounds needed stitches, but... not right now. It was getting harder and harder to stand, and I felt like I was going to pass out. Should I call an ambulance? Call someone else?

I picked up my smartphone, which was charging, and checked for missed calls. My parents, a couple of acquaintances, my parents again... there weren't many calls, so I wasn't considered missing. I selected the last number and pressed call.

"Hi."

"Why weren't you answering?" My father had picked up the phone. "Mom was getting worried."

I knew that he was equally worried but Dad didn't like to admit it. My disappearance would have upset them greatly. I certainly wasn't going to panic them with tales of goblins.

"My phone was on silent and I couldn't find it," I lied. They hardly used the internet, so I didn't need to fear the question 'Why didn't you answer any messages on social media?'

"What's wrong with your voice?" my father asked.

"I'm tired. I think I'm getting sick with the flu." I told him. "Listen, let's talk later, I'm dying to sleep."

I hastily said goodbye and hung up. I was incredibly sleepy, but first, I went into the kitchen and stuffed myself with whatever was in the fridge. Hobbling to bed, I resisted the urge to simply collapse into it and laid myself down gently so as not to disturb my wounds. The pain didn't stop me from instantly passing out. I dreamed of goblins.

✿ ✿ ✿

I woke up, drank straight from the kettle and walked to the window, still slightly unsteady. It was early autumn and everything looked quite ordinary. No matter what had happened to me, it hadn't affected the others. Children dashed around the playground, their parents sat on benches and the car park was full of vehicles. Nothing had changed.

I focused my attention on a guy passing beneath my window. Information immediately popped into my head.

Human. Male. Outside of the System.

The message was in a neutral gray color. It was the same for the other people, with only the gender visible, which would be useful in Thailand, I suppose. I couldn't see any information for those located further away. Did the skill only work for 30-40 meters?

I refilled the kettle and turned it on, trying to figure out what to do next. The easiest option was to call a taxi and go to the hospital. I would receive all the necessary help and maybe even get admitted to the ward, but the police were bound to get involved. They wouldn't believe that I had sustained an accidental injury like this. I'd have to make up some random attack and they'd open a case, but of course, not find anyone. I didn't have any evidence, anyway. If the government found out about the players in the future, they'd establish a date and start tracing people...

I had to set my priorities, right now. It wasn't hard to figure out what I wanted most of all – to survive. Then to ensure that my loved ones and I were safe. Thirdly, to get the maximum benefit from the System. Independence was only in fourth place, and then came minor things like curiosity, a desire to help other players and a thirst for discovery.

Would it be so bad to ask the authorities for help? I always tried to remain neutral, not idealizing but also not demonizing those in power. Most of the people at the top are pragmatists, and I was sure they would be interested in what had happened.

The problem was that I doubted that the System had appeared long ago. Small details like the title and local ID made me suspect that the authorities were not even aware of what was happening, which created a lot of uncertainty. There were no rules for interaction. The survivors of the first wave would have to find ways to reach those in power, then prove their sanity, and it still wasn't clear how it would all turn out for them. Everything was possible, from the expected help to being forced to cooperate, confiscation of 'alien artifacts' and a secure cell. Even if the latter was a temporary measure, the timer in the depths of the interface indicated that nothing was over yet. If the decision wasn't made after a month, there was a possibility of going on the next mission with no equipment at all. So, before I contacted someone, I needed to gather my strength and, at a minimum, leave behind a spare set of gear and weapons.

"I'll think about it tomorrow," I muttered. Although, in my case, 'tomorrow' would be in about a month from now. So far and so close at the same time.

In the meantime, I had to assume that I didn't want to be discovered, and thought about what else might give me away as a player. First, abrupt changes in behavior and lifestyle. After all, hundreds of people had disappeared for a whole day, and didn't show up for meetings, answer calls or turn up to work. Absenteeism was suspicious in itself, but even people who had a day off yesterday were unlikely to continue working as if nothing had happened. Most players would probably quit their job soon, which meant leaving behind evidence.

Luckily or not, this wasn't an issue for me since I had resigned a week earlier. My savings account held a pretty decent sum, some of which was still left over from my college days. More precisely, three accounts in three different banks. Plus, a card with a bit of money for current expenses. The amount might seem ridiculous to someone from the capital, but in my city, it was enough for a couple of years of modest living. I wasn't planning to look for a job until a couple of months later, when my non-paid vacation ran out, so I didn't expect any problems there either.

Nobody close to me will notice anything suspicious. I didn't have much contact with my relatives, and preferred not to bother them. My parents didn't even know I'd quit my job. No wife, and I broke up with my last girlfriend three months ago. What else? Plenty of acquaintances, good colleagues, but no friends for a long time. Life had taken me away from people I could truly call my friends seven or eight years ago, and communication was now limited to messages on social media and formal announcements. It was a bit depressing but now worked to my advantage. Perhaps I was just being paranoid and getting worried over nothing? The capabilities of the special services are often exaggerated...

My computer produced a welcome chirp, indicating that it was ready to work, and I returned to the room. I went online and checked the news, looking for anything unusual. The price of oil was falling, the dollar was going up, the political situation was unstable, experts were making guesses, et cetera... There was nothing about an alien invasion, the System, levels, skills, or the hundreds of dismembered corpses found in their beds this morning. It really seemed like yesterday's events had affected only a small percentage of the world's population. For now. Even a thousand people going missing wasn't very noticeable on a global scale, although less than a hundred had returned. And it didn't look like they had rushed off to tell their story to the media. Even if there were several sets of players and the next ones were more successful, it would take time for traces of what had happened to appear online.

Well, since there was no news, I needed medicine. I was hesitant to go outside in my state since I doubted that pharmacists would respond positively to my appearance. Fortunately, the city was full of pharmacies offering home delivery. I searched online for another five minutes, copying several phone numbers into a text document.

I unplugged my smartphone from its charger, held it in my hand for a minute, then thoughtfully put it back. If I was going to play a game of spies, I would do it properly. I dug through my closet and found a nearly flat — there was only one bar left — old Nokia with a burner SIM card. There were less and less of them with every passing year, so I had bought one about a year ago, just in case. I rarely used it, just enough to keep the number active, and I didn't call friends and family on it. Amazingly, this utter waste of money was going to come in handy now. It took only two calls for me to find everything and to arrange for the order to be delivered within an hour. I didn't give them my address, but rather the apartment number of my neighbor several floors below, who lived alone and was almost never home during the day. Twenty minutes later, I left my apartment and went to stand beside the right door. As I had expected, he wasn't home, so I stood and waited. There was a tin full of cigarette butts attached to the railing. I went to get a lighter and burned a couple more right down to the filter, adding to the smell of tobacco in the air. I lit the last one when I spotted the courier through the window as he drove up to the entrance.

"Wow, someone's been done over," commented the delivery guy as he stepped out of the lift.

"They got it worse," I joked grimly, stubbing out my cigarette on the edge of the can and tossing it inside. "You're from the pharmacy, right? That's a delivery for me, then. I'll take the bag. How much will it be?"

"Dmitry?" the guy asked. Incidentally, the name was neither mine nor my neighbor's. "Four thousand, eight hundred and forty-three rubles."

"Here you go," I handed over a note and took the change. Luckily, I always have some cash in the apartment, so I didn't need to run to the ATM.

While we were talking, the lift left so the courier went back down on foot. The entrance door slammed soon after. After making sure that the guy had left the building, I went back up to my apartment. The performance had been rather exhausting, but it gave me a chance of remaining hidden if someone started hunting down the players. Or it at least created the illusion of a chance. Not bad either...

Surgical thread, needle, bandages, plasters, antiseptics, painkillers... I needed the medications one way or another, so it was simply a matter of how to get them. Only time would tell whether I had made the right decision and if I should have bothered at all.

∗ ∗ ∗

The longer I delayed treatment, the worse I felt. My head ached, I developed a fever and started shivering, but I was still able to move around.

I sat in front of the mirror and, remembering my arts and crafts classes at school, used a needle to sew closed the edges of a long but shallow gash on my chest, trying to keep the stitches neat. I was not very successful. I wouldn't have even attempted this a couple of days ago, but the *Medicine of the Earth* skill, combined with some experience, gave me the confidence. My grandfather had a dacha back when I was little, and sometimes sewed up animal wounds himself, using me as an assistant. A piglet with its leg sliced open on a nail, a goose with a punctured head... They had all survived the surgery and died closer to winter, slaughtered for their meat. Still, they hadn't needed to stitch themselves up... When I finished, I spat out the blood from my bitten lip, and then examined my brow. I didn't want to risk trying to sew it closed but the cut wasn't deep so I decided to put a plaster over it. It would be good to develop the *Regeneration* skill soon.

I still hadn't distributed the points for Level 3, and considering my current state, I was tempted to increase *Vitality*. As I understood it, the parameter was responsible for healing wounds, increasing immunity, slowing down aging, increasing life expectancy, and that sort of thing. Investing the two free points into it would give me outstanding health and add twenty years to my life. Which would make sense if it was all over, but I only had a month. It was enough time to recover naturally, and this parameter wouldn't be much use in skirmishes against goblins.

Although there were no useless parameters here in principle, and increasing any of them potentially had huge advantages. I read the descriptions again, which had expanded slightly since I increased my *Intuition*. I'd already mentioned *Vitality*. The benefits of *Strength* were obvious enough. *Stamina* allowed me to not only fight for longer and increased my chances of escape, but also partially numbed pain. *Perception* increased reaction speed and the ability to detect danger. *Agility* made me more flexible. *Luck*... I wasn't sure how it worked, and I wasn't going to waste precious points on it. I couldn't improve my *Intuition* yet, but even if it were possible... I suspected that a couple of points would not produce obvious effects. I wanted to increase my *Intelligence* since the possibilities here were the most promising, but I didn't think the goblins would care about the size of my brain when they scraped it off their clubs...

What was the point if I'd already made up my mind? With a sigh, I put both points into *Wisdom*, raising it to three. This time, the increase felt like pins and needles all over my body and sharp flashes of pain. For a few minutes, I was hot and cold, until it suddenly stopped. The feeling of something strange and hidden in my stomach became much more pronounced. Exactly three times stronger, just like the amount of mana, I bet.

I considered whether I wanted to test my *Invisibility*, or swallow another handful of tablets and go back to bed. The urge to sleep was stronger, but I forced myself to activate the skill. It wasn't like waving a magic wand, I felt the energy flowing through me, transforming in strange ways and finally bursting out of me. I didn't disappear all at once, but in sections, as if dissipating in space together with my clothes. Ten seconds later, the mirror showed only the wall behind me. I took a few steps, but nothing moved in the mirror. Fantastic. Contrary to the hypotheses of some scientists, my sight remained the same. The mana bar slowly crept to the left. Based on the speed, it would indeed last for about five minutes. Maybe even a little more, since I replenished the mana at the same time as I spent it. Although the speed of regeneration was too slow to be much use at the moment.

OK, next experiment... The camera on my smartphone also didn't record anything, which cheered me up. There are cameras on every street corner these days, so this was important.

The skill felt quite strange, to be honest. I could sense the field surrounding me, and could manipulate it to some extent. I lifted a chair and made the field envelop it as well. The speed of mana consumption increased dramatically, but I succeeded. Interesting... how far can I extend the field? I tried the same trick with the couch, but about halfway through, the field cracked and burst before I could draw it back in, rewarding me a flash of pain that nearly knocked me unconscious. The mana bar abruptly ran out.

Attention! You are suffering from magical depletion. Mana regeneration has slowed down.

This was the last straw. I collapsed on the same couch and allowed myself to either fall asleep or pass out. I dreamed of goblins again.

* * *

I spent the next few days in a kind of delirium, taking tablets, sometimes staggering into the kitchen to eat something, and then back to bed to dream about goblins. It seemed that the delirium was partly due to all the knowledge I had acquired, because the dreams were incredibly detailed and when I woke up again, I knew much more about these vile creatures than before. Not only about goblins, but the world as a whole...

If the dreams were true, the goblins had quite a progressive medieval society with their own kings, nobles, officials and priests, until relatively recently. Sar was the capital of the largest empire, but then the world was attacked by... well, let's call it Chaos. A faction known as the Lords of Chaos considered the System evil, but did not disdain from using it. The battle took place both in certain higher spheres and on the planetary surface.

The city defenders lit a beacon in their attempt to stop the assault, calling for help from the players, who were mercenaries of a sort. Or demons, depending on the way you looked at it. However, not many were willing to come to the aid of a dying world. The goblins and their allies retreated to the center of the city, and when hope was gone, used higher magic to turn themselves and a large part of the fallen into bloodthirsty zombies. The Goblin gods were defeated, but the enemy suddenly retreated. Without a will to spur them on, the creatures of Chaos also retreated or simply scattered across the world.

And chaos descended on the planet. Countries fell. Most altars were destroyed and the Gods stopped responding to prayers. The strongest players died, System weapons were lost, and the rest mostly lost their status and power, becoming simply "heroes". There weren't many of them. Without the status of a full-fledged player, enemies dropped almost no loot. Those who raised their level using System weapons received only the points, but did not have access to the skill base. The average level of the goblins, which used to be ten, began to drop rapidly, which affected their minds and then the general level of their civilization. Without the power of the System, most goblins died before they were fifty. Powerful magic almost completely disappeared, leaving them with only ancient shamanic tricks. They were saved from descending into complete savagery by a racial peculiarity, when individuals with an Intelligence bonus were born among them from time to time. Plus, there were hobgoblins among the leaders, whose abilities equaled humans. New states appeared, but they were smaller, weaker, poorer and more primitive.

Yet hope remained. The priests proclaimed that if an altar could be found that had not been destroyed by the enemy or stolen by greedy aliens, they could resurrect one of the old Gods or, as the heretics said, summon someone new. The hero would then be rewarded and return his or her people to the ranks of full-fledged players.

I somehow doubted that these Lords of Chaos would allow the resurrected to live long enough to fix anything, since they had destroyed all the Gods of Order to snatch the world from the control of the System.

In any case, the goblins had so far failed. Places where altars could remain had either been destroyed or access to them was extremely difficult. Apart the undead, the area around the Celestial City was populated by Chaos creatures, which made life very difficult for the goblin tribes living nearby.

Nevertheless, the city's wealth beckoned. All

kinds of adventurers plundered the city outskirts. Rulers and priests sent out expeditions that often reached the middle zones, but most of those who headed to the center never returned. In recent years, the System would occasionally summon small groups of players, who fell prey to the goblins or the undead. It was clear that the goblins couldn't let the aliens reach the altars first...

It was a very interesting story, yet it was difficult to say which parts was true and which were the results of my delirium. Ultimately, it wasn't a voice from above telling me this story, rather I had reconstructed it from a whole bunch of scattered and sometimes contradictory fragments.

After finishing everything edible in the refrigerator, I threw a bag of pasta into the slow cooker. Such a convenient device... Ten minutes later, I drained the water and began to eat straight from the bowl. I still felt weak, but once my hunger was sated, I no longer felt like lying down and dying. I changed my dressings and treated the wounds again. They were healing surprisingly well, and according to the interface, complete recovery was not far off.

The magical depletion had also passed, which meant that I could continue my experiments. I activated the skill, feeling the invisible energy run through unseen channels and escape through my hands and feet, creating a cloaking field around me.

I then deactivated the field and tried to do something without the System's help... No, not the same thing, that would be impossible, but something. I wasted an hour but the mana ignored all my attempts. At best, I made it waver slightly. Which could have been my wishful thinking. Nevertheless, I was sure that I could master magic with the proper training and without these 'skill crutches'. I just needed to start with something basic.

"But not today," I muttered to myself.

I gave up, went online, and checked the news again. Although a thousand people wasn't a lot on a global scale, some traces had to appear sooner or later. It was only a matter of time. By the way, how long had I been lazing about? The calendar showed the date, and I swore. Tuesday, October 3rd. I had wasted almost a week due to a dozen superficial scratches. Not that I'd completely forgotten what had happened. I remembered changing bandages a couple of times, taking medication, and periodically answering calls and complaining about the flu. And dreaming. Yes, mostly about goblins.

My eyes fell on a ballpoint pen, and I applied my second skill, which I had almost forgotten. *Identification.* Energy flowed to my hands, enveloped the object, and gave me almost the same information as a normal *help note*:

Unknown object. Outside of the System.

My mana dropped by a third. It didn't make sense to use this skill on normal items. Should I try it with System objects?

My hunch was correct. The skill allowed me to identify them quite confidently, and often provided more thorough information. For example, the skill recognized the starter kit as individual items, and although most objects were identified as **System items**, without any properties or descriptions, the flasks turned out to be artifacts.

Eternal Flask

Class: *F.*
Status: *System artifact.*
Description:
Newcomer's flask. Included in the basic kit.
Properties:
— Gradually converts a liquid poured into it into a System item. Conversion speed depends on the composition.
— Liquid can be stored for longer without losing its properties.

It was as unexpected as finding a pile of gold while digging in your own backyard. Considering how many I had... I gathered the flasks and counted them — nine. I was, however, only able to check two more, but both turned out to be artifacts, which convinced me that this was no exception. My mind raced with all the possibilities.

After all, I could fill them with liquids other than water, such as alcohol, gasoline, kerosene, some kind of poison... The list was almost endless. It was a pity I didn't have access to liquid explosives or really strong poisons.

Well, there was still plenty of time to consider the options.

After I recovered from my wounds, I wallowed in a kind of melancholy for a while.

Few are happy with their fate, and people often pray for a chance to change everything. I guess I was no exception, but one would have to be a raging optimist to view what had happened as a chance to gain might and power, or something else from the eternal list of human desires. Anyone who had ever played computer games knew the chances of completing the whole game on the first go, without saving and without ever dying in the process. It wasn't high, to put it mildly. In my case, this was an understatement, since no one could guarantee that this game even had a storyline or a theoretically possible happy ending. Even if I completed the global goal by capturing that damn altar, there would be no end credits and the game wouldn't finish. More likely, we would simply be cast into another, possibly even more dangerous place. And I would remember the goblins with nostalgia...

There were no saves or extra lives, and death would be final. It was a miracle that I had survived the first time. Perhaps I would survive the next time, but how long could one walk on a knife edge? A year? Two? Three? It was like a fatal disease in temporary remission. It was unlikely that I would live even ten more years.

I could try to become stronger, but this increased the risk in the short term and didn't guarantee my safety in the long term. It was likely that as my power grew, so would the complexity of the tasks. On the other hand, it would be even worse if the difficulty increased and I remain at the same level. It felt like a race that most players were doomed to lose. Death was the only ending I could see ahead of me.

Was it possible to control my movements and refuse to complete the missions? I couldn't see a way as yet, but my dreams held hints that high-level goblin players possessed such an ability. Could I trust my dreams, though? Especially if they contained no definite answer?

Was there a way to leave the game? Hmm... Funnily enough, I knew of one way. Failing the mission and remaining in the goblin world. It didn't seem much better than death right now, but if the players recaptured the city or reached an agreement with the locals, the situation might change. Learn the skills, increase my parameters and stay in the other world... Not a very enticing idea. The status of Hero didn't offer much freedom.

Still, even that looked better than forever wandering through the worlds, fighting to stay alive for another month.

How many players were there in total? I suspected that my group had been the first but would it be the only one? A thousand people is nothing on a global scale. What if there were at least ten groups? What about a hundred? Who knew how many more people would be kidnapped? Even if only a thousand people were added each time... I imagined my family being 'chosen', then discarded the idea. The likelihood of that happening was so far too small for them to get involved in this mess. If I saw that the situation was changing, I would warn them.

In any case, I wasn't going to give up, so I needed to use the remaining time to maximize my chances of surviving the next time. It was enough to start with.

CHAPTER 7

PREPARATION

WELL, IF THERE WEREN'T many players yet, it gave me a certain head start. After giving it some thought, and failing to find anything online, I decided to create an information portal for everything I knew about the System, the goblin city and, in the future, to somehow unite the players. It's not too difficult these days, especially if you have money. Buy a domain name, pay for hosting and use one of the numerous website builders. User registration, open part and closed parts of the forum, ability to configure access rights. Someone else would do this sooner or later, but being the first meant I would have access to all the information posted there.

I wasn't so deluded as to think that I would maintain control of the resource once different governments got involved. I may not get to use it at all, depending on how fast the response would be. The main goal was different — to unite the players and increase our chances of survival, including my own chances.

I didn't need any extra attention, so I presented the portal as a platform for developing a hypothetical game. I put a description of the concept and a scanned map of the goblin city itself, but without any extra notes. A few photos of the equipment and System items, so that a player would understand that these coincidences weren't such. Now for the rules... I added a point that the game creators were very invested in it and asked users to communicate as if it was real. I moved this statement to the main page of the portal, since no one ever reads the terms and conditions anyway.

Now for the content. It would be naive to expect everyone to rush over here and share all their information. Since returning to the real world, I'd lost my connection to the Server, and therefore had no access to the skills database. I opened a new document and started listing everything that I could remember. Name, type, mechanism of action, and rank. Healing skills, combat skills, summoning spells... There were many sections and I couldn't remember them all. I made three dozen entries, although, given that the names weren't fixed and could differ from person to person, this would only slightly facilitate the search. I couldn't remember the numbers, of course, as there had been too many. I didn't include my own skills in the list. Nevertheless, considering how sparingly the System provided access to the Server, any information was valuable. I therefore added the possibility of exchange. A player could offer the administrator information and get something equivalent in return. Given that I would be at the center of the web, I might be able to find out something interesting. Theoretically, I could also make money from this, but I didn't provide my card details. Unlike the SIM card, I didn't have an anonymous bank card, so it would be easy to track such transfers. Anyway, that wasn't the point.

It was funny, although I knew that the government might intervene I had little faith that they would actually search for me. The events seemed more like a game of Elusive Joe than a real threat...

The truly important information would initially go into a separate closed section. For example, combat forms that allowed you to unlock parameters. This skills category allowed you to ignore the limit, read the parameters of other players, yet allowed you to invest free character points into combat skills at the same time. Something like shapeshifting, when the second form is much stronger than the first. In fact, many of the options resonated suspiciously with human legends. Unfortunately, I hadn't had enough time to study the list, so I could be wrong about the details. In short, combat forms were also limited in development, but their limit was higher and depended on a specific choice. For example, the 'basic combat form' allowed you to pump all the parameters up to twenty. For specialized combat forms, the limit could be higher or lower, plus there were special bonuses. Like having claws or a tail. If I wasn't mistaken, there was a restriction, so you could only get this perk at Level 10.

Why was this even necessary? On one hand, it was a disadvantage, since by investing points in a combat form, you couldn't use them on your primary body, but on the other hand, it allowed you to avoid negative consequences. Let's say that if you increased your *Strength* to ten, you'd become like Hercules, but if you raised it to fifteen, would you even look human? I would have to find out.

There were also opportunities to break through the first limit directly. From using the System points directly to applying specialized skills. Interestingly, after I had reached my limit for *Intuition*, I'd discovered that the locks had different colors. While *Strength* and *Agility* were marked red, *Perception*, *Intelligence* and *Stamina* were yellow, and *Vitality*, *Intuition* and *Wisdom* were green. The first required a hundred System points to be removed, the second eighty, and the last only fifty. The hint was quite clear — the greater the requirements, the more important the restriction and the higher the danger. *Luck* had a black lock, and trying to remove it cost an insane one thousand points.

I had to assume that characteristics shouldn't be increased willy-nilly since they were interrelated. For example, if I pumped up *Perception* without *Intelligence*, there could be problems with processing incoming information. I suspected that excessive *Strength* had to be balanced out by *Agility*, and together they needed to be reinforced by *Vitality*. Of course, I was basing this on logic and intuition, but I had begun to trust the latter. Even if I was slightly exaggerating the risks, it never hurt to be careful.

The next step was creating a formula for calculating 'experience', for which I had enough data. To begin with, I wrote out the parameters of everyone I had killed, their level and weapons used, and then began to look for patterns. For example, I received two SP for killing a first-level goblin, and four SP for a second-level one. The amount was exactly double, so it was safe to assume that the creature's level was the multiplier in the equation. Then the level of weapon absorption had to be taken into account. The number of experience points was greater if an E-rank dagger was used, but as practice showed, not by ten, but by twenty percent... Why? After a moment, I realized my mistake. I needed to divide, not subtract, and the difference between 40 and 50 was exactly 20 percent.

What else was part of the equation? To get the right numbers, I had to multiply the result by twenty for humans but only by five for goblins. The only thing that came to mind was the value of the first limit, which could probably be five for goblins. But then why did human points increase fourfold instead of doubling? This discrepancy was evident in all cases.

I had to assume that there were not three but at least four multipliers in the formula. For goblins, the fourth multiplier was one, while for humans it was two. So, what was the last, fourth multiplier? Perhaps some nominal 'strength ranking'?

In any case, if I accepted this as fact, the formula for calculating experience points looked something like this:

level × value of the first limit × strength ranking × absorption percentage.

I double-checked using those I had killed, and the numbers matched each time. Was it so simple? I didn't wish to blow my own horn, since I had basically adjusted the formula to the results and much of it was based on assumptions. The main thing was that it worked. At least with goblins and humans. If I was to run into someone else in the future, I wouldn't have any problems with the calculations as long as I collected a little statistical material. And apply some Grade 9 math knowledge.

I didn't see any point in hiding this 'secret formula' and added it to the open section. One small step for man, one giant leap for mankind. Perhaps I'd get a Nobel Prize for this one day? Heh... or a life sentence for the genocide of an alien race.

The video editing was nearly finished and it was time to evaluate the result.

An ordinary kitchen table covered with an oilcloth, on which lay the naked goblin corpse which I had brought with me. A man in baggy clothes and a green mask stood nearby. Several video cameras recorded what was happening from different angles.

"Let's get started," said the man. "We see... a goblin. Humanoid, 6'4" in height, had been Level 8 in life. Died relatively recently. The neck incision is quite deep, the artery was nicked, but he died due to a penetrating blow to the back. " Since I'd killed him myself, I knew what I was talking about.

Turning the body over, the 'doctor' showed the wound and dug out a piece of chain mail. It wasn't part of the System, but the bag had allowed me to bring it with the corpse. The corpse itself seemed to belong to the System, but turning a goblin into ingredients seemed amoral.

"It's difficult to ascertain the age, but the goblin was quite young. His build is lean and muscular. The skin is dark, but not black, and the texture is slightly different from human skin. Increased hairiness. The shape of the ears is different, and the teeth... " The pathologist reached inside the mouth and pulled the lip up. "There are twenty-eight of them and the fangs are pretty sharp, but they don't pierce the glove."

Looking at the confident figure, it was hard to believe it was me.

"All right, let's begin the autopsy." Taking a scalpel, the man set to work, managing mainly due to the knowledge gained from the skill. "I have made an incision. The blood isn't flowing, but it's the usual shade of scarlet, take my word for it. Overall, the goblin's structure is similar to a human, but the organs are slightly different, the heart is more central, and there are fewer ribs — ten pairs, but they are wider. The bones are quite light..."

The autopsy lasted for five hours, but a little more than an hour remained after editing. Not all the information was worth sharing. For example, I found a **mana crystal** containing 943 units of energy in the goblin's heart, and this finding didn't make it into the video. I had basically obtained an item that allowed me to quickly replenish magical energy. It wasn't difficult to figure out how it worked. With this stone alone, I could use

Invisibility for almost 16 extra minutes. A trump card that could save my life.

I uploaded the video to the closed section of the site. Nobody had registered over the past couple of days, but this wasn't surprising, given the lack of advertising and inbound links in general. It was almost impossible to find the website.

Well, that would change after the next round.

I stood on the roof of a twelve-story building that towered over its nine-story neighbors. It was quite cold this high up, and the wind was much stronger than on the ground.

Now that my health was more or less back to normal, I had taken up something that I rarely had time for before: stretching, regular exercises and training, morning runs... I had to assume that if the System was akin to a game, then it was possible to boost my parameters naturally.

Besides, I needed to reinforce my knowledge of *Spear fighting*, and I felt more confident with each session. Now, with only the second level of skill, I could quite easily match an experienced veteran of medieval wars and perform professionally in all kinds of medieval reenactments. Sadly, awing audiences with my skill wasn't part of my plans, so I found a secluded place for training. It needed to be in the city, so I didn't have to travel far every day, and I didn't want to skip training. After considering the options, I decided to use the roof of one of the neighboring buildings, after carefully sawing off the lock and replacing it with my own. There was little danger of being spotted. If someone suddenly showed up in the middle of training — I could always kill them and hide the body in my bag.

Funny joke. Haha.

I lunged forward, piercing the air in front of me, then paused, holding the spear with one hand. Then moved to the next stance. The training was comforting, filling me with confidence that I could survive the next mission. Even though the numbers didn't visibly change, I was getting a little better every day, and my training felt a little easier. I was almost sure that the result was there, but the display error was too large. Under normal circumstances, one unit of *Strength* would be the result of months, if not years of hard training, and it didn't look like the System accelerated them in any way. I guessed that I would see the improvement only when the parameter reached the next limit.

It wasn't the best news, but it was just a fly in the ointment. After all, I was much more afraid of regression than a lack of progress, especially in my physical parameters. Every person knows how easy it is to get out of shape just by skipping a couple of training sessions. The System pushed the body to the limit, which was nearly impossible to maintain for an ordinary person. Nevertheless, although I had spent almost two weeks in bed, my parameters hadn't dropped and I didn't experience any deterioration. This led me to think that either there was no regression, or it was so slow that I simply couldn't spot it. If I was right, it was cheating in a way. Wasn't this the dream of millions of athletes? To know that your progress, no matter how small, would always remain with you? Wouldn't that be a reason to push yourself to the maximum?

In the end, I visited the hospital for a variety of tests, and was pronounced almost completely healthy. It appeared that Earth was not in danger of a global epidemic of goblin flu or a zombie apocalypse. For now, at least.

I paused for a moment to catch my breath, then lifted the spear again, threatening an invisible opponent.

"Die, blasted goblin!"

The imaginary goblin obediently died in agony, and I continued my dance, lost in thought. All this time, I hadn't stopped looking for traces of other players, and the search had not been completely unsuccessful. Reports of strange disappearances had cropped up a couple of times in local news around the world. A husband who disappeared from his wife's side in the middle of the night. An apartment locked from the inside, with the keys still in the lock, and the owner gone without a trace... People disappear all the time, so there was no guarantee that these unlucky individuals had disappeared through the fault of the System. However, I could thus assume that the dead did not return. Hundreds of mutilated and decapitated corpses would have made a lot more noise than the strange but familiar disappearances.

Not long after, several magicians had appeared on YouTube, whose abilities looked too convincing to be tricks. Unfortunately, I didn't have much luck in trying to contact them. They didn't respond to my veiled emails and soon disappeared altogether. It was the first hint that the stronger your abilities, the more you'd be tempted to use them to get rich.

I also thought about ways to turn my skills into profit, but my thoughts were mostly of a criminal nature. What could I do with invisibility? Robbery, theft, espionage, unlawful entry and so forth. Something that only an idiot would risk doing in my position. Using System abilities for petty crime was like hammering nails with a microscope.

I wasn't planning on selling the trophies I'd brought back from the goblin world, either, so I hid them for the time being. I did plant the herbs I'd gathered in pots. Some of them even survived, although I had no idea what good they would do me, and hopefully they weren't poisonous.

In any case, I still had some money left over,

and if I died, I wouldn't need any more. I decided to postpone dealing with my finances until I returned. If my powers increased, I could reevaluate my options. After all, five minutes of invisibility wasn't long enough to get in and out unnoticed, and the risk had to be worth it. Plus, I wasn't inclined to break the law unless I absolutely had to. Maybe I should try to find something valuable in the goblin world? Or I could take out a loan. I probably wouldn't get a chance to pay it back anyhow.

By the end of the third week, I spotted a dramatic news item CHICAGO SWORDSMAN KILLED! POLICE SHOOT A MANIAC RESISTING ARREST! It was accompanied by a photo of a six-foot-tall black man with a dozen bullet wounds and a sword lying beside him.

> *Inside the apartment, police discovered the murder weapon, clothing with traces of blood and a golf bag, in which he had carried the sword...* blah blah blah... *Twenty-six victims confirmed in the last month alone, but citizens can finally sleep in peace. As a reminder, his first victim was Jack Red, one of the world's leading economists....*

Police had already arrested a suspect three days earlier but hadn't found a weapon.

Nevertheless, "they were certain of his guilt", and the media predicted the death penalty. Suddenly, the police admitted their mistake and released the detainee, and today had found the "real killer". I couldn't determine the suspect's level through the TV, but I'd bet that the first detainee was a player and that he'd struck a deal with the government. I doubted he had killed just for the hell of it. Was he leveling up? Probably.

In any case, I had to assume that they knew about the System overseas. This was the first sign. Now that they had a player, it would be much easier to screen other suspects. The System wouldn't let us hide our status from each other. While there were only a few of us around the world, governments could only catch these deviants or those who gave themselves up. But if the number of players increased, sooner or later they would find all of us. Sometime in the distant future. Well, I had never intended to hide forever.

"Time to die, human," the goblin said, raising his spear. I tried to summon my weapon, but the System didn't respond. "You don't think you can hide a spear in such a small card, do you?"

"It's a dream," I said.

"You think so?" While the goblins in my earlier dreams simply killed me, now they preferred to mock me first. "Then it won't be an issue if I kill *you?"*

The issue was that I wasn't sure if I was really sleeping. I couldn't remember. Perhaps I'd already returned to the goblin city and everything was real? Then why wasn't my card working?

System message! Your luck is too low to activate.
Beep... beep... beep...

I sat up in bed. A dream, it was only a dream. What did luck have to do with such things? What a load of crap.

The alarm had pulled me out of my nightmare, but I didn't feel any better. I could hope that the goblins weren't real in my dreams, but no longer. I closed my eyes, checking the internal timer.

Time remaining: 2 hours 59 minutes 01 seconds

If I wasn't mistaken, I'd be transported to a new mission when the timer reached zero. There wasn't much time left. Just enough to eat, shower, pack and sit down to wait...

The first alarm was joined by two more. Although I always got up when the first alarm went off, the fear of ending up in the ruins with no weapons or equipment was too strong. That was why I hadn't taken any sleeping pills, and had slept for only nine hours instead of twelve. It would be enough for me to spend the next 24 hours on my feet, even without the stimulants poured into one of the flasks.

The Marauder's Bag didn't let me bring anything from our world. Except for the bow and new arrows, converted into System ones using the weapons card. Although it had eaten up a lot of my money, I now had a great compound bow, much better than the one I'd gotten from the goblin. It was one of the few technological things that I could bring with me, thanks to the card. The quiver hadn't stood idle and was now filled with System arrows – for both bows, since I was bringing the goblin one too.

I ought to arrange a cache in the ruins. Once I brought goblin items into my world, I couldn't return. Most items weren't recognized by the System, and would thus be destroyed during the transfer. It was a shame since decent chain mail wouldn't hurt.

I put a large sealed envelope on the table, together with some papers and one of the two reserve bags. There was no point in carrying everything around with me, and if I died, it would serve as proof of my words. I was sure my father would find a use for the artifacts and information. Should I have told him everything in advance? I glanced at my phone, but it was too late, both for my call and for any regrets.

I was suddenly ready and there was nothing

left to do except to sit and wait. Well, I preferred lying on my bed and staring at the ceiling as I reminisced about my life. My heart was pounding. Then the world went dark.

✳ ✳ ✳

Surprisingly, I fell asleep again. Fortunately, the alarm clock woke me up just before the transfer. I was lying in the center of the white room again, and the timer was showing me that I had an hour.

"How generous."

I got up and dropped the last *Bottomless Bag* onto the floor. It contained a spare set of equipment and weapons, in case I ever returned here empty-handed, whether due a loss in the goblin world or some kind of force majeure in the real world. Or I should say in my home world, since I had proven to myself that both worlds were real.

First, I decided to check the seven gates that I didn't have time to explore last time. The gates looked like stone slabs covered with faint mythological designs. If there was a gap in the center, I couldn't see it.

Obeying my wishes, the System highlighted the objects. As I had suspected, the gates were connected to different gods, but it was a strange list.

Gate of Hera. What did I remember about Hera? Wife of Zeus, goddess of fertility, in fact, a supreme female deity in the Greek Pantheon. Very vindictive.

Gate of Guan Yu. It was easier with Guan Yu since I knew nothing about him, except that he had originated in China.

Gate of the Great Seth. Seth is a god in the Egyptian Pantheon, and an evil one at that. I think he was responsible for desert storms, serpents, and the death of his brother Osiris. This was where my Grade 5 Ancient History classes came in handy.

Gate of Shiva. Shiva was from India, had many hands and many swords, and I had only a vague idea of what role he played in the religion. Was he the God of Destruction?

Gate of Quetzalcoatl. Oddly enough, I knew about Quetzalcoatl. He was an Aztec god, and very fond of blood sacrifices, butterflies and pyramids.

Gate of Inti. Inti... I associated him with the Incas, but I wasn't sure. Was he the Sun God?

Gate of Odin. Of course, Odin, the one-eyed leader of the Nordic Pantheon. I knew quite a lot about him... But I couldn't for the life of me remember which eye he was missing. Was it the right or the left?

All the gods were pagan and had nothing to do with Christianity. Why them? Another question with no answer. There were also no Slavic gods, so Odin was probably the closest to me. Geographically. I didn't particularly like the Scandinavian god. Could the gates be activated?

The Gate is closed. Do you wish to force open the gate to Odin's abode? (100 SP)

I didn't have the points nor the stupidity for that. I doubted that Odin would welcome a person kicking down the door to his house. What use was it to me, anyway?

Despite knowing the result, I checked all the other gates, making sure they were closed and required a similar number of points to 'force open'. They had definitely been activated last time, and I could have passed through any of them. Perhaps the gods didn't want to waste time on those who probably wouldn't return? Or was this the result of my **Atheist** status and their attitude towards me?

"Whatever," I muttered. "I didn't want to visit you anyway."

I wasn't convinced I should go there at all. The pagan gods had one thing in common in all the legends — they didn't usually give mere mortals anything good. Even those they favored rarely enjoyed a long and happy life. What could be said about those who had angered them?

The other question was, who were these seven? I didn't believe they were the real ancient gods. Gods are fiction, a part of folklore and history. Hence, these entities may be impostors, masquerading as something familiar to us. Or an embodiment of people's ideas, created by the System. Or even players who had received certain abilities, perhaps somehow related to their adopted names.

I didn't know which idea I liked the least... Strangers who had come with some unknown purpose? People who suddenly gained power but don't know how to wield it? Or seven incarnations of the twisted imaginations of our ancestors?

I looked at the Gate of Quetzalcoatl and imagined if it was the real god from the legends. Would I like to pass through these gates and talk to him? Hmm... I didn't feel particularly enthused. I doubted that a nice god would be called the Feathered Serpent. The rest were hardly better. Which one could even be called a kind god? To hell with kindness, which one of them was fair? I needed to re-read the myths and legends when I returned.

I checked the timer, discovered that I had already wasted fifteen minutes, and headed to the *Summoning Portal*. As I glanced across the floor, I suddenly found something that hadn't been there before. To be more precise, the System gave me a prompt, highlighting a section of the floor near the portal. I bent down and picked up a small, opaque stone the size of a chicken egg. Where had it come from?

"The Ring perceived its time had come and abandoned Gollum," I replied to myself. I'd heard that talking to oneself was a bad sign.

In any case, the stone was listed among the rewards for the first mission, so it wasn't difficult to guess where it had come from. I had missed it last time, too busy lying unconscious after falling through the portal. Let's see now.

Soul Stone (83%)...

Rank: *1.*
Properties:
— *Condenses the Nascent Soul.*
— *Can be dedicated to one of the deities.*
— *Probability of attracting the soul of a dead player: requires an anchor.*
— *Probability of resurrecting a player: requires an anchor.*
— *Ability of improvement (0/ 100 SP).*
Owner: *none.*

I mentally prodded the ellipsis next to the name and saw a list of other potential names: **Minor Altar Fragment** (74%), **Tombstone** (53%), **Phylactery** (65%). The concordance percentage for these terms was lower, and quite significantly for some of them. Why were these options displayed at all? Perhaps each of them contained a piece of the puzzle lacking in the other? Was the truth somewhere in between? All these riddles, hypotheses and theories were beginning to give me a headache and permanent paranoia. How much did the picture I was building of the world correspond to reality?

The System remained silent, refusing to

specify the concordance level as it normally did. As a percentage. Instead, when I mentally went through the list of properties, a different message popped up:

Would you like to bind your soul to the stone? Yes/No

I thought about several things at once. For example, did I really have a soul or was this just another translation error? The number 84% immediately appeared next to the word "soul". So, the notional soul that notionally exists. Let's leave that for now...

Did I want to bind my soul to a rock? I listened to myself. I didn't like the idea but I wasn't totally against it. It was more simple caution than a warning from my *Intuition*. As for the voice of reason, I had never been particularly religious. If resurrection was possible using this stone, then there could only be one answer. **Yes.**

This time felt very unpleasant, as if someone was trying to pull out and cut off a piece of something vital inside me. I checked the timer when I regained my senses to find that the binding had taken a whole five minutes. So, how had my chances improved?

— *Probability of attracting the soul of a dead player: 1%.*
— *Probability of resurrecting a player:*

0.0001%.

I laughed hollowly. Great. I felt like I had run into a mousetrap to eat the bait and found a block of plastic cheese inside. My disappointment was so great that I had to resist the urge to crush the stone as tightly into a pile of fragments. I would have probably succeeded, because I hadn't felt such a jolt of fear in a long time. Since my last meeting with the goblins.

Attention (Intuition)! High probability (82%) that destruction... clarifying terminology... of the phylactery (85%)... will lead to damage to the player's mind. Moderate chance (52%) of death. Low probability (5%) that the soul will be completely destroyed. It is recommended that the phylactery (85%) is placed in a safe place.

I noticed that the concordance percentage for the term "phylactery" had risen sharply. What the hell? I tried to find a way to unbind my soul from the stone, but the System did not respond to these attempts. Well, not surprising if this was a trap.

"What a poor Horcrux you are," I muttered, looking at the stone egg in my palm. At least Horcruxes worked. I clearly shouldn't take the stone outside of this room. Could I consider this room sufficiently safe? I didn't know where I was, or if anyone else could access it, but I was inclined to assume that this piece of space was mine alone.

The System reacted suddenly:

Attention! Only the owner has access to the Private Room.

How suspicious, I'd say, or even clumsy. I was tempted to look for a trick in this statement. So, this room was safe. Should I leave the stone here? Even if the stone was in a safe location, there was a 1% chance that my soul would be brought back if I died. To a place nobody had access to. Wouldn't that mean that my soul would be locked up here forever, with no chance of resurrection or rebirth? Or even a final death? Was that the trick? If I died, would the System get my soul? Should I consider it a kind of artificial devil or was I becoming delusional and paranoid?

Despite all the risks, it was far more dangerous to carry the stone on me. I studied the description of the phylactery again, trying to find any hidden functions. Its level could be increased. And another thing...

Would you like to dedicate the altar fragment (74%) to one of the deities?
Yes/No

Oh, so now it's an altar fragment? Not a phylactery? How convenient. I didn't want to, but

I assumed that since there were many gods, the decision wasn't final and could be reversed. I carefully indicated Yes.

The list of seven gods appeared again, along with a list of bonuses they bestowed on their followers. Rather measly bonuses, such as increasing *Immunity* by five percent within a meter of the stone. Which may be useful if it could be worn on a chain like a pendant, but who would risk such madness? Even in our home world?

However, all seven options were unavailable to me due to "low reputation". I wondered how this "reputation" worked if the local gods were not software scripts and possessed intelligence. Did they refuse me personally? In any case, I seemed to be left without divine protection. Whatever, this was for the best.

I looked at the timer, counting down in the corner. I still had ten minutes left to sit and enjoy the last few moments of safety. I wondered what would happen when the time ran out. Would I get a chance to return? Or die? I focused on the dwindling numbers, trying to get a clue. A minute passed, then another one... Finally, the System responded.

Attention! Access level insufficient to obtain additional information.

A message that, for all its neutrality, did not encourage experimentation. Knowing the System,

I was sure that the answer wouldn't be good. Despite the risks and suspicions, I decided to leave the stone here. I placed the phylactery by the wall and reminded myself to bring a box from the goblin world, then went back to the portal. What do we have here...

This time, the System gave me no choice in either destination or level of difficulty. Only one option was available for both.

Task No. 2

> **Type**: *looting*.
> **Information**:
> *This is the Celestial City of Sar, which once belonged to the **goblins (83%)**. Their **gods (57%)** lost and were defeated. Although the enemy has retreated, a curse hangs over the city. The central city districts are overrun by the **undead** (93%), and the outskirts are raided by the surviving goblins. Once allies, the living and the dead are now locked in a battle for access to the altar.*
> **Global goal:**
> *Difficulty level: A.*
> *— Capture the altars of fallen deities and dedicate them to a new owner.*
> **Reward:**
> *— Variable, depends on the choice.*
> **Allies:**
> *— Players.*
> **Proposed adversaries:**

— System creatures.

— The undead.

— Goblinoids.

Local goal:

Difficulty level: E.

— Survive at least 3 days.

— Receive at least 1 SP.

Reward:

— Temporary access to the Server (50%).

Additional goal:

— Survive 9 days.

Penalty for failure:

— Player (E) status reduced to Hero status (84%).

— Inability to return.

CHAPTER 8

THE GOBLIN

THIS TIME, the activated portal didn't look so impenetrable and I could discern the outline of a street through the murky haze. I activated my *Invisibility* mode since I was quite vulnerable whcn I appeared, and stepped into the portal. Let's go.

I landed on the cobblestones and immediately leaped to the side. It was a simple precaution, but when I looked around, I spotted a goblin standing on the roof nearby. He was looking directly at me. Perhaps he couldn't see me, but the portal was hard to miss. The fact that it closed almost immediately seemed to further alarm the observer. His gaze darted around, trying to find the one who had come through the portal.

Now what? Time was ticking away, sapping

my mana, so there was no point in just standing there. I took a cautious step to the side, then another and another one. The goblin's gaze froze, then slowly shifted to follow me. Damn it! My footprints. Although I was invisible, the pavement was covered with a layer of dirt and dust, and the native evidently had excellent eyesight. So much the worse for him. I stopped hesitating and ran resolutely in his direction, without inactivating *Invisibility*, of course. The goblin snapped out of it, gave a startled yelp, and vanished from sight. But I was too close and there was nowhere for the watcher to go.

The goblin didn't even try to fight, choosing to run instead. He jumped out of the first-floor window on the far side, since I was already inside the building. I heard the crash and raced through the house to follow him. I was on the ground floor, unlike him.

I didn't have to chase after him — the goblin had hurt his leg and was limping away, glancing nervously behind him. The perfect victim. Like a bird dragging its wing, leading the hunter away from its nest. Was I being too cautious again? If he wasn't alone, I'd be stabbed in the back as soon as I ran after him. I listened but it was quiet upstairs, and I decided to risk it.

Obeying my wish, the *Invisibility* faded and I whistled to get the fugitive's attention. The goblin turned and froze. My appearance alone would have only made him run faster, but I had a bow in my hand. Or was he impressed by the mask I was wearing? The goblin's eyes darted around in search of cover, but there was little chance that I would miss, and we both knew it.

"Come here or you will die." I said softly, while also listening to my surroundings. I hadn't completely left the building, so even if the goblin had a partner on the roof, he'd have to come downstairs to get me. I kept my spear close by, leaning it against the wall by the doorway. Considering my rank, low-level goblins shouldn't pose much of a threat.

"How do you know our language, Player?" The goblin asked hoarsely but calmly enough. Without challenge, flattery or obvious fear. A very noble reaction, it would be a pity to kill him.

I motioned for him to come closer. When I didn't reply, the goblin gave up and walked slowly towards me. He kept his hands away from his weapons, which were only a knife and a hatchet at his belt. Knowing that goblins had lower parameters than humans, I expected them to be stupid, but there was nothing so far to indicate that.

OK, let's start with... **Identification**. The skill consumed a third of my supply, but now I felt it was justified.

The Nameless Goblin*

Status: System creature.

Type: Copper.
Creature Rank: F-.
Level: 1.
Danger: very low.
Emotions: fear, resolve, pride.
Parameters:
Agility: 5.
Strength: 4.
Intelligence: 6.
Vitality: 3.
Stamina: 4.
Perception: 5.
Luck: 1.
Race Parameter:
Wisdom: 1.
Special Features:
Goblinoid blood — one or more parameters may be higher than the race parameter allows.

You can give him a Name (10 SP, 150 mana units, and the creature's voluntary consent).

There was an unexpected amount of information: status, type, rank, danger, not to mention the parameters and emotions. The ability to give him a System name was interesting, but who would spend SP on a goblin? Unless it allowed me to gain his loyalty and turn him into my minion, which I doubted.

I looked at the *Goblinoid blood* feature. Although I had never heard the term before, I knew that goblins could have parameters above the natural limit. It was nothing to be envious of. An increased parameter was all well and good, but the limit for goblins was half of what it was for humans. Five. This was partially compensated by the fact that over years of selection, their parameters had become close to maximum. Like in this case, where almost all the physical parameters were fours or fives. Although he hadn't been very lucky with the bonus, which had been added to *Intelligence*. Despite having decent stats for a Level 1 creature, it didn't look like it had brought him happiness... or even the money to buy it. The eternal problem of those who are only slightly smarter than those around them is that they can't hide it, and being a *little smarter* is not enough to achieve real success. It doesn't compensate for a lack of wealth, good teachers, power, or the help of influential relatives. Plus, the secondary characteristics, including *Luck* and the bonus *Wisdom* were minimal, as opposed to the physical ones. He was the underdog.

"Don't be afraid," I began and stopped, realizing how false it sounded.

"I am not afraid of death, human," the goblin's voice was unexpectedly firm. "I have already lit the signal fire, and my duty to my people is done. You can now kill me."

I sniffed and finally caught the smell of burning. That's why I had intercepted him so easily. The goblin didn't have an accomplice or a devious plan, he had simply delayed to send a signal. "Whom did you warn? When will the others arrive?"

The goblin said nothing, raising his head proudly and staring into space. A partisan... I reminded myself that I hated goblins, but the dreams... Paradoxically, the dreams had weakened this feeling, so that I could no longer perceive them exclusively as monsters.

"Okay, how about a deal? If you answer my questions, I won't kill you. You're only at Level 1, so your death won't do me much good."

"Well, what level do you have, player? Second?"

"Possibly. You shouldn't know too much if you want to stay alive. Come into the house, and if your answers are true, I'll let you go and reward you."

I pulled one of the cards out of my pocket, twirling it between my fingers. It's difficult to accurately read an alien's facial expression, but the goblin's face was filled with conflicting emotions, greed being the most obvious. He clearly knew what it was, and hesitated.

"This is your chance to change your life. With a System weapon, you'll be able to become much stronger. You will reach your potential."

"Alright," said my prisoner. "I swear in the name of the Great Y that I will answer your questions truly, in exchange for my freedom and the magic card. If you are honest with me, Player, then swear it in the name of your God! You should already have a patron."

I couldn't help admiring the goblin's audacity. He had been ready to die as a hero a minute ago, and now he was willing to reveal any secret in exchange for a card. Yet he had the guts to demand something. I wondered if it was bravery or desperation. Well, easy enough for me to do. Whom should I swear by? One of the seven gods? I would probably lack sincerity in that case. "I swear in the name of my Lord Jesus that I will fulfill our bargain if you give me no reason to do otherwise. Answer my questions and you can leave with the card."

Attention! System failure, oath was not accepted.
Relations with the Earth Gods have deteriorated!

"What do you wish to know, Player?"

"Call me... Cain," I chose one of my three names. The goblin couldn't see my status anyway. "First, I need to know how soon your kin will arrive, and how many of them there are."

"Not soon. There are many observers scattered around the city. Those who will see my smoke will light their own fires, and so on, until the smoke columns are noticed by the chiefs. These signals will let them know that the players have returned, but they will need time to set out."

I didn't scrimp on mana to check that his emotions match his words. It didn't look like the goblin was lying. Well, if I was wrong about him and this was an attempt to stall for time, he would die, and I had a mana crystal left, which would allow me to escape a possible chase while protected by *Invisibility*. "Then we have time. Come inside, we're not going to talk in the street, are we?" I changed weapons and stepped aside, indicating the far corner with my spear. "You can sit on the floor."

Perhaps it would have been wiser to tie the goblin up, but I doubted he would agree, and he'd trust me even less after that. Torture, of course, loosens the tongue, but I had neither the time nor the desire to engage in it. The goblin calmly walked to the corner and kneeled.

"Were you here alone?"

"Yes. What is the point of putting two watchers in one place? Most of us will die, so why give the players more experience?"

He believed that he had been left here to die? No wonder we had come to an agreement so easily.

"Tell me everything. How many warriors have your leaders gathered? How far away are they? Who's in charge?"

"The army is being led by the First Prince himself, the mighty and invincible Ra. He is a hobgoblin, the eldest son of our king and his most likely heir."

"How many warriors does he have?"

"I can't give you exact numbers, but they say there are more than ten thousand of them. Hundreds of hobgoblins, including even *Named Heroes*."

"Who are these named heroes?"

"They are mighty warriors who are only one step below you. Former players who lost their status, or those who received their System Name from the hands of kings or high priests. However, there are few people in our time who can do this. Even Prince Ra, they say, is no longer capable of this."

"Who else is there except players and heroes? What does this System Name give you?"

"You don't know even the simplest things. Has your world has only recently entered the Great War? In that case, what has happened here may soon happen in your homeland. I am an ordinary goblin... **terminology adaptation**... a System creature, but if I get at least one point of... experience, I will become... a unit. I will be able to see my own strength and a range of other possibilities. Then, given a name, I will become a *Named Hero*. I will be able to become much stronger than ordinary warriors, and gain not only... experience, but also a divine reward for any slain enemies. If I don't fall in battle, I can easily live to be a hundred years old. My children may even be born with a Name themselves. Being a Hero means glory, power, honor and wealth! Prince Ra promised weapons and a name for those who distinguished themselves in this campaign."

"Is that why you're here?"

"These rewards are for experienced and powerful units. I am here only because I did not have a choice. I am not so stupid as to hope for the impossible. But if I had a Name, my clan would regain its glory!"

"At least you'll have a weapon and then, who knows? Alright, back to business. Where is your army now and how soon will it arrive?"

"In the camp by the Outer Wall. It will take them less than a day to get here. The leaders will not delay, either, because the players arrive quickly and disappear just as quickly. I think they will arrive before nightfall and start hunting in the morning. Most of you will be dead by tomorrow evening."

I smiled crookedly. The goblin had gotten into the flow and made no attempt to hide his opinions or soften the wording. This suited me just fine. The information about the army alone was enough to pay for his life and a low-ranking card. If I had learned of the army's arrival when they had come here, it would be too late. So, I had to leave the danger zone by tomorrow morning. The only question was, where should I go?

"Where are we now?"

"In the Sixth Ring... Between the fifth and sixth walls."

Unfortunately, I didn't have the trophy map so that the goblin could point to our location since

I couldn't bring it back from Earth. I remembered it quite well and spent a few minutes asking questions to decide which way to go, and along the way, learn to navigate by several local signs. Mostly navigating by the sun, of course, but the goblin shared a few other ways. Moreover, he didn't even conceal the existence of the fortress blocking my way to escape. It was time to end my questioning and get going, but I decided to find out as much as I could.

"How did your ruler know that the players would return?"

"A divine task," replied the goblin. "We still have prisoners, and we know the truth, that you are here for the temples. Since the Great Y perished, many *Free Players* have tried to reach the altars. Now your gods have become involved. We cannot let them succeed."

"Why?" I decided not to ask about the fate of the prisoners. I could clarify that a bit later.

"This is our city. Although there is a Curse hanging over it, our dead ancestors protect the temples. We kill them, but our hearts are heavy. Although their bodies prey on the living, their souls languish in the altars. Only we, goblins, have the right to control the temples! If strangers control the temples, our gods will never be able to reawaken. The souls of our ancestors will be destroyed for the sake of experience. Even the soul of my venerable grandfather is perhaps kept in the altar of the Great Y! Without our gods, we will weaken completely and be nothing but food for the others. We will be hunted by players and creatures of Chaos for centuries. You, the aliens, are still weak, but you will grow stronger if given time. By coming here again and again, you will destroy the surrounding settlements, invade the center of the city, take over our altars, and we will never be able to resurrect our past..."

"Kept in the altars? Your players can be reborn?"

The goblin's stare clearly said, 'You don't even know that?'

"The chance is small but it exists, and a god can recreate a destroyed body. At the time of the Great Y, one in ten of his followers was given a new chance after being slain by enemies! Didn't your patron, whose name you recently invoked, allow you access to his altar?"

In other words, the gods could somehow increase the chances of attracting a soul, and then endow the player with a new body. A truly divine ability — but the odds were still rather low.

"I'm the one asking the questions here. You said your grandfather was a player?"

"He was a mighty hero who was allowed to touch the altar. His name was Duk! His name had one letter more than the Prince and only one less than the King."

"What is the name of the King, by the way?"

"My family is too lowborn. I am not allowed to utter his sacred name."

"Nevertheless?" I said. The goblin knew plenty of interesting things and, quite obviously, didn't consider his origins to be that low. "I can't believe that the grandson of a *Named Hero* doesn't know the king's name."

"You're right. His name is Fyyr, like many of his predecessors, most of whom he is not even related to. When the King dies, the Crown Prince will put on the crown and take this name."

The way this was said had an air of intrigue, old grievances and possibly even struggles for power. In this respect, the goblins were the same as humans. But what use were their internal power struggles to me? None of them would agree to an alliance with the players. This was obvious after all that had been said. Even peace was unlikely.

"So, the main reason you're here is to protect your god?"

"Correct. Your arrival has merely hastened events. Your weapons and the obtained energy will enable our army to become stronger, so it can move further towards the center of the city. If we can reach to the Central Temple and bring the Great One back to life, everything will change."

"You said that the players kept appearing. When and how many times have they appeared recently?"

"Seven times. The first time you came was more than thirty days ago. There were six more squadrons of a thousand men, and fewer and fewer left each time. Then nobody came for many days, but we knew that sooner or later, you would return. Your gods will not give up. This is the eighth assault and perhaps nobody will leave this time."

Seven waves — because of the seven gods? It sounded like the goblins have already grown significantly stronger by capturing a lot of System weapons, as well as killing or capturing about six thousand players. If less than a hundred people had returned from my wave, I had to assume there were about 700 'veterans'. A thousand people, at best, since the goblin might be lying about the losses. Plus, there was no guarantee that all the veterans were here now, and wouldn't arrive in the next few days.

Remaining players: 982/1000.

The maximum hadn't changed, and, compared to last time, losses were low. If you can say that about the death of eighteen people in half an hour. In any case, it clearly wasn't enough against ten thousand troops, united under a single commander. Even if all the veterans were suddenly united in one squadron, instead of some 'fresh meat' being added to the survivors of my wave. If there were nine hundred newcomers, we wouldn't survive three days. It was going to be a massacre, compared to which the results of the first mission would seem like a nice Christmas story...

"There is a fortress deep in the city. What do you know about it?"

"The fortress," the goblin sighed wearily. Our conversation had dragged out. "It protects the inner suburbs from being overrun by hordes of the undead and serves as a base for long-distance campaigns. The garrison is quite small, no more than three hundred warriors, but they are all experienced veterans."

"Will they attack if people try to go deeper into the city?"

"If there are few players, certainly. Your weapons are very expensive."

"What if there are a lot of people?"

"They will attack anyway," he admitted after a moment. "If there are a lot of people, you may try to reach the temple. It is unlikely that you will succeed, but the risk is unacceptable. To pass unhindered, there should probably be not too many and not too few."

"How many?"

"I don't know. Not enough to make the fortress war chief think that you can capture the altars, and not too few to be an easy target. A hundred? At least. Three hundred? No more than that. It is difficult to predict such things. Even if they let you pass, they will follow you. But you have a useful skill — you can easily slip past the fortress alone. Even if all the other players die, you have a chance of surviving."

"I appreciate your frankness."

"I swore an oath," the goblin shrugged in response.

"All right, let's drop this subject. What happens to the prisoners?"

"It varies. Some of our sages use them to learn your language. Although human women are hideous, they are chosen by chiefs and strong warriors as they will bear strong children. Goblins with two or three attributes, maybe even hobgoblins. I believe the men will be given to widows, and later will be sacrificed using sacred weapons. However, that's for the future, they're still alive so far."

I nodded. I had expected something like this when I saw, during the first mission, how the goblins tried to capture the humans rather than slaughtering them all.

"Where are they being held?"

"In different places," the goblin shrugged again. "In settlements around the ruined capital, in the neighboring cities, some were even sent to distant lands as gifts or slaves for sale. However, most of them are with the Prince right now. I think they'll be executed before the army heads to the altars. It will significantly strengthen our Champions."

There were seventy-six people who had failed to return from my squadron, and if you multiplied this by the number of groups, you'd get five hundred and thirty-two Heroes. Even if the Prince sacrificed only half, it was an impressive number, especially when converted into System points. Unfortunately, I didn't see any way to help the prisoners.

I asked the goblin a dozen more unimportant questions and finally fell silent. There was no point in prolonging the conversation. I had to decide.

Funny, although I hadn't even learned the goblin's name — not the System one, but the "true" name — I could no longer view him as a faceless and malicious enemy that had to be killed.

I looked at the task assigned to me again. The goblin before me was a chance to obtain the required point of experience, but that wasn't the main difficulty. The problem was how to survive three days in these ruins... Without food or shelter, surrounded by thousands of goblins and the undead... As soon as I imagined what the next three days would be like for other people, I wanted to swear. Or cry? I had to admit that this little goblin had managed to scare me. Why was the maximum limit so high? Nine days...

Considering the seven waves of a thousand players mentioned by the goblin, and comparing it with the current time frame, I could assume that a new one thousand players would arrive every day. After three days, everyone would have a choice: stay in this world to help the new arrivals or leave. I wasn't sure I was right, but... this set-up gave us at least some hope.

"Do you have any more questions, Cain?" the goblin broke the long silence. He was aware that his fate was being decided right now.

"No, no more questions. I'm happy with your answers. Here." I threw the card to him and the goblin snatched it eagerly out of the air. Ten seconds later, a Cossack saber materialized in his hands. I watched him curiously, waiting to see if he would try to kill me. I even put away the spear that I had kept beside me throughout the conversation, ostentatiously putting the card into my pocket.

"Thank you, it was a fair deal."

"Good. You are free to leave." I didn't add any threats or promises — he was smart enough as it was. The goblin bowed briefly, without taking his eyes off me, and sidled over to the door. He didn't even try to attack me. Shame. I raised my hand and leaned as if onto empty air, standing up and letting the masking field fall from the spear. Something itched inside me...

"Hey, wait! I shouted after the goblin had taken a dozen steps.

"If you want to hit me, hit me in the back."

I wasn't offended. When I had begun this conversation, I was planning to kill the goblin, even if I had to break my vow to do it. He hadn't really believed me either. The world is far from fair, and excessive nobility only leads to death. Nevertheless, I let him go and also gave him the card, which didn't contain some axe that the goblin would have trouble lifting, but a blade that suited his size. It was stupid, illogical, and short-sighted, but my gut told me that letting him go would do me more good.

Attention! Do you wish to give the creature a Name? (10 SP, 150 mana units) Yes/No

"I name you Dinar," I sighed, saying goodbye to my precious experience points. "Go and remember. I gave you a weapon. And now your name has one more letter than the king's."

"We will still be enemies."

"I haven't chosen a god yet. If I reach the altar first, I'll think about letting your Great Y return to this world."

"What do you want in exchange?" The goblin looked incredulous, but relaxed. By giving him a name, I had made it clear that I wasn't going to kill him.

"If you can help to keep your prisoners alive..."

"I shall try. If we meet again, I will not try to kill you."

I watched the goblin go, trying to figure out what I'd just done. Did I just waste ten experience points and a lot of mana? Or had I laid the groundwork for negotiations? Well, I could think about it as I walked.

* * *

I didn't leave immediately. I first checked the roof, making sure that there really was nobody else there. Then I took off the mask, put out the fire, and collected all the things the goblin had abandoned during his escape. A blanket, a small pot, a flask containing some dubious brew, a bag of grain, salt, some herbs, strips of dried meat and berries. Plus, what I thought might be pemmican, a strange-looking mixture of dried meat, berries, nuts, and something else. I doubted that the meat included human flesh since players were quite rare here, and goblins weren't savages, but I still wouldn't eat it without a laboratory analysis. Or the threat of starvation.

Ultimately, I had gained quite a lot. The goblin had been on duty for a while, and needed something to eat. I didn't know how much of it was edible for humans, but the pot would come in useful. I'd see about the rest. After all, I could always treat another person and see how long they lasted... just kidding.

Well, what was I planning to do? I didn't see many options. I could continue alone or try to form a group with someone else. The decision depended on which direction I planned to go and what my tactics would be.

This city had seven zones separated by circular walls. According to the goblin, I was currently in the Sixth Ring, between the fifth and sixth walls. The System hadn't failed this time and had chosen the safest place for players to appear. If you could call the position between the hammer and the anvil that. The anvil here were the undead in the center of the city, and the hammer were the thousands of goblins waiting for players to arrive, somewhere in the seventh zone or outside the city walls.

Should I stay in the sixth zone, given that the goblins would be arriving soon? I may have been a pessimist, but I was sure that humans couldn't withstand such a force, even if my captive had exaggerated its size. Should I try to escape the city? This was a solution with a chance of success. It seemed stupid to head into enemy territory, but the ruins were vast and the goblins couldn't possibly block all the exits. The army would head through known territory, using breaks in the walls, so all I needed to do was reach the wall and descend somewhere further away. Easy enough to do from the inside, the main thing was to get some rope.

If I succeeded, I could get out of this trap and even visit one of the goblin settlements. Most of the warriors would probably head to the ruins to slaughter players, which meant that only women, children and the elderly would remain in the villages. An almost defenseless source of "experience points" that only my morals could prevent me from accessing. It was also an opportunity to free the prisoners. Who, unlike me, had nowhere to run. As far as I could remember, I had seen skills that would allow them to return home, such as a Slavery or System Squad card, but this was all purely theoretical for now. I doubted anyone would chose something like this out of all the available E rank skills. Plus, only a few people could be saved this way.

What was the point of saving them if all I could do was put them out of their misery and score some precious experience points? Moreover, goblin women could also fight, and some guards probably remained behind in the settlements. Even if I somehow managed to get out of the city, a fight with hundreds of weak enemies would end in my death rather than with a stack of easy experience points. Perhaps the situation would change once I reached a higher level, but for now, it was just another way for me to die. I needed a whole squad but then we wouldn't be able to pass unnoticed. Well, I wasn't planning to mess with the settlements and had simply considered the possibility.

I was much more interested in the second direction — deeper into the city, into the area controlled by the undead. While the goblins were busy slaughtering the other players, I had a good chance of getting away. Of course, I still had to get past the fortress, but it served more as a transit point for the goblins, rather than actually blocking the road. There were four breaks in the wall, and the fortress controlled only one of them. The other three were protected by barricades and small teams of goblins. These squads would likely retreat to the fortress as soon as the signal fires were lit, which would leave the way pretty much free.

On the other hand, it was too dangerous to venture into the territory of the undead alone. I needed a squad... Preferably one that could sneak past unnoticed, without alerting the garrison. Or a really large group so that the goblins wouldn't dare to engage. For that I would need to gather more than half of the players, and there wasn't much time. Nor did I believe that a crowd had much sense. Even if I openly announced the danger, many people would not believe me, would be afraid, or would decide to do their own thing. Given the extremely low requirements for experience points, personal survival would come first. I'm sure many people would conclude that the easiest thing to do would be to lie low and wait out these three days. The city was large, and some would succeed...

But one couldn't hide forever, and cowards are doomed to extinction in the long run. Hence, I wasn't going to follow that tactic. Perhaps I wasn't the strongest player right now, but I was definitely among the leaders. If I avoided fighting, I would become one of many, and then lose my advantage altogether. Playing hide-and-seek with goblins was no guarantee of survival.

What would happen next? If I was to the

predict the outcome, the death of many high-level players would allow the goblins to get our weapons and experience. The loot would attract thousands of new "adventurers". The goblins would become stronger and stronger, while their opponents would be mostly newcomers and the rare surviving veterans. My chances in the first mission were quite high because the goblins hadn't been expecting us, but this round would be a massacre for beginners. The same picture as the goblin had described, but in reverse...

I preferred the option where humans were strong enough to drive the goblins out of the ruins. Then those who lost could continue to live, and the players would have a better chance of reaching the temple and ending this thing... Or at least finding out what would happen next.

Of course, it was unlikely that everything would be solved this time. My goal was much more modest — to survive and boost my bag up to the Level 3. After all, if the first level allowed me to transport only System items between locations, and the second level allowed me to bring trophies back to Earth, I had to assume that I could carry something from our world to the goblin world in the future. Normal armor, equipment, medicine, and most importantly, firearms. As they say, you can get much farther with a kind word and a gun than you can with a kind word alone. If I replaced "gun" with "automatic weapon" and "word" with "spear", the wisdom of this phrase only increased.

Of course, I didn't have access to a military arsenal, and the bag's size was limited, but problems should be solved as they arise. To begin with, I had to find another forty Level 1 bags. Perhaps it would be wiser to negotiate with the other players, but knowing people, I doubted that they would agree to 'chip in' and give away such a useful artifact. I was unlikely to volunteer such a thing either. The second possibility was robbery. Given my skill level, few of the newcomers would be able to put up a decent fight, and the mask would allow me to avoid identification. I didn't even have to kill them. Not a great option, but I'd keep it in mind.

I pulled out a flask and uncorked it, checking the contents. Different liquids took different times to be accepted by the System. Blood needed only one day. This flask contained exactly that, chicken blood, if it mattered.

I took a piece of cloth, wrapped it around a stick and wrote the address of my site on the wall with large strokes. We had to unite if we wanted to survive, but we needed to do this in advance and not during the mission. Even if I didn't return, the players would be able to collaborate on the open forum. Moreover, the closed sections would open in a week's time, and all the information that I was able to find and translate into English would become available. My knowledge of the language had made my school teachers cry, and it hadn't improved much since then, but anyone who needed to know would understand. And forgive me.

As always in times of danger, I wanted to crack jokes. If I was honest with myself, I was afraid. Shit. I had narrowly escaped death last time, and I wasn't sure that I would be able to do so in this round. It's why I had chosen *Invisibility*, so I could hide. To hide and then strike a sudden and deadly blow.

Unfortunately, I didn't have enough mana to fully use the skill. The only way to fix this was to increase my level by earning SP, which meant killing. Goblins, undead, monsters, even other players. Fear breeds cruelty, and as I had said, I was afraid. So was everyone else, I suspect. Was that the reason for what happened next?

CHAPTER 9

CHANCE MEETINGS

THE FIRST PERSON I met was a stocky man, wearing the standard but rather battered player outfit. He was about thirty, fair-haired and of European appearance. He wasn't holding any weapons and his name glowed green, but I didn't let my guard down. The sleeves of my jacket contained 'fast slot' pockets, allowing me to touch a card and summon my spear within seconds. I suspected that other veterans knew this trick as well, and the experience of the last mission had shown that I couldn't trust anyone. A significant number of veterans had completed the previous mission by killing their allies, but the mark was long gone by this time.

The stranger smiled, but his gaze lacked confidence in me, betraying his wariness. He'd probably also had some bad experiences. We paused for a moment, then walked toward each other, while also keeping an eye on our surroundings. *Identification*

Jack

Status: player.
Local ID: hidden.
Level: 2.
Home Location: Earth.
Race: human.
Gender: male.
Parameters:
Strength: 7/10.
Agility: 7/10.
Intelligence: 7/10.
Vitality: 8/10.
Stamina: 8/10.
Perception: 10/10.
Luck: 7/10.
Race Parameter:
Intuition: 4/10.
Additional Parameters:
Faith: 5.
Features:
Mark of God — this person is under the protection of a higher entity. Other features hidden.

His parameters were impressive, despite only the second level. It was clear that the man had been keeping in shape even before this. Strange that he had decided to boost *Perception* to ten first, and not the other parameters. His *Intelligence* was also a little concerning, since numerically, Jack was smarter than me. And much, much luckier. The only thing in which I had a competitive advantage was *Intuition.* What kind of parameter was *Faith*, anyway? I mean, it wasn't hard to guess that it was related to the gods, but... We were now too close for me to get distracted.

"Hi," he said hoarsely. "I'm Jack Snow, from Nebraska. Is this your first time here?"

The question came as no surprise. My clothes were intact, and with his four in *Intuition*, he could see almost no additional System information. By giving me his full name and mentioning his city, he seemed to be trying to provoke me to return the courtesy...

"Hi, I'm Blake. Just Blake," I lied automatically. "If you want to talk, let's get off the street. I wouldn't want to be interrupted by goblins."

"Sensible." Jack smiled broadly as he studied my face. "You're a careful guy, aren't you? Clearly not a newbie."

"Other types don't survive here long."

"I bet that's not you real name, huh? And this isn't your first time here. What's your level? Second? No? Third. Really? Third level, then..."

What sort of trick was this? I stifled my irritation and turned, heading for the nearest building on my left. Jack followed, keeping a safe distance between us, a mixture of caution and courtesy.

"You're very good at guessing." I finally stopped and looked around. "Is it a type of skill, like detecting the truth?"

"You guessed it. I'd say that I wasn't very lucky with the mission reward, but sometimes it's good to know when you're being told the truth and when you're being lied to."

I smiled, aware that he was in fact lying to me right now. I was willing to bet that he did have such a skill, but that he had received it for having a 10 in *Perception*. And why did he say "bad luck" when he mentioned the mission reward? Didn't he have a choice?

"Yes, I don't like liars either."

"Then we'll be friends," Jack replied. "You weren't planning to kill me for the experience points, were you?"

Despite the joking tone of voice, it was a serious question. What does one say in response? Especially when I didn't really know how his skill worked, and which trump card he had up his sleeve.

"Of course, I considered it," I pretended to admit with a smile. "I always consider all my options. I think my chances of succeeding are pretty good, but why would I want the red status? The mission has just begun, and we have three long days ahead of us." I could have gotten around this rule by using the mask, but my opponent didn't need to know that. After all, he had started this game first.

"You're telling the truth," the American said. "You see, it's quite useful. It helps to avoid misunderstandings. Now I know that you are unlikely to attack without good reason. I can trust you, up to a certain point."

"The question is whether I can trust you?" I responded. "So far you're just annoying me."

"All right, all right, cool it. Shall we show our cards a bit?" he held up his hands. "It's my second time here, and the first thing I did when I returned from my last mission was to surrender to the government. There were a lot of skeptics there, of course, but I had more than enough evidence. So, I'm not just Jack, I'm Captain Jack, with the right to recruit newcomers. How do you feel about money, Blake? Our government literally prints it, so the new bureau will have no problems with funding. Do you want to be rich?"

"Who doesn't? Why don't you ask me if I'm a patriot, too?"

"Patriotism is great and all, but I'm betting on pragmatism. Even if you're not Blake, but some Ivan from Russia... sorry, you don't look like a citizen of North Korea and Iraq, and I can't think of anyplace else. You can obtain citizenship and support from the most powerful country in the world. We've already found six players, back on Earth, I mean. No one has refused yet."

The 'agent' spoke rather convincingly. Money wasn't the most important thing in our situation, but state support was a pretty strong trump card. If we could gather a large enough group of players, we could combine their bags, and then bring modern weapons into this world. Probably not much since ammunition is heavy, but enough to deal with the goblins. As well as the players who would stand in the way of a new power. I couldn't say that I was overly happy about it.

"Listen, Jack," I said. "Your offer sounds intriguing, but I don't like making hasty decisions. There's a lot to consider. Let's talk about this later, when this is all over. How can I contact you?"

"Via e-mail, of course." He dictated the address. "It's not just me, this is the office e-mail. Can you share this information with others if necessary? By the way, the guys from the Analytics Department advised me to write it on the walls. Even using goblin blood, if nothing else was available."

I nodded. Our ideas were similar, but our approaches differed. If my site was meant to unite all the players, e-mail allowed them to work with each person individually. Such a simple idea had occurred to me, too, but one 'little thing' had stopped me — the chance that I might not return myself. I guess the dead shouldn't care what happened next, but I was still alive and I didn't want any pointless deaths. Funny... I was planning to kill dozens of goblins and was seriously considering hunting down other players, yet I was worried about their safety? It was idealism verging on stupidity.

"E-mail me. If you agree to talk, you'll get ten thousand dollars on your return," Jack persisted. "Just for talking, no strings attached."

"I'll keep that in mind," I said. The amount mentioned was considerable, but not excessive. I thought that many people would agree, and bank transfers weren't difficult to trace.

The conversation had tired me out. Despite the man's light tone, I never forgot where we were. The constant need to figure out the purpose of the conversation, while at the same time making sure that I didn't get stabbed with a sword... Or has he got something else? I noticed that the distance between us had been imperceptibly shortening during the conversation. I could probably get him with my spear from this position. A second to remove it from the card, then a strike...

The smile on Jack's face suddenly disappeared, he took a step back, and a gleaming gold bastard sword appeared in his hand. Judging by the ease with which the American held it, the sword was made of something else.

I also stepped back and the spear appeared in my hand. Had something gone wrong? It wasn't a terrible place for a fight — although my choices were limited, I had chosen the building well. The ceilings were high enough that the length of my weapon was not a disadvantage.

"What's the matter?" I decided not to attack first. "You've decided to kill me?"

"Don't even try to trick me!" Jack exploded. "I trust my powers of observation, and I can see that you're not interested! Do you have a problem with my plan? You don't want me to succeed, enough to try to kill me, right?"

"You're mad," I replied. The absurdity of the situation was kind of depressing.

We slowly circled each other while keeping our distance. I quickly glanced at the sword and then focused on my opponent.

"Don't try to lie to me! Why did you decide to attack?"

Had I decided to attack? How... sad. Either Jack was simply looking for an excuse to kill me, or he was plain wrong. Well, I had considered the possibility of a clash, but in theory. I wasn't planning to kill him.

"You're wrong about that, but I don't like being threatened," I responded grimly, activating my *Invisibility*. "We better leave it at that."

Jack didn't wait for me to disappear completely and pounced, trying to reach me with his sword. I dodged and performed an automatic thrust with the spear in response. Jack managed to brush it aside and slid along the shaft, forcing me to retreat abruptly. I'd need my fingers for later. The American tried to build on his success by swinging his sword around at random, but I was now completely invisible and had slunk off to the side. The fight had lasted only seconds, but my heart was racing. The asshole had almost gotten me!

I suppressed my emotions. I had the advantage now, and had to figure out what to do next. Do I leave? Negotiate? Finish him off? I had to decide quickly since *Invisibility* only lasted five minutes.

However, there was only one choice left to me. I removed the mask from my bag and put it to my face with a sigh. Whatever had motivated the American, I couldn't forgive such behavior. People don't like to admit their mistakes, and even if I left now, the whole situation could misfire the next time I met him. I had to end the problem.

✡ ✡ ✡

Once he realized that fighting an invisible person was a bad idea, Jack backed up against the wall and was intently studying the dust-covered floor. Well, it was naive to expect that he would be more stupid than the goblin... I took a couple of steps to the side, and his gaze followed me. Damn, this invisibility was useless! But who said that I had to approach him? I retreated again and took out my bow. I may be less skilled with it, but it was hard to miss at this distance. Plus, I had a quiver full of arrows.

"Wait! Look, we both overreacted. If this was a mistake, it's not too late to negotiate!" Judging by Jack's strained voice, he wasn't pleased about the current situation. "Your ability is impressive. I can offer you more! How about three hundred thousand? Maybe even a million! We can simply go our separate ways." He'd certainly changed his tune! All it took was for circumstances to change, huh? Go our separate ways? Nevertheless, I took my time to make up my mind. How sincere was Jack? Everyone I'd killed before had given me good reason to do so. They had wanted to kill me, leaving me with no other option. Here, it could have been a simple misunderstanding. "Hell, there's no point in us killing each other! The goblins are our enemy. Come on, say something!"

"Why did you draw your weapon?" I asked.

"It's all because of my skill! My *Perception* is too strong. I can't tell the truth from a lie, I can only see the intent. There were too many negative emotions and hostility in you. After all, everyone here is trying to kill each other."

I was no longer listening to Jack, noticing that the sword in his hands had begun to glow suspiciously. He had just been buying himself some time! I wasn't going to wait for the ability to activate – the bastard hadn't considered the possibility that I was no longer holding a spear.

Jack jerked when he heard the snap, but he couldn't deflect the arrow. Dropping the sword, he gripped the shaft with both hands, trying to hold the wound closed. There was little blood, however, and a faint greenish glow appeared beneath his palms. Another ability? Healing? Even if that was the case, it was too late. Although I still had a choice a minute ago, I could no longer let him live.

"Damn you... What you're doing is an international crime. They'll find you."

I ignored his words, since the man was smart enough not to be babbling such nonsense seriously. Rather, he was biding his time in the hope of a miracle, for nothing else could save him.

"You don't believe that, Jack," I said, dropping my *Invisibility.* "They won't find me. No one will even know how you died. Come up with something more convincing."

"Wait," he croaked. "You can't kill me. I'm protected by Inti... I'm his High Priest... Who is your patron? If it's Hera or Odin, we have an alliance..."

Another piece of the jigsaw. Unfortunately, now wasn't the time to continue the interrogation. I had to hurry, since the last thing I needed was a miracle from the gods.

"Wrong guess," I said, putting another arrow in him, right beside the first one. Jack fell on his side and stopped trying to speak, grimacing in pain and glaring at me with hatred. Only the glow beneath his hand told me that he hadn't given up yet. Honestly, I felt like a villain. So be it. "I'm sorry, it's nothing personal," I muttered. "I just need the experience points."

I dropped to one knee, drawing my dagger. He tried to bite my hand, but the movement only helped my blade to sink deeper into his neck. A few seconds of agony, and a wave of heat washed over me.

Attention! You have gained 20 SP! (20/60)

Attention! (global alert, hidden) The Inti High Priest has died his final death!
You receive an additional 20 SP. (40/60)

Forty points? Being a villain seemed quite profitable. No wonder there was never a shortage of them.

It was rather ironic that Jack had been a priest of the god of the Incas. I didn't know if modern Americans were descendants of the conquistadors, but Europeans had been responsible for the Incas' extinction.

I suddenly received a flurry of new messages.

You have attracted the attention of the God Inti!
Attention! Inti has declared that he hates you... adjustment (mask)... Cain.
Attention! Inti has declared you a Heretic. A bounty has been placed on your head.

Right, so this was a reminder of why villains rarely lived long. What a vengeful deity. I looked at what I had 'obtained'.

Personal Enemy of a God (tied to the mask) — *you have insulted Inti. You will die and your soul will be destroyed. A bounty has been placed on your head.*

Heretic (tied to the mask) — *relations with the gods of Earth have significantly deteriorated. Henceforth, all followers of the Sun God Inti are your enemies.*

Will of Chaos (tied to the mask) — *you have killed the high priest of a God of Order. The Lords of Chaos and their followers approve of this action. There is a possibility that when you meet the* **followers of Chaos** *(51%), they will not kill you at once.*

It was the notes in the brackets that kept me calm. When I took off my mask, I was relieved to see that my new statuses disappeared. Damn... So, the artifact was just an E rank item that hid me from divine retribution? The *Note* did not show anything new, so I took out the slightly 'melted' mana crystal, replenished my energy, and cast *Identification* again.

Mask of Cain (cursed)

Material: *unknown leather.*
Class: *D.*
Type: *System artifact.*

Description:

The rules are the same for everyone, but the weak will die anyway. Why shouldn't they serve as a stepping stone for your ascension?

Properties:

— Hides the face and all System information about the player.

— Changes the name to match the mask.

— Temporarily severs the link with the altars, depriving one of the right to resurrection.

— In the event of death, the soul is absorbed by the System. The killer doesn't receive SP.

Additional Features:

— Will of Chaos.

— Personal Enemy of a God.

— Heretic.

The artifact's class had increased, but the reasons for this were unclear. I didn't see any hints in the description. Did the mask somehow absorb the power of the divine curse? An interesting concept, but it was now even more dangerous to wear than before.

* * *

After checking the mask, I immediately put it back on and began sorting through my loot. Despite his high status, the priest hadn't dropped much. He also had very few possessions, just the bag, standard equipment, and a sword card. The latter was the most interesting part of the loot. As soon as I picked up the weapon, a message appeared before me:

Attention! Faith parameter is available!
Would you like to convert Wisdom to a similar Faith parameter?
Yes/No

I understood that the *Wisdom* parameter would disappear in this case. I would still have the same mana, but it would no longer be personal, but rather 'divine'.

Attention! You lack a divine patron, so the Faith parameter is blocked.
Would you like to accept Inti as your patron?
Yes/No

Of course, I declined this 'wonderful' chance. The sword was extremely interesting, however. ***Identification.***

The Sun Sword

Rank: *D.*
Material*: gun metal, unknown leather, true gold.*
Weight*: 1 kg.*
Type*: divine artifact, scalable.*
Features:

— Enables the owner to absorb 60% of the spiritual and life force of the victim.

— 19% of the energy absorbed by this weapon goes directly to Inti.

— 1% of the absorbed energy condenses on the sword.

— 40% goes to the owner.

— 40% is absorbed by the System.

Dedication to Inti (locked, requires binding):

— Unlocks the Faith parameter. Faith +1.

— Ability to convert similar parameters to Faith.

— Symbol of power. Allows you to dedicate new adepts to serving Inti (10/ 10).

— Able to absorb light.

— Able to emit the True Light, which reveals that which is hidden.

— Gives Inti the chance to draw the soul of the murdered owner to his altar. The chance depends on the god's power.

— Beacon.

Additional:

— Linked task 'Return the divine sword to the temple of Inti'. Reward is variable.

Owner:

— Absent.

I wasn't planning to convert *Wisdom* into *Faith*, especially since it was blocked, but the weapon was far from ordinary. Grade D and scalable? Of course, Inti took a big chunk of the energy, but the bonuses made up for it. In addition, I thought that few of the other players even had E-ranked weapons at this stage. I, myself, had a dagger, but I'd gotten it from a dead goblin, not from the System. The dead priest had nothing to lose...

The ability to absorb and emit light was also quite fascinating. If I had waited for the skill to activate, Jack would have not only dispelled my invisibility, but also blinded me with a flash. I doubted he would have held back. No matter whose fault it was, I had done everything right, and hesitation, on the contrary, had almost cost me my life. The priest's set of skills was impressive and seemed honed against me. Could this be considered a sign of his *Luck*?

I shrugged and went back to studying the sword. What else... An additional chance to draw the owner's soul to the patron god after death? Not bad for a priest, but not good for a thief like me. The most interesting feature was the ability to initiate new adepts. No wonder Inti was so angry. Even ignoring the death of his priest, I doubted that Inti could hand out such artifacts left, right and center.

Do you wish to bind yourself to the Sun Sword and become its owner?

Yes/No

I looked at the last line of the description and declined. I didn't see the point. Considering that the sword now lacked an owner, the binding could easily be removed by death, but were there other ways? If not, the binding would significantly reduce the value of the sword and limit possible maneuvers. I returned the artifact to its card, thought about it for a moment, then hid the 'evidence' in one of my jacket pockets. The wrath of the gods made me hesitant to use such a conspicuous sword, but I could always gift it to some goblin. Or set up an enemy by giving them the mask and then bringing the head of the 'killer' and 'irrefutable evidence' of the crime to the resentful deity. All this needed careful thought.

In any case, given the American's identity, I needed to keep my role in his death quiet. Even ignoring the gods, murder was murder. I didn't know how US law applied to the murder of its citizens on other planets, but I didn't really want to know either.

"Well, rest in peace." The anger had dissipated, and I didn't feel any hatred towards the man. Perhaps I should have buried him, but for that I needed three things: time, stupidity, and a shovel. Instead, I cut off the corpse's head so that he wouldn't turn into the undead, and hid it further away in the bushes. It sounded simple, but, despite my skills, the procedure took a while and was not in the least pleasant. I felt utterly surreal for a few seconds. The System, another world, goblins, a severed head. Was this really happening to me?

Deep in thought, I unscrewed the top of the flask, raised it to my lips, and stopped. It wasn't water.

An unknown elixir, created by the indigenous people of Earth.

Its properties weren't shown, but the label color was yellow with a greenish tinge. In other words, it was safe to drink. I weighed the trophy flask up in my hand and considered wasting energy on *Identification* of the elixir, but then took a cautious sip. Ugh... Disgusting. Fire ran through my veins, and my senses grew sharper. A few minutes later, when the potion finally took effect, a message appeared,

Status: action of elixir No. 0003. Stamina +1.3. Perception +1.1. Duration: 17 minutes. Warning: prolonged use may have negative effects.

Clearly, I wasn't the only one who had worked out the hidden property of the flasks. I guessed that the potion was originally some kind of medical stimulant. Not great for my health, but I was unlikely get hooked since the flask wasn't that big, and I didn't have access to the source of the 'magical liquid'. I checked my stats. Funny...

My *Perception* had jumped from seven to eight as expected, but *Stamina* had risen by a whole two points. It appeared my theory that the System didn't display fractions and rounded up instead had been confirmed. This was important.

I scratched a mark on the flask and put it in my bag. It was time to move on.

✵ ✵ ✵

Once I had put some distance between the corpse and myself, I picked an empty house, found a secure spot and closed my eyes. I had received a surprising amount of experience points for killing the priest, enough to take the next step on the path to power and survival.

Attention! Increase the *Spear fighting* skill to Level 3? (40 SP)
Yes/No

Of course, I wanted to reach the next level, but this required finding another twenty SP, while I could improve my skill right now. I confirmed the choice and my experience bar dropped to zero **(0/60)**.

Remembering how it worked last time, I began to move around, consolidating the knowledge as I received it. It was harder but much more effective than just lying on the floor, writhing in pain and waiting for it to be over. The card gave access to the basics, and the specialization was too broad. It was up to the player to decide whether they'd obtain a bunch of general skills, most of them unnecessary, or whether they focused on their own weapon and style.

"I hate goblins."

Each level provided more and more knowledge, and required more and more time. It was no longer abstract experience. I saw and remembered hundreds of fights, without any 'censorship' this time. Compared to some of the opponents I saw, the goblins no longer looked so dangerous. After all, there were few master fighters among them, so they were mostly dangerous because of their number. Even the undead were a more difficult opponent for a spear fighter.

The masters in these visions didn't always win, on the contrary, the battle often ended in their death or injury. Sometimes it could be predicted, when the opponents were much stronger and more numerous, or the weapon wasn't suitable for the fight. Other times, it was unexpected, with an arrow shot from behind a corner or flames falling upon the battlefield. Quite often it was due to simple stupidity, from a desire to show off or a minor mistake. A reminder that one could never relax in a fight. Even an 'puny goblin' could kill a great warrior, if the stars aligned right.

An hour later I stopped, panting and feeling stronger than before. I had chosen duels among all the options, and now I had a much better understanding of the advantages and shortcomings of my weapon. I could probably call myself a spear master now, even by the standards of days when spearmen were everywhere. And there were still two levels left...

"Phew," I wiped the sweat off my brow and checked the requirements for the next level of *Spear fighting*. The first level was worth 10 SP, the second was worth 20, the third was worth 40, but the fourth was only 60, not 80 SP. Which was a relief, since I had worried that the progression would be geometric. This meant that 80 SP would cost as much as the last, fifth rank. In any case, I needed experience – a lot of experience, and the ways to obtain it were limited. The rules were simple — kill or be killed.

We froze, watching each other. A dark-haired guy of about twenty, European in appearance, with a narrow sword at his belt. His nickname was hidden, even though it was possible to display it in the settings. ***Identification.***

Lone Swordsman. Level 2

Well, the nickname was rather stupid, but certainly not the worst possibility. At least when displayed in the System language, it didn't reveal any information about his origins. His attributes were average, his level was also low, but nevertheless, it was clear that this wasn't the guy's first time here. The second veteran in a row. Was I lucky or was it a trend? After all, who was to say that the System hadn't gathered all the survivors in one wave?

"Glad to see a human being here!" the guy shouted. Still, he hadn't approached me and his hand hovered over the hilt of his sword. Sensible. Those who didn't comprehend that trusting strangers here was dangerous wouldn't survive for long. Not that caution was a guarantee of survival...

"I'm pleased to meet you, too," I said ambiguously. I tapped the card, drawing out my spear, twirled it and swung it to the right, using the point to draw a semicircle in the pavement dust. "Defend yourself or die."

I was getting tired of these games, but there was a way to solve all the issues on the spot. I slowly walked forward, holding the spear back and giving the young man a chance to react. I was also trying to figure out the easiest way to kill him. If I was really going to do it, of course.

"What are you doing?" The guy backed away, drawing his sword from its scabbard, and the smile on his face turned into a snarl.

He was getting ready to fight. Bad idea, in my opinion. Spear against sword, only the second level, so his weapons skill was no more than two. Moreover, given his six in *Intuition*, he knew almost nothing about me except my level. Was he counting on his skill? In his place, I would have tried to run away, or at least retreat indoors, where he would have the advantage. I didn't activate *Invisibility*, deciding instead to check how much my *Strength* had increased.

The guy sped up, trying to circle around the spear and get closer to me. I swung the spear, striking it flat against his hand. His fingers loosened, and the sword fell onto the road. He screamed and tried to grab it with his left hand, but stopped when my spear touched his neck.

I could wound him, place the Mask of Cain on his face and then kill him, not only receiving the gratitude of Inti, but also the legendary trophy sword...

"You..."

I shook my head, stepped back and rested the spear on my right shoulder. I had principles, too. Everyone I killed had given me good reason to do so, to save my life. The swordsman was not an enemy, and if I killed him simply for profit, I wouldn't be able to convince myself that it was justified.

My opponent picked up his sword and backed away. However, he didn't point the weapon at me or display any other hostility. Not a fool, then.

"You're not bad. At least you're not a

coward." I gave him a friendly smile. "How about we team up? We humans should stick together. If you're not too angry at me."

"I was all for it anyway. Why did you attack me? Did you want to see what I could do?"

"There were many reasons... Test my own skills, find out which of us is stronger. Besides, now you can be sure that I won't kill you just for the experience points."

"What if you'd lost? Do you think I wouldn't have killed you?"

It seemed that the guy had finally remembered that the System didn't approve the killing of allies. However, this wasn't a completely insurmountable ban. Considering how few experience points were awarded for goblins, most people who had made it to the second round had clearly broken it. Even if one could reach Level 2 by killing goblins, my third level literally screamed that I'd had to kill people. "Is that what you're asking me?" I said. "I just thought the risk was acceptable."

"Right. Are you in charge?" he changed the subject, rubbing his neck.

"It doesn't work that way. We all have a common goal here, and that is to survive and return home. I'm not interested in power per se, I just think it will be difficult to survive alone this time. If you decide that we won't get along, you can always leave."

"That sounds quite... honest. I agree."

"Great. I'm, um, Vasily," I said. I had to get used to my nickname, so that I wouldn't accidentally use my real name.

"The Lone Swordsman."

"Seriously? Are you a, um," I snapped my fingers. "Native American?"

"It's my nickname." He hesitated, but apparently decided that the name alone would do no harm. "My name is Dmitry. I'm from Moscow. My surname is..."

Russia? A lucky coincidence, but not so surprising, considering that there were a thousand players from all over the world. If I was to assume that the distribution was uniform, then around thirty players would be from Russia.

"I don't need to know your last name, Dmitry," I didn't force him to lie. "I can see that you have Level 2, but what about your skills?"

"Second rank swordsman, plus *Regeneration*."

Not bad. This was likely what had prompted the guy to take me on. My level was higher, but it suggested that I had invested very little in Spear fighting. The probability that I had already reached third rank was extremely low.

"Can you tell me more about Regeneration?" I asked. I had seen a similar skill, but it required a 10 in *Vitality*, which the guy didn't have.

"It's a passive skill based on *Stamina*. It's not much use at Level 1. Blood clots only a little faster, so even a slight wound take about half an hour to heal. At the same time, the skill saps strength and requires food. Still, I can regrow a severed finger in a month. Well, theoretically. Or a tooth, which I've tested in real life." Dmitry gave me a Hollywood smile, followed by a questioning look. It was my turn to open up.

"Third rank in *Spear fighting*, *Archery*, *Minor magical ability*, and first rank in *Identification*. *Identification* is a lot like *Help*, but provides more details. But it only works with System items. It's linked to *Wisdom*." I wasn't going to lie, but I decided not to share information about my *Invisibility* for now. What could I do if I was getting more and more paranoid with every person who wanted to kill me?

"You didn't score the best option, did you?" Dmitry said sympathetically. "The random is pretty bad here."

"Depends on how you look at it," I replied. He was the second person to mention random. I needed to figure out what it meant. "Information is useful, too. For example, the flask in the basic set of artifacts allows you to transport any liquid with you. Not just water. By the way, I almost forgot to say that I've also learned the local goblin language. Come on, we'll talk on the way."

It was the first time I could talk freely with a 'fellow victim', and learned plenty of interesting things at once. For example, although Dmitry received a free E-ranked skill at the end of the previous mission, he hadn't been able to choose it. He simply woke up in his private room at the end of the mission, with a *Regeneration* skill card next to him. The guy hadn't gotten access to the Server either, judging by my careful questioning. Why was that?

He had also received the Soul Stone, but his level of *Intuition* was too low to understand exactly what it was. Dmitry called it 'a small altar fragment' and didn't know of any other names.

In any case, he found a new gate upon his return to the room. The first thing he did was visit Odin's abode, which wasn't surprising, given the other options and the fact that the Scandinavian gods were best known after the Greek ones. Beyond the gate stood a temple where the other players were already roaming, but they didn't have much time to talk. Odin offered to dedicate Dmitry's 'small altar fragment' to him, promising patronage in return. Many agreed. It was much easier to agree to give an 'altar fragment' to some random god than a 'soul stone'. Your own soul, since you can't dedicate an inactive stone. What did it mean? Was it a translation error? An accident? The more I learned about this game, the stranger it seemed to me.

Dmitry didn't agree immediately and spent the time allocated by the System visiting the temples of other gods, where he received similar offers. Nevertheless, he ultimately returned to

Odin, and now his stone, among many others, served as part of the Norse deity's altar. This was how they build up their strength, apparently.

"Why him?" I asked. I didn't want to upset the guy by telling him that he had placed his own life in a stranger's hands.

"I don't know, Odin seems closer, somehow, culturally-speaking. There were no Slavic gods and Odin easily admitted that he was just one of the players who was a bit luckier than the others. Plus, he offered to make a deal straight away, while the others were kind of weird. As if they really believed that they are ancient gods. Whom did you pick, by the way?"

"No one. I got hit on the head, lay unconscious for who knows how long, and when I woke up, it was too late to visit the temples. I wasn't up to it, you know... I barely managed to reach the portal back to Earth. The timer had almost run out, and I didn't want to find out what happened next."

"Then you should definitely choose Odin. I think it'll be easier for acolytes of the same god to stick together. It's harder when you're alone."

The conversation was abruptly interrupted by a goblin rounding the corner. First level... He froze, then raced into a nearby building. We looked at each other and gave chase, but gradually began to fall behind. The goblin was running for his life, even dropping his weapon. He knew that nothing good would happen to him if he was caught, so he climbed onto the roof at the first opportunity and began to draw further away from us, making some very dangerous leaps with no hesitation.

"Nah, we won't catch him," Dmitry was the first to admit defeat, watching the goblin bound over roofs ahead of us.

I silently pulled out the old bow and sent an arrow after him. Given the low skill level, a hit could only be attributed to randomness, or if the goblin's luck was even worse than mine. The wound wasn't fatal as the arrow struck his leg, but now the goblin's fate was sealed.

We caught up with him five minutes later, by following the drops of blood. The goblin crouched against the wall, shaking with fear and holding the broken arrow in front of him. He was cursing obscenely as he tried in vain to give himself courage before he died.

"Wow, listen to that swearing. Are you going to finish him off?" Dmitry asked, watching the 'source of experience points' hungrily. It was like a drug, in a way. Or was the reason that he hadn't yet obtained the points he needed to avoid becoming a hero? In the literal and figurative sense.

"He's wounded, unarmed, and he knows that he will die soon. Don't you feel sorry for him?"

"Sorry for him? He's the enemy." Dmitry frowned. "It's either us or them. Better to think of it as a monster from one of those online games. Each of us has already gotten their hands dirty."

I sighed. He was right, it was easier, and yet I felt that such an attitude would be a mistake. Not that I was going to wag my finger and preach to him. We had made our choice the previous time, when we decided to kill for the System. I was sure that most hadn't limited themselves to goblins... "He's yours, then. I've already killed one, so you can finish this one off."

Dmitry stepped forward and slashed the goblin's arm with his blade, making the creature drop the arrow, then plunged his sword into the goblin's chest without a second thought. It was the first time I'd watched someone kill using a System weapon up close, so I tried to spot the energy we absorbed each time. It didn't work. Well, it would have been naive to expect otherwise. "Done."

Right. I dropped to one knee, bared the corpse's chest, and made an incision. I dug around in the wound with the dagger and pulled out a small, dull blue stone.

Mana Crystal. 34 units

That's it? It seemed that the amount depended on the goblin's level.

"What's that?" Dmitry asked, not even trying to look away.

"A mana stone. It's used for skills linked to *Wisdom*," I wiped the blood off the stone and tossed it to my partner. He caught it. Not a squeamish one, that's for sure.

I decided to take the goblin's body with me and put it in my bag. Although it added about three kilograms in weight, I already had some ideas for what to do with it in the future. While I was wiping my hands, Dmitry strolled to the edge of the roof and suddenly pointed down. "Look! I think it's a website address."

I followed his finger and saw a crooked inscription that I had left on the wall not so long ago. It was large enough to be seen from afar.

"Let's take a closer look."

It didn't make much sense, because you could see it from here, but I decided not to argue. We didn't want to jump across roofs again, so we found a staircase that hadn't completely collapsed, and carefully made our way down to the street. Once we reached the wall, Dmitry touched the 'pain', sniffed his fingers and announced, "It's blood."

Bingo. I could have brought paint into this world, but blood raised far fewer questions. Plus, unlike paint, I could drink it. Well, if I was truly desperate, I wasn't a vampire, after all.

"It's a pity we've got no internet here, there may be something useful on this site."

"We'll have a chance to check it out once we get back home, but I wouldn't count on finding all the answers there. It's probably a player who decided to get in touch with the others. I guess it won't do any harm to exchange information."

"You might be right," Dmitry said gloomily. "If the goblins are coming, as you said, it'll be hard to survive these three days. There's no food here, either, I'd only ever seen some sparrows. And insects. Do you think goblins are edible?"

"Let's not check," I said, smiling to show that I got the joke. "Even if we don't find any other food, we won't starve to death in three days." I'd taken the body for purposes unrelated to cooking.

I remembered a joke about a cannibal, who'd survived a plane crash. He was found sitting under a palm, surrounded by human bones. "I did it to survive," he said. "But the plane only crashed yesterday," the rescue commander objected. Yeah... Food was hard to come by here, so what seemed like a joke now might come true one day. Especially if the missions continued to increase in length. However, there was no point in thinking so far in advance and worrying about what might never happen. I didn't tell my companion about the flasks, some of which didn't contain blood but rather a much more nutritious liquid. Out of greed, I suppose?

"Let's go and have a look at the place where we encountered the goblin. His hiding place should be somewhere nearby, and therefore his personal belongings." Hadn't I seen tendrils of smoke in that direction? Another set of 'watchman's gear' would certainly come in handy.

CHAPTER 10

THE DUEL

FINDING AND PLUNDERING the goblin's camp wasn't too difficult. The encounter hadn't changed our plans, except that by running away, the native had made us deviate slightly from our route. Given the circular design of the city, players could only travel in two possible directions, either northwest or northeast. If I had correctly determined our location, we needed to go 'left' to get into the city. Going in the opposite direction, we would have to circle all the way around and would also reach the breaches in the wall sooner or later, but it would take much, much longer. Plus, we would have to cross the gaps leading to the outer part of the city, which was goblin territory.

Considering the size of the city, there was

absolutely no way we could have completed the main task and reached the temple last time. The trip alone would have taken longer than a day.

Since I had picked a direction and the local objectives had become easier, it made sense to team up with other players. Fortune smiled upon us soon enough, even before we reached the point where we had spotted the goblin. Nevertheless, when fortune smiles upon me, I get nervous.

"Thank goodness, people! Hooray!" shouted a rather attractive young woman of about twenty, pressing her hands to her breast. "Do you know what's going on here?"

"Right. Where the heck are we?" echoed her companion, making it abundantly clear that he wasn't scared. It was quite convincing. Well, even if he wasn't pretending, the fear would come later, together with the first corpses.

I, for one, was constantly afraid, and that was probably why I was still alive. Fear only made me stronger, forcing me to pull myself together and consider all possible risks. Both players were Level 1. They were obvious newbies, so I didn't see the point of wasting my mana on *Identification*, but I didn't let myself relax. It was still possible that they would attack, even if unlikely.

"We recently saw some weirdo... um, African-American here," said the girl with 'impressive' tolerance. "He was short and hideous-looking, and immediately ran away when he saw us."

Sometimes running isn't the best option. It was quite possible that it was the body of their goblin in my bag. Afrogoblin... Hmm... I wondered if this could be considered racist.

I glanced at my partner and suddenly noticed that Dmitry was looking anywhere but at the girl. Seriously? I wasn't that shy, so I didn't have to sneak glances at her. She really was something. The petite blonde was more than just pretty, and even the baggy clothes couldn't hide her shapely figure. But I was viewing her in a totally different light. She was short, with an impressive bust and not very long legs... Even without knowing her abilities, I could see that she was completely unsuited to fighting or running. To be brutally honest, I was looking at a future corpse. Or a breeder, if she was unlucky enough to be captured by the goblins.

In my mind, it didn't make any sense to start a romantic relationship with another player at this stage. Even 'just sex' was fraught with problems and hidden obligations. Like villains, knights didn't usually survive for long. The risk of making a mistake and dying was too high. Admittedly, I myself had finished off a goblin commander not that long ago, and had almost died at the hands of his followers. No matter how much I tried to convince myself that it had been based solely on logic, I couldn't fool myself. Who was I to stop others from making mistakes?

"Dmitry!" I tried to snap my partner out of it.

"Explain what's going on here to the newbies."

"Of course. Ahem... this is only our second time here. None of us players know where we are or what's going on, but it's all real. I advise you not to treat this as a game, a dream, or anything like that. Death is real here. If you don't complete your mission, you will remain in this world and will probably never return to Earth. The dark creature you saw was a goblin, and the goblins are our main enemies. Vasily, will you show them?"

I thought about it, then pulled the body out of my bag and let them examine the native. Their reaction to the corpse dropping onto the road was... different. They went equally pale, but the guy also suddenly threw up.

"Don't feel sorry for him," I said coldly. "If there had been more goblins, they would have attacked you, killing you for the cards and experience points. Although they prefer to take women prisoner, as they say that human women give birth to strong children."

I nodded at Dmitry to continue, and watched their reactions. "What's your mission?"

"Get one unit of experience and survive for at least three days," the girl replied. "The reward is a rank E skill and a doubling of the points earned..."

Although the reward was basically the same as the one I had received, there were several significant differences. Last time, I had spent a day in this world, and I had to look for the goblins. This time, the newcomers have three to nine days, and the enemies would find them. Those who hold out long enough, prove themselves in battle and survive, can easily become much stronger than the veterans of the "first wave". I wasn't too pleased with this idea. In simpler terms, to remain at the level of the second wave leaders, I had to either fight twice as hard or stay here twice as long. The newcomers could also stay for longer, although given the low experience requirements and high risks, most were unlikely to do so. Perhaps nobody could. If I didn't help them... In addition, newcomers weren't tainted by the murder of their allies, which meant that they were less likely to get stabbed in the back. I considered the 'suicide squad' before me with fresh eyes. While I had previously planned to recruit veterans to my squad, I now revised my plans.

"The only way to earn System points that we know of is killing," Dmitry continued. "And you must use a System weapon, the one you received as a card."

"Murder?" the girl's eyes grew moist. I could have sworn there was a flicker of guilt and helplessness on Dmitry's face. It looked like the girl could wrap him around her little finger, if she wanted to.

"Otherwise you'll stay here forever and be killed by the goblins," I interrupted. "We had to obtain twenty System points on our first mission. For that we had to kill ten goblins. You'll only have to kill one. In addition to the goblins, there's also the undead. The creatures are stronger, but also give you more experience points." I sighed, feeling the slight twinge of headache. It was like a warning, since all newbies would have similar questions. "Tell us about yourself. Your name and nickname, which weapon you choose."

The young woman's name was Lisa, she was from the UK, and she had chosen a rapier as her weapon. Not a bad choice for a woman, and there was every chance she could finish off a goblin in a one-on-one skirmish. If the goblins fought fairly, of course, and didn't attack en masse or throw stones or arrows at them. Still, the rapier was a duelist's weapon, and lost most of its advantages in a group fight. Nevertheless, it was a surprisingly good choice for a woman who didn't want to kill.

The guy's name was Hans and, according to him, he was a full-blooded German. Like me, he had chosen a spear as his weapon. It was hard to find fault with this choice without questioning one's own, although the shape... His spear was overly ornate.

Their nicknames, were different, however: the girl called herself Elle, and the guy Siegfried. At this point, I was sure that the German guy had noticed how Dmitry was looking at his companion, and seemed a little jealous. Even though he had met her for the first time only an hour earlier! What a bloody melodrama. For a moment, I wanted to solve this nascent love triangle by murdering all three of them.

"Alright, since we've introduced ourselves, I suggest that we keep going. We'll discuss the rest on the way."

The conversation was a long one, so Dmitry continued to describe the situation on the move, trying to make it clear what difficult circumstances they were in. However, they could only truly appreciate it through experience. The undead, goblins, gods, the high mortality... I listened to some of his thoughts with interest myself. Not forgetting to monitor the situation around us, however.

After the first meeting, we began to encounter individual players, and even groups, quite regularly. Some squads were even larger than ours. My suspicions turned out to be wrong. Most of the players were, sadly, beginners with no idea of what to do or where to go. There were far fewer veterans, and they weren't much better, differing only in that they looked warier.

Conversations and more conversations... I understood their concerns, but repeating the same thing for the tenth time brought me nothing but irritation. If I could smuggle something in here from our world, I'd definitely try to print some information brochures, as well as bringing weapons.

However, we didn't exactly waste our time. The information about the upcoming goblin invasion, which Dmitry and I shared freely, convinced most people about which way they should go. If, at first, we had to explain this ourselves, the information then began to spread faster and faster, acquiring rumors and further details, without our involvement.

Not that I could call the players gathered around us a squad. It was just a crowd going in the same direction, without a single commander or a global goal, for that matter. People stuck together only because it seemed the safest option for everyone. The fact that I had chosen the direction didn't make me their leader. Many of the people who joined later were unaware of this fact. Once the crowd exceeded fifty people, I decided to try and sort things out a little and stopped, raising my hand.

"Listen up!" Even if they couldn't see my hand, my shout was sure to draw their attention. "You may not know this, but I was the one who obtained the information about the goblin army and chose the direction to go! However, it's too dangerous to continue travelling this way. We need lookouts and scouts. Are there any volunteers?"

The players began to exchange glances and talk, but none stepped forward to volunteer. At once, there were those who didn't like my attempt to take charge. I knew this would happen, didn't

I?

"Why are you suddenly giving orders?" protested a pot-bellied man of about fifty, with an impudent and discontented face. He looked like such a politician. Level 1? This was ridiculous, he wasn't even holding his spear properly, rather leaning on it like a stick. I think he simply didn't quite understand where he was and what was going on, and was acting resentful out of habit. A very bad habit, since it gave me a chance to teach the others a lesson.

"You have a problem with what I've just said?" I asked coldly while giving him a disparaging look. Once upon a time, I had spent ages practicing this expression in front of a mirror. It was meant to incite my opponent to want to punch me in the face, or shut up instead. "Would you like to cross spears? Or can you only use yours as a walking stick?"

I pointed my spear at him. The man took several steps back and looked around for support, but most people just stepped away from him. His eyes shifted around frantically. He wasn't going to fight, and I wasn't planning to kill him. Now all that was left was reinforce the idea.

"Are you picking on the weak?"

I had been afraid of something like this, as a proverbial Batman stepped forward. Figuratively speaking, as my new opponent's name was Bai Hu. Even if I didn't know what it meant, the System kindly provided me with a translation:

White Tiger. His looks hinted at an Asian background, but he was also very solidly built. Third level... Even without using *Identification*, I could guess that he had invested most of his points in *Strength*, and the rest into *Agility*.

Basically, I was being challenged by one of the strongest players here. The majority were Level 1 novices, and even the veterans had mostly reached only the second level. To reach Level 3, they would have had to kill a ridiculous number of goblins in their search for 'good and justice'. Or a much more modest number of people. Now this man, whose hands had to be covered in blood, was trying to tell me how to behave?

"And if I am, my stripy friend?" I chuckled, letting my first victim disappear into the crowd. It was obvious that the Asian man was looking for an excuse to fight and I had readily provided one.

"I don't like your behavior. Just because you have a big spear doesn't make you a general. I agree that it is time for us to organize ourselves, but what about the principles of democracy? What about choosing one who is worthy?"

Was he seriously planning to fight me for power? I didn't believe it. All my instincts told me that he hadn't come out here to talk at all. "Shall we hold a referendum, then?" I snorted. "How are you doing with independent observers?"

"You shouldn't laugh at what our ancestors have achieved," Bai Hu said with a sanctimonious shake of his head. "You're European, aren't you?"

"If you really need to know, I'm Russian."

"Oh, I see... Vodka, babushka dolls, dictatorship," he smiled like a cat that got the cream. As if I had confessed to some terrible crime.

"You're Chinese, aren't you?" I ignored the taunt. Hello, dictatorship. "How does your communism combine with your ardent commitment to democracy?"

"Not all Han people live in China and believe in communism and the wisdom of the Party. Russians don't believe in it either, do you? Why shouldn't I have my own opinion about this?"

The whole situation smacked of surrealism. We were in the middle of who-knows-where, the goblins were coming, and we were discussing politics? Which I never gave a damn about. I'm sure the other guy didn't care either. Then what the hell?

"Enough of this crap," I sighed. "Get to the point. What do you want?"

"I don't like you. I suggest that we resolve our differences in a fair fight."

"Might makes right, as our ancestors believed?"

The Asian man gave me a grim smile as he pulled a bastard sword out of a card and slung it over his shoulder. I almost felt relief, since the conversation had been getting tiresome. So, he wants a fight. Since he had gone this far, I doubted that he would be satisfied with a simple show of force. How was he planning to circumvent the

System's ban on murder? Perhaps he had one of the ten masks? I wasn't going to pull my own mask out in this crowd, but it would be useful to obtain a second one that lacked a divine curse...

"You know how to get around the ban?"

"My skill is called *Duelist* and will allow us to solve this little problem. An honest one-on-one match, with the System itself monitoring the rules. The winner gets everything. By the way, let's agree right now that since my E rank ability is not a combat skill, you won't use yours either."

Attention! The Player Bai Hu, No. 325, challenges you to a duel.
There will be no punishment for murder in this match.
Accept/Decline?

I said nothing. I wasn't planning to make any promises, but if he had announced the rules, was the System going to monitor their compliance? In any case, there was no way to retreat honorably. While we had been talking, the other players had formed a wide circle around us. People were always ready to watch someone else fight while they remained safe. Only now we were in a city filled with goblins and the undead, and since nobody was in charge, none of the players were even keeping watch. It was... annoying. How many people did I have to kill to make the others listen to reason?

"Well? Are you going to fight or are you afraid?" Bai Hu threw back his head. Such big words!

"A fight to the death?" I clarified, studying the inscription floating somewhere at the edge of my consciousness.

"Of course not, it's just a friendly match," Bai Hu replied, in blatant disregard of his own intentions. Yet there were those who believed him. "But the sword lacks eyes, so don't blame me if I don't stop in time."

I pulled a face. Seriously? The man was nearly thirty and was clearly planning to kill me, yet didn't shy away from uttering such pretentious phrases. The sword lacks eyes. Why don't you shove that sword right up your...

Naturally, I kept this wish to myself and only waved my hand, snatching the spear 'out of thin air'. Fine, why not? "If you want a fight to the death, there's no point in making excuses. By the way, this will be my eleventh fight. I didn't lose any of the previous ten."

Accept. Out of the corner of my eye, I noticed a circle of light appear around us and slowly expand, causing the audience to back away.

"Make room, I need space for my skill!" Bai Hu shouted belatedly.

The people backed away faster. The slowest ones, who were held in place by the back rows, found themselves inside the circle, and their nicknames began to slowly turn yellow. From the haste with which they left the area, I wasn't the only one to suspect that the yellow would be followed by a different color — red.

Attention! You are forbidden to leave the Circle until the end of the match.

The System didn't explain what breaking this rule might entail. The circle stabilized, and Bai Hu suddenly leaped forward, hoping to catch me off guard. It was very obvious... I was frankly surprised that he had the guts to challenge me directly. He was probably betting on his skill level in *Sword fighting*, which was the maximum for our level. Plus the points he had invested in his physical parameters. Still, it wasn't enough. A few blows, one of which almost got him, and he quickly retreated out of range of my weapon.

"What's going on?" I shouted. "Leaving already?" We had exchanged only a few blows, and I was already sure that he had the same rank as me. But I was stronger. Didn't he have any other tricks up his sleeve?

"You have the third rank!" he exclaimed, as if I had deceived him in some way. "Qing Long, you dog, you tricked me!"

I only smiled wryly, not allowing myself to get distracted by further bickering. It sounded like the White Tiger had been set up. I took a step forward, and the man jumped back. Bai Hu might have wanted to stop the fight, but I didn't give him the chance. We paused in front of each other, straining every muscle and our attention. In a real battle and without armor, the outcome is determined very quickly. One mistake and blood will flow, and then time will work against you.

"You remember that I didn't promise not to use my skill?" The provocation worked and Bai Hu rushed forward without waiting for me to reveal my skill. I swung my spear forward to meet him, then stepped aside and abruptly changed the trajectory of the spear. The sword that tried to parry my blow sliced through the air, and its owner spun after it. Realizing that he had made a mistake, the man screamed and tried to jump back, but my spear was faster and struck him hard in the back. Bai Hu desperately tried to jab his sword into my flesh, but failed to reach me. I put a little pressure on the shaft, causing my enemy to fall down. My foot landed on his hand, which was still clutching the sword. His fingers snapped, and his scream made my ears ring. I kicked his weapon to the edge of the circle and could finally believe that it was over. I had won.

"Mercy, mercy," there was nothing but horror in the man's voice this time. "Don't kill me."

Sometimes we notice the strangest things, and now, as I looked around me, I noticed that although many in the audience had shuddered, almost nobody turned away. A battle to the death, a victory... Why didn't I feel any satisfaction? There was only intense fatigue.

Mercy? How did he think that would work? I didn't need to be a doctor to know that he was in a bad way. I hadn't held back my blow, and although the spear was still plugging the wound, it was bleeding profusely. As soon as I pulled the weapon out, his blood would start gushing. Even if he didn't die of blood loss or shock, he wouldn't be able to last three days here. Still I hesitated... "Which god do you serve?" I asked, buying myself time to think.

"Guan Yun." the Chinese man admitted. How predictable. "Mercy."

Attention! Your opponent has surrendered and begs for mercy! Complete the fight? Yes/No

I ignored the notification, taking my time with the answer. The anger had mostly faded. It was hard to stay mad at a person who was practically dead and who hadn't even managed to wound me. But what next? I suspected that if I accepted my victory, the spear in the body of my enemy would be somehow unacceptable to the System. If I pulled out the spear, the man would be dead within a minute, yet I wouldn't receive any points... Some would call this terrible cynicism but it would be hypocritical of me not to make use of the fruits of my labor. If you catch a fish or kill an animal, you must eat it, otherwise their death has been in vain, and your act is nothing but senseless cruelty. So why should I let the White Tiger die for nothing?

"Is there anyone here with sufficient healing skills who wants to help this loser?"

Several players who had traveled in the same group shook their heads and retreated. One of them, also possessing Level 3, sneered and I saw his lips whisper something. "Kill him", perhaps? Well, well, well, Qing Long, I presume?

My guesses were unnecessary since nicknames could be seen in the settings, and the player wasn't hiding his. The other spectators remained silent, although I noted several who had at least reacted to my query. My future group would need a healer, preferably one who could also fight, and not just have the appropriate skill. This was one of the reasons why I hesitated. The other reason was that I wanted to shut up my potential accusers, so I was giving them a chance, and if they all kept quiet, they would share the responsibility for his death. It didn't matter that their skill level was too low to heal such a wound. I wasn't sure that he could be saved even using modern medicine. They could join forces, right? But for that I needed an order and not a request.

"I... I'm studying to be a doctor," Lisa suddenly offered. "I could bandage him up, if..."

She indicated the border that kept her from getting any closer. I shook my head. I could have applied a bandage myself, even sewed up the wound, but the White Tiger would die anyway. "Do you really think a dressing will save him?"

The girl looked away, confirming the verdict. Well, it was time to end this farce. I pulled the spear free, shifted my grip and struck again. A short cry, and a wave of heat ran down my arm, leaving behind a couple of system messages in my peripheral vision.

Attention! You have gained 24 SP! (24/60)
Attention! The fight is over! All restrictions have been removed.

"Sorry, the spear doesn't have eyes either," I paraphrased the dead man. I felt neither happy nor guilty. It was becoming easier and easier to kill.

The circle that protected us from interference faded. Then a light flashed over the corpse, leaving a softly glowing card hanging in the air. The light was brighter than during previous times.

Duelist skill card.

Rank: E.
Level: 1/5.
Description:
— Allows duels with allies. Requires the consent of the opponent.
— Allows dueling conditions to be established.

— Creates a **field of battle**. Interference from outside players is prohibited by the System.

— Upon the death of the owner, the Duelist card drops out with a 99% probability.

— Significantly increases the chance of the loser dropping the strongest available ability.

Saturation:

100/100 SP

An E rank skill card that was ready to be learned? This was slightly suspicious, especially considering its purpose was to permit fights between players. Was I being paranoid, or was the System preventing us from killing each other with one hand and pushing us to do the same with the other? Nevertheless, the temptation was too great and the card too valuable for me to pass up this chance. I was sure that as soon as I picked it up, many people noticed that it was slightly different from the standard one.

Study. The card flashed and faded in color, indicating that it had already been used. The process took place without any unpleasant effects on the body. I carefully put the card in one of the pockets – they were surprisingly strong, and if I filled all the slots, I'd have a decent armored jacket. I closed my eyes a little, examining the new possibilities...

Mana was not required for activation since the skill was completely System-based. As I had suspected, it was possible to choose the terms of the match. My conscience could be clear – the bastard had really been planning to finish me off in a death match. Otherwise, Bai Hu would have chosen another option. The reason? The reason was obvious, greed. He hadn't been overly lucky with the advanced card, and he wanted my skill.

I dropped to one knee and closed the corpse's eyes, then quickly searched him, removing the bag and pulling several maps from his pockets. One card was for his sword, the other for a fancy short dagger. Considering his level, there wasn't much loot. It looked like he had left the other cards somewhere else... Or with someone else?

"My name is Vasily!" I suddenly proclaimed as I stood up. "This was the fifth player I'd killed. I know this figure will horrify many of you, but I have nothing to be ashamed of. I didn't stab my allies in the back, and everyone I killed had wanted me dead. I didn't just fight people! I have killed at least fifteen goblins. Including two chieftains, who had Level 8 and 9. I also saw and personally laid to rest one of the undead!" I gazed over the crowd, assessing the results of my short speech. There might have been fewer goblins, since I had shot a large number of them with arrows and they might have survived, but in that case, I could have even said that there were twenty of them. Nevertheless, even this estimate was impressive, and not just to me. Although I had to admit that not everyone looked at me with approval. "I don't like long speeches! I possess the *Goblin language* as one of my skills. I captured one and learned a lot about the goblins' plans and where we are now. Does everyone know that the natives have gathered a huge army and will soon come for us? It will be difficult, if not impossible, for us to survive alone. This was why I had stepped forward and asked for some scouts. What did I get in return? This man wanted to kill me, and all of you just stood by and watched to see how it would end."

I felt a growing anger. Perhaps not everything in my speech was true, but here and now, I almost believed my own words. "I won't be responsible for all of you, and I don't crave power. I'm not going to comfort newbies or make excuses for myself! My squad needs people who can help each other survive and become stronger. People who are ready to fight and who are ready to kill. Who will not abandon a friend or stab him in the back, too! If there are such among you, think about it and come with me."

"Qing Long?" I guessed, looking at the man who had come up to me. He seemed to be between thirty and forty years old. He also didn't suffer from excess modesty. The Azure Dragon... Second animal in the zodiac. Big name. How many other 'dragons' were in the crowd, I wondered.

"Congratulations on your victory, Vasily."

"I assume you had a hand in what happened? You don't you feel sorry for your... ally?"

"Not at all. Although we are technically on the same side, it would be more accurate to call us competitors. Bai Hu was half-Chinese, had been born in the United States, had never been to his homeland, and did not even speak Chinese properly. Nevertheless, he sought to be the high priest of Guan Yu!" Qing Long shook his head in disapproval. Well, I wasn't the only one here with the ability to justify any wrongdoing in my own eyes. I was more interested in something else, however.

"I hope he didn't get the job?" I queried. It would be extremely unfortunate to run into another curse. The question was more rhetorical, since I had received no curse after the death.

"If you had killed a priest, you would have felt it," the man reassured me. "No, Guan Yu is wise and did not rush into making this choice. He has no priests. The one who will achieve the highest results this time, will become the High Priest. You've made things a lot easier for me."

"You're very, ah, frank."

"Why not? I do not want any misunderstanding or animosity between us. You are not stupid. I will admit that thanks to my *Eye of the Serpent*, I can see other people's skills, so I convinced him that you were only at Level 2. Greed blinded him."

I wondered what had blinded Qing Long to make him decide to get rid of a competitor using someone else's hands? Why wasn't he ashamed of it? "Well, happy to help," I said, accepting the apology.

"I am glad you do not hold grudges," replied the Azure Dragon. "Although he was not my friend, I would like to take care of the body."

I glanced at the corpse. I wondered if mana crystals were found only inside goblins, or if the players had a similar anomaly. Still, my curiosity wasn't so great as to cut out the dead man's heart in front of dozens of players. Under normal circumstances, I would have stripped him of all his other equipment, but now such pettiness seemed out of place. "Certainly. You can take the body."

"Thank you. I think we can discuss our plans later in the evening, once more players have gathered. Until then, the others and I will keep order."

The Azure Dragon did not get his own hands dirty. Several of his companions approached the corpse, stripped it and placed the body in a bag. All that was left on the ground was a pile of stained clothing. They didn't attempt to take any of my loot.

"You can share the rest if one of you needs something." I had a spare set in my bag, but not everyone was able to keep their equipment in one piece, so there were immediate takers. A brief scuffle broke out over the boots, after which the winner tried one on, then threw the boot at his bloodied rival. The left boot. I looked at the winner's status. Strangely enough, the System didn't react to this behavior. Did it only respond to murder? Or when one received energy from the dead? It was an interesting question that could only be tested experimentally. I wasn't quite ready to kill people for the sake of satisfying my curiosity. Why? Because I believed in humanity. I was certain that someone else would satisfy my curiosity sooner or later.

My victory in the duel, in addition to my loot, brought me twenty-four of the sixty points needed to reach Level 4. The eternal choice between what was best now and what would be advantageous in the future. I could save them or invest them in one of two skills, increasing my *Archery* or *Magical ability*. The first would increase my long-range ability, while the second would allow me to use *Invisibility* for longer. Both were good, but the increase in parameters that I would get once I went up a level was also very tempting. Maybe if I increased my *Intelligence*, I'd stop doing so many stupid things.

The speech also bore fruit. Although no one was in a hurry to join my team yet, people were clearly assessing me, and the crowd began to look much more like a proper squad. At least groups of scouts had set out in both directions, and veterans had positioned themselves along the flanks, allowing the newcomers to take cover inside the formation. It was rather pointless at present, since the goblins were supposedly far away, but it was better to get used to this sort of thing in advance.

"Wooooo..."

I winced at the harsh sound. One of the veterans had found a horn, which he periodically blew into, playing some modern tune. I couldn't identify the melody. Both the instrument and the bugler's musical hearing left much to be desired, but it became much more difficult to miss our approach, and we began encountering players more often.

We didn't see any live goblins, on the other hand. The signal fires had long since burned out, and the watchers had either fled or died. I stopped beside two bodies of goblins who had the misfortune to meet people before us. Very greedy people, it seemed, for the corpses had been stripped down to their underwear. Why the hell would they need goblin clothing? I didn't think other goblins had done this, since the heads hadn't been cut off, which meant that the corpses could turn into the undead at any moment. A source of increased danger and increased experience. Hmm.

"The goblin's corpse is almost whole," Dmitry said quietly, but he didn't rush to disembowel it.

I nodded. Although 'whole' was an

exaggeration since they had sustained a number of wounds, but there was no characteristic hole in the chest. The killers obviously hadn't known about the mana crystals. Just like most of the players.

We weren't the only ones interested in the bodies, and many newcomers who had never seen a goblin gathered around them. Some found it hard to look at the dead, and some even appeared to feel sorry for the goblins. I felt a flash of annoyance. Over the next three days, many of us were bound to be killed by the relatives of these 'poor buggers'. "When I first landed here, I had hoped to make a deal with the natives," I said to nobody in particular. "But the very first goblins I met had been standing over the body of the player they had killed. There were half-erased drawings on the ground. He didn't want to fight them and had tried to negotiate with them. The goblins pretended to be interested, then attacked, broke his legs, and hacked him to death with his own sword for the sake of the experience points. There were three of them, and they were the first goblins I had killed. That's why today, when I look at these corpses, I don't feel sorry for them. I feel satisfaction. We're in the middle of a war, and the sooner you accept it, the better!"

"Well said," Dmitry responded, clapping his hands and thereby reducing the melodramatic tone. "You're starting to enjoy making speeches, aren't you?"

I looked at the bodies again. There were too many people around us to hide the extraction of the crystals. Of course, we could have taken the bodies with us and extracted the crystals later, but I didn't think there was a point in hiding this information any longer. Otherwise, how many of these stones, which could increase our chances of survival, would remain inside the dead goblins? How many would I be able to extract myself before this information becomes public? After all, money's no use to you if you're dead. "That's not all you need to know! Apart from the cards that sometimes fall out of the dead, there are also mana crystals inside the goblins. Here, near the heart."

I drew my dagger, cut open the goblin's chest with a few quick strokes and carefully dug out a blue stone. I repeated the process with the second corpse, pulling out a very similar but slightly larger stone. "The higher the level, the larger the crystal. They are very small, as you can see. This one contains forty mana units, while this one has fifty."

"What do you do with them?" someone asked.

"There are skills that use mana. The veterans have them, and you may obtain them in the future. If you find and kill a goblin, I recommend extracting the crystal. I'm sure they'll be in demand in the future."

I placed the goblin corpses in my bag, which immediately grew five kilos heavier. I didn't touch the other corpses I saw, leaving them for those who wanted to check the truth of my words. Although not everyone wanted to dig around inside dead goblins, there were always a few who were willing to do so. All I had to do was make sure that the bodies were put into bags. "We must take the goblin bodies with us. If we leave them like this, they will turn into the undead sooner or later. The bags stop this from happening. We can cut off their heads, but we need the whole bodies."

"What for?" asked one of my recruits. A bag is not a backpack, and even a couple of extra kilos were very noticeable. Nevertheless, I was in no hurry to reveal my plan.

"You'll see when we find the right place. I'm sure you'll like it."
If we were lucky, some of the corpses would rise up as the undead, and the newbies would be able to acquire the experience points that they needed for this mission. Even a training match, with veterans controlling the situation, was worth a lot.

CHAPTER 11

THE GATHERING

THE MORE PEOPLE gathered, the more difficulties we were having. People got into arguments, developed blisters on their feet, and simply wanted to eat, drink, and rest. Less than ten hours had passed since the start of the mission, yet most players had already emptied their flasks, and it wasn't easy to replenish water supplies in a dead city. Of course, I had enough water left, but only if I considered my group. If I was to divide it among everyone, there would be no water at all.

"Thus they went into the ruins full of monsters and all died of thirst," I muttered.

"And an hour later turned into the undead." Dmitry added grimly.

Things weren't quite so dire yet. The goblins

used to have a primitive plumbing system that supplied water to the public fountains and even private homes, but it hadn't survived to this day. Now these remnants of former, but not so distant, glory served as a reminder that the local goblins weren't savages.

A second source of water were the stone basins in wealthy homes, designed to collect rainwater. The water didn't inspire much confidence since the tanks hadn't been cleaned in a long time, but there were drains provided, so it was still possible to drink it. Some people had been willing to drink it and they didn't look like they were going to drop dead just yet. Morons.

The third option were the public wells, some of which were still being used by goblins. Many were covered and equipped with ropes and even buckets. The problem was that there weren't that many wells, and there wasn't enough water in them to sate everyone. In addition, the goblins knew that the players were coming and could have easily prepared by poisoning the wells.

"I hate goblins."

Of course, the last and safest option was the sky. I doubted the goblins could send down toxic rain. Unfortunately, the clouds didn't look ready to share their life-giving moisture. Even the puddles had dried up since the last rain.

"A well! A full well!" The returned scouts shared the good news, and the column changed its route slightly and accelerated. We soon came to a large square. The first thing that caught my eye was a massive pile of partially burned wood, coals, and ash, with a lot of charred and cracked bones. Not only goblin bones, but human ones as well. The skulls were hard to mix up.

"A funeral pyre," Dmitry stated the obvious.

It was a clear answer to why the whole city wasn't littered with corpses and where they went. The goblins couldn't leave the bodies lying around since they would turn into the undead sooner or later. Burying them was useless. Even cutting off the corpse's head was only a temporary measure that would prevent it from rising up for a few days. Take the dead out of the city? Too difficult, given the size of the capital and the number of players who have died here in the past month. Just as many goblins had probably been killed, too.

I suddenly wondered what seven thousand dead in a single month meant to them. This figure was a drop in the ocean for Earth, but a serious loss for this medieval state, likely significantly devastating the neighboring settlements. At least the army of the Goblin Prince was clearly gathering somewhere else, and surely had fewer locals. This meant that even if we were all killed, yet the System continued to make up for the losses and send in new players, the goblins would eventually lose control of this city, and either die or retreat.

"Unfortunately," I muttered, "neither you nor I would be alive by this point." How many of us would survive the coming carnage, and would it be the last one? I doubted it. It was important to remember that capturing the temples was a matter of principle for the goblins. Even if they were defeated, they would return again and again.

I could only guess at the actual goblin losses. This square, for example, contained just a few hundred corpses, which had been hurriedly burned, with half of them human. They had been burned a while ago, about two or three weeks... The fire hadn't been touched since.

If I were a goblin, I wouldn't have put so many bones in one pile, but since they had done this, they were sure that the remains wouldn't turn into some kind of 'bone dragon' one day. Or whatever the undead turned into here. To think that they had set this up as a trap for us would be exceedingly paranoid.

"Time for a rest!" I shouted, not really caring how many players would follow the suggestion. "Look for shelter and water, and rest!"

Although the duel had strengthened my reputation, my opinion was only just *listened* to. Because they were afraid of me, I guess. Now I had a better understanding of why the group that the goblins had slaughtered in the previous mission had been led by an obvious player killer. There hadn't been a leader who had dared to challenge him... and remained alive after that, of course. I was in a much more precarious situation, and I felt that if I went even a little too far, the people would turn against me. Nobody would arrange a 'fair fight' this time. There were plenty of other people in this crowd who wanted to give the orders. We still had to reach an agreement, somehow.

So, I wasn't going to push it, but I didn't see anyone who decided to continue walking. Several voices took up the call. Everyone knew where we were heading, and people clearly weren't keen to approach the goblin fortress in a proud but small group.

According to my calculations, we were getting close to the fortress. Quite a lot of players had gathered, but they weren't ready for battle in their current state. It was quite possible that we would stay here for a while, at least until we figured out what to do next. At worst, I'd take the people wanting to come with me, and we'd slip into the city on our own. It was risky, but better than waiting for a goblin horde. In the end, I was just trying to give the others a chance, and it was up to them how they used it.

"We'll take this house. Siegfried, make sure none of the others get in here."

Despite the pile of bones close by, it was a good place to rest. The square was surrounded by solid buildings that provided shelter from the weather, and their walls were thick enough to protect us from enemies, if needed. In addition, the goblins seemed to have repeatedly conducted burnings here, and had gathered enough wood for us to build fires. Or could we try and heat the indoor stoves? The well was full, and the rich houses contained reservoirs of rainwater that we could try to boil. There were plenty of trees bearing fruit that, as far as I knew, the goblins ate... They looked almost ripe. It was the perfect place to rest. If I were a goblin, I would have set a trap here, or at least put something in the water.

"Be careful with the water!" I shouted. "The goblins could have poisoned the wells. Fill up your canteens, but don't drink yet." All I could do was share this thought with those around me. Those who would listen. I couldn't stop the others from drinking, but I could wait a while and see if my fears were well founded. Too cynical? Perhaps. Even if I could dissuade someone from inadvertently eating alien fruit, it was harder to deal with thirst. After all, if we didn't learn to drink the local water, we wouldn't last even the three days.

"I can check the water," One of the nearby veterans suddenly admitted. "My skill allows me to distinguish the edible from the inedible. But I don't want my ability to be widely known."

"That would be great... Sahel. Come with me."

Although his skill couldn't help to annihilate the goblins, it was extremely useful here and now.

✳ ✳ ✳

After checking the well and making sure that the water was clean, we left without announcing the results. If there was no risk, why deprive people of the chance to perform a feat? I was certain that someone would try the water soon. We left a couple of people to fill our flasks and headed for the fruit trees. Most looked vaguely like apples.

For some reason, I suddenly remembered a poem I had learned at school many years ago. It told of a caravan that found an oasis in the middle of the steppe, but cut down the three palm trees there to make a fire. The caravan left, the spring disappeared without the trees, and the oasis became just another piece of desert. The goblins, even though they were frequent visitors here, were smarter and hadn't touched the fruit trees. Even if it seemed much easier to chop them down for firewood than to hunt around for suitable branches. Would anything remain here after we left?

Sahel turned an apple around in his hands for a minute, and a green inscription suddenly appeared above the fruit:

Apple (63%)... Edible.

In other words, his skill didn't just show what was edible, it also made the object part of the System. If I had this skill, I could bring food into this world in my bag. Sahel couldn't do so, since I could see that his skill was only at Level 1.

Sixty-three percent of correspondence? Without thinking about it, I tapped the three dots and renamed the fruit *Goblin apple*.

Attention! System expansion... Database update... Please wait...

The System froze for a second and then abruptly labeled all the trees around us. Judging by the surprised shouts, the labels were visible to all.

"Can everyone see this?" I asked.

"Goblin apple?" Lisa read, plucking one. "Do you think they taste good?"

"We better start with making sure they're edible. Sahel?"

The correspondence percentage had disappeared. I narrowed my eyes, and the number reappeared a second later. One hundred percent? In other words, the System accepted this term as being correct? Weird.

"They're edible." Sahel wiped the fruit on his sleeve and bit into it. He grimaced but kept chewing. "They're even good for you but they're sour. I hope none of you have stomach problems."

Perhaps I should have waited a couple of hours to make sure my test subject didn't die in agony, but there were some things the System didn't cheat on, so I took the chance. You couldn't be afraid of everything, could you?

The apples were very sour, and it was hard to tell why. Maybe they weren't yet ripe, maybe they'd gone wild, or maybe it was their normal taste. They reminded me of green apples and weren't bad on the whole, but only as a snack. The thought of these apples being a major part of our diet for the next three days was rather depressing. The others couldn't resist trying them too.

"All right, enough grimacing, let's harvest these fruits. I recommend gathering a three-day supply, because soon there won't be anything left."

Was I born to say the obvious while looking wise? Nobody tried to argue, and we deftly stripped a few trees. I was right in my assumptions, and not a single apple was left by the time evening came, although there had been plenty of them.

The house I had chosen as a temporary base was relatively small, but it had three floors, a rainwater tank, and, most importantly, a basement. It was deep, dark, and cold. The owners had probably stored food here once upon a time, but almost nothing remained after all these years. Only an empty 'honeycomb' in the corner, similar to what people used to store bottles of wine on Earth. It was the perfect place for an undead nursery.

"Unload the bodies."

Although the bag significantly reduced their weight, the goblins weren't that light and still ended up weighing 4-6 kilos. Few people wanted to carry around such a weight, so the bodies had been distributed among 'volunteers'.

I had a second-level bag that reduced the weight even more, still, I was happy to get rid of the bodies. We had managed to collect twelve corpses with varying degrees of damage. The sight of some of them made me want to turn away, but I kept my outward composure.

It was unpleasant, but we had to get used to it. This was our future. Battles, murder, and, quite possibly, a violent death. Just like these goblins. Each one had been alive only a day ago, with their own dreams and aspirations and... I didn't care. The memory of them killing other players and pursuing me was a good way to erase any stupid feelings of pity. Even now, the goblins were holding hundreds of our people captive. Any one of them would be glad to kill me, given the chance. I didn't feel any real hatred, however. Only the determination to survive and give my allies the chance to survive as well. Even if they stubbornly resisted it.

There were probably a lot more observers in the area, but the bodies we found were enough for my idea. After all, all necromancers had to start somewhere, right? I rubbed my hands together as it was cold in the basement. "Now we need to tie them up," I revealed the next step in the plan.

Due to a lack of alternatives, we bound them with ropes made from their own clothing. It might have been easier to chop off their hands and feet and knock out their teeth, but apart from the ethical aspect, I worried that it might affect the likelihood of success. In addition, crippled goblins couldn't be used for training. Even most veterans hadn't seen the undead and didn't know what they were capable of. The newcomers knew even less, of course.

Each of the undead would allow one of the newbies to significantly increase their chances of survival. They could be used as a kind of SP reserve. In addition, this was a good opportunity to study the undead, arrange training matches and develop tactics. All in all, the idea seemed reasonable enough to try.

"We need a couple of volunteers to watch the bodies. As payment, they will be allowed to fight one of the resurrected, under my supervision."

"I'll find some suitable candidates," Dmitry said.

It didn't take long to find them, and the two newbies remained in the 'morgue' to keep an eye on the dead. Of course, there was a risk that the undead would rise too quickly or that the guards would decide to take all the experience points, but there's never a carrot without a stick. They had seen me fight and understood that nothing good would come from cheating.

As I left the basement, I suddenly thought of another use for the captive undead. We could feed the undesirables to them. I winced at the thought. All right, what was the next step in my plan? Vitamins?

✿ ✿ ✿

I took out a white card and turned it over in my fingers. It was an 'empty' and, according to the description, I could record a low-level skill on it. I now had to decide which skill I wanted to obtain. I needed something for fighting in close quarters.

My bow wasn't bad at long range. The spear was good for middle range, but it needed quite a lot of space. *Invisibility* allowed me to escape, but required mana and couldn't be activated instantly. Five seconds wasn't a terribly long time, but it was long enough to die in a sudden attack. It meant that I was almost defenseless up close, and even a first-level newb had a good chance of killing me. Was this one of the reasons why I was so reluctant to let the other players get close to me? The System's defenses only worked against direct murder, and after everything I'd seen, I was reluctant to trust them.

Of course, I had accumulated plenty of cards with suitable weapons, but what use was a sword if all I could do was slice my own throat with it? Yes, I was exaggerating a little, I could use an axe to some extent, but unlike firewood, the enemy wouldn't wait for me to hit them. I was thus weaker than even first-level people who had the corresponding skill.

I was hoping to learn all the basic skills one day, but for now I was limiting myself to the classic weapon — the sword. Given my current position and level, I doubted that any player would refuse a veteran's request to copy their skill.

I searched for the appropriate 'donor' with all seriousness. First, I studied my trophies, choosing the sword I liked best. Not too short and not too long.

Then I began the search. I was keen to find a specialist who had taken advantage of the original card and had studied their weapon in detail, rather than skimming over everything. It wasn't easy, given that most players stored their weapons in the cards and didn't go around displaying them.

"I need someone with a similar weapon!" I said and raised the blade above my head. The sword was very popular, which was largely why I had chosen it as an additional weapon. Success was only a matter of time.

The first two candidates dropped out after a brief conversation. One only possessed general knowledge, and the second admitted that, although he had discovered how to focus on specific information, it had been too late.

The third one was suitable. Of course, I didn't arrange a duel to check. Our weapons were real, and even with the *Duelist* restrictions, I couldn't guarantee that he wouldn't get hurt. I simply took his word for it. Why couldn't I just trust a person? Especially when he was aware of the consequences of lying, and I possessed the *Identification* skill?

I held out the card, and after closing his eyes for a short while, he returned it to me.

Sword fighting (copy)

Rank: *1/5*
Accuracy: *98%**
Features:
— Specialization: simple one-handed sword.
Saturation:
0/10

*If the copy accuracy is below 90%, you will not be able to improve the skill. If the accuracy is below 80%, the skill will not be recognized by the System.

Accuracy seemed to indicate how much the copied skill matched the original skill. Judging by the footnotes, ninety-eight percent was an excellent result. Perhaps the original card was better, but they were rarely dropped, and you couldn't buy it.

"All right, you can take a weapon of your choice." I laid out the cards I didn't really want before him. A pair of katanas from the ashigaru's companions, a sword and a saber taken from the goblin rider. I had decided to keep the rest. The cards were probably not very useful, but the player didn't complain and took the saber after a moment's thought.

"You're good. Would you like to join my squad?"

"Thank you, but I am loyal only to Allah."

I nodded, accepting his decision, and said goodbye, my thoughts turning back to the card. It was relatively safe here, so there was no need to delay. **Study.**

The card didn't fade this time but simply crumbled in my hands, flooding my mind with information. I started moving. Although the skill had been firmly fixed in the mind of the first owner, it helped to better consolidate the information I received. You couldn't get more out of a card than there was, but you could definitely get less.

When I stopped five minutes later, the sword in my hand no longer seemed so foreign.

Sword fighting (F, 1/5)
Accuracy: 96%

I was a bit disappointed with the drop in percentage, but I still thought it had turned out well. After all, the received information had been adapted for a completely different user. Once I got access to the Server, I could improve the skill and make up for the four percent lost along the way.

I sat at the edge of the roof of 'my' house, clutching

a wooden mug and drinking compote made from goblin apples, leaves, and some other edible fruit. It was surprisingly delicious. I wondered if poisoning the compote would be considered murder by the System, then sighed, aware that I was being paranoid. Why would Lisa poison us? She wouldn't even get experience points for that. If she used sleeping powder, however... Stop, stop, stop.

Although I was joking right now, I had to admit that the events here had left their mark on me. Like they had left their mark on the others. The newbies were actually the most reasonable people here. Dmitry, for example, although he blushed every time he glanced at Lisa, was no longer as naive as before and could finish off an opponent if needed. The Lone Swordsman had reached the second level, and although he kept the story rather vague, he didn't deny that he had killed another player. Siegfried, on the other hand... He may have been a decent guy, but he didn't even have a single goblin under his belt. Not many people could literally stab someone in the back without emotional turmoil, and I suspected that most of them were in prison somewhere.

Many newcomers were still being tormented by doubts about "whether it was right to kill the goblins". I had also hesitated when I had arrived here for the first time. I asked around, and few had received the bonus that I had obtained from the card, in the form of 'murder experience', and it only eased the consequences. Each person had to make the decision alone. These events were changing us, and not always for the best. No matter how you looked at it, I was a monster in the eyes of ordinary people. Most veterans were monsters, too.

My principles were quite simple: don't stab your allies in the back, respect your interests, and react appropriately. But who was to judge whether my actions had been reasonable? They didn't exactly fall under 'necessary self-defense'. How long would my principles hold under constant pressure? The desire to survive was rather insidious, and impunity corrupts. It was why the players needed to unite and develop some kind of rules. Laws that would be enforced not by the System, but by the community itself.

I shook off these sad thoughts and looked down. The view below me was encouraging. What I had initially considered a temporary stop was rapidly turning into something like a proper camp. The smoke of a dozen fires attracted attention from afar, and by evening, about five hundred players had gathered in the square, with new groups arriving. The overall losses were small.

Remaining: 956/1000

This wasn't an accident; the landing zone had obviously been much smaller this time. Not even the entire sixth ring, it seemed, but only a narrow section of it. Otherwise, given the size of the city, the players wouldn't have been able to gather here so quickly and in such numbers.

I took another sip and lazily watched a tall, solidly-built man move around the perimeter of the square, periodically raising a black sword and shouting something. He was loud, but the space was too large to make out more than a few words. From time to time, in response to his shouts, a player would come out of the crowd and join the procession. By the time he got close enough to me, eight people had gathered behind him. They appeared to be all veterans.

"I am the high priest of Quetzalcoatl! All who are loyal to the Serpent, join me!"

Another priest? Right. Given that the seven gods shared about a hundred veterans between them, and assuming they were distributed more or less evenly, this Quetzalcoatl must have about fourteen or fifteen followers. And nine of them, counting the priest, had gathered here. Not bad.

I squinted slightly, and a level appeared above the priest's head. Level 5? A chill ran down my spine, I choked on the compote and started coughing. Had I been calling myself a monster? I was an innocent lamb compared to this man. His nickname was green, so I couldn't accuse him of anything, except the possession of a mask or some other skill that allowed him to circumvent the System restrictions. I didn't hesitate to spend the mana. *Identification.*

Bill Michigan

Status: player.
Local ID: hidden.
Level: 5.
Home Location: Earth.
Race: human.
Gender: male.
Parameters:
Strength: 9/10.
Agility: 8/10.
Intelligence: 8/10.
Vitality: 9/10.
Stamina:10/10.
Perception: 8/10.
Luck: 5/10.
Race Parameter:
Intuition: 5/10.
Additional Parameters:
Faith: 5/10.
Features:
Mark of God — this person is under the protection of a higher entity. Other features are hidden.

It was terrible. The problem wasn't just the fifth level, his parameters must have been above average from the beginning. *Stamina* was a ten... Although I couldn't see his skills, the level and parameters were enough to know that this guy was extremely dangerous, and I preferred not to cross him unless I absolutely had to. Not because I was a coward, but because he could probably kill me quite easily. My only chance was a surprise strike using *Invisibility*, or to bring a machine gun from Earth. Why did I think that we'd have to fight? Moreover, an honest fight, one-on-one?

The priest suddenly lifted his head and looked directly at me. I smiled and nodded, saluting him with my mug and taking a sip. I had a vague feeling that I had already seen him somewhere.

"Yesterday, the notorious Chicago Swordsman was arrested, accused of more than ten murders. His peculiarity is that although he actively used a firearm, he preferred to finish off his victims with a sword. The name of the suspect has not yet been disclosed as the investigation is ongoing, but our editorial office managed to obtain an exclusive photo..."

"Fuck."

The suspect was walking around below me. A man who had been 'falsely accused' of the most high-profile murder spree of the decade. A priest of one of the seven gods. The strongest player. Potentially, the leader of one of the largest groups. A bloodthirsty maniac?

"Won-der-ful, " I muttered, finding that the compote was all gone. Did I need to expose him and try to finish him off before things went too far?

Or pretend that I didn't know anything and hope for the best? For a 'hero' like me, the answer was obvious. Well, the situation was certainly getting more and more interesting.

INTERLUDE

THE NINTH

CHICAGO IS A CITY with a fascinating history. The Chicago Swordsman, as the media called him, wasn't a maniac. Bill was a criminal and a hitman, but he had previously only killed for practical reasons. For money, reputation, and to sort out the problems associated with the 'business'. After ten years of a very busy criminal career, he had only eight bodies to his name. Five of them had been criminals like him, and the rest were just greedy scum. You could say that Bill's hands and conscience were clear. He certainly never dreamt of those he had killed, and, like any good Catholic, he planned to go to heaven after death. Well, why shouldn't he? The important thing was to repent in time and be granted absolution by a friendly priest.

He was quite happy with his life overall. He had a good credit history, a house he was paying off in the suburbs, a beloved wife and three children. Everything that a respectable ...economist should have. This was his official position at a serious investment firm. After all, criminals also needed health insurance, retirement savings, and the ability to freely manage their money.

However, the police arrested his bosses six months ago, the company was teetering on the edge of a cliff, and the once respectable made man found himself in a rather difficult situation. If a business doesn't make money, the employees end up starving. Bill knew how to 'solve problems', but murder itself didn't bring in money. Unless you did it to steal the victim's wallet, but Bill felt nothing but disgust for such behavior. Ending a person's life for a hundred bucks? The scum capable of such a thing simply devalued his noble work. To descend to the simple robbery...

He nearly added a ninth corpse to his count — a person who loved asking passers-by for directions after dark. Fortunately, Bill was a professional and didn't kill for free, so he had stopped in time. The other man had been lucky, for as a disabled person, he enjoyed numerous advantages: parking in specially designated areas, had medical insurance, and a decent disability pension. Every month, Bill visited his 'friend', looked him in the eye and took a hundred bucks.

He didn't need them, but one had to pay for services... and for mistakes. In addition, the rumors of what had happened had been good for his 'business reputation'. All the street trash knew him by sight, and he could walk down the darkest alley without being asked for the time.

This was real respect. It was almost like the good old days, when the Outfit practically ran the city. However, Bill wasn't even thirty years old yet, so he hadn't actually seen that time with his own eyes. Still, it was useful to nod in agreement with the incessant grumbling of old men, if you wanted to move higher up the ladder. The shooting hardly stopped in the "good old times", and his eight bodies wouldn't have impressed anyone. Nowadays, it was not customary to kill people at the drop of a hat. After all, the dead brought in no money, and money was at the center of everything. The crisp green bills with the American presidents. Even if the bills were no longer quite so green after the last reform.

His bosses had committed the worst possible crime in the United States. Murder, bribery, smuggling, manufacturing and trafficking of drugs... All this paled before the greatest sin of tax evasion. A legitimate business, once created only for money laundering, suddenly began to bring in tangible profits. Real college graduates suddenly appeared among the 'economists' who could shoot accurately, conduct heart-to-heart conversations with debtors, and solve all sorts of problems. One of the graduates eventually wormed his way into management, got carried away, and then ratted out the shady business when under investigation.

Bill was tasked with dealing with the traitor, but he never managed to finish off his ninth target. Without going into the details, he screwed up, the traitor escaped, and the company started having some serious problems. Some mistakes, however unintentional, cannot be forgiven. The traditional cement shoes on his feet were proof of this.

"You know I have nothing against you, Billy," said his old friend Tom. He was an equally experienced made man, although with fewer corpses. Only five, if he wasn't lying. "But our people are very angry with you. I understand why: twenty-five years without parole, after all."

Bill could have said a lot in response. About an unfortunate series of events, good security and the initially tiny chance of success, but when your feet are soaking in rapidly hardening cement, and you're on a yacht in the middle of a deep lake, all excuses somehow pale in significance.

"You were the best, Billy, and you let them down. You let us all down. The bosses asked me to tell you that your family will be next. Your wife, you son and two daughters..."

"You bastard! You're their godfather!"

Tom took a step back and waved the gun at him, glancing at the cement. "We're old friends, aren't we? Don't worry about that. I'll be honest with you, no one is going to touch them, the oldies are just angry and want you to, well," he scratched his nose. "feel a sense of despair? After all, it's because of your mistake that they'll have to sit in jail for the next few decades. So put on a sad face, we need proof."

The camera held by the third mobster clicked several times. Jack. Young and ambitious, he was going to fill the newly vacant position. It was useful for the fellow to see what happened to those who let the bosses down. But also, how they pay for ten years of spotless service. What conclusions he would draw from this would depend on whether he had a brain.

"All right, Jacky, send the photos to the cloud. Has the cement set yet? Hey, friend, can you move your legs around?"

Bill didn't move at first, but then he remembered his family and obediently tried to shake his legs. Yes, the cement was holding fast.

"Right, I'm glad you understand. Any last words? A cigarette?"

His wife didn't like it when he smoked, and Bill had quit about a month ago. Had it been the third time or the fourth? What difference did it make? He didn't say no this time. He accepted the cigarette with his lips and waited for the light, then leaned back in the hard chair. Three minutes of life…

The sun was setting, turning the sky crimson. The glow reached the filter, almost burning his lips, and Bill spat the cigarette out.

Jack stepped on it to put it out.

"You know, Tom, you can still shoot Jack, help me get out of this fucking cement, and we'll figure something out together." They both knew it wasn't going to happen, but Bill had to try.

"Shhh... You know how I feel about you, Billy, but that's not how things work. I have a family, too, and they need my salary. We have a mortgage on our house, we recently bought a new car, our eldest is going to college in a couple of years. You know how it is."

"Then come on, you bastard," Bill said bleakly. "Hurry up already. Do your job, I won't reach the edge myself."

"Don't be stupid, okay? If you try to escape, we'll shoot you in the knees. Unfortunately, you must go swimming alive, the orders were strict about that. Jack, take him by the elbow and help me drag him."

A minute later, the cement shoes began their journey to the bottom of Lake Michigan. Bill looked up through the water and saw his successor leaning over the side, trying to get another good camera shot. He tried to move his legs, but the cement was high-quality and time-tested. They had tied the rope around his wrists well, too. No chance. Not wanting to prolong the agony, he opened his mouth, letting the air bubbles escape. Somewhere on the verge of losing consciousness, when the mind gave way to a desire to survive, a line of text suddenly appeared...

Game Over. Try again?
Yes/No

Tom really was a good friend. He had lied about Bill's family, for his wife and son were already dead. They had been killed by Jacky, who had to earn his position as the new 'economist'. The traitor's heir had to die, but Tom had protected his goddaughters by convincing the bosses that they were "just girls". Feminism wasn't traditionally strong among the leadership, so he was allowed to take care of the future orphans. Nevertheless, they had noted his weakness and drew the appropriate conclusions.

After uploading the last photos of the execution to the cloud and deleting the originals, Jacky turned around, pulling out his gun. He fired immediately. No pause. No words. Three more shots followed, for the new made man wasn't going to risk coming closer. Then a final shot to the head... The deck would have to be scrubbed, but it was better than getting a bullet in return or fishing the body out of the water to tie weights to it. He looked at the fishing rods lying by the side of the boat. It looked like only the fish would benefit from today's fishing.

An hour later, once the mess had been cleaned up, the yacht headed back to the dock. There was a difference between cause and reason. Tom didn't die because he was weak. It was just that the 'senior economist' had become too well-known in recent years, and he knew too much to simply retire. In addition, the Outfit wasn't going through the best of times, and there wasn't even enough money for bribes. It was nothing personal, just business, and the business was being restructured.

CHAPTER 12

THE CIRCLE

THE MORE PEOPLE are involved in a discussion, the longer it will take to reach a decision, and the more questionable the result. We didn't have much time, so only eight players had gathered on the roof of one of the buildings. The strongest ones. Given that experience points could only be obtained here by killing, it wasn't the best selection method.

"Well, friends," Qing Long began, bowing slightly. The Chinese man had been the main initiator of this meeting. "We don't know each other very well yet, so we don't trust each other very much. Let's follow certain security rules. Do you see this circle?" He pointed to a large white circle drawn with what looked like lime, pieces of which I had seen on the floor below. The circle was divided into eight, roughly equal sections by four intersecting lines. Another circle was drawn at their intersection, and the lines inside the circle had been erased. "Let each person stand inside one of the sections. I have left a space in the center for the speaker, but I suppose you can speak from your spot. It is forbidden to leave your section before the end of the negotiations or try to cross the borders into another sector."

"Seriously?" said Marcus, the 'wolf in sheep's clothing', summing up his opinion about the idea. He was the leader of the very group I had tried to warn about the goblin attack.

"If you disagree, you can leave. Since we have agreed that the meeting will be confidential, there are no guards. The other participants will have to stop a violator of the rules."

How thoughtful. This design, despite its absurdity, allowed you to speak without raising your voice, but it didn't allow you to suddenly attack. Of course, it was unlikely that any of the participants would be stupid enough to attack an opponent, but the rules were reassuring.

I stood in the center of the section with a number eight drawn inside. Qing Long took the section to my left, with the number one. The Chicago Swordsman stood beyond him. Then a Middle Eastern man... Then an African man... Someone from India, perhaps? Then a fair-haired European, and finally, the 'wolf in sheep's clothing' on the right. And not a single woman. Although the System lacked prejudice, and each batch of newcomers had about 50% women, but there was barely a third among the veterans.

Despite the seriousness of what was happening, I couldn't help but smile a little as I realized what this reminded me of. Such rituals were popular among various evil organizations in anime and manga. Although the baddies who weren't yet important to the plot and to the main characters usually remained in the dark and the viewer could only see their outlines.

"Let's start by introducing ourselves," Qing Long said, "and describing our abilities at least in general terms. You don't have to reveal everything, but please don't lie. I will begin first, to set an example." This reminded me of school and students introducing themselves in front of the class. I wouldn't have been surprised if it turned out that the man was a teacher in normal life. "My name is Qing Long. I am thirty-six years old and come from the Celestial Empire. My patron is Guan Yu. I have reached System Level 3 and the second level in sword fighting. My gift or E-ranked ability is called the Eye of the Serpent. It allows me to see what is hidden. In particular, other people's abilities and special skills."

Was this an overt hint that there was no way of hiding your abilities? I couldn't read them even with the help of *Identification* in most cases. And what did "see what is hidden" actually mean? Could he see through *Invisibility*? Sense lies?

These were questions that would remain unanswered for now. In any case, his ability was unlikely to be passive, which meant he couldn't use it continuously.

"Furthermore, I currently have forty-three players under my command. Nine of them are second-level veterans." I noted that my word had caught on. "Well, that is all."

It appeared that Qing Long had assumed the role as leader of the 'Chinese faction' after the death of his competitor. At least, his supporters looked the part, and the group seemed to be formed based on religious and national principles. As far as I could, players had been gathered evenly across the planet, so there were quite a few Chinese people among us. Every sixth or even every fifth player. They preferred to stick together here, creating the appearance of unity. Nearly all the Chinese veterans have chosen Guan Yu as their patron, and the newcomers were sure to follow their example.

The Korean and Japanese players could have provided a bit of variety, since they also respected this deity, but political and cultural differences forced the Koreans to keep themselves a little apart, and the Japanese even more so. If some of them were among the supporters of the Azure Dragon, I couldn't tell. Plus, everyone was using the same language provided by the System.

Could I trust this man? It was hard to say. I doubted Qing Long genuinely felt grateful to me for eliminating his competitor, but he didn't seem to have any reason to retaliate.

"Who would like to speak next?"

"Let's go in order," said the Swordsman. "My name is Bill Michigan, and while my first name is real, my last name... Let's just say, it's a tribute to an important event in my life. Some of you may have recognized me as the Chicago Swordsman, but the authorities in the United States, where I'm from, have already admitted their mistake and cleared me of all charges..."

I noted that he said, "cleared me of all charges", and not "I'm innocent". The fact that he had chosen to confess wasn't particularly surprising, since the case had been a high-profile one and people would inevitably find out. At the same time, the confession hinted that he was following the rules and avoiding complete lies.

"I am also the high priest of Quetzalcoatl," Bill continued, "I am twenty-nine years old, Level 5 and have fourth rank in *Sword fighting*. My ability... Let's just say it's a form of *Invisibility*. I have sixteen people. Half of them are veterans."

It wasn't that many. Perhaps more people had wanted to join the strongest player's group, but he only accepted the followers of the Aztec God. Plus, people they had vouched for. Given that most of the newbies in his squad were women, I secretly suspected that he was preparing a mass sacrifice. Joke.

I thought about it again, trying to decide how

I felt about a man who was responsible for dozens of deaths. A killer who could strike at any second. Hmm... The description also suited me too well. I hadn't killed back on Earth, of course, but murder was murder. This wasn't a dream or a game, and the goblins were real. In fact, the only difference between us was the number of corpses. I'm sure we'd both say that we had killed out of necessity. I didn't have any warm feelings toward the Swordsman but neither did I feel disgust. I tried to treat everyone with equal prejudice.

After all, he didn't look like a psychopath, mad with fear or power, and ready to kill everyone. I felt wary more than anything else. Perhaps he was just good at pretending.

"I suppose I'm next?" the young Arab man raised his head. "My name is Saud bin Salman, I'm originally from Saudi Arabia and I'm nineteen years old. Second level and second rank in sabers."

One could ask what this youngling was doing among the other 'wise men'. Despite his youth and only the second level, he was the formal head of the largest Muslim party. They were Sunni. He had assumed leadership not so much through force as through cunning and his background, which was rumored to be noble. Some even called him "Prince", but I doubted this very much. The Saudi royal family was extensive, of course, but the chance that one of them had ended up here was ridiculously small. The youth himself made no such claims, either.

"My skill is identifying poisons and their properties," Saud continued.

At first glance, it was similar to 'determining edibility', since knowing what couldn't be consumed made it easy to understand what could be eaten. However, if you looked deeper, it had a much broader application. He could easily gather some herbs by the roadside and then poison half the camp. A useful skill for a dark sorcerer. Or a witch. I remembered that even in our time, his homeland continued to fight against magic, using the most progressive methods – decapitation. How would they react to the appearance of the players? Would the country declare them sorcerers and start hunting them? Or would they call it a 'gift' and try to use it? Frankly, I didn't believe that any of the powers that be would refuse the opportunities offered by the System. If heads did roll, it would only be at the start.

"I believe in Allah, but I can't be certain of how many of the faithful here are willing to listen to my words. I think I can only count on eleven people for serious matters. However, if we are talking about the total number, there are about thirty."

Although there were more Muslims in the world than Chinese people, and they were technically the largest faction, they lacked even a shadow of unity. Sunni and Shiite... People from Africa, the Middle East, Europe, and who knows where else. Everyone had their own, only right idea of how to believe in God.

Perhaps the Muslim players could help in the fight for independence from the System gods, but I had no desire to get involved. Nor did I wish to accept Islam. Moreover, there were both fanatics and moderates among them. Some believed that abandoning Islam was punishable by death, while others argued that the new gods were not real and feigned consent meant nothing. I suspected that the *Faith* parameter wasn't so rare after all among them. Many had probably agreed to accept the 'false gods' while continuing to believe in the One God. I wouldn't have been surprised if one of them tried to develop a new branch to fit what was happening into the familiar picture of the world.

"Sulu," an dangerous-looking black man said, slapping his chest. "I am from Africa. My home is Somalia. My weapon is axe. My level is three. I can sense danger, believe in God, and serve him!" The man stabbed his finger at the Arab youth, while maintaining his most serious expression.

What a speech! What an accent! I resisted the urge to applaud his acting. He spoke as if the System language matched his 'primitive English'. I spent the mana needed for *Identification* to check that his *Intelligence* was in fact OK. He had a seven. This joker was no more stupid than I was. He also had the *Faith* parameter, which meant that his god wasn't Allah, but one of the seven impostors. I wondered if the Prince knew about this.

He probably didn't. As far as I could tell, the African man was the second leader of the Muslim faction. It was difficult to say how many of the faithful listened to the words of the Arab youth because the older man stood behind him. Although Sulu's muscles and height may have been shaped by the System, it was unlikely that he had ever suffered from hunger. Looking at his intimidating face, it was easy to believe that he was a pirate back home, but not his adherence to Islam. Far more likely, his alliance with the Prince was dictated by mutual interests. Something basic, like money and the opportunity to escape the hellhole he had been born in? The desire to leave one's homeland and move to a better place was common for half of the world's population. He was a shady character.

"Well, thank you for that," the Chinese man said, giving him a sharp look.

"I am a brahmin from India," said the fifth man, bowing slightly. "I am forty years old. I have reached Level 3, first rank in clubs and third rank in magic. I can control the undead. I am also the High Priest of Shiva. I am served by two dozen people, including five veterans. The same number will join me very soon, I think."

The brahmin glanced at me, and I suddenly remembered Sahel, who had joined my band while avoiding his kinsmen for some reason. Was the reason standing before me? Well? Did I make a fuss or try to negotiate? I could offer the Indian man one of the dead goblins, for example. To be honest, considering the extracted mana crystals, I had some doubts about whether my necromancy would succeed. If the bodies didn't reanimate by tomorrow morning, we'd just have to get rid of them. There was no point in dragging them around any further.

Out of all the leaders who had introduced themselves, this man repulsed me the most. His ability sounded extremely useful, but we really needed to know the specifics and limitations of the skill.

"Xander," said the sixth guy, a handsome blond. "Or Alexander, if going by name and not by nickname. I'm twenty-four years old and from the EU. Level 3. My weapon is a mace, but only the second rank. First-level magic. The special ability is Earthen Armor. My patron is Odin. I have twenty players in my squad, including two veterans."

Despite the impressive head count, the unit consisted almost entirely of newbies, so their fighting ability was dubious at best. I would even say they were ballast, clinging to a high-level player.

I turned my head to the right and looked at the last player in the circle. The 'wolf in sheep's clothing', as I kept calling him. I doubted he had recognized me without the mask and bow.

"My turn, huh?" he said. "Well, you can call

me Marcus. I'm twenty-seven years old. Italy. Like most of you here, my level and rank is third. My weapon is a sword. My ability is linked to time, but I won't go into the details for now." Linked to time? Boastful bastard. It sounded impressive, but could easily turn out to be something useless, like a 'superpower' that allowed him to determine when the local sun would rise or set. I'd seen it before. Even if we were talking about Time, the ability's impact would be minimal, given its rank. "There are seven players in the squad besides me. Two veterans. I could have recruited more but someone is spreading unflattering rumors about my... military talents and personal qualities. If you find out who it is, please tell me. Oh yeah, and I worship Hera."

"Vasily," I said. "Eastern Europe. Third System level. Third rank in *Spear fighting*, first rank in *Magical ability*, *Sword fighting*, and *Archery*. I also know the *Goblin language*. My special abilities are *Duelist*, which allows me to participate in duels under the System's protection, and a type of *Invisibility*. I have ten people with me, only three of whom are veterans. That's it, I think."

"You forgot to name your god," the Azure Dragon reminded me. For some reason, I didn't want to reveal my godless status after his words.

Odin, Hera, Shiva, Guan Yu, and Quetzalcoatl. Five gods out of the seven. The late Jack, as the High Priest of Inti, would have occupied a worthy place in this circle. Six. Only a representative of Egypt's God of the Desert was missing... Unfortunately, the Great Set was not very popular among the people and, from what the players were saying, was dark-skinned in his current incarnation. A suitable patron for Sulu, perhaps? In any case, only one position was definitely vacant.

"True." I scratched my nose. "I'm connected with Inti." Well, wasn't our fledgling feud a connection? Moreover, I possessed the *Faith* parameter, even if it was blocked, so Qing Long could find no fault with my answer.

The negotiations themselves were successful, although rather boring and predictable. Each of us had pondered the situation for a while, so our thoughts tended to follow the same lines.

"Now that everything has been decided, I propose forming an official alliance," Qing Long said in the end.

"I'm in," the Swordsman replied first.

I looked around the circle skeptically. I didn't even like any of these bastards.

"Of course," the Arab man said. We'd somehow continued speaking by going around the circle.

Sulu simply nodded. The brahmin bowed slightly, his hands folded. Alexander, then Marcus.

On the other hand, we were united by a desire to survive, our personal strength, and a willingness to fight. I trusted their skills in killing their own kind. Wasn't this the basis for a strong, even if short-lived, union?

"I also agree, " I nodded, not wanting to be the last. "Shall we discuss the terms?"

Contrary to my concerns, everything here was quite standard. Joint actions, protection from outsiders, considering the interests of allies, and revenge for killed members of the circle. Any internal conflicts were to be resolved through mediation by other participants. Plus, a lot of small details, which took about ten minutes to discuss.

"I think we should give our group a name," Alexander said with a flash of his pearly whites.

"The Justice League?" Marcus snorted. I'd already noticed that the Italian had an acerbic sense of humor. "Or the Avengers?"

Oh no, he'd say Akatsuki next. Thank goodness there were no Japanese people among us. Then I thought that it wouldn't be the worst option. Warriors of Jihad? The Panthers? The Firm?

"What about the G8?" I suggested the name of the largest 'band of evil' in our world. The laughter that arose defused the situation, and after five minutes of discussion, my suggestion was unexpectedly accepted.

I thought it was a clear indication that

nobody expected much from our treaty. An alliance created for three days, which was unlikely to last more than a day. The future didn't inspire much optimism. Although we had agreed to cooperate, would it be enough? Only time would tell.

CHAPTER 13

PLANS

WE STOOD ON THE PORCH of a large building that had probably once housed the local government, which now served as a makeshift podium for the, eh, popular assembly. The square was big enough to hold thousands, and the approximately six hundred players occupied only a small portion of it. I checked the interface.

Remaining players: 943/1000

We'd managed to gather about two-thirds of the survivors here. Another third, scattered somewhere in the surrounding area, had not reached the square. The overall losses were low compared to the previous time, but it was worth remembering that we had landed close together and in a relatively safe zone. Except for a few goblin observers, who had been killed early on, the only danger was the fortress in the vicinity. Yet almost sixty humans had managed to die. How? It was a rhetorical question, considering that two people on the list were my doing.

Frankly, I was bored. We had already discussed everything that was being said here in our select group, and were now communicating the information to the 'voters', giving them the opportunity to make the 'only right decision'. Or leave if they didn't like it. I must have demonized the circle members excessively, since none of them offered to kill the potential renegades. I had a minor role in what was happening. I stood behind the speaker and looked stern, demonstrating my full support for his words.

"The situation is critical!" Qing Long proclaimed. "You have all heard that numerous goblin bands are on their way here from the city outskirts? There may be up to ten thousand of them! And these won't be scattered groups of looters, whom we met last time, but trained combat units."

Although information obtained from a single source couldn't be considered reliable, we decided to act as if it was true. Then came a series of simple calculations. News of our arrival should have reached the goblin army almost immediately, and they had probably set out without delay. The players spent only a day in this world last time, so the goblins risked not finding anyone if they delayed. On the other hand, if there were several waves, they could be targeting the next ones. Plus, the remnants of the previous wave, consisting of failed players.

"Some of you think you can negotiate with goblins, but you can't! Nobody makes deals with the weak. Don't feel sorry for them. Each goblin will come here to kill us, collect our gear, and gain experience. This is war!"

I nodded automatically. If we had encountered random clusters last time, now we would be facing goblins who were coming for our heads. It was a small advantage among a huge pile of disadvantages.

"There's only one path we can take!" the Azure Dragon went on. "We must go further into the city."

That's what the circle had decided. Turn the players into a force and go deep into the ruins, sending scouts ahead of us. Force our way right through the gaps to save time. There were only three hundred goblins in the fortress, so they were unlikely to attack the significantly larger number of players. But if the army caught up with us, they would surround us and simply crush us. Perhaps not everyone, and some would escape, but the united players will be finished. The goblins would spend the remainder of the time hunting us down like wild animals, and the new waves would fall right into the trap...

The existence of these waves was no longer an assumption, for the priests had received some additional information from the gods. Every day, at around the same time, we could expect reinforcements to arrive in the form of a thousand fresh players.

"The breaks in the wall are two hours north from here. They are controlled by the fortress, but only notionally. We don't need to storm its walls, just walk past it. Yes, we may meet the undead in the next zone, but it is better to deal with the occasional monster than a goblin horde."

The idea of capturing the fortress had also been discussed, but was rejected as too difficult. Theoretically, we could try to lure the goblins out of the fortress, crush them, and then use our abilities to try to capture the fortress gates and finish off the others. If successful, with only a few hundred players lost, we would almost certainly be able to hold out until the end of the required period. But not with our troops, and not with the goblin army close on our heels. I think that if Qing Long had announced an assault, our units would have scattered in all directions, like cockroaches beneath a slipper.

The same was true of the proposal to climb the wall and set up an 'elevator' somewhere else. It was potentially safer, but we had neither the time nor the materials.

So, the plan was to pass through the breaks in the wall and keep moving, while sending out scouts in all directions. If we were lucky, we'd be able to find a suitable place to make camp and defend ourselves. We would have to hold out there for three days, leveling up newcomers using the weaker undead and goblins. Our goal was not only to survive, but also to save as many other players as possible. However, if the information about the size of the goblin army was accurate, holding them back in a random place would be madness. We would be forced to break up into hundreds and run away, continuing as independent units. If the situation became dire, we could continue to split up into smaller groups, hoping that the goblins would also split up and not kill everyone.

"We have already interviewed the players who came from the north. The gaps in the wall are not defended, and there are only three hundred goblins inside the fortress. They won't dare attack our party with such numbers!"

I nodded again, but with considerable doubt this time. Looking at the crowd, I didn't share the confidence in Long's voice. I didn't think he felt it himself. Yes, there were more of us, and the average player was stronger than a goblin, but I wouldn't bet on the results of a face-to-face battle. Napoleon once said that "one Mameluke can kill ten Frenchmen, but one hundred Frenchmen will kill one thousand Mamelukes" because the French were soldiers. Perhaps the goblins were medieval savages, but they were also warriors, while the human players fell short of even the Mamelukes. Although the System had given us combat skills, most were ordinary people who had suddenly found themselves on the battlefield. They paled at the sight of blood, were afraid of death, and would vomit if they saw a corpse....

"Nevertheless, the goblins may test us. We must be ready to fight. There are fewer goblins, they are weaker, and most of them lack the System skills!"

Right. But the goblins had normal armor, weapons, and training. We were light infantry, with our mismatched weapons, and a lack of armor and shields. How could we counter a well-coordinated formation shooting arrows at us? The players had almost no ranged weapons since there were none in the basic list. No bows, no crossbows, and certainly no firearms. I wouldn't have been surprised if I was the only archer here. Our hope was not so much in our numbers — given the unwillingness of the members to sacrifice themselves, it meant very little — but our special abilities. Poorly developed, randomly dropped, and often not very useful, they were still an advantage.

"If we work together, we will win!" Qing Long continued to lie enthusiastically.

Sure we will. If we fight, of course. Perhaps the players would be willing to kill to survive. But battles weren't only about murder, but also the constant threat of death. Most soldiers die or flee before they finish off a single enemy. How to get them to fight when push came to shove? Of course, over the centuries, humanity had developed a method by which soldiers gave their lives for the Motherland. Punishment and reward. Carrot and stick. We didn't really have either.

The carrot? Of course, experience and loot were good, but it wasn't enough. As for the stick, the situation was dire. By lowering the experience point requirements to almost zero, the System had really tripped us up. Once a player killed their first goblin, they were no longer bound by the mission requirements and could simply run in the face of danger. If one ran, another ten would follow. Even threats wouldn't stop them.

A soldier had nowhere to go, with people on every side, family back home, and deserters being shot. Here, a coward just needed to run away and survive for the specified period, and any threats after that were useless. What could we do about it?

"We have discussed this and have developed a plan for fighting the goblins."

We didn't have the power to force people to obey orders, but we could give them an order that they'd want to follow. The tactics used by barbarians against the armies of civilized countries suited this place almost perfectly. Feigned flight followed by a strike against the pursuers... Goblins were probably stronger in formation, but they wouldn't be able to catch anyone while in formation. As soon as the goblins broke rank and began to pursue us, the number, bravery and personal strength of the soldiers would come to the fore. There was a good chance that a false flight would turn into a real one... Yet who would obey if we ordered them to attack the goblins head-on?

"We have also developed a system of signals," the Chinese man continued, raising the familiar horn above his head. Sounds cut through the air: long, short, and intermittent. It wasn't much, but even this would make coordination much easier. "It is time to make a decision. Those of you who agree with our plan should go to the right," given the relativity of this direction, Qing Long gestured as well. "Register your name and obtain a personal number. The rest can go..."

"To hell?" someone in the crowd suggested.

"Left," Lung contradicted. "But that's about the same way. These players will not be protected by our Alliance. They will have to leave."

"What if we don't want to leave?" someone different shouted. "Who are you to give us orders, anyway?"

"Then I will kill you," the Swordsman stepped forward, putting on a familiar mask and drawing his sword. Today, Bill had to play his usual role of a villain. His nickname turned red and changed:

Faceless Killer No. 3...

Wow, they even had numbers? If I was right, almost everyone in our group of eight had such a mask. Another stick. I automatically poked at the three dots, and the Faceless Killer became simply the Faceless. I wasn't sure if the change worked just for me or for everyone else.

"Of course, it will be a fair fight. You can defend yourself."

"Hey!" the speaker backed away. "I didn't... I was just asking! It... it was a joke."

It would have been better if he'd just kept quiet. While he was an anonymous voice from the crowd the first time, now we could clearly see who had decided to ask such a clever question.

"I'll say it again, for the dumbasses," the Swordsman launched into his speech. "The situation is critical! Powerful undead await us in the center of the city, and a multitude of goblin units are heading towards us from the outskirts! We are caught between a rock and a hard place, but we must somehow hold out for three days. Strength, experience, and skill are all a lie. If there are idiots among you, who think they are the 'chosen ones', then I have news for you. We're cannon fodder that the System is trying to swamp these ruins with. There are many people on Earth, and if you send them here, thousand after thousand, month after month, sooner or later they'll clear the outskirts. Then the survivors of this hell will head into the center of the city and capture the altar. They will be the 'chosen ones'!

And we'll probably all be dead by then. If we want to survive, we must unite. My daughters are waiting for me back on Earth, so I have someone to fight for. I will kill anyone who threatens my return. If you're not ready to fight, then piss off! But if someone tries to get in my way, I will personally save them from unnecessary suffering!" Silence met his words, and I clapped my hands automatically. Qing Long joined in a second later, and soon almost everyone was clapping. It was a good speech. "Make your choice," the Swordsman repeated coldly. "I remind you, idiots go to the left."

It may be that some would decide to leave after this speech, but it was better to weed out such 'gentle souls' now. They wouldn't fight anyway.

The first to head to the right were our own people, whom we had spoken to earlier. Almost one hundred and fifty people. The veterans followed them. Humans show herd behavior and tend to follow the majority. The newcomers drifted after them... As soon as the number of people who had made the choice passed three hundred, the rest of the crowd moved almost wholly... Almost.

Frankly, I didn't think there would be people who would choose another option, but I had underestimated humanity once again. Almost three dozen players stood to the left. They could be proud of going against the majority if it hadn't been so stupid. Well, let's consider it natural selection. The meeting had gone surprisingly smoothly overall.

"We set out tomorrow at dawn!" Qing Long announced.

Alliance Stats

Total number of Alliance players: 563.
By level:
— Fifth level (V): 1.
— Fourth level (IV): 0.
— Third level (III): 6.
— Second level (II): 63.
— First level (I): 493.
Weapons:
— Pole weapons (p): 56.
— Bladed weapons (b): 252.
— Knives and daggers (k): 62.
— Axes (a): 71.
— Crushing weapons (c): 63.
— Magic (m): 42.
— Exotic weapons (e): 11.
— Ranged weapons (r): 7.
Skills...

I sat by the break in the wall that used to be a window, looking through sheets of rough paper covered in tiny handwriting. The paper had come from the goblins, the feathers from birds, and the ink from my canteen. Unfortunately, there wasn't enough paper and the 'clerk' had tried to save it as much as possible, so not only was the text small and crooked, but full of abbreviations. At least the copy that I had received was so. The original kept by Qing Long had more details. I could discern the general meaning.

8/Vasily/III/p3-r1-b1-m1/Invisibility/ M25-E-1.85-B/vasia23123396@gmail.com

I was eight... The first eight places were occupied by the 'leaders', but the other positions in the list didn't mean anything, with the numbers distributed randomly. True, the veterans were at the top of the list, and only then came the newcomers, but that was mostly for convenience.

I turned a piece of wood with the number 8 and a squiggle carved into it around in my hands, then put it back into the designated jacket pocket. By morning, each player had to carve a similar Alliance token. People love such symbols, plus, there was a practical benefit, since it would be easier to identify the bodies.

I returned to studying the papers. The sun was setting, and I had to strain my eyes to make out the text. The statistics included a serial number, nickname, level, combat skills, special ability, and finally a brief visual description.

The first seven had also listed their email

addresses, where other players could send a request and get a copy. Provided, of course, that one of us survived. Our email addresses were also listed on the wall of the 'Government House'. Naturally, no one wanted to reveal their real email address, so we had simply invented new ones, planning to register them on our return. The important thing was to choose a name that wasn't already taken by someone else. This wasn't so difficult, if you didn't chase after an attractive email address. I hadn't forgotten about my website either, and left its address on the same wall. However, given how quickly information about the players had spread, I was no longer sure that I should go back in there.

OK, what next? Levels? The information wasn't very useful overall, but it allowed us to see the ratio of newcomers to veterans. The weapon stats that should have, theoretically, helped us to divide people into groups, were practically useless at present. The players had accumulated too much stuff and the generalizations were too crude. Sabers, swords and rapiers were lumped together as 'bladed weapons'. Spears and halberds of all shapes and sizes were called pole weapons.

Appearance? In my case, the abbreviation meant "male, 25 years old, European, 1.85 meters tall, brown hair". I had fibbed about my age by rounding it up. Given that an increase in *Strength* significantly affected height and other parameters, this information only made sense in the short term. Theoretically, it could help to expose people who tried to appropriate someone else's number, but skills were more important than appearance here... Plus, it's not like the goblins would make very good spies.

The most interesting, no doubt, was the list of abilities. It was a pity that my copy only contained the names, but at least they weren't abbreviated. I planned to study it so that I knew what to expect from my allies.

The long day finally drew to a close, leaving behind nothing but fatigue. The players had spread out among the houses, where they had settled down for the night. Sparse bonfires flickered in the square, with the sentries keeping them going. My bed, made of grass and twigs, didn't look very inviting. To be honest, I had no confidence in tomorrow.

The same thoughts, the same fears... I felt like I was on track to developing soldier's syndrome. Yet this was only my second time here. How soon before the first players began to lose their mind? Or would we adapt?

"Can I come in?" a quiet voice said.

I turned my head but could barely make out the outline of a girl who had slipped into the room. "Lisa?" I had no trouble identifying the visitor. "Why aren't you asleep?"

"I can't sleep. I'm... I'm scared."

I nearly said, "Me too," and a shiver ran down my spine.

"Can I sit here with you?"

"Sure" I replied.

Given the lack of light in the corridors, she had made her way here almost by touch. Lisa sat down next to me, pressing her hip against mine as if by accident. I already had an idea about the purpose of her visit. Was the love triangle turning into a square? Or should I pretend to be an idiot and ignore all her hints?

"Beautiful stars," she noted. I glanced at the scattering of dim lights and mumbled, "Yeah."

This world must have been located unbelievably far away from Earth, somewhere at the edge of the galaxy. Was I imagining it, or were there now more stars and they were brighter?

Lisa put her head on my shoulder. I looked at the stars again, feeling how with every passing second, the question of their location relative to our world was paling in significance. Who needed the stars anyway?

"I got the hint, I catch everything on the fly," I mumbled melancholically. "But I don't know exactly what you mean."

"What?" She looked up at me. Here, by the window, I could almost see her face, and our lips were very close.

"Why?" I tried again.

"We may all die tomorrow." The girl drew

back a little, sounding slightly offended. "So why not? You don't like me?" Of course, she didn't mean love, but I'm sure that was mutual. You don't need love to have sex. So... why not?

"I do."

I pushed my thoughts aside and walked straight into the honey trap. I'd worry about the consequences tomorrow, unless my jealous competitors stabbed me in my sleep tonight.

INTERLUDE

THE RENEGADE

N THE EVENING, another player entered the square in the gathering darkness.

Leon. Level 1

About twenty years old, European in appearance, nothing interesting... The few sentries patrolling the area only glanced at him indifferently. New groups of players regularly approached the makeshift camp in search of protection and information. They spotted the smoke, stumbled on it by chance or were directed toward it by the scouts sneaking around. Another newb didn't surprise anyone. He might have looked a little more nervous, dirty, and exhausted than the others, but who knew what the guy had gone through?

"Hey, rookie! First time here?" one of the sentries waved. "You need to go to Government House, register yourself, and get a number. Ask someone down there and they'll show you. It's mandatory!"

Leon nodded nervously, murmured his thanks and kept walking. He didn't ask for directions to Government House. After standing in one spot for a while and making sure that no one *truly* cared about him, the guy calmed down. *He could... He could...* Slowly, feigning curiosity, he reached the center of the square with the mound of charred bones. The other players avoided this spot, a reminder that we were all mortal, but it was Leon's goal. He got down on one knee and, taking a small pouch from his bag, emptied a handful of blue crystals into the dirt and surreptitiously buried them. "That's it," he whispered to himself under his breath.

When Leon was sure that no one was paying him any attention, he stood up, dusted himself off, and wandered away with his head down... If someone had checked the newbie's status, they would have found that he was a hero rather than a player. One of the few who had failed the last mission but survived.

Leon knew that his actions wouldn't bode well for the humans, but he didn't have a choice, did he? No. He couldn't stay with the other players. They were doomed. Some would die quickly, and some, like Leon himself a month ago, would be captured by the goblins. Even if a prisoner survived, there was no way back. The thought of his lost homeland caused a flash of envy and anger. Not at the goblins, but at the players who had no idea how lucky they were. Anger at himself.

No, if he wanted to live, he had to serve the Master faithfully. A month ago, the very idea that Leon, an EU citizen, could have an owner would have aroused nothing but disgust, but now it was a reassuring thought. He was under protection.

He could leave already, but the more he learned here, the higher the reward. As he wandered among the people and listened to their conversations, Leon became lost in his own memories.

It had started with a mistake. Leon was an avid gamer and knew that nothing was stronger than magic in games, so he immediately chose the *Minor magical ability*. A sword as well, because the System didn't offer any magic staffs or spells. Without the accompanying skill, of course, but swinging an iron stick in the direction of the enemy didn't require much brains. Or so he had thought. What an idiot he had been.

The magic didn't live up to his expectations. To bring down enemies with *Chain lightning* or *Fireballs*, you had to reach the appropriate level and then get these spells from somewhere. While the sword... The very first goblin dodged Leon's clumsy swing and hit him over the head with a club. The warrior awoke already undressed, bound, and unarmed. He was lucky that the goblins didn't kill him, but had taken him to a nearby fortress. If the fortress had been far away, he would have been slaughtered.

As it turned out, some goblins knew the human language. And human anatomy. There was a short interrogation, interspersed with torture, in which he told the goblins everything he knew, and then some. He was thrown into the dungeon, beaten, broken, and crying with pain and self-pity. A day later, his mission failed, Leon finally realized that this nightmare would never end. He had become a hero. It sounded like a cruel joke in his present circumstances.

Gradually, the neighboring cells filled up with new prisoners, allowing the fear to be diluted with communication and some news. They were periodically beaten for talking, but they could still converse if they didn't get too carried away — the guards were too lazy to punish the prisoners very frequently. There were almost no wounded, for the goblins killed people whose survival was uncertain, for the sake of experience points.

Some of the prisoners were women... It was then that Leon realized how lucky he was to have been born a man. The goblins were not interested in men, but they visited the female captives regularly and for specific purposes. Not that they found human women particularly attractive — they didn't — but there was a shortage of females in the fortress. Visits to the captives quickly became a reward for distinguished warriors. The rapists felt no shame in front of the people in the neighboring cells. Some of the captive women committed suicide, but most accepted their fate.

The men had another problem, for they were rarely fed. In the weeks that followed, Leon grew skeletal, and the fate of the women ceased to concern him. They were given food and water, and even allowed to wash in between 'client visits'. The conversations that brightened up the first few days gradually stopped. Leon grew weaker and weaker, and death loomed before him. It would come on the tip of a blade, for the goblins would slaughter him as soon as the they thought that his days were numbered. When he had almost resigned himself to his fate, he got lucky.

The prisoners were visited by the 'top brass', and a shaman took a shine to Leon. A mistake when choosing his skill, which had cost him his freedom, turned out to be a stroke of luck. His *Minor magical ability* allowed him to leave the dungeon, becoming the slave and disciple of a goblin who was not yet old. He immediately took up the shaman's offer, without the slightest shame or hesitation, catching a few envious glances from the other prisoners. Many of them would have been happy to serve the victors, but few had the chance.

Leon began his studies with unprecedented enthusiasm, absorbing new knowledge like a sponge. The shaman regularly praised him for his intelligence and soon promised that he would give him the hand of his only daughter. If she agreed, of course. The small, dark-skinned goblin was no beauty queen, but the Frenchman was no racist. He'd seen worse girls, and once, when he had been drunk, he even... In any case, his time in the dungeons had taught him to value a woman's soul. And her powerful parents. Although he wouldn't have minded if the shaman's daughter had bigger tits and a prettier face... These thoughts didn't stop him from reading her "his own" poems, which praised the beauty of the "most beautiful of maidens". He was far from perfect in her eyes, too.

He had no choice, in any case. The shaman made no secret of the fact that the studies were only a side goal. He needed an heir, and the captive was viewed as a stud, first and foremost. Humans and goblins could produce offspring. Even hobgoblins were sometimes born. Human genes were highly valued. The goblins preferred to acquire these genes from the women, of course. But the shaman only had a daughter, so he was counting on many strong grandchildren. In the future. The girl had only recently begun to bleed, and an early pregnancy could end badly for both of them. The shaman would never forgive the death of his only daughter. Leon had to wait until she grew a little older.

Unfortunately, Leon only enjoyed his new position and security for a week. The commander of the fortress, the hobgoblin Un, then entrusted him with a very important mission. If Leon completed it, he would become a proper goblin and could officially ask for the hand of the beautiful maiden. If he returned from the mission.

"Hey, where are you going?" the sentry called after him this time. "It's almost night time."

Leon didn't answer as he walked away. His head was pounding. There was another shout behind him, but he could no longer hear it. Tears ran down his cheeks. However, the road was long, and by the time he reached the fortress, the tears had long since dried. Leon had made his decision, for he could only survive with the goblins. If he had to betray his own kind and get the shaman's daughter pregnant... Well, he was prepared to do more than that.

Morning was approaching when the heap of ash stirred, and a monster made up of bones crawled out of it. Although there wasn't enough material to create a Bone Dragon, according to the System classification, such a creature was called a **Bone Horror**. They were rarely found in the outer city districts.

The creature gave itself a shake and headed to where it could sense life. Even though it had just been born, it knew exactly what to do.

CHAPTER 14

THE BONE HORROR

I WOKE UP, UNSURE of what had awoken me. The bed made of twigs and grass was uncomfortable, but my sleep had been much better this time around. Although I had dreamed of goblins again, they had been on the losing side.

"What's the matter?" Lisa propped herself up on one elbow.

I didn't get a chance to answer. A desperate cry came from the street, then stopped abruptly, indicating that the sentry had done his duty until the end. The nightmare was becoming real.

"Get up! Danger!" I repeated, with no idea of what was going on. "Get your weapons!"

I stood up, pulled on my pants and threw on my jacket, then ran to the broken window. The fires cast small pools of light so I could barely make out something large nearby, about the size of a small truck and made up of nothing but bones. **Identification...** The System hesitated for a moment, as if unsure whether certain conditions had been met, but then the skill worked.

Bone Horror... (93%)

Status: *undead.*
Type: *bronze.*
Creature Rank: *D.*
Level: *10.*
Danger: *deadly.*
Parameters:
Strength: 20.
Agility: 10.
Intelligence: 3.
Durability: 7.
Stamina: 20.
Wisdom: 20.
Perception: 20.
Instinct: 10.
Features:
Undead — *this creature is already dead and has been created using magic, with all the following consequences.*

Regeneration — *if material is available, the bones of this creature can repair themselves.*

Aura of Terror — *instills unconscious terror in creatures of lower rank.*

Life-seeking — *can sense living creatures*

within a certain radius.

System Creature — *belongs to the System.*

Holy shit... I felt a chill of fear run down my spine. It wasn't due to the skill, I just imagined myself in the place of the sentries for a second.

"Danger!" someone shouted again from the darkness. "Help!"

I heard the horn sound. Raising the general alarm? The Bone Horror caught up to a player and, piercing him with one of its paws, threw the corpse aside, immediately losing all interest. The undead creature didn't seem interested in blood and flesh, just murder... And experience points, probably.

For a moment, I could see the creature in the firelight. The Bone Horror reminded me of a three-meter-long lizard made up of fused bones: six legs, with the front two resembling arms, a meter-long tail dotted with sharp fragments, a short neck ending in a massive head, with a huge mouth filled with teeth. The limbs varied in length, and the whole thing looked ugly, crooked, and unbalanced.

"Bloody hell! I can't see shit! What's happening?" Dmitry's voice rang out. "Is it the goblins?"

"No, it's a strong undead," I said, once I ascertained that he wasn't going to ask about Lisa. "Tenth level. Rank D. Twenty points of *Strength*, ten of *Agility*, three of *Intelligence*."

Another short cry came from the darkness.

It should have been the last one, since most sentries had disappeared into the buildings by now, and the monster was too large to fit through the gaps. Unless it was strong enough to break down the walls, but even then, the victims would have a chance to escape...

"What do we do now?" Lisa broke the silence.

I didn't know the answer to that question myself. There was barely enough firelight to track the monster's movements. There was no way we could go out there and fight the creature. Was this sort of beasts waiting for us in the center of the city? Trying to distract myself, I calculated how many experience a hero would receive if they managed to take down such a creature. The creature's rank (3) is multiplied by level (10), multiplied by the limit (20), then by the weapon absorption level (0.4). I got 240 SP. Defeating the Bone Horror would immediately raise me to Level 6. I listened to my gut but greed could not overcome fear, for the risk was too great. There was only one undead creature, so we could quietly leave the building and head far away. Not that I had much faith in such a plan.

"We'll wait until morning," I made the most obvious decision. "We'll decide what to do when it's light. Everyone back to bed!"

⁕ ⁕ ⁕

I sat in my usual spot, legs dangling over the edge of the roof, and stared at the square. The sun rose slowly, allowing me to assess the situation and count the mutilated corpses. There were four. Not that many for such a monster. The creature itself lay in the center of the square, on a pile of ashes. Was it my imagination, or had the mound really shrunk since yesterday?

The players were already awake, some gathered on the roofs, some peering out of the windows. Now, in the light of the sun, I wasn't so sure we could run.

"I don't think we should mess with it," Dmitry said dryly. He was hurt. Perhaps he even wanted to push me off the roof, but I didn't sense any real danger. "We can just leave."

It made sense, but would the creature leave us alone? If the undead followed us, we'd still have to fight it but under totally different conditions. Either we would destroy it, or the players would scatter, putting an end to our joint mission.

"Let's see what the others decide." I didn't hurry with my answer. "We can always leave."

While I was thinking, Qing Long came out onto the square, surrounded by his men. They kept close to the entrance so that they could return to the house quickly in case of danger, but if I understood correctly... The Asian man raised the horn to his lips and blew.

"Get ready for battle?" I wondered. Had Long really decided to fight? Strange, since he had seemed overly cautious to me. Was that the point? Or was it a test? There were six hundred players gathered here, against a single Level 10 undead. If we couldn't deal with it, did it make any sense to venture deeper into the city, where we might encounter hundreds of such creatures?

I turned and glanced at my people, most of whom looked scared. Not that I wanted to risk my life either, but I felt a little disappointed by what I saw.

"According to the agreement, I must join the battle. Let each one decide for yourself whether you're ready to fight." I looked at the girl. "Lisa, you'll stay in the house and take care of the wounded if necessary."

The girl nodded, not even trying to pretend that she wanted to fight. It wasn't surprising, really, I'd assumed she'd come to me in the hope of protection. Pragmatism mixed with instincts. This thought left a bad taste in my mouth. If I died, which one of her admirers would get lucky next?

Possible neither of them, since both of my 'rivals' decided to go into the square. To my surprise, the others followed. Well, it was their choice. I had put the group together to increase my chances of survival, not to risk my neck for everyone else.

"Stay behind me and don't go charging in without my orders."

The creature lay motionless on the mound of ashes and didn't react when people appeared in its range. Had its run out of energy? It couldn't sense our presence? It was too good to be true. Was it drawing us closer? Waiting until there were more of us? Given the 3 in *Intelligence*, it didn't have enough brains for an overly subtle plan. Why chase after us if it could catch us all at once?

Meanwhile, similar groups of players were gathering in front of the other houses. Nevertheless, there were too few of us, much fewer than expected. Two hundred, perhaps? The only good thing was that all the top players were present. When I was sure that I had been spotted, I saluted the other 'kamikaze' with my spear.

The players who had decided not to risk it remained on the roofs and in the windows as useless spectators. We had almost no long-range weapons, and except for a few mages, they could do nothing to help us. Unless someone built a sling, but even that would be useless against the bony beast. I should have felt mad, I guess, but their behavior was rather predictable.

Attacking from a distance was not a bad idea. I pulled the modern bow from its card and slung my quiver across my back. It looked alien among the ruins, but my Archery card was no longer a secret, so it didn't raise any questions.

Nevertheless, Long hesitated to attack. Without waiting for his signal, the Brahmin came forward, surrounded by his followers. "Listen up!

My skill allows me to control the undead! Don't interfere. If I can subdue the creature, we won't have to fight it. Moreover, it may help us in our fight against the goblins."

The square was quite large and I may not have heard his words, but the other players repeated the message. The undead creature still didn't react. Was it deaf as well as blind? Anyway, how did this bag of bones sense its surroundings? How were the bones connected to each other? Did the creature have a set of magical organs, or just a sort of 'life force'? Would my *Invisibility* work on it? Take the head, for example. This was a critical spot for almost any living creature, but I assumed that the most important part here were the teeth...

"May the rakshasas devour him." Sahel muttered, and added, noticing my questioning glance, "The Brahmin is a bad man. Very mean."

"Don't worry, we have an agreement. He won't bother you." I'd managed to exchange a few words with the Hindu man yesterday, settling the conflict. He had 'gifted' Sahel to me. I did have to promise him one of the potential zombies in return, though. He was an unpleasant character, but my necromancy experiments had clearly interested him.

"Really?"

I nodded and stared ahead of me. The Brahmin walked slowly forward with his left hand outstretched. He held a kind of long staff or club in his right hand. He had picked magic as his first skill, and yet, despite having no magic spells, had managed to become one of the strongest players. And a leader. Almost his whole squad was following him.

The Bone Horror suddenly leaped to its feet and darted toward the approaching procession. I closed my eyes instinctively, not wanting to see the monster impale the man on its bone talons, but then opened them so as not to miss anything. The Bone Horror stopped five paces away from the group, as suddenly as it had moved.

"I'm holding it!" the Brahmin shouted. "I'm holding him! Don't interfere!"

Now that the Bone Horror was standing still, I could see a blue ball deep inside the tangle of bones. Hidden in the center of the body and covered by a dense network of bones, it clearly meant a lot to this undead. This must be the 'weak spot' I was looking for. I wondered if I could hit it with an arrow. Frankly, the chances were very slim, and I couldn't do it now without getting a bunch of complaints in return.

The creature's stillness had a calming effect on the players. Many began to draw closer, and people who hadn't initially planned to get involved came out of the houses. The sneakiest ones, to be blunt. They stayed close enough to the houses to escape if something went wrong, yet they would later describe how bravely they had come to fight against the powerful undead.

"Obey me!" the Brahmin shouted. "Come on!

I! Am! Your! Master!"

Judging by the strain in his voice, the taming process was not going well. Perhaps the man should have started with something smaller, but he had decided to go all-in. If he succeeded, the Brahmin would become the strongest of us all, and I sincerely wished him good luck. There was no time for envy. We had one common enemy, the goblins. Well, if the Brahmin totally lost his mind and decided to turn against us, his bone pet wouldn't protect him from an arrow flying out of empty air...

"I... I can't do it. Kill it! I can't hold it any longer. Attack!"

I raised my bow to take advantage of the monster's stillness, and the Hindu man's retinue surged forward, but the Brahmin had taken too long to admit his defeat. Three of his followers were thrown aside by powerful blows. The creature leaped forward, swung its paw, and the Brahmin's head was flung far away. A fountain of blood rose into the air.

"I've only see this in games, until today," I muttered.

The monster's tail rose into the air and struck the crowd, who stood frozen under a shower of blood. The creature didn't stop for even a moment, smashing into the bewildered group and showering blows right and left... It was a massacre. Humans were slower, weaker, and their weapons were ill-equipped to fight such monsters.

The horn sounded again, and I looked for Qing Long. A general attack? Seriously? Despite the order, most players remained still, and some even backed away. Everything hung in the balance...

"Attack!" the Swordsman shouted. "Let's all attack it together!"

I was distracted for only a second, and then I lost sight of him. His ability made it hard to lead people into battle, and would his *Invisibility* have an effect on this thing? Would mine?

"Hold," I repeated my order. None of my people had the abilities to fight this meat grinder. The charred bones were now splattered in blood. If I survived, I'd probably have more than just goblins visiting me in my nightmares.

One of the battle mages threw a fireball. A few more people cast spells, but the monster didn't seem to take much damage. Despite looking impressive, their abilities were too weak. Plus, the mages had terrible aim. I let an arrow fly and although it struck the creature, it got caught in the tangle of bones. The monster ignored it, sinking its teeth into the player in front of it.

Less than half of the people who had accompanied the Brahmin remained, and that was only because the Bone Horror couldn't attack everyone at once. The other players drew closer, and the creature spun, as if trying to decide who would be its next victim. For a moment, its gaze lingered on me, but then it turned towards the approaching players. Hmm... Whether the creature could see or not, its behavior reminded me of a living creature.

The Bone Horror jumped. I let out another arrow. Then another one, and another one. Really, there was no way I could aim properly at the continuously moving creature, but I half emptied my quiver before I admitted to myself that I was only wasting arrows. Had I been hoping for a miracle? Or using an excuse to stay away from this thing?

A two-meter-tall golem leaped forward, striking the creature's face with its club. Teeth flew in all directions, but the monster didn't seem bothered by the loss. The Bone Horror swept its paw and flung the golem far away. Alexander rolled along the cobblestones, losing his 'earthen armor' before our eyes. Nevertheless, the System could still identify him when he stopped, which meant that the idiot was still alive. What was the point of striking the head if its 'heart' was inside the body?

The horn howled again, urging people to attack. Qing Long was right, for if we retreated now, there'd be no chance of defeating the monster later. I took out my flask and took a sip of elixir No. 0003. Of course, one could track the increase in characteristics, but mostly theoretically. Plus, what conclusions could people draw from this? Who would connect the elixir to the dead priest? Even my paranoia didn't go that far.

"Are we going over there?" Dmitry asked and licked his lips, as I put away my bow and took out my spear. Although the spear seemed completely unsuited to fighting the undead, I thought it was the most appropriate weapon in this situation. Perhaps I could reach the 'heart' with the right now. True, the blow had to be a truly masterful one, yet it would be much more difficult to do with a sword.

The alternative was to take the creature apart, piece by piece, which is what the players were currently doing. Their blows caused the bones to crack and come off, but there were too many of them, and the retaliatory blows left corpses in their wake... If there had been fewer players, we would have already run away.

"I'm going," I said, shifting into *Invisibility* and reluctantly breaking into a run. I had strong doubts about whether my skill would work on the undead, but I had to test it. To my surprise, I ran towards the battle, and not away, as my voice of reason instructed.

We can't win... It's too strong... I must run... I'm going to die...

I stumbled, belatedly realizing that it wasn't my cowardice, but the Aura of Terror. It was difficult to get close to the creature, but once I recognized this, running became easier. The overwhelming feeling receded, although I'm sure

I'd have run faster in the opposite direction.

Attention! Your parameters have temporarily increased!
Stamina +1.3. Perception +1.1.
Time remaining: 17 minutes

Finally. The elixir wasn't based on magic, so the effect wasn't immediate. I would have noticed the change even without the notification, for I could now see my surroundings much more clearly, and my strength had obviously increased.

Once I reached my target, I didn't rush forward but decided to wait. It seemed that my *Invisibility* worked on the beast, for it was ignoring me. Unfortunately, my allies couldn't see me either, so I had to make sure that I didn't run into someone or receive an accidental blow. I also had to pick the right moment to attack. If I missed, I didn't think I'd get a second chance.

Should I use the bow again? The thought sent a chill of foreboding down my spine, indicating that this decision was a mistake. My skill was too weak, and the creature wasn't that dumb, so an arrow flying out of nothingness may incite it to strike the area with its tail, for example. Or jump in my direction and deliver a dozen blind blows. This was just an attempt to find a reasonable explanation for what my intuition was telling me.

"Fine." I gripped the spear, and the chill

eased, as if agreeing that my chances were much better with it. The horn blared again, calling to attack, but I could see that the players were ready to run. Frankly, I didn't understand why we were still holding on. Was it one of the skills? Maybe I'd seen a *Fighting Spirit Aura* on the list last night? Otherwise, it was hard to explain why I was willing to take such a risk.

"No!" shouted a familiar voice. The chimera lifted another player into the air, piercing his body, and with a flick of its paw, flung him aside. Marcus? That would be three out of the eight leaders. Five leaders now... Damn!

These dark thoughts didn't stop me from striking when the creature paused for a moment as it tried to dislodge a player impaled on its tail. I sensed that the moment was close to ideal.

Someone screamed again, but I couldn't get distracted. The blow was a success. The spear grazed several bones, but kept going until it finally felt resistance. The monster twisted, the bones inside it shifting to grip the spear, but I didn't even think of letting go as I continued to push it in further. Come on! A rush of energy swept through me, almost making me scream with pleasure.

Attention! You have gained 240 SP!

You have obtained Level 4! (80/80)

You have obtained Level 5! (100/100)

You have obtained Level 6! (14/120)

Attention! You have earned Shiva's favor!

Attention! You have avenged the death of the High Priest of Shiva. Go to one of the temples to receive your reward. Bring his weapons and receive an extra reward.

My *Invisibility* faded, and I dropped to one knee. Only half of the spear remained in my hand, for it had snapped. The tip and a piece of the shaft were somewhere inside the pile of bones.

It was as if the sound had been turned back on, and I heard moans, cries, and calls for help. I got back to my feet and looked around. This battle had cost us dearly, leaving about four dozen dead and seriously wounded on the ground.

"Is it dead?" someone asked. Well, if it was still alive, I wouldn't have received the experience points, right? "It's dead! We won!"

Someone took up the cry, and the shouts soon merged into a united roar, which grew in strength. I looked around and found the Swordsman standing next to the monster's head, which was lying separate from the body. It seemed that we had launched our attack almost simultaneously, only I had struck the 'heart' and he had gone for the neck.

"I suppose I should be congratulating you." The Swordsman said grimly. Right, his level remained the same, all the experience points had gone to me. He'd performed a feat, all to discover that he'd been a little late. It was unfortunate. I was now a level higher, but it was just numbers somewhere in the depths of the interface. This was a moment of my greatest vulnerability. I hadn't become stronger just yet, but the price on my head had increased dramatically.

"It's OUR victory, " I said, resisting the urge to retreat into *Invisibility*. "That was a good strike."

"Don't," he frowned. "The monster wouldn't have died from its head being cut off, and we both know it. It would have only weakened the creature. I just couldn't reach that blue sphere."

I put the broken spear in my bag and took out the spare one from the ashigaru. It felt strange in my hand, but it suited my fighting style. Better than a sword, in which I only had the first rank.

No one tried to stop me from removing the second piece of the spear from the mound of bones. Even if there was no way fix the weapon, I was going to hang it up on the wall at home. The pieces of blue crystal had crumbled into fine dust, mixing with the earth and ash, but I gathered them up as well. There were also the arrows, but I could collect them later…

The main reward, a card, hung above the monster's corpse. I snatched it out of the air and glanced at it.

The Calculating Mind skill card

Class: *E.*

Level: *1/5.*

Description:

— *When activated, suppresses emotions for rational thinking.*

— *Consumes mana or Vitality.*

— *Continuous use of the skill can have negative consequences.*

— *???*

Saturation:

86/100 SP

The skill itself seemed quite useful, given that I could feel myself slowly losing the plot. Being able to calm down at a critical moment could save lives more than once. Eighty-six points? Just the right amount so that I could spend all the remaining SP and obtain this skill. It was a very odd coincidence, but life could be weird...

"Well, what is it?" Marcus asked. Although the Italian sported a bloody hole in his chest, he looked disgustingly cheerful for a dead man. As if it wasn't him who'd been run through and thrown to the side a minute ago, breaking half his bones on the cobblestones.

"Take a look," I handed him the card. It was a sign of trust and a test at the same time. I doubted that he could study it, and if he tried to keep it...

"Not bad," the Italian man said, handing the card back to me. "By the way, I almost died without saying thank you for your help last time. You were that archer on the roof, weren't you?"

"I was glad to help," I said, seeing no point in denying it. "How did you survive?"

"Back then or this time?" Marcus asked.

"This time."

"Thanks to my skill. I wanted to keep it a secret, but there's no point now. It's called a backup, and if I die, it rewinds my body back a little in time. About three seconds. Alas, it doesn't apply to my gear," he touched the hole. "I'll have to take a new jacket off some corpse."

"Then you'd better hurry," I said, indicating the approaching crowd of competitors with a jerk of my head. "I think the dead will soon have heirs."

The monster's death aroused widespread interest, and players poured in from everywhere. They hadn't touched the bodies yet, but it was only a matter of time.

"Attention!" Qing Long shouted, apparently coming to the same conclusion. "Bring the card and bags of the dead over here! Their property will be distributed later. Take care of the wounded! Firstly, look after Alexander!"

I regretfully gave up on the idea of collecting more bags. I couldn't be too greedy. Also, in addition to the messages about experience and levels, wasn't there something else relating to Shiva? I looked around and found that Michigan had already reached the headless body of the Brahmin and, taking advantage of the fact that his followers had run off, was searching it. Bag, cards, staff...

"I must return the priest's staff to the temple of Shiva," I said as I approached.

"I also have a mission to bring the staff to the temple of... Quetzalcoatl." The swordsman returned the staff to the card, then suddenly handed it to me. "However, I'm not going to break our agreement. Here."

He didn't share the dead man's bag, however, and slung it over his shoulder.

Great, another divine artifact. Lucky me! I took the card and studied the characteristics.

Spirit Staff/Khatvanga

Rank: *D.*
Material: *wood, steel.*
Weight: *1 kg.*
Type: *divine artifact, scalable.*
Features:
— *Enables the owner to absorb 60% of the spiritual and life force of the victim.*
— *19% of the energy absorbed by this weapon goes directly to Shiva.*
— *1% of the absorbed energy condenses on the staff.*
— *40% goes to the owner.*
— *40% is absorbed by the System.*
Dedication to Shiva (blocked):
— *Unlocks the Faith parameter. Faith +1.*

— Ability to convert similar parameters to Faith.

— Symbol of power. Allows new adepts to be initiated (0/10).

— ??? (0/10).

— Beacon.

— Gives Shiva the chance to draw the soul of the murdered owner to his altar.

Owner:

— Brahmin.

Interesting that the owner hadn't reset. This was probably why the abilities were blocked. It was odd that the block was linked to the owner and not the patron. I could easily use the Sun Sword, for example, despite not being initiated into the service of Inti.

Oh, and had I jumped to conclusions and none of our eight had been eliminated? Even Alexander was now awake, moaning heroically, surrounded by a trio of girls from his squad who looked at each other jealously. What a hero.

"Looks like the Brahmin is alive," I said confidently. It was difficult to say this about a man whose decapitated body lay half a meter away. "To be precise, he is dead, but his soul was captured by Shiva, and I think Shiva will resurrect him."

"Some day. According to Quel, resurrection is a costly process, and our gods are still young."

Quel? It appeared that I wasn't the only one who had trouble pronouncing the name of the

Aztec deity, since even his high priest had chosen to use an abbreviation. It sounded much better.

"Were you given a second task?"

"Deliver the staff to the Inti temple?" I said, noticing the questioning look. One lie begets another. If I had a 'patron', then it was logical to assume that he would also want to get his hands on someone else's artifact. "Of course."

"I thought so," he said. "The gods don't get along very well. It seems the first task was assigned for killing this creature, and the second is assigned to anyone who picks it up. So be careful. I hope you make the right choice."

"Of course. Can you answer one question for me?"

"Shoot."

"Which skill did you get for a ten in *Stamina*?"

"It's called Marathon Runner. It slows down how quickly I tire, so I can run for longer... or swim..." Bill winced visibly at the last word. He didn't seem to like swimming.

"Thank you," I said. "What does a ten in *Strength* give you, do you know?"

Sulu had a ten in Strength, but I didn't really want to pester the African man with such questions yet.

"The *Explosion* skill, I think. It allows a person to become even stronger for a short time, overcoming the first limit. However, it causes damage to the body, so it can't be used often."

"Thank you."

The Swordsman nodded and walked away, leaving me to be accosted by people wanting to congratulate me on my "outstanding strike", "new levels", or exchange a word or two. Speaking of levels, I had to decide what I wanted to invest my points into. Of course, I had a draft development plan, but after getting so many free parameters at once, it made sense to adjust it.

In general, the choice was between *Strength*, *Agility*, *Intelligence*, and *Perception*. It didn't make sense to level up "a little bit of everything" if I could increase two parameters to the maximum and get bonuses. Although there was also *Wisdom*, which could be increased to nine. It wouldn't reach the cap, but it would dramatically increase my magical abilities.

"Goblins! The goblins are coming!"

I swore. Judging by the panic in the voice, they weren't just individual scouts. All our plans were going to hell. Why didn't that surprise me? It was naive to hope that this bone bastard had appeared here by chance.

APPENDIX

CHARACTER TABLE NO. 2

VASILY

General ID: unknown.
Local ID: Z-8.
True Name: Ivan Susanin (hidden).
Age: 24 years.
Race: human (97%).
Gender: male.
Level: 6 (14/120 SP).
Available: 14 SP.

Parameters:
Strength: 6+1=7/10.
Agility: 7/10.
Intelligence: 7/10.

Vitality: 6/10.
Stamina: 6/10.
Perception: 7/10.
Luck: 2/10.

Race Parameter:
Intuition: 9+1=10/10.

Additional Parameters:
Wisdom: 1+2=3.
Faith: 0/10 (blocked, no patron).
Free points: 6.

System Skills:
Player (E):
— Intuitive interface (E, 1/1).
— Help (E, 1/1).
— System language (F, 1/1).

Combat Skills:
— Spear fighting (F, 3/5).
— Archery (F, 1/5).
— Sword fighting (F, 1/5).

Secondary:
— Camouflage (F, 1/5).
— Medicine of the Earth (F, 1/5).
— Goblin language (F, 1/1).

Features:
— Minor magical ability (F, 2/5).

Rank E Skills:

— Identification (E, 1/5) — allows one to determine the properties of objects.

— Invisibility (E, 1/5) — creates a cloaking field around the hero.

— Duelist (E, 1/5) — allows one to conduct a duel according to certain rules.

Achievements and Titles:

— **Eighth (personal, unique)** — sometimes bad luck is so great that great luck passes very close by. Features unknown.

— **Atheist** — reduces the favor of the gods.

Cards:

Rank F: spear — 1, spear fragments, sword, axe, saber, sword, katana — 2, sword, dagger, Goblin language.

Rank E:

— **Archer's Kit:** renewable quiver (E), goblin bow (-), archer's ring (-), spare bowstring (-).

— **System Dagger (E).**

— **The Calculating Mind (E).**

Rank D:

Mask of Cain (cursed).

— **Khatvanga (Shiva)** — the sacred weapon of one of the seven gods of Earth.

— **Sun Sword (Inti)** — the sacred weapon of

one of the seven gods of Earth.

Other:
— **Marauder's bag (E, 1/7).**
— **Bottomless bag (F, 3/7).**
— **Eternal flasks** — 11 items.
— **Broken spear (F--).**
— **Faded cards** from studied skills. Can be used as armor, other use unknown.
— **Modern bow (-)** — transformed using the Archer's Kit.
— **Player kit (x11)** — various levels of completeness.
— **Mana crystals.**
— **Crystal powder** — dust mixed with earth, from the destroyed magical hearts of the undead. Purpose unknown.

CHAPTER 15

THE RETREAT

"KEEP CALM!" Qing Long shouted, trying to quell the rising panic. "Take the wounded and withdraw to Government House!"

He raised the horn to his lips and blew a long note, inviting the few who hadn't yet done so to join us. Most of the players had already spilled out onto the square, keen to see the fallen beast, but the fate of the rest was in their hands.

"Retreat!" others shouted in support. "Don't panic! There aren't that many goblins!"

I noticed that some players ran away instead of joining the main group. They were probably hoping to remain hidden while the goblins slaughtered the rest. Should I follow them or retreat with the main force? The right decision depended on the number of approaching goblins. If it was the promised army, then immediate flight was the only way to survive. The goblin squad that appeared on the other side of the square didn't look like an army. Three hundred warriors, no more. However, it could have been the advance party, with a few thousand more hiding behind those houses...

I listened to my gut, trying to decide whether I was more drawn to the dubious security of Government House or to just getting away from the square. My *Intuition* remained treacherously quiet, refusing to give me any clear hints. On the other hand, I didn't feel the same sense of deadly terror as when I'd seen the Bone Horror. There was, however, another problem.

"Eighth squad! To me!" I shouted, looking around to make sure everyone was present.

Who was I kidding? I was interested in a particular member of our squad, who'd remained at the base. Funny that I'd fallen into the same trap I thought the others would fall into. I knew perfectly well that we had to retreat and leave the girl to her fate, but I couldn't let her fall into the goblins' hands after what had happened. I could, of course, but then a new character would be added to my nightmares. What should I do now? Abandon everyone and go 'save the princess'? I almost hated her at that moment — an irrational but powerful feeling.

"Lisa?!" I shouted again, hoping for a

miracle, and I got one.

"I'm here," the girl said, emerging from the crowd and holding out a bundle of arrows. "I collected as much of them as I could."

"Well done," I said, putting the arrows back in my bag. My irritation dissipated, replaced by a pleasant surprise. I knew she wasn't stupid, but still... It was very helpful. The Bone Horror hadn't kept still so the arrows had been scattered over a large area, and I hadn't had time to collect them. To do so now, with the goblins in the square, would have been simply stupid.

"Are there any wounded?" she asked, belatedly remembering her role.

I shook my head. There weren't many left after the Bone Horror, and most of them need a priest rather than a doctor. To grant them absolution. "Withdraw!"

* * *

The goblin formation split, letting out fifty archers who were running very fast in our direction. The spearmen were moving more slowly, but they also picked up speed. I was most concerned about the cavalry, but the three dozen riders chose to split into two groups, cutting off the flanks. Well, it seemed like the fugitives had made the wrong choice.

"Arrows!" someone shouted. "Look out!"

It was a timely warning, for steel rain pelted

the crowd a few seconds later. Strangely enough, some of the players carried handmade shields, while others tried to roll themselves into a ball or cover themselves with their hands or a bag. Some of the arrows struck the paving stones, but some found their targets. There were screams of pain and pleas for help.

"Collect the wounded!" When I saw one of my people fall, I corrected my instructions. "Grab Nick under the elbows and drag him. Don't leave anyone behind!"

It didn't make much sense, because if a player couldn't walk by themselves, this would only delay the inevitable, but logic never worked well in such instances. Just like a conscience. Most ignored the wounded, not wanting to risk their own lives.

"Throw the wounded on you back!" Marcus shouted, hoisting a dead body onto his shoulders. "They will protect you! The arrows can't penetrate a body!"

I remembered that d'Artagnan had done something like this once when getting out of the firing line. The idea turned out to be quite attractive, at least, many people liked the concept of 'human shields'.

"Collect the arrows!" I shouted. The bow gave me an advantage, but what was one quiver? Thirty arrows. Three minutes of combat, under normal conditions. Two minutes considering the lost arrows.

To set an example, I scooped up a couple more arrows as I ran, and dropped them into my bag. I didn't even think of getting out my bow, since the main thing right now was speed. The loss of a couple of warriors wouldn't slow the goblins down, but they needed to stop to shoot. The distance between us was almost at the limit of their bows, and we had to make use of this.

It also didn't make much sense to activate *Invisibility*. The goblins fired at random and almost without aiming, so it wouldn't protect me from the arrows, but an invisible person could be knocked down by their own people. Unless I moved out of the crowd, but this certainly wouldn't improve my squad's fighting spirit. On the contrary, leaders needed to exude calm and confidence, regardless of how they really felt. Damn it.

"Get inside. Quickly! Quickly!"

We were winning this race since the goblins weren't moving fast enough. The problem was that the entrance was too narrow to let everyone in at once, and the arrows only added to the panic.

"Through the windows!" Qing Long commanded. "Those with the shields, cover the back rows! Remain calm. Drag the corpses inside, too!"

"The women and wounded go first," the Swordsman chimed in. For a maniac who'd killed a whole bunch of people, he was being terribly noble.

I snorted as I watched him try to get the

players to keep at least some semblance of order. Sulu and the Middle Eastern man had already disappeared into the building. Quite pragmatic. Alexander had 'put on' his earthen armor again as he tried to cover the others. The arrows couldn't touch him, but how long could he pretend to be a golem?

The delay, small as it was, allowed the archers to close the distance between us and fire a full volley. "Arrows!" I yelled, and took a step to cover Lisa with my body. There was no heroism, just simple logic. What difference did it make where I stood if an arrow could fall anywhere?

Well, I shouldn't have forgotten that I was rarely lucky at cards. The gesture, which should have cost me nothing, was almost my last. I felt a sharp twinge of fear and instinctively swung up my spear, deflecting the arrow. How?

"Th-thank you," the girl said and put her hands on my back. It must have looked quite impressive. A chill ran down my spine again, a belated realization rather than a premonition. Three days... Even if that arrow hadn't kill me, it would have still been the end.

"Don't just stand there!" I growled. "The building is rectangular. There are windows on the other side, too!" The crowd dispersed rapidly, and I felt a stab of cold anger, having almost died. "I hate goblins," I muttered. "Go! I'll hold them back for a bit."

Clutching my bow, I faded into *Invisibility*

and stepped aside, firing a dozen arrows one after another. Fortunately, the goblins had provided me with plenty of them, so I didn't need to scrimp. Four enemies fell, and I hurriedly took cover behind a pillar. Invisibility was poor protection from a shower of arrows, even if they weren't aimed directly at you.

One of the goblins, covered in necklaces of bones and amulets, pointed at the spot where I'd been standing, and several dozen arrows flew there at once. I squinted... Wow, seventh level!

"It's rude to point," I muttered, sending an arrow his way. Unfortunately, it pecked at the goblin's chest and bounced off the armor hidden under the cloak.

The shaman turned in my direction, but didn't point this time, preferring to hide behind two bodyguards. No, it didn't look like he could see me. Had he reacted to the arrows coming out of thin air? I didn't want to push my luck any further, preferring to lie low and watch for a while. By this point, the last players had already climbed through the doorways and windows, taking cover inside the building. The goblin spearmen sped up, but still didn't make it, stopping fifty meters away.

What now? Unfortunately, the goblins didn't try to follow the players inside. The archers remained in place to monitor the doorways, while some of the infantry went to check the corpses. Their method was simple but effective – a kick, then a dagger to the eye. The three who'd managed to beg for mercy in time were dragged away.

"Bastards."

In any case, there was nothing left to do here. Jumping into a window and moving slightly to the side so as not to get struck accidentally, I dropped my *Invisibility*. Several players gasped, but calmed down when they recognized me. It seemed that I was becoming famous. I didn't know whether to be happy about it or not.

I didn't have to look for my people for long, for they had taken up position on the ground floor, closer to the other side of the building. It was a smart move, since they had higher chances of escaping if something went wrong. Lisa was bent over the wounded man, examining his leg.

"It's obvious that Vasily is dead!" Siegfried argued fervently as he held the wounded man. "Otherwise, he would have returned by now! The goblins will soon attack, and we must..."

He faltered when he saw me approaching. I could have listened to the rest of his plans, but I doubted that I'd have heard anything interesting.

"How is he?" I asked, indicating the guy lying on the floor. Judging by the fact that the System still recognized him, he was simply unconscious. What a delicate flower.

"Well, he's unlikely to die from this wound," Lisa stated. Was it good news? I wasn't sure since a natural death would have made things much easier.

"Are you going to remove the arrow?" I asked and she nodded. "Do you need any help?"

"We'll help her," Dmitry said. "The other leaders were looking for you. They're somewhere on the first floor, discussing how to get out of this mess."

How? There weren't that many options. I didn't need a fortune teller to tell me that we'd have to fight soon. It was better to go into battle with increased characteristics. So, the choice between this need and participating in yet another meeting was obvious. I pulled out one of the flasks with the nourishing cocktail and drained it in one long swallow. Something was telling me that I'd need it.

"I went up three levels, so I need to spend the points. Don't let anyone approach me," I ordered, sitting down against the wall and closing my eyes. This made it easier to work with the interface. "Send someone up to tell the others I'm busy, they can decide without me."

I doubted the respite would last long, so I needed to be quick. I had decided on my overall strategy of raising one more parameter to the maximum, and distributing the remaining points more or less evenly. I'd decide exactly how as I went along. Expending everything at once was madness, given how painful the procedure was, so I had to move step-by-step. What did I *definitely* need to increase?

> **Parameters:**
> *Strength: 6+1=7/10.*
> *Agility: 7/10.*
> *Intelligence: 7/10.*
> *Vitality: 6/10.*
> *Stamina: 6/10.*
> *Perception: 7/10 = 7.*
> *Luck: 2/10.*
> **Race parameter:**
> *Intuition: 9+1=10/10.*
> **Additional parameters:**
> *Wisdom: 1+2=3.*
> *Faith: 0/10 (blocked, no patron).*
> **Free points:** *6.*

"Whoosh!" I muttered, putting the first point into *Intelligence*. Of course, I wouldn't be able to destroy the goblins with my mind, but increasing this parameter was important. At least to evaluate the effect. Perhaps it would also help me to better distribute the remaining points?

It felt nothing like waving a magic wand. The process was far from instantaneous, and the sensations were very peculiar. As if a bunch of ants were running around inside my skull, occasionally biting off pieces of my brain. My vision blurred for a moment, but then everything returned to normal.

As for the result... Well, there was certainly

a change. It was easier to think and my thoughts were clearer, but the difference wasn't so marked that it couldn't be due to wishful thinking. Nothing global, like abruptly rethinking my whole life or a desire to blink my third eye. How about some math? Well, two plus two was still four. To hell with it, I'd postpone the tests until later. What was next?

"Whoosh!" I repeated to myself, increasing my *Agility*. The stick clenched between my teeth made it difficult to speak. There was a reason why I'd put it there.

It... was... very... unpleasant. Back when I was child, I'd done some martial art, and one of the most unpleasant parts was the stretching. In the same way, ligaments and tendons were being slowly but steadily stretched all over my body. The process wasn't very long but it was excruciating.

I lowered my head, stifling a cry. Somewhere at the edge of my awareness, the wounded man howled, but I was too wrapped up in my own suffering. It was all over after a couple of minutes, and I unclenched my teeth, spitting out the splintered wood. It was time to make the next selection.

"Mother f..." I changed my phrase slightly as I increased *Stamina*. This time, it was my heart, lungs, and muscles that hurt. The latter all over the body, of course.

I tried to remember the theory to distract myself from the pain. According to scientists, muscles consisted of three types of fibers. Slow oxidative fibers, containing a type of mitochondria that allowed them to interact with oxygen, and made the fibers red in color. These fibers can withstand a load that isn't too heavy for a long time, and the mitochondria process all the harmful products accumulating in the body. When the load increases, the intermediary or pink fibers come into play, whose mitochondria are much smaller, and do not cope so well with processing the toxins. If the load becomes even greater, then the third type of fiber comes into play, the fast glycolytic white fibers. A short time after they kick in, the body stops coping with the end products, and it becomes not only almost impossible to continue at this pace, but also harmful.

If I was to summarize all this scientific mumbo-jumbo, endurance depended on the red fibers and, to a lesser extent, the pink ones. Power depended on the white fibers. The number of fibers couldn't be altered, but it was possible to increase their size and density, which is what the System was going to do...

Strangely, my muscles didn't increase in size, but even decreased slightly. It didn't fit the theory. Or was it just me? Perhaps by pumping up this parameter alongside *Strength*, I could avoid turning into a two-by-two meter hulk?

I spat out the badly damaged piece of wood and took a new one out of my bag. This was the end of my obvious conclusions. I had three points remaining. It was time to decide which parameter would be raised to ten. *Strength* (7), *Agility* (8), *Intelligence* (8), *Stamina* (7), or *Perception* (7)?

Intelligence? Just two points so the temptation was great, but if I understood correctly, this parameter affected cognitive processing, ease of learning, and so on. It wouldn't make me smarter right now, it would only provide me with the potential. I also felt no desire to invest another point in this option.

Perception? It should give even better results together with *Intuition*, but I was already suffering from bouts of paranoia. It was hard to remain calm when you constantly sensed danger at the edge of your consciousness. As I recalled, Jack had increased his *Perception* to the maximum and had suffered from something similar. Would I experience the same thing? After all, it wasn't enough to notice everything around you, you also needed to process and filter the received information. I wasn't yet ready for such an experiment on my psyche...

The next choice was less simple. *Agility* (8) or *Stamina* (7)? Should I flip a coin?

"Dmitry, heads or tails?" I asked.

"Tails," the guy said without even thinking.

The coin showed tails... Like the Bone Horror's whipping tail. I shook my head to drive the image away. *Stamina*, then. Only an idiot would trust an important choice to chance. The point of tossing a coin was to help me understand what I wanted. I felt no disappointment or a desire to flip again, which meant that I was happy with the choice.

I increased my *Stamina* by three more points, one by one, feeling ready to eat a couple of goblins by the end of the process. Metaphorically, of course. Who in their right mind would eat such filth?

Congratulations! Your Stamina parameter has reached the limit for your race.

Connection with the Server... Select a bonus skill from the list:

— *Marathon Runner (passive, by default).* *You fatigue more slowly.*
— *Second Wind (active, random).* *Allows you to instantly relieve fatigue once in twelve hours.*

Two skills at once? I looked at the timer, which showed that I had a whole thirty seconds to make this fateful choice. This hadn't happened last time. It looked like the first option was the default, and the second was a kind of bonus due to my *Intuition*?

"Lisa, heads or tails?" I decided to resort to the tried and tested method again. "Quick!"

"Heads?" The girl had chosen the opposite option. An accident? I didn't think so.

Marathon Runner, then? This time, the

internal resistance was obvious. I didn't want to take the standard skill. Then let's assume it was tails again. Who was I to argue with fate? I chose *Second Wind.*

I could have stopped there, but I still had one card left.

Would you like to learn the "Calculating Mind" skill?
Yes/No

I confirmed my wish, spending all my remaining experience points. The name and description of the skill sounded a little dubious, but after a moment's hesitation, I decided to test it right away. After all, I could always disable it. **Activate.**

It was as if a veil had fallen over my mind, pushing unhelpful emotions far into the background. The habitual anxiety receded. Yes, the goblin world was dangerous, but the hazard was far enough away to be *rationally* ignored. What a simple thought. I rather liked this state of mind... well, time to act.

＊ ＊ ＊

"How are the goblins?" I asked, adjusting the straps to fit my new build and looking around. "Have I missed a lot?"

A few fresh corpses lay by the wall nearby,

and there were bloodstains under the windows. An Asian man standing by the opposite wall caught my eye and hurried away.

"They're waiting. Shooting at the windows if they spot any movement." Dmitry replied.

He'd replied first again. This time, I noticed how the other members of the group were looking at him. His position as my deputy seemed secure, and even our discord hadn't changed that. He could be potentially dangerous. However, it would be *irrational* to kill him now.

"I went around all the players and collected the arrows, since no one else has a bow, anyway."

"Thank you," I nodded. "Lisa, how's Nick?"

"I removed the arrow, stopped the bleeding, and bandaged the wound. But he can hardly walk on his own."

Right. I found myself being scrutinized. The others were expecting us to leave him. It was *rational...* and *irrational* at the same time. *Insufficient data. Choice* is available.

"I'll go and talk to him. Try to figure out how to make a stretcher of this, we'll take him with us." I took the broken spear and goblin cloak out of my bag and handed them over. Even if emotions were *irrational*, one had to take them into account. Nick was sniffling in the corner, clutching the leg that had been pierced by the arrow. He'd been lucky, for the wound was clean, and the arrow had been pulled out once the tip was broken off. However, if he couldn't walk properly, then he couldn't fight, either. Therefore, even if he survived for three days, he wouldn't be able to fulfill the System's requirements. Unless I brought him a goblin to dispatch?

"How's your experience?" I asked. "Have you killed anyone yet?"

"No," he sobbed. "When would I've had the chance? I hadn't even seen a live goblin before this morning."

Hmm... A walking dead man. He'd set a bad example for the others. We had a battle ahead of us, but it'd be hard to fight without holding back, knowing that the smallest scratch meant death.

"If you keep wallowing in self-pity, you'll die for sure," I said, not feeling sorry for him in the slightest. Pity was *irrational*.

"As if there are any other options," Nick mumbled grimly, pulling himself together. Still, I hadn't accepted people in whom I hadn't seen any potential. He'd just been unlucky.

"You're a member of the eighth squad, and we won't abandon you. For as long as possible, at least," I said with a shrug. "Tears won't help. If you want to live, you've got to fight to the end. If you want to die, you don't have to wait for a sign. Go outside and the goblins will grant you your wish. I think you're strong enough for that?" I stood up and turned away, not wanting to continue this conversation. It was *irrational*. If he decided to die, great. If not, he was still unlikely to survive, but then it wouldn't be my fault. I expected the others to soon get tired of looking after Nick and abandon him when things got tough. But I'd give him a chance.

"I'll go and see what they've decided." I didn't have to go far, as Qing Long met me at the top of the stairs. So, it hadn't been my imagination, and that Asian guy had been watching me? A dangerous sign. It seemed that whatever plans they'd made, I had an important role to play in them... "What have you decided?" I smiled. "Are we going to fight?"

"You've seen what their archers can do, haven't you? We shall retreat first, and then we will see. How many points do you need to raise your *Archery* skill to the second level?"

I noted that he didn't guess, but knew exactly what level my skill was at. It would be *irrational* to deny the obvious.

"Twenty," I said, smiling again and wondering if I should kill him given the opportunity. It was bad when someone knew so much about you. However, this was also *irrational.* "I've spent everything else."

"That's not good." The Chinese man rubbed his chin thoughtfully. "However, we can solve this problem. Come on, let's go to the hospital. We need to hurry, so I will explain everything on the way."

I exchanged nods with the other leaders as I walked. The meeting seemed to be taking place next door to the 'hospital' room. Although it was more accurate to call it the morgue. They may have initially gathered the most seriously injured players here, but only one of the six 'patients' was still breathing. The System no longer recognized the others. Or, more precisely, it identified them as corpses. Even when they died, the players remained a part of the System. It would be *rational* to cut off their heads.

"Lin Jun," Qing Long said, bending over the dying man. "Can you hear me, brother?"

"Yes. Is this... him?" the younger man rasped out, spitting blood onto the floor. Judging by the shaft protruding from his back, the arrow had pierced a lung, and the man was in a bad state. "You promised..." Qing Long nodded silently and looked at his kinsman, inviting him to continue. "I'm going to die anyway. Soon... Kill me... Take my strength... Avenge my death on these hideous black creatures."

I snorted at this sudden racism. However, its origins were somewhat different. People in China were fixated on white skin, which was considered a sign of aristocracy in older times. Tanned, and dark skin in general, was considered unattractive, so the ebony goblins were ugly by Chinese standards.

This whole scene had been obviously set up so that I wouldn't refuse to kill an ally for moral reasons. It had been a waste of energy since I was under the effect of the *Calculating Mind*, and only expediency mattered to me. The main obstacle right now wasn't morality.

"I appreciate his willingness to sacrifice himself, but I don't want to get slapped with a red status." I couldn't use the *Mask of Cain* in front of witnesses, so it was up to the other man to decide the next move.

"We've thought about it," Qing Long nodded, pulling out another mask. As I'd suspected, many of the council members had been among the first 'traitors'.

I'd only hoped to gain some time to think things through by refusing the offer. Getting the experience points was *rational*, but putting the mask was dangerous. I'd lose the System's protection, and anyone could stab me in the back with impunity. Were the experience points just bait?

"For killing a Level 1 player, even with a dagger, I'd only get eight experience points. Ten if it's an E-ranked weapon. I have a suitable dagger. Do you have another sacrifice for me?"

"One is enough. Lin Jun will wear the mask."

Qing Long helped his companion to put on the mask. It was impossible to do this against a person's will, for the mask simply wouldn't activate. A second later, it molded to his face like a second skin. I'd seen something similar in a very old movie, but this mask didn't cover his entire head or give him any supernatural powers. **Faceless No. 6?**

"What's the point? Will I get more experience now?" I asked, glancing at the crimson nickname. The intensity of the status color depended on the severity of the crime. If you believed the description, no experience points were given for masks.

"Not quite. Look at it for ten seconds and you'll understand."

Attention! Faceless No. 6 has broken the Rules! Reward for killing: 20 SP!

A System quest, eh? Twenty experience points... A very round and tempting figure. Especially for beginners, since it was the number needed to reach the second level. I wondered if the number depended on the criminal's level or if it was the same for everyone?

"Just... Do it... Quickly..." the wounded man found the strength to speak. "No pain..." The man was willing to sacrifice his life, but as far as I could remember, the soul of a masked player would be absorbed by the System. Was the price too high? On the other hand, who knew if this was worse than a normal death? I didn't know if rebirth was possible, but I always thought that nothingness lay beyond the threshold. The hesitation flickered and disappeared. It was *rational* to kill him. I drew my dagger and stabbed him in the heart. My *Medicine* skill included knowledge of anatomy and helped me to avoid the man's ribs, so the blade went in smoothly.

Attention! You have eliminated a Criminal! You have received 20 SP! (20/120)

A long, branching crack appeared in the center of the mask, and it split into two halves. The artifact was damaged beyond repair. We should have guessed that the System wouldn't give anything for free. Qing Long cursed. The activated *Calculating Mind* skill prevented me from feeling properly satisfied. By the way, why was it still active?

Would you like to deactivate the Calculating Mind skill?
Yes (irrational) / No (rational)

Irrational? Hadn't I planned to only test the skill and then disable it? Right, that was also considered *irrational*, so I had decided to get a better feel for it. The goal had been achieved. If I could only act *rationally* under its influence, how could I disable the skill at all? Is seemed somehow... *irrational?*

The text swam before my eyes, changing slightly.

Would you like to deactivate the Calculating Mind skill?
Yes (rational) / No (irrational)

This made sense, so I confirmed deactivation. As soon as the skill stopped working, I realized what had happened. It was as if, by blocking my emotions, I'd also been brainwashed. Feelings had almost completely disappeared, leaving only my *goals*. Rational, irrational. Ugh... The most frightening was that as soon as I thought something was rational, I acted without hesitation. Nothing held me back but pure logic and personal gain. All I had to do was decide that I'd found the optimal solution, and even someone's death wouldn't stop me. However, there was no guarantee that the decision would be the right one. Everything depended on the ability to calculate the possible consequences.

If I'd allowed myself to show emotion, I'd have sworn harder than the Azure Dragon after he'd lost the mask. I'd spent precious experience points on this blasted thing?

✹ ✹ ✹

After raising my *Archery* to Level 2 and calming down a bit, I decided that everything wasn't so bad. Although the *Calculating Mind* didn't work quite as I would have liked, it performed its main function perfectly. The constant fear of death, the weight of responsibility, and feeling of tension had all receded into the background, and although the pressure was back on now, I felt much better mentally. As if after a long rest. The accumulated psychological fatigue was gone, which meant that I would make fewer mistakes. In the long run, it meant that I wouldn't go nuts even if all my allies died in front of me, and I was standing knee-deep in blood.

When activated, the skill couldn't force me to act against my will, and it didn't make me more stupid, but simply removed emotions and moral restrictions. It was dangerous, but not as dangerous as it seemed at first glance. The main thing was to know how to disable the skill in time, to convince yourself that it would be *rational.* We didn't have much time, so I decided to postpone this experiment to a later date.

I shook my head, coming back to reality. Yeah, I probably shouldn't skip our G8 meetings without a good reason. I doubted these leaders would have nominated me for the role of 'hero' so easily if I'd been present at the discussion. However, could I complain when I'd agreed to it myself? A deal was a deal.

I glanced at the corner where several fresh, arrow-riddled corpses of my predecessors lay. One of them looked familiar. A 'battle mage' who could cast lightning and who'd decided to compete with the goblins in accuracy. He had even hit someone, but ended up with an arrow in his eye. Nine more had missed, but one was enough for him. He served as an instructive example of how stupid it was to engage in a shooting match with such a difference in 'firepower'. If you don't have an ace up your sleeve.

"Well, let's start with a prayer," I muttered, checking my bow and sorting through the arrows. I hate goblins. I suspected it was mutual. Taking a deep breath, I activated my *Invisibility* and approached the window. The goblins outside didn't respect us at all, and were going about their business. The archers kept the building in their sights, but only formally, while the infantry were lighting fires. Beside one huddled three human figures, the prisoners.

The enemy didn't seem to be leaving anytime soon. This wasn't a full-on siege since the goblins hadn't split up and had just placed sentries around the building, but the next move was up to us. Qing Long was right, attacking them directly was madness.

I slowly drew the goblin bow and set the arrow I'd chosen. Perhaps the modern compound bow was better, but my skill focused on the classic goblin bow. I was sure that training could smooth this out, but I didn't have the time right now. If I wanted to take full advantage of the increase in my skill, it was better to use goblin weapons.

The first arrow soared upwards, made an arc and struck the neck of a brightly dressed goblin. Level 4. He probably had chain mail, but it was an armor-piercing arrow, so he was a goner. The goblins ran around, allowing me to calmly release a second arrow. I didn't pick this time and struck a random archer. Without waiting for the result, I moved away from the window. A single arrow came from outside, hitting the wall. It wasn't even my window, but the next one over.

"They're dead!" our lookout shouted happily, observing the goblins through a crack. "To be more precise, the first one is dead, the second one is still moving."

I changed windows and, leaning out for a moment, released another arrow. The goblins responded in kind, but now more arrows flew through my window, and through the other windows. The goblins were unsure where the arrows were coming from, so they tried to hit me at random. Well, well, good luck with that, fellows.

"Another one's dead!" announced a second lookout. The building had plenty of cracks through which one could observe the outside.

"I don't think so, more like seriously injured," the first one disagreed. As a matter of principle, I guess. "See that leg twitching?"

Bloody commentators… I moved around the building, changing windows at random, sometimes going back, and generally tried to shoot arrows from unexpected locations. Spearmen joined the goblin archers, trying to cover them with their shields, but the overall score was clearly not in their favor. Zero to nine, if you counted the wounded, which were more than half. Still, the goblins were on guard, and a Level 2 in Archery wasn't that much, so not all my arrows found their target.

I felt a chill and paused, while an arrow flew through the window right in front of me. *Whoosh... whoosh... whoosh...* Arrows flew through the other windows as well. The enemy had changed their tactics and were shooting at random, no longer trying to catch me after the shot. The likelihood of wasting arrows was much higher than their chances of hitting me, of course, but I didn't want to play Russian roulette with my luck.

"They're leaving!" the first watcher spoke up again. "Also, they seem to have finished off the wounded."

"Open your eyes. Only two out of the three, they've taken the girl."

Bastards... I drew close to the window and sent another arrow after them. Not very successfully. The last goblin fell with a cry, catching an arrow in the leg. One of his friends rushed to help him, but a second arrow brought him down. Permanently, it seemed. There were no more takers, and the other goblins chose to hurry up, leaving their comrade to his fate.

I shouted a few insults after them in their own language, but didn't finish off the wounded goblin, letting him crawl back to his own people. Not out of kindness. I wouldn't get any experience points for killing him anyway, and I had turned him from an enemy warrior into a burden with this injury. It was a sort of revenge for Nick.

It was useless to continue shooting from this location, for the goblins had moved out of range. That's what they thought, at least. It was time to change weapons. The modern compound bow could shoot much further than a goblin bow. If I also added our height, it should just be enough.

"Looks like it's time to head up to the roof." I said to myself.

Unfortunately, this plan had a flaw. If the goblins realized where the shooting was coming from and decided to shoot back, I'd have no place to hide. A couple of volleys would be enough to turn me into a dead hedgehog. I had to plan ahead.

"Can I borrow your shield, buddy? I'll return it later." I cast off *Invisibility* and approached one of the newcomers, who was sporting a huge shield half as tall as a man. Viking 2001?

There weren't many players who had such awkward names, not only because there were so few of us, but because the System didn't demand uniqueness. It did issue a warning if there was a match. There were none among veterans, for we had been given a one-time opportunity to change our nickname after completing the first mission. I had been too busy lying unconscious to change mine. We'd had a time limit, just like for everything else.

"H-here. It's an honor for me! Just give it back after, okay?"

I examined my acquisition. It seemed to have been a table until very recently, to which the man had somehow attached a handle. This so-called shield was too heavy for combat, but protected well from arrows. For example, the guy was among the last during our retreat and his shield had caught at least three arrows, which served as a quality guarantee.

"Don't worry, I will." I smiled. "I'll be glad to see you in my squad, if you haven't joined anyone else yet."

Of course, if he wasn't killed by the goblins in the upcoming battle. Or if I didn't die. Hell, I was turning into an awful pessimist.

The precaution turned out to be unnecessary. I only managed to release a few arrows before the goblins took off again, without even trying to get back at me. One of them, wrapped in a cloak, cast something onto the stones, and their departure was obscured by clouds of thick smoke. Wasn't it the ignoramus who had been saved by the armor?

Well, I'd succeeded with the first part of our plan by driving the goblins away. It was a pity that their losses hadn't provoked the goblins to attack. Cautious bastards.

"Time for plan B, then," I concluded. Wasn't it?

I wasn't the only one who thought so. The

horn sounded below, and players tumbled out of the doors and windows. If the goblins had been closer, they could have tried to block us or shoot us again with their bows, but they couldn't do it now. It was time for a strategic retreat, or, simply put, a getaway.

CHAPTER 16

THE AMBUSH

E DIDN'T REALLY HAVE a chance of getting away from the goblins. My actions only bought the others enough time to leave the building in an organized fashion and head deeper into the city, following the previously explored route. Obviously, if the goblins had decided to attack, I couldn't have stopped them. How long could a single archer hold back nearly three hundred warriors? They let us leave.

As soon as the column was out of sight, I hurried after it. The withdrawal was a temporary measure. In theory, goblins were less hardy than humans, but unfortunately, we were dealing with veterans, so most of them were second or third level, while some had reached Level 5 or higher. Not to mention the leaders, one of whom had Level

9, while the shaman had Level 7. Besides, goblins were smaller and lighter than humans. Even with lower parameters, they possessed almost the same speed and seemed to recover faster. How else could they have chased me to that damn tower?

"I hate goblins," I mumbled habitually, pushing the unpleasant memory away. If I ever acquired a coat of arms, I knew the motto that would adorn it.

This situation was different, for we were being slowed down by the wounded. A group travels at the speed of its slowest member, and while the goblins could leave their 'weakest link' behind and pick them up later, for us, it meant condemning a person to death. To get away from the goblins, we would have had to leave not only the wounded, but also the weak. Many newbies had a *Stamina* of only five, and some overweight members even had four. Disregard for one's physical health had already cost many people their lives, for our enemies hadn't given them a chance to level up.

In a way, the goblins reminded me of a pack of wolves harrying a herd. Their first victims were usually the sickly and weak individuals. Predators could afford to wait, following the trail and biding their time.

We couldn't avoid a battle, so it was a question of under what conditions it would take place. There were fewer goblins, but we didn't have much chance of defeating them head-on. Fifty archers could fire several volleys in the time it would take us to reach them. Naturally, not all arrows would hit their target, but without armor and normal shields, any hit, even if it didn't kill, would almost certainly incapacitate a player. Let's suppose the people didn't lose their nerve and reached the goblin formation. How many would will risk rushing the wall of spears? I strongly suspected that the players would stop. Because you can hurl yourself at spears, breaking them with your weight, only if you are wearing proper armor or are ready to die. Any delay would mean continuing losses from arrows. Perhaps we would win, thanks to our System abilities, superior strength and numbers, but it would be a Pyrrhic victory.

No, we needed a better plan. We had one, on the whole. The question was, would the goblins let us put it into action?

It would be a mistake to consider goblins stupid just because their original parameters were lower than human ones. Although their first limit was only five, there was no lock on it. Any goblin who managed to acquire a System weapon and gained enough experience points could go beyond it. Their leader was a hobgoblin, which meant that he was as good as a human. Considering that he was Level 9, he actually surpassed most of the players.

Perhaps defeating the Bone Horror had gone to my head, since I decided to perform another feat and dispatch the goblin leader. There was even a chance I'd succeed.

Taking cover on another roof, I waited for the main squad to appear, then stood up and fired an arrow while remaining invisible. Unfortunately, the hobgoblin was very careful: he wore good armor and was constantly protected by his bodyguards. The arrow got stuck in the upper part of one of their shields, and I was forced to escape when several dozen enemies rushed towards my position. There weren't many mana crystals left, so I had to use them sparingly and only activate *Invisibility* in critical situations. Given the goblins' rage, the risk was too great, and the likelihood of a subsequent attack being more successful was vanishingly small. I did what I had to do, and withdrew. Or ran away, if you prefer. My maximal *Stamina* served me well, allowing me to easily get away from my pursuers. However, I was in no hurry to rejoin the main forces.

So far, both sides had acted quite cautiously. The humans were retreating while aiming for the city center and the fortress, while the goblins stayed on their tail, waiting for reinforcements or just a good opportunity to stab us in the back. Of course, the natives sent scouts ahead of them, who, in addition to checking the way, peppered the retreating humans with arrows, popped up unexpectedly here and there, and generally kept us on our toes. It was a sensible but rather predictable move.

The players, in turn, also set up a rearguard, whose purpose was to cover the main forces and kill the most arrogant goblins. Short scuffles broke out every now and then, resulting in a fresh corpse being left behind in the ruins, often stripped almost down to the underwear. If there was one thing humans and goblins had in common, it was greed.

Sitting on the second floor of a four-story building, I watched the street while trying to be aware of what was behind me. Using *Invisibility* would be a waste, but I felt vulnerable without its protection. I pictured goblins creeping up behind me, but when I turned around, there was nobody there, just nerves.

Although our retreat had only been going on for a couple of hours, the fighting had been continuous, and I'd already seen five veterans who'd turned out to be weaker than the goblins. They had underestimated the enemy and paid for it with their lives.

A couple of minutes and I'd need to keep moving. There was no point in staying in one place. The troops kept moving, and an attempt to set up an ambush could easily result in me finding myself behind the goblins. A tempting but unhelpful thought. If I'd wanted to run away, I shouldn't have organized all this in the first place.

"Okay, stop," I muttered, slipping back into *Invisibility*. I hadn't imagined it.

The bushes in front of the neighboring house moved and I saw two goblins sneak along the wall. An archer and a swordsman. Although the players had almost no archers, the goblins preferred to avoid open spaces.

I stood up slowly and nocked an arrow. The goblins couldn't hear any rustling or spot any telltale signs at this distance, which was the optimal situation for *Invisibility*. It also compensated for one of the main drawbacks of the bow, the inability to shoot lying down or in hiding.

I let out the first arrow and almost immediately the second. The archer fell, clutching his chest. I didn't have many System arrows left, but unlike goblin arrows, they could easily penetrate normal chain mail. The swordsman reacted with commendable speed, and the second arrow only pierced his arm as he dove through the building's opening.

"Damn it," I grunted. Despite the advantage of surprise, one of the scouts had escaped. There was no chance of catching him, since the goblin would probably run like mad with such an injury.

I glanced at the dying goblin, fighting my avarice, and lost. He wasn't the first goblin I'd shot in the last few hours, but it was usually too risky to get the experience points. I typically used ordinary arrows, not only to avoid temptation, but also to avoid pumping up the goblins. Therefore, despite the overall success of my actions, I hadn't received any experience points until now.

When I descended to the ground floor, I activated *Invisibility* again and headed towards the corpse, trying not to leave any footprints and watching my surroundings warily. One of the veterans, whose body I saw about twenty minutes ago, had died in a similar situation. It was perfectly possible that another pair of eyes was watching the goblin right now, waiting for the shooter to come for their loot.

The goblin jerked convulsively and lay still, the System no longer recognizing him. Ready. All the better, I could put away my dagger. I touched the arrow lightly...

Attention! You have received 4 SP! (4/120)

As expected, since the archer had been only Level 2. The goblin who'd escaped had Level 3. A semitransparent card appeared above the corpse, but to my disappointment, it was empty. It was only the second time I'd seen a 'clean skill card', but according to the statistics, it was the most common type of loot. Well, if one didn't count no loot at all, which was most often the case with first-level goblins. I could count myself lucky. Speaking of luck, I still wasn't sure if the *Luck* parameter affected whether cards were dropped, or even their quality. So far, it seemed that the effect was minimal, if any. I had scored loot quite regularly.

I didn't touch the body right away. I entered the building, and checked that the second 'experience carrier' had indeed run away. This was obvious from the occasional drops of blood running to the window and continuing into the grass. I'd gotten the goblin well, but I wasn't going to chase him since he wouldn't be a threat to us over the next three days.

Well, no need to stay here any longer than necessary. I returned to the corpse and looked around again, trying to find the hypothetical observer and see if I had really sensed a threat or if it was just the nerves. I probably should have left the arrow sticking out of the body and just walked away, but I decided that it was safe. I hooked the bow over one arm, grabbed the corpse by the leg with the other, and pulled it inside the building. My heart was pounding, as if I'd done something really dangerous. It seemed to be only paranoia...

I froze. The goblin was dead, but now there were two arrows sticking out of it. Had I felt a breeze on my face when I'd grabbed the body? The street outside remained quiet, but I now knew that there was a shooter lurking out there.

It was an ambush. Especially for me, it seemed. The archer knew that someone invisible was working against him. Nevertheless, the archer appeared to be alone, so the danger was...

moderate. I listened to my gut. I didn't want to go looking for the sniper to avenge my own stupidity and greed. It was easy enough to find a reason to retreat. I'd already tarried too long, and soon there would be a dozen or more goblins here, thanks to the one who'd gotten away. To hell with this.

I threw the corpse in my bag and left the building through one of the back windows. Five minutes later, when I was far enough away, I stopped briefly to sort out the trophies. The body weighed a lot even when in the bag, so I decided to get rid of it and take only what was useful. In addition to my own arrow and the one that landed as a gift, I had inherited a full quiver, a new bow, a slightly blood-stained cloak, a belt, a dagger, a bag of small items, and a little mana crystal. Not bad, although, alas, I found no System artifacts.

The hunt went on.

* * *

A player's headless corpse lay in the dust beside the road, wearing only his underwear. As I'd already said, not all our 'hunters' were doing well. Goblins knew their way around the ruins, were cautious, operated in packs, and, most importantly, had long-range weapons.

Nevertheless, the goblins were slowly but surely losing this game. Having lost about three dozen scouts, they now stuck close to the main group, checking only their immediate surroundings. The only exception were the horseback riders, who operated openly, with little or no fear, and could thus monitor the movement of our forces.

The cavalry was the elite part of the goblin army. The riders were all at Level 5 or higher, with good armor, weapons, and shields, and many even had System bags. Thankfully, only a few had bows, since the local nobility seemed to consider this type of weapon not prestigious enough.

They operated in groups of ten or more. And yet, and yet, they had their weakness — the horses. Unprotected by armor and covered only by a thin blanket, these magnificent animals could do nothing against an archer who was unscrupulous enough to attack them. A villain like me. Did I feel sorry for the horses? Of course, since my potential dinner could have walked along on its own four legs as well as carried our wounded, but was going to be nothing but a dead weight in my bag.

I held my breath and released the bowstring. The horse reared, throwing off its rider, jumped several times, and fell over. I must have hit an artery. I remembered that in the Middle Ages, aiming for the enemy's horse was considered ignoble. Given their cost, it was also an economic crime. Greed had ruined many a life...

"But I'm not like that, huh?" I snorted.

I hadn't chosen my target at random, for a human head hung from his saddle. I raised my bow. The next arrow struck a shield that had been raised at the wrong time. The third bounced off his armor.

"What the hell?" I muttered, feeling indignant that the enemy refused to die. My fourth arrow missed again.

I wasn't allowed to finish off the goblin. The other goblins didn't abandon their comrade, with several riders surrounding him, and one even dismounting to help the wounded goblin mount his horse. The goblin who had dismounted ran alongside the horse, holding on to the stirrup... Had I shot at someone important? A pity that I couldn't finish the job. I sent several more arrows after the riders, but the goblins hung their shields on their backs, and the horses only sped up after getting an arrow in the rump.

What bad luck... Of course, there was a dead horse and saddlebags lying on the road, and I'd gotten revenge for the human head, but I'd learned my lesson today and wasn't going for the trophies. The riders had retreated, but what if they decided to return as I approached the street? They'd surely spotted my position.

Theoretically, I could have tried to ambush them, but... a horn sounded in the distance, sparing me any further decisions. It was time for battle, and time to return to the main force.

"I hate goblins," I breathed out. The phrase seemed to give me strength, but it no longer carried any real emotion. It was only now that I realized how tired I was, and everything was only just beginning.

✾ ✾ ✾

"Hyung... nim," the youth stumbled. "Boss. I've heard that you have a spare bow, and arrows to go with it."

I looked up at another Asian guy before me. Hyungnim, boss... Right-o. Judging by the honorific, the youth was from Korea. There two such countries, so North or South? A question of little importance, but probably the latter. That's where they shoot all those doramas, right?

"Let's say you're right. What then?"

"Let me borrow it! I've heard a lot about your exploits! We have an intense battle ahead of us, and another archer will definitely come in handy."

I thought about it. He was right, I didn't need three bows, and we'd obtain several dozen more as trophies after the fight. But to hand them out willy-nilly... Going by the fact that the guy's weapon was a spear, his sudden passion for archery was quite obviously related to a reluctance to stand in the first row. Yes, the spear didn't only have advantages.

"Do you possess the *Archery* skill?" I asked. "A blank skill card? Ten available SP?" As expected, the answer to each one was negative. "Then what are you going to do with a goblin bow?"

"Don't underestimate me. Archery is a national sport in my country. I've been training with a bow since I was five, and I was a university champion!"

I pulled the newly obtained bow and quiver out of my bag, and drew out three arrows.

"See that pole about thirty meters away? If you can hit it even once, the bow's yours."

The Korean guy politely took the bow from me and examined it, bending it and pulling the bowstring back a couple of times. It looked like he knew what he was on about. The youth took the first arrow, nocked it, pulled back the string and then released it. It looked very impressive, but the arrow flew two hands to the left of the target. The second one flew one hand to the right. The Korean guy paused for several seconds before firing the last arrow, and it struck the very edge of the post.

"Well done!" I clapped my hands. "Were you really a champion at university?"

"Well," He scratched his nose shyly, "It was a small university."

"Alright, take it," I said. "The arrows are yours, too. Here are five more... Sorry, I don't have that many."

"Thank you, boss!" he bowed. "My name is Kim, boss. You won't regret it, boss."

It felt like I'd just given him a job rather than a bow. I smiled patronizingly and nodded, resisting the vague urge to let the guy kiss my ring. Possibly because I wasn't wearing one?

Lisa came up behind me and put her arms around my shoulders. A convenient gesture to cut someone's throat, but I liked it. I didn't really believe it was likely, simply some mild paranoia.

"Maybe I should take a bow too?" she asked. "I'll have to fight anyway."

"I'll consider it if that Korean guy survives the battle." In my mind, he was safer fighting at the forefront if he didn't have *Invisibility*.

* * *

We stood on the roof of a fairly high building, which offered a good view of the enemy forces. The scuffles over the last few hours had battered them considerably, and out of the three hundred original goblins, only two hundred or two hundred and fifty remained. It was hard to know exactly.

About one hundred and fifty players stood blocking the long but narrow street. There were some makeshift shields in the front row, but they didn't look very convincing. I hoped the goblins would think the same thing.

Hiding in the neighboring houses were people useless in direct combat: those with light weapons, women, the wounded and those unsuited for battle. Of course, they were lying low, but could this 'ambush regiment' really deceive anyone? Life was different from computer strategies, and these 'bots' were clearly playing at a high level. Even without sending scouts to check the road ahead, the goblins had stopped and were in no hurry to climb into such an obvious trap.

“Come on,” Marcus muttered and licked his lips.

A lot depended on the goblins’ decision. It was possible that they would stop and wait for the arrival of their reinforcements. Then we’d have to take off again and hurriedly retreat. The entire plan hinged on the fact that we’d almost reached the breaks in the wall, and the goblins would have to keep pursuing us through neutral territory – if you could call the part of the city filled with the undead that.

Each of the eight leaders led a large group. Qing Lung oversaw the overall course of battle, Alexander headed the main squad, Saud was in charge of the sling shooters on one side of the street, the Swordsman on the other side, and Sulu led the ambush squad and was responsible for springing the trap. Marcus covered the rear, while I remained in reserve back at ‘headquarters’. I was nervous, too, although I tried not to show it. Waiting for combat was a torturous activity.

* * *

Nothing happened for a while, but then the goblin riders turned and sped off down the street. The lancers formed a square with the archers hiding in the middle, and slowly began moving forward. The scouts headed out again, cautiously checking the houses.

“So, they decided to fight after all,” Qing

Long muttered with a faint smile. "Then the riders have gone around and will obviously attack from the rear. How long will they need?"

"No more than ten minutes," I said. "It's hard to know without a map."

Although the city didn't boast any straight streets and the development was chaotic in places, it wouldn't be difficult to find a detour. It was bad, because we were counting on a head-on attack.

"We'll have to change our plans a little. You still have some napalm left, don't you?"

I nodded. It seemed wrong to call the quick and dirty incendiary mixture I'd created 'napalm', but now wasn't the time to discuss terminology. The important thing was that the mixture burned well and was hard to put out.

"One more flask," I said, pulling it out of my bag. Unfortunately, there weren't that many flasks, and only two had contained napalm. The second one had helped to cover our retreat and was now empty.

"Good. Take your people, grab Cthulh and another person, and cover our backs. The riders must not be allowed to attack us from behind."

Cthulh used to be a member of Marcus' group, was the last of our 'battle mages', and could create a *fireball*. Not very fast or powerful, but it flew quite accurately and exploded rather spectacularly, which made it useful in this situation. Interestingly, the mage had initially wanted to be called Cthulhu, but the System hadn't let him. Considering that he'd been in the first wave, it was unlikely that the name had been taken by another player, and doubles were allowed anyway. I was inclined to think that some of the names were reserved for the gods. Fire magic in someone who'd wanted to name himself after an aquatic deity seemed like a sort of joke. Nevertheless, he'd been lucky since most of the first-wave mages hadn't survived the first mission, and not all of the remaining ones had received a useful skill. *Faith* was indeed an analogue of *Wisdom*, and only the lack of appropriate skills prevented us from having hundreds of mages. Mana was mana, whatever its source.

"I'm coming with you," Marcus said. "I'll go and warn the boys. I'll also recruit another two dozen volunteers from the main group, since our squads won't be enough."

"Just don't bother the ones with the shields," Qing Long said, and turned away after receiving a nod. Hell... Was it just me, or was the Chinese man enjoying what was happening?

It was harder to watch the battle from the new position, but still possible. The goblin square moved slowly forward, protecting its archers. Knowing that we had practically no archers, I understood why the goblin leader had taken this risk in the first place. Yes, the goblins knew that there were players hiding in the buildings, but they assumed that they could repel the attack.

"Fire," I whispered, translating the signal I'd heard. What would we have done without the thing?

Thus it began. Numerous players appeared on the roofs and in the windows, pelting the goblins with stones. The bags had allowed us to collect a fair number of projectiles, and the narrow street made it impossible to hide from the 'shelling'. Some players cast stones with their bare hands, but most were using handmade slings. They did this with varying degrees of success, but accuracy wasn't needed when shooting at a crowd. The goblins tried to respond with arrows, but there were only a few dozen archers and hundreds of stone throwers. Though our accuracy was a joke, and the throws weren't strong enough to break through the shields and armor, soon the first victims began to fall on the pavement. Their number increased with each passing minute.

The goblins froze, their shields raised, unable to move forward or back. It wasn't that they didn't shoot back – the arrows flew, taking the lives of the sling shooters and making the players hesitate. This was bad.

Suddenly, one of the goblins collapsed with an arrow in his neck. His companion shouted something, pointing to a roof in the distance, where an archer stood to his full height. When he saw that they'd spotted him, the archer deftly hid behind a parapet as a rain of arrows fell on where he'd been standing.

"Poor Kim," I muttered, feeling a little guilty that I'd been right. "I hope he brought a shield."

It was very unlikely, since all the shields had to be down below, with the infantry. The goblins didn't stop, and a second volley followed the first. A chill ran down my spine. They must have mistaken the guy for me, otherwise, it was difficult to explain such a well-coordinated reaction.

"Yeah, they really don't like archers," Marcus drawled as he backed away. "Or you in particular? You should, uh... Save your arrows for now."

"They're too far away," I said, smiling politely to show that I got the joke. "What do you have to fear? Aren't you practically immortal?"

"As if," the Italian man shook his head. "Time isn't a trick. My skill hasn't reset yet. If I die, I'll never taste my momma's pasta again." He made a slight grimace at this. Perhaps this respectable woman's culinary talents were questionable.

"Okay, I'm going down there," Marcus sighed. "There are a lot of riders, so we'll attack them from both sides."

"Good luck," I said. "Try not to die out there." Odd, but I was starting to like the bastard. It would be a pity if they killed him.

"Hey, don't jinx it," he chuckled. "You're the one holding a bow! It's bad luck!"

I turned away, focusing on the battle again. The goblins were backing away, having decided that fighting on such terms wasn't in their best interest. The horn sounded again, and the 'ambush squad' led by Sulu rushed out onto the street, cutting off their retreat. There were only about fifty people, but it was enough. A wall of fire, originally meant to be a trap for the cavalry, blazed up in front of the goblins, cutting them off from the main force, which also worked out well. Another signal sounded and our main squad moved forward, trapping the goblins. Now, to break through, the goblins had to cross a wall of flame and fight their way through our troops, all under a hail of stones and with a force about to hit them from behind. If not for the cavalry, I would have said that victory was already ours.

"Riders!" Lisa, who was serving as the lookout, shouted as she rolled away from the edge of the roof. Just in time, since several riders had bows and reacted to her voice. Fortunately, the arrows were fired almost at random and didn't hit anyone. They only made me angry.

One quickly gets used to a good thing. I calmly walked to the edge of the roof, sure that my enemies couldn't see me. Three dozen riders. Twenty-nine, to be exact. Not that many, but if they attacked now, they could easily turn the tide of the battle. At the very least, they could turn the approaching thrashing into a modest defeat.

Perhaps even a draw?

The riders also took stock of the situation and gave a signal, turning around to attack. I think this formation used to be called a 'swine array', or a blunt wedge. The most heavily armored horsemen rode ahead, followed by the others, spreading out in a wedge across the entire width of the street. Not the most effective formation, if you believed the history books.

The goblins paused for a moment, then started their horses again, slowly picking up speed. I looked at the narrow strip of liquid crossing the street. Our plan hinged on getting the timing just right. Three, two, one...

"Come on!" Cthulh beat me to it, and a fireball shot out from the opposite roof. The incendiary mixture burst into flame, causing the horses to rear. The rear riders crashed into the ones in front. Some of them did race through the flames, since the effect was mostly psychological, but this didn't save them. I started shooting without even trying to aim, just emptying the quiver: arrow after arrow, until they were almost completely gone. The mage provided fire support with several *fireballs* flying into the crush of goblin and horse bodies.

"Go!" Marcus shouted. "There are enough enemies for everyone!"

Players poured out of the houses, eager to take advantage of the panic among the riders and gain valuable experience. There may have been enough loot for everyone, but, alas, the river of experience points flowed past me today. Looking at how quickly the goblins recovered, perhaps that was for the best.

The horsemen were strong warriors, and they fought fiercely even when ambushed. I spent the last dozen arrows carefully, trying to cover the combatants. To my mild annoyance, I spotted Lisa among them. What the hell?

I calmed down after a moment, for she was right in her own way. I couldn't protect her forever, and cowards and pacifists were the first to die out here. Unfortunately, the brave often didn't live very long either.

Lisa stood still for half a minute, clutching her rapier and not daring to wade into the fray, and then a goblin leaped at her. Level 5. The warrior easily knocked her down and would have killed her if not for the arrow that pierced his arm. He paused and then the rapier struck him from below, right into the heart, easily passing through the rings of chain mail. Ten points at once...

Irritated, I fired the last arrow, drew my spear, and ran downstairs. By the time I reached street level, the battle was almost over. About ten horsemen had broken out of our trap, but this time, they weren't inclined to return and raced away down the street. Another goblin fought with his back against the wall, but his fate was sealed.

"Don't kill him!" I shouted. "We need a prisoner!"

The last goblin soon fell with my help, and was deftly disarmed and tied up. Perhaps too roughly, I had to remember to loosen his bonds. Later, though.

I looked around the battlefield, picking out the dead and the wounded. Although there was still fighting on the other side of the street, we had clearly won. It was time to assess our losses and profits. "Horse with baked apples," I said dreamily as the smell of burnt meat wafted through the air. Perhaps it was also burnt goblin, but I preferred to think of good things. Meat, trophies, and the upcoming torture. What else did one need to be happy?

CHAPTER 17

THE SPOILS OF WAR

MM, THE SWEET SMELL of victory," I muttered. "But more in a figurative sense."

Once the initial euphoria had passed, I didn't want to take deep breaths any longer. It stank of burnt flesh, blood, and entrails, and although I didn't want to vomit, the sight of mutilated corpses didn't bring me any joy, either. The sight of our 'brilliant victory' was complemented by the neighing of crippled horses, and the groans and cries of the wounded.

I was tempted to activate the *Calculating Mind*. My eyes roamed over the street, strewn with bodies. Thirty horsemen against forty foot soldiers. We wouldn't have stood a chance if we'd met out in a field somewhere, while here, we'd not only sent goblins running but also lost barely a dozen dead, although there were almost as many wounded.

Because I'd tried to protect my own people first and foremost, the losses in my squad were minimal. Nevertheless, minimal wasn't the same as none. Lancer lay on the ground with a shattered skull, and although the System still recognized him, he had no chance of surviving. They say that in ancient times, a warrior acquired a helmet first and only then armor, and looking at the guy before me, I understood why. I could practically see bits of brain...

The player's nickname was rapidly fading, reflecting the plummeting likelihood of resuscitation. It was only because he'd been struck with a conventional, rather than a System weapon, and it was still possible to get XP from him.

"He's dead," I told Lisa, who was trying to resuscitate the guy. "Chest compressions are useless. Even mouth-to-mouth won't help here." Given what happened to Lancer's skull, I doubted anything other than powerful magic would help. But this wasn't a fairy tale. A beauty's kiss would only work if she was a witch and specialized in necromancy.

"I know," Lisa said, removing her hands from the dead man's chest. "He was still breathing a minute ago." It was like rubbing salt on the wound. Even it wasn't my fault as I couldn't protect everyone, it was my first loss in a new role. Inappropriate thoughts were just a way to stay calm.

"His name was Lance. We even lived somewhere near each other. He was from London."

I decided not to upset her by revealing that the 'Brit' had told me he was Ukrainian, and that his nickname was based on the fact he was a freelancer. To hell with it. Whoever he'd lied to, or for whatever reason, it no longer mattered.

"I feel sorry for him, too," I sighed, sitting down beside her and closing the man's eyes. "But we should take care of those who can still be saved. I saw Cúchulainn take a hit. It's nothing serious, but he'll benefit from your help." Despite Cúchulainn's very particular nickname, he was Belarusian rather than Irish. Although he could have passed himself off as the latter thanks to his fiery red mane. Plus, his axe really fit the image.

"You're right." She stood up resolutely. "I'll ask Alf to help."

Alf was actually named Gandalf and was one of the newbs who had chosen magical abilities. Deciding to stick to the concept, he had selected a spiked mace as his 'magic staff'. Also called a morning star in olden times. Why did I take him into my squad? Well, he was young, sensible, in good physical shape and had convinced me that he could be useful. So far, there was nothing to reproach the Norwegian for. He fought clumsily, but bravely, and had managed to not only survive, but to get off with only scratches. Most of the other novice mages just whined about how unfair life was...

"I saw him over there," I motioned. "You can enlist everyone you see. And... we need to help all the wounded, not just our squad."

"Of course," Lisa nodded. "I'll see you later."

I paused and watched as a player dragged a goblin's body to the side and tried to remove the chain mail. I looked around me, already knowing what I'd find. Another player was laughing as he tried on a helmet, clearly searching for one that would fit his healthy but empty head... Bad behavior is contagious, and several more people began to wander among the corpses, looking for something interesting.

"Listen up, everyone!" I shouted, sensing that soon it would be too late. "Stop looting, right now. No fighting over the goods. All the loot will be distributed by me personally. For now, you can only take the card that fell from a goblin you'd killed! There's work to be done, so help the wounded, finish off the injured horses and drag the corpses to the wall. Keep the goblins and humans separate!"

The players froze, not quite sure if they wanted to follow my orders. Although the System protected against direct murder, there were plenty of ways to circumvent the restrictions. A rope was an obvious one. I sighed, then continued, "That's an order! Anyone caught stealing will be deprived of their share of the spoils. The most impudent ones will be hanged!"

For all my big words, I still had to negotiate the division of the loot with my ally. I looked around again and headed for Marcus. The Italian was sitting with his back against the wall on the opposite side of the street, blood caked in his hair. A woman fussed over him, carefully trying to wash the wound with water from her flask. He was alive.

Judging by the fact that I hadn't seen him get injured, he must have been hit at the very end of the fight. It wasn't difficult to guess the culprit, as I'd just stepped over the body of a goblin covered in wounds, but still clutching a bloody mace.

"How is he, Cleo?" I asked the 'nurse'. I didn't even need a System prompt to remember her name. Funny how in the real world, I could struggle for weeks trying to remember the name of a new colleague, but here I only needed to hear it once. Faces, names, occasionally even minor biographical details, all this was easily and firmly etched in my memory. Perhaps it was because I'd been indifferent to my colleagues, by and large, while here, my very life depended on the people around me?

However, there was a downside to everything. As I passed by a corpse, I'd see a familiar face and not just a nameless player. At least three of them had belonged to Marcus' squad. Maybe even four. Considering that he'd only recently gathered ten, the losses were significant.

"I'll be fine," the patient replied, but he didn't open his eyes. Yeah, sure.

"You picked the wrong time to get clubbed over the head."

"It was an accident," the Italian waved his hand weakly, then dropped it again. "The mace almost missed me. He got me with the very end, the bastard."

"Well, we don't speak ill of the dead," I said, once I'd made sure that Marcus wasn't going to die. "What's wrong with him?"

"Concussion," Cleo responded. "As well as a cut, but I think the bleeding will stop soon."

"Still, we better not move him yet," Cthulh interrupted, coming up from behind us. Wow, he'd survived. I had thought that 'long-range units' wouldn't survive for long without *Invisibility*. The arrows had definitely flown in his direction. "Good shooting, by the way. Great speech, too. I especially liked the bit about hanging people. Very persuasive."

"That's probably because I wasn't joking," I snorted, glancing at the mage a little doubtfully.

Marcus and I were about equal in level, but he clearly wasn't going to be any help right now. He'd be useless for at least a day, and would need two or three days to fully recover. If the Italian survived them at all, of course. In any case, it meant that I'd have to sort out the problems on my own for the time being.

"I'll get up soon... Just need... to sit for a bit. Cthulh will help you." Marcus bent over abruptly, ending his speech by showering the pavement with the remains of his breakfast, which was mostly apples. A concussion for sure.

"Rest up, I'll take care of everything," I nodded. "By the way, I saw you kill two of them. Once you feel better, don't forget to collect your cards. If the goblins dropped them, of course."

"Yeah, right, thank you."

I shook my head. I was definitely getting myself a helmet.

✹ ✹ ✹

Speaking of cards... Although I'd wounded a lot of goblins, I hadn't received any XP since they'd been finished off by other players in the heat of battle. The others had also collected the loot. I wasn't going to claim those cards. You couldn't divide them in half, and taking them by force was stupid. Hadn't the ancients considered generosity as one of the most important qualities in a leader, alongside luck? If anyone obtained an interesting skill, it'd easier to make a copy.

Plus, the cards were much less valuable to me than to the others. I'd get access to the Server again at the end of the mission, which meant that I could learn any skill, as long as I had enough points. If I found it in time in the almost endless list of options.

"Catch it!" a familiar voice shouted. "Grab the bridle! For the love of..."

Several players down the street were eagerly trying to catch a dappled horse. I recognized two of them as Roland and Ilyas were members of my group. A Frenchman and a Kazakh, if you could still take people's word for it in these woeful times. The horse had probably belonged to my recent victim.

Dead goblin

The System outlined the body in gray when I approached. A good sign, since it ignored corpses that had been 'drained'. It seemed that the warning given before battle not to touch my arrows had worked. I quickened my pace and knelt to touch the shaft.

Attention! You have received 10 SP! (14/120)

The goblin's label faded and disappeared, indicating that he was no longer of any interest to the System. Slowly and almost reluctantly, a semitransparent card formed in the air.

I paused for a moment, another question in my mind. What would happen if the killer died and didn't collect the card? Would it dissipate after a while? Or, on the contrary, grow solid? Well, we'll soon known anyway. What have we here?

Horseback riding

>   **Rank:** F-.
>   **Level:** 1/?
>   **Description:**
>   — *A skill allowing you to learn how to ride and handle* **horses**.
>   — *???*
>   **Saturation:**
>   *0/10 SP*

Well, not the best option, but it'd be a sin to complain. I suspected that cards were dropped for a reason, and were tied to the skills and knowledge that the mob had acquired during their lifetime. This goblin must have been good with horses, perhaps even very good. It was also clear that sufficient knowledge was only one of the conditions for the loot, otherwise, why would empties fall out at all? The System could be considering the level, our differences, *Luck*... anything at all, really. To be honest, I was tired of building castles in the sky on a foundation of endless assumptions. Why couldn't the creators of this fucking game given us a manual? For that, I'd have even changed my usual approach and read it BEFORE something went wrong.

I looked at the question marks. The lack of an upper limit was probably due to no "connection to the Server". As for the hidden item, it looked like I didn't have enough rights to see the full description. It wasn't the first time. The others didn't see the hidden item at all – I'd checked. There were two options. Either I didn't have enough *Intuition,* or I needed a special skill. Did I need to increase the *Identification* level and try to identify the card?

I turned the card over thoughtfully, then put it in my pocket. The experience gained for the goblin was just enough for me to learn this skill, but I didn't really need to ride under the current circumstances. What I needed a lot more was Level 2 in my *Minor magical ability.* Yes, it required twenty SP, but if I kept wasting points on all kind of nonsense, I'd never level up my specialized skills. If I needed to ride off into the sunset in the future, I could still learn it, as long as I had the card.

"Grab it, grab it!" another cry of desperation and excitement showed that the horse refused to be caught. As soon as the hunters came closer, the horse trotted away but didn't escape completely, shifting slowly in my direction. "What a shaitan!"

Shaking my head, I bent over the dead goblin, rolled him over, and yanked at the arrow. It didn't come out straight away, remaining stuck below the shoulder blade. I tried to dig it out with my knife, but then discovered a very good suit of reinforced chain mail beneath the cloak. Unfortunately, the plates had covered only the chest, so it hadn't protected its wearer against an armor-piercing arrow in the back. A shield was probably meant to cover the rider's back, but the goblin hadn't had time to lift it into place. The shield lay a few paces away, as well as a mace, which had traces of blood on it. And possibly something gray..

"Bloody hell!" Ilyas shouted. "Should I just shoot the animal? At least we'll get some meat, and have some fun. Let's get a bow and..."

"Do you know how to use a bow?" Roland asked skeptically, hefting his sword.

"Of course, you know my second name!" Ilyas proclaimed passionately. "Or let me throw a spear!" The Kazakh man shook the spear above his head. I chuckled. What a performance. They'd noticed my presence, and this was an unobtrusive way to show that they needed help. Should I give them some wise advice?

"Don't touch the horse, Legolas!" I shouted. Yes, this was the nickname Ilyas had chosen for himself. A Light Elf with Asian features.

"Oh, commander! I knew you'd eventually notice your loyal henchmen!" Ilyas proclaimed. "We need your divine arrows. Just shoot it in the knee, and I'll do the rest myself."

"What about your nomad genes?" I asked. "Your innate love of horses?"

"It's all there, commander." Ilyas smirked in

response. "I love horse meat. As a descendant of Genghis Khan, I proclaim that this is an incorrect horse! The least it can do to make up for our suffering is to allow itself to be eaten."

I grinned in reply. Easy character, good sense of humor, smart. Despite the clowning around, his 8 in *Intelligence* clearly showed he wasn't stupid. In a place full of danger, being able to distract yourself from dark thoughts and have a laugh was useful.

"Watch and learn," I chuckled, activating *Invisibility* and slowly approaching the horse. It grew nervous when I drew closer, but I grabbed the reins before it could escape, and became visible again. A little behind it, so as not to frighten the animal. Well, that's what I thought. Shaitan tried to bite me, justifying its nickname, but didn't succeed. I'd always been good with animals. The main thing was to show them who was boss. I smacked the horse between the eyes, making it back up a little and try to kick me with its hoof. Its front hoof, which was interesting. "What are you waiting for?" I yelled, hanging on to the reins and dodging the creature's snapping teeth. "Help me!"

The horse lunged forward, lifting me off the ground for a moment, and tried to kick me again. It seemed that the books I'd read as a child about wild mustang tamers had lied. Or had I misremembered the details? I was greatly tempted to release the reins, but something told me that the animal wouldn't allow itself to be caught a second time, and would run away to wherever its home was... The depths of hell, no doubt. Ugh, I could have learned that damn skill, or simply shot it with a bow. "I name thee Kebab," I said grimly when the three of us had finally managed to subdue the beast. "If you keep behaving badly, I'll make one out of you."

Unimpressed, the horse snapped its teeth Was I beginning to hate horses, too?

Of the twenty-nine goblin riders, ten had managed to escape. One was taken prisoner. The other eighteen were dead and laid out in a row along the wall. In armor and with their weapons, as befits the dead whose property hadn't yet found new owners. The saddles, harnesses and saddlebags lay nearby. Our spoils were plentiful and varied, and needed to be divided quickly and, if possible, fairly.

This wasn't easy. I had to simultaneously consider the interests of five parties. The interests of the Alliance, my own group, Marcus' squad, and the 'non-factional' players assigned to us. And, last but not least, the interests of my inner dragon. For others, it might have been an inner toad or hamster, but I'd always preferred reptiles – they aren't so petty and prefer gold as a minimum. Hmm.

"Eeny, meeny, miny, moe, catch a tiger by

the toe," I mumbled as I considered the options.

Unfortunately, there wasn't enough time to really think it through. We still weren't sure where the goblin squad had come from and how far away the main forces were. We needed to interrogate the prisoners, and then decide at what speed and in what 'strategic direction' we should head. It was possible that the best choice for me was to get on a horse and ride hell for leather away from here. Alas, the captured goblin had so far refused to talk, and we needed time to conduct the interrogation. I was sure the main squad also had prisoners, but there was the matter of finding an interpreter. In theory, the dead should have dropped plenty of cards, so someone else could have scored a language one.

"Attention, please!" I shouted, raising my spear above my head. "Listen up, everyone. I'm going to describe the principles by which the spoils will be divided." My words sparked plenty of interest, and the crowd drew closer. I resisted the urge to lick my lips as dozens of eyes stared at me. I wasn't afraid of public speaking, but this was an important matter, and I couldn't make any mistakes. Everything had to be fair. "Alright," I began, with only a vague idea of what fairness meant in this case. "To begin with, I will indicate the things that will not be shared and will serve the entire Alliance. Firstly, the horses. Live animals are a strategic resource for transporting supplies and the wounded. The dead ones are a solution to our food problem. Six of the eight surviving horses will serve the army. One will remain in my squad and one in Marcus' squad. Any questions?"

"Why don't we get a horse?" one of the 'mercenaries' shouted. His name flashed overhead. Mario. "I killed a goblin, too!"
This so-called faction was disorganized and didn't pose much danger. Of the twenty-one 'mercenaries' that Marcus had brought in, six had been killed. Another five were injured badly enough to be more interested in survival than loot. Only ten players remained, who could only be united against me by my own stupidity and greed. All I had to do was make sure that everyone got a piece of the pie.

"No, Mario. The horses will be handed over to Qing Long for distribution. If you think my decision is unfair, you can complain to him later."

"Yes, a written complaint, in triplicate," Cthulh spoke up suddenly. Although, why was I surprised? My offer wasn't detrimental to the interests of the seventh squad. A horse, given Marcus' condition, would come in useful.

"Oral complaint, of course," I chuckled, once I made sure there was no follow-up. "Perhaps if you, Mario, create your own squad, Qing Long will take your merits into account. In the meantime, everyone can take a two-day supply of horse meat! The rest, as I said, will serve the needs of the Alliance."

It was hard to call it a bonus, since there was enough meat for everyone, but the players had a chance to choose the choice cuts. Wherever those were located on the horse, in their opinion. Meat... My mouth started watering, which gave me another idea. "Just keep in mind that you mustn't build fires until we clarify the situation. The goblins could be close by."

There were no objections to this. The support expressed by Cthulh had firmly positioned the mercenaries as a minority. I could continue.

"The crystals obtained from the goblins will also be pooled together and distributed among the holders of key magical skills."

This was a crucial point. If we allowed the crystals to remain in the hands of players, most of whom didn't even possess magical skills, the Alliance would lose its main trump card, the ability to use high-ranking abilities for a long time. Where would I be with my bow but without *Invisibility* and the ability to quickly restore my mana?

"That's right. However, I'd like to get five crystals at once," Cthulh said. "In case we run into goblins all of a sudden. Mine have run out." The mage had played a significant role in the recent fight, so his demand was fair. Just a bit untimely. Why couldn't he have asked me a little later?

"All right," I nodded. "Then you should oversee their collection."

"I will," Cthulh agreed readily. Among other things, it gave him the opportunity to choose the largest crystals. A trifle, given that most goblins had the same level, but still nice.

As far as I knew, the mage hadn't received any experience points for the goblins he'd killed. It was hard to imagine how they leveled up at all. Was a mage supposed to wound the enemy and then finish them off with a System weapon? It was even worse than a bow. There may be a solution to the problem, but so far it looked like a wild imbalance. Although, who said that this game should be balanced? This gave me another idea.

"Bows and arrows will also be a strategic reserve of the Alliance." There were no questions, but I still decided to clarify the reason. "None of you have the right skill now, so they're practically useless. However, anyone who receives an *empty skill card* and accumulates ten SP can come up to me and learn *Archery*. This person will then be allowed to choose a bow from the arsenal."

"Even me?" Lisa raised her hand. I could guess what she'd gotten from that goblin. It seemed that the example of the dead Korean youth hadn't taught her anything.

"If that's what you want," I smiled, suppressing mild irritation, which was mainly directed at myself. "You can choose a bow that you like straight away. The rest come by later!" I sighed, catching my breath and gathering my thoughts again. This was the easy part. Everything I'd said up to now was reasonable, and there wasn't much point in arguing about it. Even if a point didn't seem fair to someone, they couldn't go against the interests of the entire Alliance. Compared to the rest, our group was already getting a big piece of the pie. It wasn't enough to eat it, you also had to not choke.

"The next item concerns the loot taken directly from the goblins. As I said, the cards they drop go directly to the person who made the kill." I was going against my own interests here. The inner dragon writhed with greed under my heel but I was adamant, having a rough idea of what would happen if I suggested that we divide the cards in some other way. Perhaps I had an overly active imagination, but I preferred to think it was my *Intuition.* "All other goblin possessions, except the System items, will be divided among everyone. I'd like to remind you that things like armor and shields should strengthen our Alliance, and not gather dust in someone's bags. Therefore, everyone should take only what they can and will use. If a piece of armor is too small for you, leave it for someone who will fit into it. If you're not going to fight in the front ranks, don't take a shield. I hope all this makes sense?" The response was a hubbub, mostly approving to my surprise. Hell, a little more and I'll decide that I was wrong about humanity.

"How do we decide the order?" Mario called out. "Are we drawing lots?"

"No. It'll be according to your number on the Alliance list," I decided to keep it simple. Perhaps it wasn't entirely fair, but the list was based on levels, and the rest was unimportant. "I don't recommend lying. If you state a false number, the penalty will be severe." I drew a noose with my finger. God, next thing we were going to do is introduce differently colored pants to classify people.

"Now, let's discuss our portions. Marcus and I, as the leaders, will get three portions each. Cthulh will also receive three, for his role in the fighting. Second-level players will receive two. First-level players will receive one."

"But..."

"If you think it's unfair," I interrupted, "we can base everything on levels, and I'll give the mage one of my portions. I'll take five myself. No? That's what I thought. Let's continue. Those who are seriously injured will receive an additional half-portion, ahead of the other players at their level. These portions will go to the people who will agree to take care of them."

The Alliance wasn't going to abandon the wounded, but we needed to give the others some incentive to mitigate the discontent. Simple humanism wasn't going to be enough when one had to drag a stretcher around for half a day. At least the wounded had tried to fight, so they deserved a chance.

While still on the roof, I'd seen that not all the players had showed their best side. Some had frozen in place, others simply waved their weapons around, forgetting everything that the System had given them. The brave had died, while many of the cowards had survived and were now getting their loot. The world was unfair, but now wasn't the time to compare achievements.

"I've lost my finger!" someone shouted plaintively from the back. "It won't grow back. Do I get one-and-a-half portions too?"

I thought for a moment. Would I allow it? Few people had come out of the battle with no injuries at all, and if I didn't set clear criteria, half the players would try to claim they were disabled. What was I supposed to do with these malingerers then? Hang them? "Not if you can move around on your own. By the way, I recommend that you find your finger and put it in a bag. You may be able to sew it back when you return."

Again, no open discontent. People! What was happening? A little more and my paranoia would die in agony.

"Let's continue," I sighed. "The property of players who were members of a particular group goes into its treasury. The property of people who didn't belong to any group goes into the Alliance treasury. The same applies to the System items taken from the goblins." I paused. "However, if someone wants to change weapons or replace a piece of equipment, they can do so freely. You should contact my deputy, Dmitry." I pointed at him. Perhaps it was strange that I publicly acknowledged his position, but if I let my paranoia rule me, the suspicions would inevitably become true. I'd push the person into betraying me with my own behavior. So far, Dmitry had given me no reason to doubt myself, which meant that I could trust him. Not completely and with some reservation, but still...

I could finally conclude my speech, there were only a couple of things left. "I'll take the prisoner, and I'll decide what to do with him after the interrogation. This matter is not up for discussion. His armor, possessions and weapons will go into the general pile. What else? Dmitry?"

"Many of the goblins had System bags with supplies, and wallets with the local currency. Mostly silver, but there is some gold. There are also the saddles and harnesses."

"The bags and the saddles should go into our supply train. We'll share the supplies at camp tonight. The money will be divided equally among everyone."

"The goblin bodies," Chulth reminded me. "What do we do with them? I've heard that if you leave them be, they can rise up as the undead."

"That's an interesting question," I spoke slowly, remembering my experiments in necromancy, which hadn't been successful. Should we 'disable' them? Take the bodies with us? Save them for the future? "Decapitate the damaged bodies. We'll take the whole bodies with us, just place them in one of the bags. Just in case, leave one of the corpse's mana crystal in place.

That's all for now, let's start divvying up the goods."

I clapped my hands, and discovered that they were quite sweaty. Damn.

✡ ✡ ✡

Surprisingly, the division went calmly enough. As a result, my worthwhile spoils consisted of the chain mail I'd had my eye on, with 'this season's trend' of an arrow hole in the back. I was larger than a goblin, but the chain mail was originally worn over an arming doublet, so I managed to squeeze into it. Without the doublet, of course. The weight felt a little strange, and the cold of the metal seeped through my clothes, but the thought of a thin layer of armor between me and this hostile world warmed my heart. Overly poetic? It was the nerves.

Using the right of first choice, I also selected a helmet, shield, and a good fur cloak. Then I replenished my supply of arrows, throwing several quivers into the bag, and instructing the others to dig my old arrows out of the goblin bodies.

I helped myself to a spear card from the late Lance's belongings, which were now in the squad's treasury. As practice had shown, System weapons didn't last forever, and it was important to have a spare.

I also obtained eleven bags at once. Five from the goblins and six from other players. According to our old agreement, 'spare' bags had to be divided among members of the G8, so I wasn't going to share anything, nor hide my trophies. Considering the total losses among players, this amount was within my share of the loot. However, I couldn't combine them all yet. One bag was used to store the bodies, one was used for the dead players' belongings, which I was planning to transfer to our supply train. Five of the bags also contained goblin supplies. For the time being, the bags were slung over the pack horse, the most peaceful one of the eight we'd captured. I'd let someone else deal with Shaitan-Kebab.

I'd already glanced through the contents of the bags and was slightly disappointed. If the goblins had a supply train, we hadn't obtained it. The bags clearly held the personal belongings of the riders. Of course, it would have been foolish to expect that the supply train had joined the attack. But inside each one of us is a child who dreams of the day a Coca-Cola truck will roll over in their street.

In addition, five more recruits had asked to join my squad, based on the results of the battle. I even accepted three who weren't found guilty of anything untoward. The 'plumber' Mario seemed to be eyeing the seventh squad.

"I'm from the venerable Qing Long," said a vaguely familiar Chinese man, and bowed slightly, distracting me from my thoughts. I couldn't remember the name, but the System helped. The player's name was Chan. "Our leader requests that you and Commander Marcus come as soon as possible to help interrogate the prisoners."

"Right," I got to my feet. "I was just on my way to see you. We'll grab my prisoner and go. Commander Marcus is injured, so he probably won't be able to attend. Nevertheless, we should visit him and ask." The fact that I'd already sorted out the biggest problems by this point was immensely gratifying.

Do you wish to record this skill on the training card?
Yes/No

I certainly did. The list of skills available for recording was small and, irrespective of my level, was limited to the first rank. *Archery,* *Spear fighting, Medicine of the Earth* and *Concealment.*

I stopped at *Sword fighting,* which was grayed out.

Attention! The original accuracy of the skill is not enough to copy!

So, the rumors were true? Copied skills couldn't be rewritten onto an empty. I'd already heard of this, but was unhappy to see it myself. This was both happy and sad news for the owners of 'unique skills'. Happy because being unique could be profitable, but sad because you had to do it all on your own. *Minor magical ability* was also grayed out, and when I focused on it, a message appeared:

Attention! Your skill level is not high enough to create an Initiation card!

The card had a slightly different name here, but I knew it was a matter of matching terms. I'd have to compare which one was more accurate later. In any case, magical ability could theoretically be transferred, which was already good news. Given that *Faith* provided almost identical mana, most mages were more likely to be priests in the future.

I ran my eyes down the list. *Identification* and *Second Wind* couldn't be copied either. The *Calculating Mind* was also unavailable, while *Invisibility* could be copied, although the likelihood of success was extremely small. I knew, somehow, that if the match percentage was too low, the card would simply crumble into dust. Okay, back to business.

Do you want to copy the Goblin Language skill? Yes/No

I had the original card, but I didn't feel like giving it to my allies for free, and the time wasn't right for bidding. So "Yes".

Like many things in the System, copying a skill was not a pleasant procedure. It felt as if an invisible tentacle was digging around in my brain, yet I had to stay focused. Fortunately, it didn't last long.

The skill has been copied. Match percentage is 99%.

"Done," I said, handing the card to Qing Long and picking up the next empty. There were plenty of them, and many people wanted to speak the language of a potential foe.

Well, no good deed goes unpunished, so now all these people would owe me a favor. Whether they wanted to or not.

✳ ✳ ✳

The results of the battle could be considered satisfactory. Out of about two hundred and fifty goblins, only twenty or thirty had managed to escape from the trap, not counting the ten or so riders. Only six goblins had been captured. It could have been significantly more, since many were only stunned by the hail of stones, but nearly all had been mercilessly slaughtered for the XP.

The loss of life among players was lower, but still significant, for thirty had been killed and around seventy were wounded. Moreover, many were seriously wounded, which further aggravated the situation. Another fifty were 'missing in action', in other words, had died, deserted, or fell behind in the recent retreat.

The situation didn't inspire much enthusiasm. The Alliance, which had numbered 563 players only a day ago, now had about 450 people remaining, 80 of whom couldn't move independently. The fate of the wounded depended on what the goblins would tell us, but so far, they refused to speak.

"If you answer our questions truthfully, we won't have to resort to torture," the Swordsman suggested. Having killed the goblin leader, he had not only increased his level to six, matching mine, but had also found a 'spare' ten points to learn the native language.

In all honesty, it didn't sound very convincing. The goblin, who had lost a hand in the battle and was covered with wounds, looked like he was planning to die pretty soon without our help. "Fuck you," the goblin rasped out and spat on Qing Long's boot. For some reason. "I won't tell you anything."

I suddenly remembered the old joke about the Chukchi man and the interpreter. *He says that he doesn't know where the gold is buried...*

"Then we will execute you," Qing Long said pensively. "Are you in such a hurry to die?"

"I'm a warrior!" the goblin responded. "I'm not afraid of pain. I'm not afraid of death."

"He's refusing to answer," Qing Lung explained to those who couldn't understand the goblin language. Although I'd copied the card for all the leaders present, only two of them had learned the skill. The rest were content with interpretation. "What does the expert say?"

Sulu claimed to have some knowledge of torture, and his skills could come in useful today.

"Pointless to torture this one. In a bad state. Will die," Sulu concluded. "Unless you cut his off fingers very quickly, and then..."

"Another time," Qing Long declined this suggestion. "Whose captive is this?"

"Mine!" One of the nearby players stepped forward. First level.

"You can collect your experience points. Help him."

Two Chinese men obeyed, seizing the prisoner by the elbows and dragging him a little to the side. The goblin didn't fight back, keeping his eyes closed. The 'owner' approached, swung his sword clumsily and cut off the goblin's head. Judging by the man's grimace, no card fell out.

"Next!" Qing Long ordered coldly.

I closed my eyes, reminding myself that the survival of hundreds or even thousands of people was at stake. Including, let's face it, my own. I wasn't going to interfere.

* * *

The main problem was getting the prisoners to talk, but after two more beheadings, things improved. No, they tried to lie and dodge the questions, but it didn't matter. We ascertained the main thing quite quickly – the army was real and was supposed to arrive soon, and this squadron had come from the fortress. There was almost no garrison left now. Several other questions followed.

"Well, that's enough," Qing Long said. He drew a finger across his throat. "We don't need them anymore."

Two goblins fell to their knees, begging for mercy, but it didn't do them any good. The players felt less and less sorry for the mobs as time went on. Especially because the prisoners belonged to the newbies, who needed the experience points for their own survival. Who knew if they'd be able to kill a goblin in the future?

"Vasily?" Qing Lung brought me back to reality. "We don't have much time, so please hurry up."

That's right, only one goblin was left, the rider that belonged to me. It was pointless to drag him along with us, but I also didn't want to get my hands dirty by killing a prisoner. Although, after all I'd seen and done, it was a bit late for chivalry.

"You want to kill me?" the goblin snarled. "If you are not a coward, then give me your sword and fight me!" I liked this idiotic suggestion, mostly uttered out of desperation. It wasn't a matter of guilt, I would have survived that. However, it'd be stupid not to use this opportunity to combine business with pleasure and to try out the *Duelist* skill, which significantly increased the chance of a card being dropped. I wondered if it would work on a goblin. I dug around in the settings and ultimately left only one option.

Attention! The conditions of the challenge do not allow you to complete the fight before one of the parties dies.
Do you wish to challenge the nameless goblin?
Yes/No

"I challenge the goblin to a System duel," I explained to the others. "A circle of six meters. Everyone stand back!"

I drew my sword and laid it on the floor, then stepped back, summoning my spear. The players also retreated, and, interestingly, nobody thought to dissuade me.

Only Saud, who had failed to reach Level 3 in the last battle, expressed his readiness to avenge me.

"If I kill you, will they let me go?" the goblin growled, looking hungrily at the blade in front of him, but not rushing to pick it up.

"You don't believe in fairy tales, do you?" I didn't want to make any false promises. "But it will be a fair fight, so you'll have a chance to finish me off. You know who I am, right?"

"I do." the goblin said and grinned hungrily. "We called you the invisible asshole." The goblin laughed, and I joined in. Funny, but deep down, I'd expected something more... impressive. Like 'Invisible Archer' or 'Deadly Arrow'. Come to think of it, why would the goblins give their enemy a glorious name? Especially if he was still alive? One could pay tribute to the dead in ballads, and then only to emphasize the valor of one's own heroes. This isn't a fairy tale, is it?

"Okay, enough fun," I sighed, wiping the smile off my face. "Shall we begin?"

"First, give me back my shield and armor!" the goblin demanded, folding his arms across his chest.

"No," I shook my head. "Why would I do something so stupid?"

"Then take off your chain mail. Otherwise, everyone here will know that you are a coward!"

"Better a coward than an idiot, especially a dead idiot." I smiled mirthlessly. "It'll be enough for you that I don't have a shield. Well, will you fight me, or am I wasting my time?"

Attention! Unit (83%) Nameless Goblin (Level 6) accepts your challenge!

Match type:
— To the death.
Conditions of completion:

— Death of one of the participants.
Circle diameter:
6 meters.
The fight will start in: 30... 29... 28...

I'd set the timer for half a minute. The circle grew slowly larger, causing the players to back away, although there was no need. The goblin lunged forward, raised the sword, and leaped back. I just grunted, not taking the chance to strike. Not only because of the timer, but because there was no point in cheating in this case. Let's be honest, right now, I was guided not so much by a desire to obtain a card, but by the remnants of my conscience.

"My name is Hmyr!" the goblin snarled. This was a personal name, not a System one. "I want my people to know that I died with honor!" The goblin had nothing to reproach himself for. He hadn't even given anything away, for his more cowardly compatriots had already done that. And he didn't ask for mercy. All that was left was to die in style, taking me with him. To perform a feat, so to speak.

5... 4... 3...

"Of course, I'll see to it," I agreed, and retreated into *Invisibility*.

Let the duel commence!

"You? I doubt it," Hmyr replied and threw a handful of dirt at me. It was a good plan, but the dirt immediately faded when it encountered my field. Perhaps he was aiming for my eyes?

I stepped to the side, letting his sword slash the empty air... Step... Strike... The spear sank into flesh, and the sword fell from his weakened hand, clattering to the ground.

**Attention! You have received 12 SP! (26/120)
Attention! The duel is over! All restrictions have been lifted.**

I yanked the spear free, letting the body fall. The fight had taken only seconds. As I'd expected, a card appeared above the goblin's body.

> ***Skald skill card***
> ***Class:*** *F.*
> ***Level:*** *1/3.*
> ***Description:***
> *— Grants the skills necessary to become a goblin skald.*
> ***Saturation:***
> *10/10 SP*

I smiled wryly at this so-called gift. It even had full saturation. Was I truly meant to write a ballad about the deceased? A return courtesy, one might say. Because I think I knew which goblin had given me that nickname. Several claps came from behind me. Skeptical ones, if you could say that about applause.

"Thank you," I bowed dramatically, waving the card in my hand. "It worked, as you can see."

"An excellent fight," Qing Long smiled and clapped his hands one last time. "Now that we have sorted this out, we need to decide what to do next. What would you say if I suggested that we try to capture the goblin fortress?"

There was a moment's silence. Although the suggestion sounded insane, we'd have a real chance if we succeeded. Instead of running deep into the city, hoping for a miracle, we could hold out until the end of the allocated time. It was a way to save everyone.

APPENDIX

CHARACTER TABLE NO. 3

VASILY

General ID: unknown.
Local ID: Z-8.
True Name: Ivan Susanin (hidden).
Age: 24 years.
Race: human (97%).
Gender: male.
Level: 6 (26/120).
Available: 12 SP.

Parameters:
Strength: 6+1=7/10.
Agility: 7+1=8/10.
Intelligence: 7+1=8/10.
Vitality: 6/10.

Stamina: 6+4=10/10.
Perception: 7/10.
Luck: 2/10.

Race Parameter:
Intuition: 9+1=10/10.

Additional Parameters:
Wisdom: 1+2=3.
Faith: 0/10 (blocked, no patron).
Free points: 6.

System Skills:
Player (E):
— Intuitive interface (E, 1/1).
— Help (E, 1/1).
— System language (F, 1/1).

Combat Skills:
— Spear fighting (F, 3/5).
— Archery (F, 2/5).
— Sword fighting (F, 1/5).

Secondary:
— Camouflage (F, 1/5).
— Medicine of the Earth (F, 1/5).
— Goblin language (F, 1/1).
— Skald (F, 1/3).

Features:
— Minor magical ability (F, 2/5).

Rank E Skills:

— Invisibility (E, 1/5) — creates a cloaking field around the hero.

— Duelist (E, 1/5) — allows one to conduct a duel according to certain rules.

— Calculating Mind (E, 1/5) — removes emotions, increases rationality.

System Bonuses:

— Identification (E, 1/5) — allows one to determine the properties of objects.

— Second Wind (E-, 1/1) — allows fatigue to be reset every 12 hours.

Achievements and Titles:

Eighth (personal, unique) — sometimes bad luck is so great that great luck passes very close by. Features unknown.

Atheist — reduces the favor of the gods.

Cards and Artifacts:

Rank F weapons: spear — 1, spear fragments, sword, axe, saber, rapier, katana — 2, sword, dagger.

Skill cards (F -): Goblin language, horse riding, empty skill card.

Rank E:

— **Archer's Kit:** renewable quiver (E), goblin bow (-), archer's ring (-), spare bowstring (-).

— **System Dagger (E).**

— **The Calculating Mind (E).**
Rank D:
— **Mask of Cain** (cursed).
— **Khatvanga (Shiva)** — the sacred weapon of one of the seven gods of Earth.
— **Sun Sword (Inti)** — the sacred weapon of one of the seven gods of Earth.

Other:
— **Marauder's bag (E, 1/7).**
— **Bottomless bag (F, 3/7).**
— **Eternal flasks** — 11 pieces.
— **Broken spear (F--).**
— **Faded cards** from studied skills. Can be used as armor, other use unknown.
— **Modern bow (-)** — transformed using the Archer's Kit.
— **Player kit (x11)** — various levels of completeness.
— **Mana crystals.**
— **Crystal powder** — dust mixed with earth, from the destroyed magical hearts of the undead. Purpose unknown.

END OF BOOK ONE

Want to be the first to know about our latest LitRPG, sci fi and fantasy titles from your favorite authors?

Subscribe to our **New Releases** newsletter:
http://eepurl.com/b7niIL

Thank you for reading *City of Goblins!*
If you like what you've read, check out other sci-fi, fantasy and
LitRPG novels published by Magic Dome Books:

Reality Benders LitRPG series by Michael Atamanov:
Countdown
External Threat
Game Changer
Web of Worlds
A Jump into the Unknown
Aces High

**The Dark Herbalist LitRPG series
by Michael Atamanov:**
Video Game Plotline Tester
Stay on the Wing
A Trap for the Potentate
Finding a Body

Perimeter Defense LitRPG series by Michael Atamanov:
Sector Eight
Beyond Death
New Contract
A Game with No Rules

**League of Losers LitRPG Series
by Michael Atamanov:**
A Cat and his Human

**The Way of the Shaman LitRPG series
by Vasily Mahanenko:**
Survival Quest
The Kartoss Gambit
The Secret of the Dark Forest
The Phantom Castle
The Karmadont Chess Set
The Hour of Pain (a bonus short story)
Shaman's Revenge
Clans War

The Alchemist LiTRPG series by Vasily Mahanenko:
City of the Dead
Forest of Desire
Tears of Alron

Dark Paladin LitRPG series by Vasily Mahanenko:
The Beginning
The Quest
Restart

Galactogon LitRPG series by Vasily Mahanenko:
Start the Game!
In Search of the Uldans
A Check for a Billion

Invasion LitRPG Series by Vasily Mahanenko:
A Second Chance
An Equation with one Unknown

World of the Changed LitRPG Series by Vasily Mahanenko:
No Mistakes
Pearl of the South
Noa in the Flesh

The Bard from Barliona LitRPG series
by Eugenia Dmitrieva and Vasily Mahanenko:
The Renegades
A Song of Shadow

Level Up LitRPG series by Dan Sugralinov:
Re-Start
Hero
The Final Trial
Level Up: The Knockout (with Max Lagno)
Level Up. The Knockout: Update (with Max Lagno)

Disgardium LitRPG series by Dan Sugralinov:
Class-A Threat
Apostle of the Sleeping Gods
The Destroying Plague
Resistance
Holy War

World 99 LitRPG Series by Dan Sugralinov:
Blood of Fate

Adam Online LitRPG Leries by Max Lagno:
Absolute Zero
City of Freedom

In order to have new books of the series translated faster, we need your help and support! Please consider leaving a review or spread the word by recommending *City of Goblins* to your friends and posting the link on social media. The more people buy the book, the sooner we'll be able to make new translations available.

Thank you!

Till next time!

Made in the USA
Coppell, TX
19 May 2021

55967737R10246